Louise Cooper beg~~an~~
school to entertain ~~...~~
and her first full-length novel was published when she
was only twenty years old. Since then she has become a
prolific writer of fantasy, renowned for her bestselling
Time Master trilogy. Her other interests include music,
folklore, mythology and comparative religion. She lives
in Worcestershire. Her latest novels, THE KING'S
DEMON and SACRAMENT OF NIGHT, are also available from Headline Feature.

Our Lady Of The Snow

Louise Cooper

HEADLINE
FEATURE

First published in hardback in 1998 by
HEADLINE BOOK PUBLISHING

First published in paperback in 1999 by
HEADLINE BOOK PUBLISHING

10 9 8 7 6 5 4 3 2 1

ISBN 0 7472 5949 6

Printed and bound in Great Britain by
Mackays of Chatham plc, Chatham, Kent

HEADLINE BOOK PUBLISHING
A division of Hodder Headline PLC
338 Euston Road
London NW1 3BH

Our Lady Of The Snow

Chapter I

E vening devotions at the Metropolis temple were a public
ceremony, and the congregations were always large. There
was a popular notion that particular spiritual credit was earned
by attending this greatest and most elaborate of the three daily
rites; and on the secular side it was certainly a sound move, for
the Fathers and Mothers took especial note of faces in the crowd
and there was always the chance that the occasion would be
graced by the presence of one or more members of the imperial
family in their galleried box high above the tiers of the temple
amphitheatre.

Tonight, too, there was an added incentive, for the anthems
and sanctification chants were to be sung by the choir of the
Court Academy. The choir rarely performed on everyday occasions, but everyone knew that they were rehearsing intensively
for the imminent visit of the Sekolian ambassador and its
attendant pomp and ceremonial. This was a dry run, so to speak,
and the choir were gathered now in the amphitheatre's great
semi-circular bowl; two hundred and thirty women and girls,
all dressed in identical gold-threaded gowns, awaiting the
arrival of the officiating High Father. In the shimmer of a myriad
lamps and candles they looked ethereal, as other-worldly as the
carved figure of the Lady, who sat eternally at the feet of her
lord and consort in the massive, high-relief devotional image
behind the altar. The figure of the God himself, towering, faceless
and utterly dominant, rose above the altar and the choir's massed

ranks like a colossus. Already a number of offerings had been laid before the image, and more would follow as people petitioned for advice or intervention or blessings.

The gazes of most of the congregation were on the choir, though some shifted upwards now and then to glance with hopeful speculation at the imperial box. The box's damask curtains were closed and the fretwork screen was in place, making it impossible to tell whether it was occupied. The Imperator and his family did not show themselves to the common gaze except on the most prominent ceremonial occasions, but the possibility that they were here tonight, albeit invisible, was a valuable sop to public contentment.

From his own lofty perspective in another screened cubicle on the elevated gallery, Exalted Father Urss had also been studying the imperial box, though his interest was cursory and a matter of habit rather than anything else. In his opinion, none of the royal family were likely to be present in the temple. The Imperator himself, burdened by the failing health of old age, rarely made the journey through the private tunnel from the palace these days; his elder son, Prince Osiv, could not be expected to do so, and Prince Kodor, his younger son, usually managed to find a plausible reason for staying away. Urss made a mental note to have another stern word with Prince Kodor on that subject, and one or two other matters while he was about it, then turned his attention once more to the patiently waiting choir.

Which one of them was the girl in question? Father Urss's sharp eyes had singled out several possible candidates, some of whom looked acceptable whilst others clearly were not; but he took no pleasure in guessing games and was growing irritated by waiting for the devotions to begin. Sound – even a whisper – carried clearly in the gallery, and he could not speak to his companion, and thus risk being overheard, until there was music and chanting to mask his voice. There was no excuse for this delay, and another mental note was filed away to the effect that the attitude of some temple Fathers towards their offices was becoming slipshod, and the failing must be nipped in the bud.

The rite did finally begin, with a cold fanfare of trumpets that brought the congregation dutifully to its feet. Father Urss did not rise, and neither did his companion; hidden as they were behind the fretwork it seemed an unnecessary waste of energy. As the ceremonial (which both knew so thoroughly that they could shut it from their minds) got under way, Urss turned at last to the small, dumpy woman seated in the chair beside him.

'We can speak now, I think, Beck. Kindly point out the girl you have in mind.'

Grand Mother Beck leaned forward with a rustle of her blue silk robe and scanned the vista below through a conveniently placed gap in the fretwork. Seventy years old – which gave her a decade over Father Urss – she had been head of the Imperial Sanctum of the Lady for four years now, and was widely regarded as the most astute politician ever to grace the post. Short, stout, with a jowly face and formidable eyes, she was well aware of her increasing value to Father Urss and his allies on the Exalted Council in matters such as this one, and her face reflected her confidence as she replied in a practised undertone.

'The fourth row, eighth from the left. The small one with the fair hair.'

Father Urss followed her direction. 'Ah . . . that one.' Had he noticed her during his private speculation? He couldn't remember. At this distance detail was sketchy, but the first impression was encouraging. The girl was young – eighteen or nineteen, he would surmise – and appeared pretty; her hair was corn-gold rather than merely fair (though that, of course, might be the effect of the lights) and, above all, she looked demure. Docile. *Obedient*.

He raised the magnifying hand-glass that he had brought with him for the purpose and held it to his right eye. The girl's face sprang into clearer focus, and he nodded, satisfied by what he saw. She *was* pretty; so delicately innocent as to be almost doll-like. In terms of her appearance, at least, she was eminently suitable.

'What is her name?' he asked.

'Nanta,' said Grand Mother Beck.

To Father Urss's certain knowledge there had not been a Nanta in the highest echelons before; but the name was not flamboyant, and it sat well enough on the tongue. He nodded again. 'And you say she is of the EsDorikye family. Which house?'

'The north-eastern.'

'Mmm.' Urss's tone implied neither approval nor disapproval; he was merely assimilating facts. 'Her pedigree, I presume, is what prompted you to choose her over any other potential candidates?'

'Yes, Father.' Beck did not mention the other factor, the uncommon and unfamiliar instinct that, for some reason which she did not trouble to question, had led her to Nanta EsDorikye. Priest he might be, but Father Urss had no time for instinct and intuition; to him they were women's foibles and thus to be disparaged. Opening a leather wallet she carried, she handed him a folded piece of paper. 'I have a copy of the pedigree here. I checked the details personally against the Crown Registry, and they are all correct.'

'You are thorough, as always.'

Beck smiled. 'Thank you, Exalted Father.'

Neither spoke for a while as Father Urss studied the paper. Beyond the screen the ceremony was progressing but they were hardly aware of it. Even when the choir began to sing, neither spared so much as a moment's attention for the spine-tingling beauty of the women's clear, pure voices filling the temple. The Academy choir might be second to none in the whole of Vyskir, but Beck and Urss had neither the ear nor any partiality for music and ignored it as they might have ignored a buzzing fly.

Eventually Father Urss folded the paper and said, 'It seems, Grand Mother, that you have made an excellent choice in every respect.' He paused. 'I trust the girl herself has no inkling of what's in the wind?'

'Naturally not.' Beck's voice was level but her eyes betrayed momentary annoyance that he should even need to ask the question.

'Good. Then it only remains to put our choice before the Imperator and persuade him to our way of thinking. Frankly, I doubt if that will be a problem.'

Beck's eyebrows lifted faintly as she noticed how, already, he was crediting himself as well as her with the choice. 'I hope not, Father. Though I understand that the Imperator would prefer Prince Osiv not to be married at all.'

'That,' said Urss with faint asperity, 'is not a matter in which even the Imperator has any choice now.' He rose to his full, considerable height. 'I have seen all I need to, Mother Beck, and under the circumstances I'm sure the God will understand and pardon our early departure.' Turning in the direction of the statue he made a deep, reverent bow, and Beck followed suit. They moved to the door at the back of the cubicle; Beck drew aside the silk curtain, stood back to allow Urss to precede her, and they walked together along the gallery towards a side staircase that formed a private and privileged link with the complexity of the temple's inner offices.

As they started down the wide, shallow steps, Beck said, 'What will you require of me now, Father?'

Urss eyed her obliquely. 'I think we can safely count on the Imperator's agreement to our proposal. So the next stage will be twofold. Firstly, the Sekolian ambassador, when he arrives, must be fully acquainted with the situation and reassured that it presents no threat to his own mission.'

'Quite,' said Beck.

'Secondly, the girl herself must be prepared for the change in

5

her circumstances. Where that is concerned, I'm sure I don't need to stress the need for *absolute* discretion.'

Beck nodded. 'Of course, Father; I understand your meaning.' Her tone suggested that she also had a strategy, but Urss knew her too well – and trusted her methods too implicitly – to demean himself by asking a direct question. He smiled, so that for a moment his saturnine face was almost pleasant.

'Do whatever you think fit, Grand Mother Beck. Just keep me informed. That is all I require.'

They continued down the stairs in companionable silence.

Flurries of snow were falling on the towers and domes of the Metropolis as the blue coach bearing the crest of the Imperial Sanctum of the Lady clattered in full panoply over the river-bridge and into the city precincts. People on foot, heads down against the wind-blown white turmoil, scrambled and slithered out of their path; an outrider's whip cracked to liven one or two stragglers and the coach with its four caparisoned black horses swept by, hurling up a bow-wave of slush and spray. A few of those they passed, recognising the crest, made obeisance or cried out for benedictions, but the cloth-of-silver curtains at the coach windows didn't so much as twitch, let alone afford any glimpse of the august passengers inside.

Behind the curtains, in gloom relieved only by a single lamp that swung wildly from the roof as the bridge cobbles did their worst, Sister Chaia, the Imperial Sanctum's messenger and emissary, glanced surreptitiously at her senior companion and wondered at the quirks of human nature that could have produced such a flaw in an otherwise sternly dauntless personality. High Sister Marine was sitting rigidly upright in one corner of the plush seat, her mantle drawn tightly around her and her face, in its frame of wimple, grey with affliction. Her narrow lips moved ceaselessly in silent prayer; despite the fact that she had never before set foot in the capital city she would, Chaia knew, have given a very great deal to be utterly oblivious of her surroundings at this moment.

Marine loathed travelling, and always had. She had discovered at an early age that she was prey to severe journey-sickness whenever she ventured more than a short distance, and for years now she had rarely left her own district. But this summons was one that could not be ignored, so for the past four days she had been obliged to suffer the bouts of nausea and the confusing agoraphobic-claustrophobic syndrome engendered by travelling in a closed carriage through vertiginously open country.

The two women had exchanged few words during their journey, partly because of Marine's sickness and partly because hers was not a personality that encouraged chatter. Now, though, Chaia leaned forward and ventured gently:

'If you have never visited our great capital before, High Sister, the view from the bridge is well worth seeing.'

Marine opened her eyes and gave Chaia a pained look. 'Thank you, Sister Chaia,' she said testily, 'but views are of no interest whatever to me. I would prefer to know how much longer we have to endure this jolting.'

Chaia raised one hand and lifted the curtain enough to peep out. 'The city is busy today.' A fond smile touched the corners of her mouth. 'And the light on the river is very beautiful. The boats—'

Marine interrupted, uninterested in such trivia. 'Can you see the Academy yet?' She had no intention of demeaning herself by exposing her own face to the common gaze.

Chaia stifled a sigh. 'Yes, Sister. The bell tower is visible. It's one of the highest in the Metropolis; with a blue dome—'

'I understand that the Sanctum of the Lady is attached to the Academy. Is that so?'

'Yes, Sister.'

'Good.' Marine leaned down and pushed away the foot-warmer beneath her seat; the coals had gone cold long since, and despite fur-lined boots her feet were numb. 'I shall be thankful for a welcoming fire. The inns on this road leave a great deal to be desired.'

'I'm sure they did their best, Sister.'

'Perhaps they did; in which case all I can say is that their best is no cause for celebration.' Marine raised her gloved hands to her head. 'Put down your veil, Sister Chaia. Court custom requires that women of rank do not show their faces unless they are within doors.'

Chaia knew that as well as she did, but didn't have the courage to point out that custom wasn't always followed to the letter. She obeyed, drawing the fine grey veil forward, and Marine followed suit. Through her veil, Chaia thought, the High Sister looked like a corpse; but at least once the veil was down she did finally unbend enough to draw the other curtain back a little and peer out. They were over the bridge now, and the outriders shouted to clear the way once more as the little cavalcade turned into one of the broad thoroughfares that followed the river bank towards the heart of the Metropolis. There was more traffic here: other carriages, traders' carts, curtained sedan chairs, opulently dressed men riding well-bred horses with servants following on foot. And on the broad pavements, among lines of market stalls, people in their hundreds: a moving, bustling sea of colourful humanity. Despite her mood Marine was fascinated; for all the tales that were told about the Metropolis she had never seen people in such enormous numbers before, and no amount of imagination – of which, anyway, she possessed very little – could have prepared her for the sheer scale of everything. Many of the buildings beside this thoroughfare were four or five storeys tall, and above their rooftops the great towers of the more exalted city centre rose taller still, climbing high enough, or so it seemed, to pierce the very clouds.

The coach rolled on, and after perhaps a quarter of a mile turned again, this time into a quieter street. Marine saw several small groups of religious women, veiled and with their hands in fur muffs, hurrying through the still falling snow, and once a velvet-cloaked High Brother walking carefully along the pavement under the protection of an oilcloth canopy carried by two pages. They were drawing closer to the towers now; façades pressed in and the horses' hooves began to echo hollowly, while the sky dwindled to a narrow ribbon between the crowding domes. Then came another turn, and ahead of them suddenly were black wrought-iron gates set into a high stone wall. Carvings covered the wall's face, depicting sacred themes and devices, and along the coping, between rows of murderously sharp spikes set to deter any would-be intruder, statues bowed their heads and upraised their hands in attitudes of prayer. Beyond, faintly unreal in the haze of snowfall and the rising vapours of the city, was the greatest structure in the entire kingdom: the gigantic central tower of the temple, its grey walls all but lost against the sky's backdrop so that its mosaic dome seemed to float ethereally above the animation below.

Marine murmured a pious word as the tower loomed high above them; then, with no further interest in the architecture, let the curtain fall again and gestured to Chaia to do likewise. Two guards in the grey and gold of Imperial service recognised the coach's device and opened the gates to let them through, and the horses slowed to a sedate walk as they entered the Academy precincts. The sound of the hooves and wheels changed, suggesting that the walls to either side were closing in, and at last the coach rumbled and squeaked to a halt.

The coachman had been given instructions to avoid the Academy's public courtyard and instead deliver his passengers to the more private reception square of the Sanctum itself. High walls, again adorned with religious carvings, surrounded them on all sides, and the only sign that this was a place of any significance was the blue canopy that arched over the door, surmounted by the Lady's own emblem of a stylised snowflake.

Servants were waiting to escort them; as they passed under the canopy Marine bowed her head over clasped hands and murmured reverently, 'The tears of the Lady are the blessing of the snow,' then looked sharply at Chaia to ensure that she did not forget the ritual obeisance. She was already feeling better. And, for the first time since the westward journey had begun, her sense of curiosity and interest in the reasons behind her summons to the Metropolis was reawakening in full measure.

The door closed behind them, enveloping them in a sense of warmth and opulence which surprised Marine until she remembered that austerity was not practised in the city as it was in more rural districts. They were conducted along a carpeted and lamplit corridor, then up two flights of elegantly balustraded stairs that took them into the heart of the Sanctum complex. Sisters of every grade glided efficiently about their business, the lower ranks pausing to curtsey to Marine as she passed. Somewhere in the distance girls' voices were raised in the massed harmony of a Sanctification Chant; they paused while a single woman's voice spoke firmly for a few moments, then after a brisk clap of hands the singing began again, fading behind the party as they walked on.

They reached a secluded part of the building, aloof and remote from the comparative bustle, and stopped outside an ornate door. The servants knocked respectfully; from the far side a voice called crisply, 'Enter!' and Marine walked in.

Grand Mother Beck was sitting in her favourite armchair, behind a desk designed to daunt more timid spirits. A fire blazed in the grate, making lamplight unnecessary; at a hearth table two postulant Little Daughters were setting out wine and biscuits under the stern eye of a chatelaine. Beck looked up from a ledger on the desk before her, and her stern expression relaxed into a formal smile.

'High Sister Marine – welcome. Come in, come in. Thank

you, Chaia; I'll have no need of you now, so you may be excused until after the refectory hour.'

Chaia curtseyed and left, and at a nod from her superior the chatelaine also departed, chivvying the Little Daughters before her. The door closed, and Beck exhaled a sigh that combined relief with faint vexation.

'Sit down, Marine, do,' she said. 'I don't need to ask how you fared on your journey; your face tells me all. There; take that chair by the fire, and I shall move from this infernal desk and join you.'

Marine perched on the edge of the chair and pulled off her ermine gloves one meticulous finger at a time. 'I'm glad to see you looking well, Grand Mother,' she replied. 'Sister Chaia gave me to understand that recent events have proved a little . . . stressful for you.'

Beck knew Sister Chaia well enough to be sure that she had told Marine precisely what she had been instructed to tell her, no more and no less, and understood what lay behind this genteel probe. Marine's curiosity had been aroused – and that was precisely what Beck had intended. For twelve years Marine had been her official amanuensis when she herself was head of the First Eastern Sanctum, and during that time she had also become, at least in private, Beck's closest confidante. Four years ago, when Beck had been elevated to her role as the highest female religious in the kingdom, Marine had succeeded to her place in the east, and since then they had met only on a few occasions. But old ties did not weaken with distance.

Father Urss would have had grave doubts about this meeting, had he known of it. He had made it clear that he did not wish Beck to involve any new players in this particular game. But Urss was not a realist – very few of the Fathers were, Beck reflected cynically – and he was not the one who would be obliged to deal with the practicalities. That, as always, would be left to the Sisters. Beck saw no reason why she should be expected to shoulder the burden alone. Besides, whether the Fathers liked it or not, Marine was indirectly involved.

'Pour me a glass of wine, Marine, if you please. And take one yourself.' She waited until Marine had complied, then cupped the delicate, faceted vessel in her hands and gave the younger woman a shrewd look. The fire lit her heavy face and a thin tendril of hair that had escaped from her linen head-cap; for a moment she looked as old as the temple itself.

'The nature of this summons,' she said, 'was, I know, peremptory in the extreme. I called you here without notice or warning, and now that you have arrived you find yourself hurried to my office with barely a moment to catch your breath.'

'I'm sure there's a good reason, Grand Mother,' Marine replied.

'There is.' A faint, hard smile touched Beck's mouth. 'You're not entirely out of touch in the east, are you, Marine?'

Marine bridled slightly. 'I hope not. We try to keep abreast of developments—'

'And I don't doubt you have your own thoughts on what lies behind the public façade. Thoughts that you don't necessarily reveal to the Sisters under your care.'

Marine leaned slightly forward, her blue-grey eyes suddenly and acutely alert. Beck continued to regard her for a few moments longer, then continued:

'I have sent for you, High Sister Marine, because I have a task to entrust. And *trust* is the key word – for what we are about to discuss now must not, and I repeat *not*, be divulged to another living soul. Do I have your assurance?'

'Of course, Grand Mother.' Marine was avid now, which was all to the good. Beck nodded.

'Very well. You know, presumably, that the Imperator has been ailing this past year or so. It's a degenerative illness, and one which neither prayer nor physic has been able to arrest. The fact is that His Majesty is unlikely to see another spring.'

Marine's tongue appeared and licked cautiously around her lower lip. 'That is very sad news.'

'Indeed. We shall all mourn him. However, it is not the Imperator's impending death that concerns the Fathers of the Exalted Council most deeply. It is the question of the succession.'

Marine said, 'Ah . . .' There was a pause, then she added carefully, 'But the succession is not open to selection . . .'

'Indeed,' Beck agreed. 'However much anyone might wish it otherwise, the Imperator can't choose who shall follow him. The eldest son must take the throne as always.'

'But—'

Marine's voice cut off swiftly, but she had given away enough to satisfy Beck. Marine knew. That was the one uncertainty Beck had had, and abruptly it was dispelled.

'You're aware of the problem, then.' Her voice was level. 'It has been kept from the populace at large, of course; to reveal the truth would have been unthinkable. But there is no such thing as an infallible secret.'

Marine smiled faintly. 'You trained me yourself, Grand Mother. I hope I'm worthy of you.'

Oh, you are, Beck thought. Aloud, she said, 'Unfortunately, the fact that Prince Osiv isn't fit to rule makes no difference whatever to law and custom. He is the heir apparent, and so he must succeed to the throne when the Imperator is called to his final rest.'

Marine nodded. 'I've never seen the prince for myself, of course,' she mused. 'Is he truly beyond redemption?'

Beck sighed. 'I'm afraid he is. He's twenty-seven years old now, but he has the mind of a little child, and a child's tempers and tantrums to go with it. How can one hold an intelligent conversation with a young man who understands nothing beyond playing with toy bricks, and who cries and screams if any attempt is made to take his toys away from him? More to the point, how can such a creature be instructed or even cajoled to perform the

Imperator's duties? The sheer *practical* problems, aside of anything else, would be an unimaginable nightmare.'

Marine stared at the fire, and chose her next words with the greatest care. 'It pains me to say it, naturally, but it seems a pity that Prince Osiv's physical health is so much greater than his mental health. If he had not survived into adulthood . . .' She let a shrug say the rest.

'When his condition was first realised,' Beck said, 'the incumbent Grand Mother suggested to the Imperator that perhaps it would be better for all if his life were terminated – without pain or suffering, of course – and an end be made of the whole matter. The Imperator might have agreed at that time, I think, but the Imperatrix wouldn't hear of it.' She tapped the glass's stem, producing a small, cold, ringing sound. 'She was a very *stubborn* woman, and while she was alive the Imperator paid her opinions altogether too much attention.'

'I was only a Low Sister at the time. I knew nothing of it, of course.'

'Oh, there was quite a furore. Grand Mother Bourne even petitioned the Fathers to have the Imperator's marriage pronounced void and a more docile wife found for him. But they were still debating the appeal when the Imperatrix bore a second son, so the question was shelved.' Beck's eyebrows lifted eloquently. 'That caused a second furore, at least in a few dark corners. It was whispered that the Imperator's line had been so tainted by inbreeding over the centuries that he was incapable of producing anything but idiots. He and the Imperatrix were first cousins, of course . . . So there *was* a rumour that she had looked elsewhere, shall we say, for the source of a healthy heir.'

Marine was shocked. 'You mean that the second child wasn't the Imperator's son at all?'

'As I say, it was a rumour.' Beck shrugged non-committally. 'But the Imperator didn't hear of it; he accepted the new child as his own. The baby bore a satisfactory resemblance at least to its

14

mother, and the tale died away as such things do. Pragmatically, the truth hardly matters, does it? All that Vyskir needed was a wholesome new prince to carry on the line. And at that time Prince Osiv wasn't expected to live beyond his fifth birthday.'

'But he did,' Marine said quietly.

'As you say; he did. And he's continued to confound the physicians ever since. Which leads us back,' Beck looked directly at Marine now, knowing that it was high time they both stopped procrastinating, 'to our present problem, and the unfortunate new development. You see, Marine, it has become necessary for the Imperator's younger son, Prince Kodor, to be married.'

Marine's eyes narrowed as she stared at her superior. 'Ah,' she said. 'There have been rumours . . . that, possibly, Sekol might be involved . . . ?'

She let the words trail off on a diffident interrogative, which was what Beck might have expected. Marine was too well-schooled to ask bluntly for the facts, but she had made a shrewd guess at what those facts were. And she was right.

Beck smiled thinly. 'The intended bride is Pola, Duke Arec of Sekol's daughter.' A note of sour irony crept into her tone. 'She is his only legitimate child, and he chooses to style her with the title of Marchioness.'

'I see.' Marine paused, then: 'Grand Mother . . . you used the word *necessary*.'

'So I did. Oh, there's been no impropriety; to my certain knowledge Prince Kodor and the Marchioness have never even met. But Duke Arec is very anxious that the marriage should take place without delay. In fact, one might say he is most *insistent*. And, unfortunately, the Imperator and the Exalted Council are not in a position to argue with him.'

'Ah,' Marine said again. 'I believe I understand.'

Beck nodded. 'Sekol has always been a potentially dangerous neighbour; they covet our fertile land and kinder climate, and for the past century they've been militarily far stronger than we are. Duke Arec succeeded his father less than two years ago, as you know, and he is of a very different mettle. He has a martial attitude and little subtlety, and the mountains between our countries are too riddled with passes to present any real obstacle to a determined invader. Sekol has always been a threat in potential, and now the potential has turned into a reality. Duke Arec has offered a proposition to the Imperator which, shorn of its fine diplomatic language, amounts to an ultimatum. He wants Sekol and Vyskir to become, effectively, a single kingdom. His arguments are very persuasive; I could recite you a dozen or more of them without pausing to draw breath. But what he's really offering, of course, is a simple choice: alliance, or invasion. The clinical term for it is blackmail.'

She could tell from the look in Marine's eyes that she had tacitly grasped a good deal more of the situation than had yet been spoken, and after a short pause to allow the information to be digested she continued.

'It is Vyskir's good fortune that our Imperator has sons while Duke Arec has a daughter, and not vice versa. This way the match will give the Sekolians what they want without threatening the security of our own kingdom. So four days ago the Sekolian ambassador arrived in the Metropolis, and the details of the marriage contract are even now being finalised.' She paused. 'However, there is one complication.'

'Prince Osiv,' Marine said thoughtfully.

'Exactly. I don't need to spell out the nature of the dilemma, do I? Obviously, even though Osiv is the Imperator's heir there can be no possible question of the Sekolian girl marrying *him*.'

'Duke Arec knows of his affliction, then?'

'Oh, yes. It would hardly have been practicable – or safe – to keep it from him. So she will wed Prince Kodor instead. However, by our law, younger sons of the royal blood are forbidden to marry until the eldest has taken a wife.' Beck made an impatient gesture. 'The measure was invented to stop a spate

16

of assassinations and usurpations centuries ago. It's a complete anachronism now, but it's so enshrined in custom that there would be a public outcry if the Exalted Council dared depart from it. We do *not* want to stir up a furore of that kind. So the only feasible way round the problem is to find a wife for Prince Osiv. That, Marine, is why I have summoned you. You see, the bride chosen for Prince Osiv is a member of your own family. Nanta EsDorikye – her mother is your cousin, I believe?'

Marine stared, her face registering shock and incredulity. Given to the religious way at the age of six, she had had little direct contact with her family through all of her life, and could barely remember the faces of her parents and siblings, let alone cousins. But as she racked her memory, a few snippets started to surface: letters from her eldest sister – years ago now – which had mentioned a cousin's marriage to an aristocratic landowner. The name, EsDorikye, rang a bell. As did the recollection that there had been one child of the marriage. A daughter, yes. Some small mystery about it as she recalled – hadn't the couple tried fruitlessly for years, before, suddenly and unexpectedly, a child had come? The details eluded Marine, or perhaps she had never known them, but there had been something special or unusual about it . . .

Beck, seeing the memory click into place, continued:

'The girl is twenty years old now, and a scholar at the Court Academy here in the Metropolis. She is also a member of the Academy choir; junior, of course, but I understand that she has considerable talent and had been earmarked for training as a soloist. She is very comely – even Father Urss of the Exalted Council hasn't failed to notice that.' Then she remembered that as yet Marine had had no dealings with Father Urss, so the sardony would be lost on her. 'These assets, combined with her pedigree, are enough to satisfy the requirements for a royal bride. And according to her tutors she is also very tractable.' This time the pause was long enough to be significant. 'Under the circumstances, as I'm sure you appreciate, that is the most vital quality of all.'

Marine saw her point immediately. 'If she knows nothing of the prince's affliction, the discovery will come as a shock,' she said.

'Indeed. So we must ensure that when she *does* discover the truth, she will not create any . . . difficulties. In other words, she must be thoroughly and carefully prepared for her new role. That, Marine, is the task I want you to undertake.'

A combination of teacher, chaperone and custodian, Marine thought. She nodded. 'I understand, Grand Mother. I'm honoured that you should consider me worthy.'

Beck smiled drily again. 'Your experience as head of the Sanctum will stand you in good stead; and the fact that you and the girl are related will help to smooth the path.'

'I've never met her, of course.'

'That's irrelevant. Blood still counts. Now: Nanta has not yet been told of her betrothal, and until the negotiations with Sekol have been completed, the Exalted Council would prefer her not to know. However, rumour has a habit of running ahead of fact, so it's vital that she should be removed from the Academy and placed in seclusion before any whispers start to circulate. She, and you, have been assigned a suite of rooms here in the Sanctum of the Lady, and you will keep her under supervision until the Council send word. It should only be a matter of a few days.'

'I understand, Grand Mother.' Marine hesitated. 'She will need to be given *some* reason for her removal. What should I tell her?'

'I leave that to your judgement and discretion,' said Beck. 'Though I see no reason why you should tell her anything; part of your task is to teach her to obey without question, so that will be a useful lesson.' She finished the last of her wine, then set the glass down and sat back in her chair with a grunt of satisfaction. 'I think we've covered the bones of the matter – or as many as we need to for the moment – and I don't doubt you would appreciate the chance to unpack and rest for a while before your duties begin.' She grasped a bell rope hanging by the hearth and gave it a hard tug. 'The chatelaine will show you to your quarters, and Nanta will be brought to you early this evening. Ask the chatelaine for anything you need, and convey any messages to me personally or through Sister Chaia. I'm dining at court tonight, so I won't be available until morning, but in my absence you may entrust Sister Chaia with any queries.'

Marine, who disliked wine and had not touched her own glass, recognised the tacit dismissal, rose to her feet and bowed respectfully. 'Thank you, Grand Mother. Oh . . . may I ask where the Sisters' chapel is?'

'Of course; you'll want to make your devotions, won't you?' Beck rarely visited the chapel herself, but Marine was tiresomely devout. 'Sister Chaia will direct you there and show you all you need. I will see you tomorrow morning. Not too early.'

'Yes, Grand Mother.' Marine bowed again. A tentative knock at the door announced the chatelaine, and with a benevolent gesture Beck waved both women out of the room.

When they had gone, she poured herself another glass of wine, then moved closer to the fire and frowned at the flames. In almost all respects Marine had lived up to her expectations; as she would have anticipated, seeing that she had trained the younger woman herself. But for all her shrewdness and quick understanding, Marine had neglected to ask one question – and that surprised Beck, for in her opinion it was the most obvious question of all. Was Marine, perhaps, being exceptionally tactful? No; it was more likely that the obvious simply hadn't yet occurred to her. It would, Beck had no doubt, for Marine was too intelligent to overlook it for long. But until it did . . . well, in truth Beck was relieved to have been spared the necessity of explaining *that* part of the Exalted Council's strategy. Marine could be told in good time. Nothing would happen, anyway, while the Imperator still lived. And even when he was dead, the girl, Nanta, need never find out the truth; not if the thing were done with proper care.

For when the Imperator *did* finally go to the arms of the God, Duke Arec of Sekol wanted more for his daughter than the role of the new Imperator's sister-in-law. Prince Osiv would sire no children, of course; so Prince Kodor was destined to succeed him eventually. But while Prince Osiv's physical, as opposed to mental, health continued to be robust, Arec would have to wait for his daughter to become Pola Imperatrix.

And that, as had been made emphatically clear to Father Urss, was something Duke Arec was not prepared to do.

Chapter II

Sister Iresya found her quarry in a close huddle with another student in one of the Academy quiet-rooms. At this hour the girls should have been studying, not whispering and twittering together like two peasant fishwives, and under normal circumstances Iresya would have sharply admonished them both for their inattention to duty. However, these circumstances were not normal, so instead she moved, silent in her slippers, across the room towards them.

As she approached, she heard a snatch of their talk.

'. . . tomorrow night, I've heard; so if we could reach the temple gallery by the west stairs, we might glimpse the ambassador for ourselves.' The dark girl who was speaking paused, then added with breathless, half-stifled excitement, 'And we might even see Prince Kodor!'

Her blonde companion's face lit with interest, but before she could reply, Sister Iresya intervened with quiet authority.

'Nanta.'

Both girls started, then scrambled guiltily to their feet and bowed to her. Sister Iresya raked the dark one with a look that promised stern words later, then addressed the other girl.

'You are to go to your room, Nanta, and pack your belongings.'

Nanta froze. 'Sister . . . ?'

'You heard me.' Iresya's tone became sharp. She had no time for explanations; besides, there was little she could explain, for she knew only what she had been told a mere few minutes ago. 'Do as I say, please, and don't dawdle.'

Even now Nanta didn't move, and the other girl, who had more courage in the face of her superiors, said, 'Sister, what has Nanti done?'

'Nant-*a*,' Iresya corrected automatically. 'We do not use diminutives here, Lulieth, as you know very well. Nanta has *done* nothing.'

'Then why—'

'That's not your concern. Kindly return to your books – and I will see you in my study after the refectory hour.'

She turned again to Nanta, expecting her to do as she was told without a further word. But Lulieth's boldness had given Nanta the confidence to speak up for herself, and she said haltingly, 'Sister, please . . . am I being expelled?'

Her tone was so bewildered and her face so distressed that Iresya relented a little.

'No,' she replied more kindly. 'You are not being expelled, Nanta; to the best of my knowledge you've done nothing to warrant that. But you are to leave the Academy.'

'Leave . . . ? For *good*?'

'I really couldn't say.' Iresya was becoming impatient again, and the feeling was fuelled by growing annoyance that she herself was almost as much in the dark as Nanta. 'All I know is that a High Sister – and a relative of yours, I understand – is here to take charge of you, and that she has received her instructions from Grand Mother Beck.'

Nanta's eyes widened. Though Beck rarely had any direct contact with the Academy students, she was known to and feared by them all. It was then that the wild, dreadful possibility flared into her mind like fire, and with it came a new terror. Had someone discovered her secret; the dreadful, guilt-ridden secret that she had striven so hard to keep from any other living soul? And if, somehow, they had found it out, what would they do to her . . . ?

Her mouth worked, but all the things she desperately wanted to say wouldn't come. At last, weakly, she managed to stammer, 'Yes, Sister.'

She went, her only farewell to Lulieth a single, helpless glance. Lulieth watched her go, Sister Iresya gliding in her wake. Then when she was sure they would both be out of sight along the corridor, she too ran from the room, agog to spread the news.

Nanta had her first sight of Marine as, clutching her valise, she came slowly down the back staircase from the senior dormitories. Standing in the shadows of the cold, cheerless hall at the stairs' foot, the first impression Marine gave was not reassuring. Tall, very upright, fair hair pulled severely back so that it barely showed beneath head-cap and wimple . . . she was well-built and might once have been handsome in a buxom way, but in middle age there was little spare flesh on her big bones, and that gave her a hard look. Her face was pockmarked, her light blue-grey eyes steady, her mouth unsmiling. Nanta shrank inwardly and might have stopped on the stairs, but a nudge from Sister Iresya, who was following on her heels, propelled her on.

'High Sister.' Iresya made a deferential bow. 'This is Nanta EsDorikye.'

Marine inclined her head, whether in greeting to Nanta or merely in acknowledgement of the introduction Nanta didn't know. Privately, Marine was a little surprised by what she saw. Certainly the girl was comely; in fact such an ordinary word didn't do her justice. But she looked more delicate than Marine had expected; almost fragile, in fact, as though she were made of china and could all too easily be broken. Which, perhaps, was part and parcel of Grand Mother Beck's thinking. Despite her resolve to be detached in this matter, Marine pitied Nanta.

However, there was no trace of pity in her voice as she said crisply, 'Thank you, Sister Iresya. You have been most helpful –

23

and at short notice, which must have been an inconvenience for you.'

Iresya blinked, a little taken aback by the considerate thought, then smiled. 'No trouble at all, High Sister, I assure you. Well, Nanta . . .' She looked at the girl, then suddenly seemed unable to find anything more to say. Another smile, more forced this time, and Sister Iresya turned and hurried away, leaving Nanta alone with Marine.

Marine, too, found herself at a loss for words. If the girl had been any ordinary postulant in her charge, there would have been no problem; experience had long ago overcome her natural reticence where they were concerned. This, though, was more complicated. Not only was the girl destined to hold the highest rank possible for any woman, she was also Marine's second cousin, and Marine was not accustomed to dealing with either high nobility or family.

She pushed down a sudden qualm that felt alarmingly like a return of her travel-sickness, and told herself firmly that, in effect, Nanta *was* no different from any ordinary postulant and so should be treated accordingly. That helped, and she said, trying to sound reassuring:

'My name is High Sister Marine. I am of the VerCoris family; your mother and I are first cousins, so I believe that makes you and I second cousins, does it not?'

'Yes, High Sister . . .' Nanta replied uneasily.

Marine searched her mind for something else that might crack the ice a little, but failed to find it. Resorting to practicalities, she said briskly, 'Come with me, child. Hurry, now. This way.'

Nanta had managed to keep her terrors at bay as she packed, but now, suddenly, they assailed her again. With an awful sense of fatalism she wanted to get the thing over with by asking Marine outright if her secret had been discovered. But, cowardly though it was, she couldn't bring herself to do it. There was a chance, even if slender, that she was wrong and no one knew: she had to pin her hopes on that and not assume the worst.

She didn't speak again — didn't trust herself at this moment — but silently and obediently followed Marine. They left the Academy by a route used mostly by the servants, crossed a bare, grim courtyard that Nanta remembered from punishment walking-penances, then went briskly along a narrow alley. Above and before them the great dome of the temple reared like a shining but oppressive vision; blinking up at it through the falling snow, Nanta felt a renewed tug of dismay. What would become of her place in the choir? She had been promised extra training, the chance of a soloist's status . . . was that, too, to be abandoned?

Then the thought collapsed as she saw where Marine was taking her.

They had reached the end of the alley, which opened into another courtyard decorated with tubs of small conifers. Ahead was an ornate door, and over the door was a blue canopy stitched with the white snowflake device of the Lady.

Nanta stopped dead. Marine was a few paces ahead and didn't notice at first. She moved under the canopy; Nanta heard her speak the ritual obeisance, then belatedly Marine realised that her charge was not keeping up with her.

She looked back. 'Nanta? What's the matter, child?'

Nanta stared back at her in consternation. 'This is the Sanctum . . .'

'Yes, it is. What of it? Come under the canopy, you foolish girl; the snow's getting heavier every minute.'

'But why. . .' She swallowed. 'Please; I'm not . . .'

Marine jumped to the natural, if wrong, conclusion that Nanta believed she was to be forced to take the veil and become a religious. That simply did not happen once a child was past twelve years old, and she said, 'Has no one explained to you? You're merely to stay here for a while; nothing more.'

25

Nanta blinked, and a trace of colour returned to her face. 'Why?' she asked.

Marine's mouth pursed primly. 'I'm not at liberty to tell you that, but you may rest assured it's not a punishment. Quite the contrary, in fact. Now stop faltering and come along.'

Nanta's heart was thudding painfully under her ribs as she obeyed. She had heard Marine's comment about this development being the opposite of a punishment, but it only registered on a vague level; at this moment her sole conscious reaction was one of relief. They did not know. She had not betrayed herself, and her secret was still intact. They did not know about the sleepwalking, and the dreams.

Marine led Nanta to the Sanctum's second floor, where the suite assigned to them was located. In a corridor thickly carpeted with deep blue plush, she opened a heavy, panelled door and walked into the room beyond, beckoning Nanta to follow.

Marine did not approve of their new quarters. She was austere by nature, and the disposition had been hardened by her years in a rural sanctum where creature comforts were few and far between. The opulence of the suite, with its polished, ornate furniture, massive chandeliers and rich fabrics that covered every inch of floor and walls, was like an assault on her senses. The suite comprised a reception room as large as the refectory of her own sanctum, two bedchambers dominated by posted and curtained beds that could comfortably have slept six people apiece, and, leading off each bedchamber, bathing rooms with marble bath and basin. This was not, to Marine's mind, the proper way of a religious house; and it was most certainly not suitable accommodation for a young and impressionable girl.

She glanced at Nanta and was a little reassured to see a look of bemused chagrin on her face. She, too, was used to Spartan surroundings, Marine reminded herself; and the thought abruptly made her feel a little more at ease with the girl.

'Well,' she said, disapproval rife in her voice. 'I believe we shall both feel out of place here, but we must make the best of it.' There was no point, she told herself, in speaking to the chatelaine about it; doubtless the suite had been Grand Mother Beck's choice, and one did not argue with Grand Mother Beck.

Nanta flicked her a look whose uncertainty was tempered by a slight hint of curious interest. Then she licked her lips and began: 'High Sister . . .'

Marine interrupted with a smile that looked more rigid than she intended. 'I think, Nanta, that as we are related, you need not address me so formally. Sister, or Sister Marine, will do.' She wondered momentarily if *cousin* would be better still, then quickly thought better of it. To address Nanta as her cousin was well enough now, but it would be out of the question in the future. Though it was hard to imagine this girl, this child, as the next Imperatrix of Vyskir. And impossible to imagine the life she would lead under the circumstances into which her marriage would force her . . .

She said, suddenly and unexpectedly, 'Nanta, are you devout?'

Nanta looked startled – and, Marine thought, almost frightened. She swallowed, then replied, 'I hope so, H . . . Sister.'

'How often do you pray to the Lady?'

An odd flush came to Nanta's cheeks. 'As often as I can.'

'That is not a very precise answer, child.'

The girl cast her gaze down. 'I go – that is, I went – to the Academy's chapel every day.' *And I prayed and prayed, until I felt I would burst with the force of my entreaties; yet the Lady never answered me . . .* But her face showed nothing of that.

Marine, with an insight unusual in her, said, 'Did you prefer to go alone?'

'. . . Yes. Yes, I did.'

'I understand. I, too, prefer my devotions to be private. But perhaps we will not object to each other's company in the Sanctum chapel?'

Nanta gave her such a strange look then that Marine was

quite nonplussed. The girl was frightened of something. Could she have got wind, somehow, of what lay in store for her? It seemed unlikely in the extreme that there could be any crack in the Exalted Council's security; but the unlikely was not the impossible. Yet Marine felt instinctively that she should look elsewhere for the answer to the puzzle. As had happened when they approached this building, Nanta's fear had something to do with the Sanctum itself.

Or with the Lady . . .

Nanta had not replied to her question about the chapel, and Marine decided that discretion might be her best course, at least for now.

'Well, you may make your own choice, of course,' she said aloud. 'I will visit the chapel twice each day: if you wish to come with me you are welcome to do so, but in either case I will expect you to attend at least once, as you have done until now.'

Still Nanta didn't speak; then bells began to ring in the distance and Marine recognised the chimes of the Sunset Devotional. The chatelaine had said that their evening meal would be served at about this hour (the timing did not suit, but it appeared there was no option), and Marine was still wearing the crumpled and travel-stained habit in which she had arrived. It would not do to sit down at table in such a state. She must wash, change. She needed to feel more presentable. And she needed time to marshal her thoughts and regain her equilibrium in the wake of this very eventful day.

Nanta was looking down at her own feet again, her expression a blank mask that might have been genuine or might have been a very well-practised disguise. Marine opened her mouth, half tempted to challenge the façade she presented, then changed her mind. Let well alone. It was not her business to probe.

'Go and unpack your belongings,' she said, unaware that her voice sounded unusually gentle. 'There'll be time enough for talking later.'

Nanta raised her gaze. Her fear had abated but her eyes were not happy as she answered meekly, 'Yes, Sister.'

Marine watched her walk away into the nearer of the two bedrooms, and felt foreboding move like a cold predator in her heart.

Late into the night Nanta sat wakeful in her new bed, propped by pillows and with a lamp shining softly beside her. She had heard the temple bells ring the Night Blessing, heard the last call of a distant watchman announcing that all was well and the city could sleep in safety; now, though, the world outside was silent and still. The fire in her room had gone out long ago, and with winter cold clamping down in earnest she felt chilled to the bone, despite the heavy, embroidered shawl she had wrapped around herself. The cold was keeping her awake, but even with warmth she doubted if she could sleep. Her mind was spinning with all the new and confusing impressions of the day, and with the fears which they had engendered. Earlier, as she and Marine picked at their meal and tried to make stilted conversation, she had found the courage to ask, directly, if this sudden and unexplained change in her circumstances had something to do with her family. It seemed logical enough, especially as Marine was a relative, but Marine had assured her – if assured was quite the word – that her family were not involved. No one had died, no one was ill, no one was disgraced. But she would say no more, and had discouraged any further questions with a terse suggestion that Nanta should concentrate on her food.

The very fact that Marine either would not or could not say more told Nanta that this change must mean something momentous. Her friend Lulieth would have pressed for answers, and she felt a sense of quick, scathing contempt at her own timidity. But she was not like Lulieth; never had been or, as far as she knew, could be. From the earliest age she had been conditioned to obedience, patience, compliance, and the habit was too ingrained in her to be overcome. A model daughter; a model pupil. Too afraid to be anything else.

Too afraid of what they would do to me if they knew what I have locked away in my mind.

She shivered then, a sudden, violent shudder that had nothing to do with the cold, and huddled deeper under her blankets. She felt lost in this vast bed, and if she closed her eyes it was horribly easy to imagine that other presences were creeping in with her. *Why* had she been housed in a place like this? She was nothing, no one, unimportant. What did they – whoever *they* were, in the hierarchy of temple or Academy or both – want with her?

She glanced at the wall behind her bedhead. On the far side of it Sister Marine was long abed in her own room. Nanta hoped she was asleep, for the thought that she, too, might be lying awake and aware in the deep of the night unnerved her. She had wanted to lock her door, lest Marine might come in to check on her, but the door had no lock or bolt. It suggested that she was not trusted, and that made Nanta feel uneasy and vulnerable. If she should walk tonight, what then? With no conscious control over her actions she might easily walk into Marine's room and, worse still, say something in her sleep that would betray the truth. Better to give thanks for an unquiet mind to keep her wakeful. Better that than risk the return of the vision and what it might lead to.

But for all her resolve, tiredness eventually got the better of Nanta. As the lamp began to use the last of its oil and burn low, her head drooped and her body relaxed back among the piled pillows. The room seemed to be merging into another vista, vague and misty and filled with alien, languidly moving shapes. The first images of a dream started to take form . . . and then, as her mind crossed over the borderland between sleeping and waking, she realised that there was another presence in the room with her.

Nanta opened her eyes. The lamp had gone out, but by the glow of a new, sourceless light she could clearly see the funeral bier that stood on the rich carpet beyond the foot of her bed. A figure lay on the bier. It was wrapped in an ice-blue shroud, the head covered so that no detail of face or hair was visible, but its hands lay free of the shroud's folds; white hands, clasped together as though in entreaty.

Nanta's heart began to pound with thick, painful intensity. The image before her was a tableau, as motionless and unreal as a painting, yet although she knew that it was not real, she also knew that she must respond to it in the way she always did. There was no choice; it was a compulsion and she could not defy it.

She rose from her bed and walked slowly towards the bier. How many times had this same pattern been repeated? Each time she tried to remember, and then tried to resist and make it happen differently, but she could never recall, and could never change the inevitable, inexorable train of events. Five steps, six. Were there always six? She was standing at the bier's head, looking down at the shape muffled under the shroud. She knew what she would see when she lifted the fold back, and terror moved in her like a cold, deep current. But still she could not stop herself from reaching out, from grasping the material that felt so insubstantial and so bitterly, bitterly cold, and drawing it aside.

The woman's eyes were closed as though in sleep, but Nanta knew she was not sleeping, for her face had the glacial pallor of death. Her lips were like clay, her skin as devoid of life and colour as alabaster, and the midnight bloom of her sloe-black hair was dulled as though with old, dry dust. A single, pale blue poppy lay on her breast, like a mourner's last tribute. She was very beautiful; more beautiful, in fact, than any human woman could possibly be. But then, she was not human, and Nanta knew her face, as did every child in Vyskir from the day it was

31

old enough to learn its first catechism. She was the divine consort of the God – the Lady of the Snow. And she was dead.

Nanta stared down at the Lady's motionless image, as she had done so many times in this same vision. The air was growing bitter, darker. Cold snowflakes began to fall from nowhere, alighting on the Lady's face and hair, flecking her shroud with silver.

And a voice without source or timbre or inflection whispered a single word in Nanta's mind:

'*Vengeance . . .*'

Chapter III

Perhaps it was just an effect of the late hour, but Prince Kodor felt a distinct sense of unreality as he walked in the midst of the procession that was making its way from the palace to the temple. The ancient tunnel between the two, customarily used only by the imperial family and the highest members of the Exalted Council, was lit by old-fashioned lanterns which gave off a thin, foggy glow, dimming the colours of faces and hair and gorgeous fabrics to a faintly unsettling neutrality. The procession looked, Kodor thought, like a parade of animated corpses. And most corpselike of them all, as though the effect were a harbinger, was the thin, stooped figure of his father, the Imperator. Arctor IX moved with the halting gait of old age and infirmity, supported by two of his personal servants while a page held the train of his heavy ermine cloak. Not for the first time Kodor felt a stirring of anger. The Imperator didn't have the stamina for this; the day had been long and gruelling, and he should have been comfortable in his bed a long time ago. But protocol had to be observed to the letter, so despite the fact that it was well past midnight, the rite of sanction must be performed and, fit or otherwise, the Imperator must attend. The procession followed the shuffling and painfully slow pace he set, and Kodor resigned himself to a further tedious hour of ritual before duty would finally be done for the day.

Since the arrival of the delegation from Sekol, Kodor had had enough of duty to last him a lifetime; and today, the final day of the formalities, had been the most taxing yet. He had sat dutifully at his father's side through the hours of talk and wrangle and rhetoric (though the negotiations concerned him more than anyone, he was not permitted to speak). Then, when the fine details were agreed and the thing signed and sealed, he had walked behind the Imperator and the Sekolian ambassador (who was overweight, loudly overcompensating for a smothered sense of his own inadequacy, and had a smell that would have been greatly improved by a thorough wash) in the progress to the banqueting hall, where he had dutifully played the expansive co-host in the feast that followed. The food, designed to please a Sekolian palate, had been too spiced and rich for his taste, and now his stomach felt distended and uncomfortable.

It wasn't just the food that had affected him. Despite the fact that he had long been prepared for this day, the knowledge that he would soon be a married man made him distinctly queasy; and the sensation was compounded by the fact that his intended bride was a complete stranger. He had always known that he would have little if any choice in the wife he would take, but when theory became reality it was still something of a shock. He had never even *met* the Marchioness Pola, and knew little about her other than that she was the only legitimate scion of Arec of Sekol, and heiress to his title when the time came (which, Exalted Father Urss had smoothly said to the ambassa-dor, might it please the God was far in the future). Indeed, Kodor had not so much as set eyes on Pola in any shape or form before this evening, when the ambassador had presented him with a miniature cameo portrait. Kodor had looked very carefully at the cameo. He was well aware that court painters kept their positions by embroidering and flattering the truth, but even allowing for that he had to admit to himself that his prospective bride was not unattractive. Skin a little sallow, perhaps, and face a little long, but she had rich, dark hair, well-modelled features and quiet eyes. She looked intelligent, which was a blessing.

Whether or not he would like her, or she him, was another matter entirely; but on first impressions at least, the choice could have been far worse.

Not that there was a choice at all when one looked at the matter pragmatically. Glancing at Father Urss's gaunt, erect back view as he glided silently at the ambassador's side, Kodor admitted to himself that, for all his long-held dislike of the head of the Exalted Council, Urss could not be faulted on any grounds for his loyalty to the crown he served. Negotiation with the Sekolians had been a long, hard wrangle, for there was no doubt that they held all the trump cards. Militarily stronger, geographically all but impregnable, and now ruled by a man with very distinct ambitions which he made no effort to hide, Sekol was rapidly becoming a palpable threat to its weaker neighbour. Vyskir, with its fertile land and well-placed sea and river ports, was a crop ripe for harvesting, and Father Urss took the view that if the harvest was inevitable, it was better to turn the scythe to advantage rather than attempt to repel its sweeping advance. What could not be resisted could, instead, be united. So one day Kodor and Pola would be Duke and Duchess of Sekol, and also joint Regents of Vyskir. That was a part of the agreement, and it was enough – though only just – to satisfy Duke Arec.

Kodor recalled the difficulty that had arisen when the question of a dynastic match was first mooted. Arec had assumed that his daughter would marry the Vyskiri heir apparent, not a mere younger brother; he knew nothing about Prince Osiv's affliction, and the first response from the Exalted Council, to the effect that such a marriage was out of the question, had resulted in a misunderstanding that could easily have turned very unpleasant indeed. Eventually, at Father Urss's insistence, the Council had agreed to tell Arec the truth. Kodor had not been party to the intense discussions and negotiations that had flown back and forth between the two countries in the months that followed, and he doubted if even his father knew the half of what had been said and done. But at last the framework of an agreement was hammered out. Osiv could never rule in anything but name; Marchioness Pola might not have the ultimate title of Imperatrix, but she would have the power and the trappings of the title, and with that proviso written into the agreement, Duke Arec was content enough.

Which left only the matter of Osiv himself.

Kodor turned his head a little, and, with a practised trick of looking without seeming to look, his restless grey gaze flicked back to another figure walking a little way behind him. He knew Grand Mother Beck by sight, of course; as head of Vyskir's entire order of religious women she often had business with the court. But it was unusual to find her included in such a private occasion as this. She had played no part whatever in the negotiations – that was not the role of any woman, however high-ranking – and her presence now did not fit with the expected form. But Kodor, whose high intelligence included a very well-developed talent for speculation, had seen Mother Beck and Father Urss keeping company together a number of times recently. They were always engrossed in talk and had never noticed him as he passed them by; and he believed he understood, now, what lay behind Beck's inclusion. With her knowledge, her connections and her well-known network of blue-robed spies among the Sanctum sisters, Beck was ideally placed to solve the problem of Osiv and the law that obliged him to be the first of the Imperator's sons to marry. Urss must have set her to find Osiv a bride; and the fact that Beck was walking in the procession tonight was implicit evidence that she had succeeded.

Kodor wondered who the chosen girl was. Not that it really mattered; Osiv's only possible interest in his wife would depend on her willingness or otherwise to play with him. For a moment, with cynical amusement, Kodor caught himself trusting that the bride would bring a dowry of toy bricks with her, then he pushed the thought aside as unworthy and in bad taste. It would be kinder to feel a modicum of pity for the girl, whoever she was. But then, no doubt Beck would have done her research well, and chosen someone whose compliance would be assured; the kind of vapid, hapless creature for whom Kodor had no time whatever. Besides, whatever the disappointments of marriage to Osiv, it was probably a preferable alternative to a future in the Imperial Sanctum.

The procession finally reached the end of the tunnel. Liveried servants waited by a door decorated in gold leaf; they swung the door open, bowing low, and after a few moments' pause to allow the Imperator to catch his breath, the group stepped through into the temple. From here a wide, shallow staircase gave on to a private upper gallery which in turn led to the imperial box. More servants waited to open the box doors, and the Imperator and his immediate party went inside. As he followed his father and the Sekolian ambassador, Kodor was intrigued to notice that Father Urss had not joined them, as might be expected, but instead was moving away with the rest of the gathering. Grand Mother Beck was walking at his side. Kodor's dark eyebrows lifted a fraction, and curiosity stirred his mind from the drowsiness that was creeping over it. But then he saw that the royal group was waiting for him, the ambassador looking back with more than a trace of impatience in his expression. Schooling his face into a bland mask, Kodor forgot Urss and Beck, and took his place in the box.

As tonight's ceremony was not a public one, the curtains and screens of the occupied cubicles were drawn back, so that all present had a clear view both of the bowl of the temple and of the occupants of other cubicles. A lesser priest was officiating tonight, so Father Urss settled to enjoy his vantage point without needing to pay any attention to the proceedings. He saw the Sekolian ambassador yawning and Prince Kodor trying not to follow suit, and his upper lip curled in private deprecation of their weakness. Everyone was tired, himself not least of all; but to allow it to show was a sign of poor discipline. Back and head erect, eyes sweeping the vista of the temple and checking that all was as it should be and nothing left wanting for this august occasion, he watched as the High Father took his place at the altar, followed by the Imperial Sanctum choir in full ceremonial dress. As the High Father's powerful voice rose in the first of the Sanctification chants, Urss murmured to Beck, in her chair beside him.

'The girl Nanta is no longer in the choir, I presume?'

'No, Father.' Beck's gaze flicked briefly to him. 'She was removed from the Academy yesterday evening, and is now in the Sanctum under the care of High Sister Marine VerCoris.'

'Mmm.' Urss's mouth hardened a little. 'I would have preferred it, Mother Beck, if you had consulted me before appointing a chaperone for her. I had assumed – erroneously, it seems – that you would undertake that task yourself.'

Beck's bulldog face remained impassive. 'I'm sorry, Father,' she said, 'but with all the other calls on my time, there simply aren't enough hours in the day for me to govern the girl as the situation demands. She must be supervised by someone who can give her their undivided attention. I trained Sister Marine myself and she was my second-in-command for many years. She has my complete trust and confidence.'

Urss's mouth pursed slightly. 'Then I must rely on your judgement, and trust in my turn that it proves sound.' He paused to give his point the required emphasis. 'Have you told High Sister Marine why Nanta has been put in her charge?'

'I've told her that the girl has been chosen as Prince Osiv's bride,' Beck said, and added before he could voice an objection, 'I considered it necessary to reveal that much, to ensure that Marine understands the importance of her task.'

'Mmm.' Urss was noncommittal. 'But you've said nothing beyond that?'

Beck eyed him sidelong. 'Naturally not.'

The choir's voices were rising in an ethereally beautiful anthem, but the sound washed over Urss and Beck and was ignored. Urss leaned forward, looking over the edge of the box. He gave the impression that he was gazing down at the priest and choir, but in reality he was covertly watching the Imperator. Beck, aware of it, said, 'His Majesty does not look at all well.'

'Indeed.' Urss's eyes narrowed perceptibly.

'I understand that his physicians are not optimistic.'

'They are not. Candidly, Mother Beck, they hold out little hope of his surviving beyond midwinter, and I see no reason to disagree with them. For that reason, if for no other, it's vital that both the princes should be married as quickly as possible. If the Imperator were to die before either one of the weddings takes place, we could find ourselves in an extremely delicate position.'

Beck nodded. With Arctor gone, Prince Osiv would be Imperator; and yet another complication of Vyskiri law stated that any royal marriage could only take place with the Imperator's express public blessing. Osiv was not fit to bless anything, least of all in public, but the law was the law and could not be flouted. If Arctor died before both his sons were safely wed, the truth about Osiv would have to come out. That was unthinkable – and not only for the obvious reason. But the second reason was not something to be directly discussed, even in the privacy of the temple cubicle. When the Imperator was dead, it would be another matter. While he lived, Beck and Urss were both too wise and too experienced to risk even the smallest indiscretion.

'For once,' Urss continued, 'Duke Arec's impatience is likely to work in our favour. It will be a strong factor in persuading the Imperator to the idea of an early marriage.'

'Do you intend to speak with him soon, Father?'

'In the morning.' Urss finally abandoned his scrutiny of the

Imperator's distant figure. 'I foresee no problems; the Imperator is a reasonable man, and as aware as anyone of the situation with Sekol. All being well, I think the Council will be able to begin the preparations without any delay.'

'Ah. Then the girl may be told soon?'

He glanced at her, a cold look that had a hint of censure. 'Soon enough, Mother Beck. I'll make sure that you're informed when the time comes.'

Beck had had too many dealings and clashes with the whole coterie of Exalted Fathers to be intimidated, and she only smiled thinly. 'I shall await your word, Father.'

Three more days passed before the word came. When it did, Grand Mother Beck sent a brief message to Marine, to the effect that she was to bring Nanta to Beck's office promptly at the first evening hour.

Marine received the summons with a feeling of overwhelming relief. It seemed she was to be spared the task of revealing the situation to Nanta and coping with the flood of questions that would inevitably follow. She had been observing her charge very carefully over the past few days, and had come to the conclusion that she would not react to the news with the wholehearted joy that might be expected. Unlike most girls of her age and station, Nanta was not ambitious. Her only real aspiration, as far as Marine could tell, was – or had been – to become a soloist in the Academy choir. Given that, and the girl's quiet piety which had unexpectedly impressed Marine, she would have been an excellent candidate for the life of a religious. It was, Marine thought, a regrettable waste.

However, it not was the place of a mere High Sister to question or even comment on court politics, so Marine set her thoughts aside and went to Nanta's room. Nanta was alarmed to learn that she was to be brought before Mother Beck, and Marine's brisk assurance that there was nothing to fear made little difference.

Nanta tried to ask questions, but her timidity, and the fact that Marine seemed concerned only with trivialities such as what she should wear and how she must conduct herself, squashed her efforts. Marine went away with a few last exhortations about protocol and decorum, and Nanta was left alone to cope with her thoughts as best she could.

She started to move towards the window, then abruptly changed her mind and instead sat down on the bed. She felt queasy with nervousness that bordered on outright fear. It seemed that she was at last about to learn what really lay behind the sudden and confounding change in her circumstances, and no matter how hard she tried, she could not imagine what the truth might possibly be. All she *did* know was that Grand Mother Beck never did anything without a very good reason. And anything in which she was concerned would not be a minor matter.

Nanta shut her eyes and pressed her fingertips to her temples, feeling the uneven throb of her pulse under the skin. Yet again she told herself that there could be no possible connection with her dreams. She had walked in her sleep on two nights out of the last three, but on both occasions she had woken before leaving her room: once to find herself standing at the window and gripping the curtains, the other when she attempted to walk through a solid wall where her dysfunctioning mind told her a door should have been. She had cried out that time, but no one had come to investigate. No one *knew*.

She opened her eyes again, let her hands drop to her lap and calmed herself with several deep, controlled breaths. Better. She would bathe, change every stitch of her clothes. Wear an unelaborate gown, Sister Marine had said. Marine would help her to dress her hair. No jewellery; save perhaps for something inconspicuous at her throat, a small jet choker or some such. Modesty. Decorum. To meet Grand Mother Beck's exacting standards . . .

Suddenly the nausea became real, rising in her gorge like a wellspring. Nanta stood up and swallowed, hard. It didn't help.

She walked quickly and a little unsteadily to the bathing room, where she was dizzily sick into a polished bronze basin. When the spasm was over she stayed motionless for a while, staring at the wall but seeing nothing. Then, quietly, she straightened, cleared away the mess, and rang for a servant to bring hot water and prepare her bath.

She fainted when they told her. Father Urss, whose presence at the interview had already horrified Nanta and intimidated Marine, was not amused; but Grand Mother Beck had half expected it. Shock and excitement were a powerful brew. Beck had little regard for the foibles of modern girls, who in her opinion lacked the backbone of her own generation, but under the circumstances the lapse was forgivable. There was a brief business with some smelling salts, and as soon as Nanta was coherent again, Father Urss continued as though nothing had happened. He spoke of the extraordinary honour that had been bestowed on Nanta; he trusted, he said, that she was wise enough and humble enough to give heartfelt thanks to the God for the blessing which he, in his infinite wisdom, had granted. He also trusted (this in a tone that made the price of disobedience abundantly clear) that she would apply herself diligently, and with the modesty and compliance properly instilled into her by her schooling, to the role and the duties of her new station.

Nanta listened to Urss's homily with bemusement, returning a glazed stare that gave her the air of a hypnotised rabbit. Now and again the muscles in her throat worked violently, but she said nothing, made no show of delight or dismay or any other reaction whatever. She nodded when she was expected to nod, shook her head on cue, and when a document was put in front of her she made no attempt to read it but signed her name with a quick, jerky movement as though her hand were being guided by an outside force.

In what seemed a very short space of time the formalities were done. Father Urss turned to Beck and said something about the public announcement of the betrothal, which would apparently take place tomorrow morning; then he stood up, gave Nanta one last, impersonal look as though he were assessing the worth of a piece of furniture, and with a general nod to the three women, left the room.

Marine felt a little of the tension ebb from her shoulders, and Beck sat back in her upholstered chair. 'Well,' she said, and eyed the frozen girl in much the same way as Urss had done. 'Nanta. Have you nothing to say?'

Nanta knew she must reply, but no words she could think of seemed adequate or even relevant. 'No, Grand Mother,' she whispered. Then something came to her; trivial in the extreme but, illogically, it mattered. 'Except . . .'

'Yes?'

'My mother and father . . . Do they – have they been told?'

'Not yet,' Beck replied.

'Then may I – may I write a letter to them? I want, you see, I *need* so much to ask them . . .'

Her voice tailed off under Beck's keen scrutiny. 'To ask them what, child?' Beck said. 'I hardly think that their permission will be lacking, and if there are any womanly questions you want to confide to your mother, Sister Marine or I can answer them as easily.' She smiled a hard, dry smile. 'I don't think it appropriate for you to write to your parents at present. They will be told of your good fortune through official channels, as is proper, and you may apply your time and energy to your own immediate concerns. Which, I might add, will be *quite* enough to occupy you from now on.'

Nanta's head drooped a little. 'Yes, Grand Mother.'

'Well. Do you *have* any questions you wish to ask me?'

She did, but the refusal of her first request had intimidated her beyond the point where she could voice them. 'No, Grand Mother,' she said.

'Good. Then I think we're done for the time being. There are one or two more formalities to be seen to, but they are minor and won't hold up preparations for the wedding ceremony.' She consulted a small gold-edged book. 'You're to begin an intensive period of instruction in court etiquette tomorrow morning, and be taken to the senior imperial dresser in the afternoon. Father Urss wishes you to make your first public appearance as the Bride-Prospective in four days' time.'

'*Four days?*' Nanta stared at her in dismay. 'But—'

Beck interrupted. 'There's ample time to prepare. You will be carefully rehearsed, and provided you pay attention there'll be nothing to fear. You must get used to such things, Nanta. You're no longer a private citizen; you have new obligations and must fulfil them readily and with dignity.' She laid her hands on the desk, a gesture Marine recognised as a signal that the interview was over. The Sister rose, touching her charge's shoulder.

'Come, Nanta. Grand Mother has a lot to do, and we mustn't take up more of her time than necessary.'

'Have a sound night's sleep,' Beck said, as though Nanta would find that the easiest thing in the world, 'and be refreshed and ready when the First Obligation chimes ring. I will have reports of your progress from Marine, and will speak with you again in a day or so.' She smiled again, an attempt this time to seem pleasant and reassuring, which did not quite work, and her fingers formed a sign of blessing. 'The Lady go with you.'

Marine said nothing as she and Nanta walked back towards the suite. Nanta couldn't judge the reason for her silence. It might have stemmed from discomfort or simply from lack of interest; Marine's angular face was far from easy to read. Not that she truly cared what might or might not be moving Marine at this moment; her own mind was too full, and there was scant room for anyone else's concerns.

She was beginning to function again as the numbness of initial shock wore off. As yet everything was still confused and disjointed; but a number of starkly bewildering images stood out like beacon lights in dense fog. *Prince Osiv. Marriage. Wife. Princess. Imperatrix. Prince Osiv. I still don't believe this. I don't, I don't. Yet it's true . . .* And overlaying them all was one frustrating question. *Why me? I am no one important. My family does not move in imperial circles, and I've never so much as set foot at court. Why have they chosen me?*

Father Urss or Mother Beck could have answered her, but she hadn't had the courage to ask either of them. Marine could also have answered, but Nanta was unaware of that. *Prince Osiv. I've never even seen him. He's a stranger. And I am to marry him.*

What *did* she feel? Confusion swelled anew as Nanta struggled to make some sense of her inner maelstrom. Was she thrilled or miserable? Excited or terrified? She had always hoped that one day she *would* marry – the match would be arranged without reference to herself, and there was a strong probability that she would not meet her future husband more than once or twice before the wedding. One expected that. It was the way the world worked among nobler families, and it usually worked tolerably enough. But to marry the heir to the throne . . . That was a prospect beyond imagination. So far removed from reality that the idea of its *becoming* reality made her want to laugh.

Or cry. Why that? She had no secret paramour, no love of her life; she was not like the tragic, misunderstood heroine of a popular story. She was simply Nanta, who until now had lived her unremarkable life and had her unremarkable ambitions, and who had been content with them.

Perhaps, she thought, *I do still believe that I'm dreaming, and will wake up soon and find myself back in the Academy with nothing more than a day of choir rehearsals before me.* She wasn't dreaming, she knew that; but her situation had so many of the qualities of a dream that it seemed more rational and more comfortable to treat it as one. In time, that would change. Let it bide until then, she thought helplessly. Let it bide. What other choice was there?

Marine, meanwhile, was feeling distinctly uncomfortable. She could no more read Nanta's face than Nanta could read hers, but she was suffering a sudden and acute attack of conscience, revolving around, as she saw it, one very major omission in today's events.

Marine had expected Urss or Beck to make at least *some* reference to Prince Osiv's condition – but they had not. From a pragmatic viewpoint Marine could well understand why it was wiser, indeed safer, to keep Nanta in ignorance for a while longer. However, to understand something was not necessarily to like it, and Marine found that kind of pragmatism hard to reconcile with her own fundamental honesty. Nanta was an intelligent girl, and if matters were explained to her properly, Marine had no doubt that she would understand her duty and submit to it quietly. There was no *need* for this subterfuge. But subterfuge was a reflex among politicians, and the higher they rose, the more deeply ingrained the habit seemed to become. Marine could no more change that fact than stop the stars in their courses, and she was not the kind of person even to think of trying. Nonetheless, she believed firmly that if the world could be purged of such deceits, it would be all the better for it.

They reached the door of the suite, and abruptly a feeling close to panic welled up in Nanta's stomach. She needed help, advice, explanations; but her only possible confidante now was Sister Marine, and she didn't think she could bring herself to make the first move in Marine's direction. However, as the door opened, revealing the oppressive luxury of the room beyond, she made a floundering effort.

'Sister . . .'

Marine looked at her as though surprised to hear her speak.
'Yes?'

'*Why* have they chosen me?'

The question was direct enough to bring a sharp, unwanted
flush to Marine's cheeks. For a moment her instinct was to
invent a quick and plausible tale to content Nanta, but then she
thought: why tangle the skeins still further? It seemed pointless.
The truth, or at least an approximation of it, was better.

'I honestly don't know, Nanta,' she said. 'Decisions such as
these are always made by the Exalted Council – and the
Imperator himself, of course – and they don't make us privy to
their deliberations.' They entered the outer room and she closed
the door before adding, 'However, I do know that it was Grand
Mother Beck who made the initial recommendation.'

Nanta digested that for a few moments, but it made no more
sense to her than anything else did. At last she said, 'What of
Prince Osiv? Did he have any say?'

'You mean that perhaps he has seen you, without your
knowing it, and that the choice was his?' Marine couldn't help
but pity Nanta's naïvety. 'No, I don't think that's at all likely.'

'Oh.' Nanta cast her eyes down as her small, vague theory
was negated. She walked slowly towards her bedroom, then
abruptly stopped and looked back at Marine.

'I've never seen the Prince, either.'

'Few have,' said Marine evenly. 'The imperial family don't
show themselves to the common gaze.'

'Yes, I know . . . but if I'm to *marry* him—'

'Nanta.' Marine interrupted quietly but firmly. 'I think you're
becoming a little overwrought.' Her conscience was squirming
again, but she had to play her part and not allow sentiment to
sway her. 'The choice is made, and it isn't for us to question it or
to make difficulties. You should be giving thanks for your good
fortune, not quibbling about details.' Then, horribly aware that
she was beginning to sound like Father Urss, she modified her

tone to something more gentle. 'There's nothing to *fear*, child. As a royal wife you'll have every comfort and privilege that the court can bestow – and don't forget that the future Imperator has many demands on his time. I doubt that you'll see very much of Prince Osiv at all.'

She wondered briefly if she had hinted too much by that last comment, but Nanta didn't seem to find anything amiss. She was staring down at her own hands now, her gaze introverted, and she said:

'All I know about the Prince is that he is twenty-seven years old. I've heard tell that he has fair hair and green eyes, but I've never seen a portrait of him.'

'Portraits rarely show the truth in my experience, so that's nothing to regret.' And the few that existed of Prince Osiv, Marine reflected, most *certainly* didn't tell the whole story. She moved across the room, smoothing her skirt briskly. 'Come along now, Nanta; have done with speculation and let us turn our minds to practical matters. You heard what Grand Mother said – you're to have a sound night's sleep and be ready for a busy day tomorrow. So no more talk, now. I'll order your supper, and you can prepare for bed.'

Nanta wanted to argue, but the will for it simply wasn't there. She moved slowly into her bedchamber, distantly aware of the sound of Marine ringing the servants' bell, and stood for a few moments staring at her window. Someone had come in and closed the curtains during her absence, and, irrationally, it felt like a trespass, an invasion of her privacy. As if she could do nothing for herself. But then, she must expect and accept such things from now on. Nanta had never had any ambitions towards true freedom – the concept simply didn't apply to girls of her age and station – but the sense of near-panic assailed her again as she tried to imagine what her new life would demand of her. *Every comfort and privilege that the court can bestow.* Every stricture and protocol, too; and all of it among strangers. She didn't know if she would cope. She didn't know if she *could*.

From the outer room came the sound of Marine's crisp tones, answered by the softer, deferential voice of the servant who had answered the bell. Nanta shivered, and for a fleeting moment an inner devil asked: *What if I should refuse? What then?*

The question, and the spark of rebellion, faded and died without an answer. There was no possibility of refusal. She had already given her consent; that document, which she hadn't even had the wherewithal to read, had sealed her fate, and she had signed it without a murmur of protest. The thing was done, and no part of it could be changed.

The same unknown hand that had drawn the curtains had also laid a night robe out on her bed, together with her embroidered surcoat to keep away the cold. Nanta loosed her hair from its pins and began to undress. She did not think she would sleep tonight. But if there was no sleep, at least there could be no dreams.

Chapter IV

Preparations for the wedding rapidly began to gather momentum, and they carried Nanta with them like a fallen leaf in a fast current. To the satisfaction of Urss and Beck, the Bride-Prospective proved as docile as anyone could wish. She submitted herself dutifully to long hours of study and rehearsal, stood silently and patiently through back-aching ordeals in the salon of the imperial dresser, sat motionless and rigid while Vyskir's most noted court painter worked on her pre-nuptial portrait. Her first public appearance passed off flawlessly; magnificent in a stiff gown and a headdress and veil that hid her face from the vulgar gaze, she was driven by the outer route from the Sanctum to the imperial palace, where in a formal ceremony she was presented to the court. The citizens of the Metropolis gathered along the route in great numbers to glimpse her, and she acknowledged them, as she had been taught, with only a decorous inclination of her head. Even Father Urss could not have asked for more.

All in all, the announcement of Prince Osiv's betrothal had brought a very satisfying public response. Rejoicing was widespread and enthusiastic; it was a long time since the populace had such an event to celebrate, and Vyskir was *en fête*. The marriage date had been set for the beginning of the midwinter cycle, now only a month away. It would mean an unseemly scramble to have everything ready in time, but the combined goads of Duke Arec's impatience and the Imperator's increasing frailty persuaded Urss that sooner was safer. It also ameliorated the problem of Osiv himself; they would have to show him in public on the day of the wedding, but midwinter daylight – or rather, lack of it – would minimise the risk of his condition being noticed by the crowds. Arec of Sekol and his daughter would be guests of honour at the celebrations; the proclamation of the Marchioness Pola's betrothal to Prince Kodor was to be made on the following day, and the Sekolians would then remain at court for a further month, when the second marriage would take place.

Then, on the eighth day after the betrothal proclamation, the Imperator took a chill. It was nothing serious, but in his state of health even a minor complaint was cause for concern, and the senior court physician told Urss privately that another such ailment could be His Majesty's last. Urss was alarmed. He had assumed that the Imperator would live until both his sons' marriages were safely solemnised, but this news changed everything. Kodor *must* be married before Arctor died – there was nothing for it but to bring the second wedding forward, to follow Osiv's by a bare few days.

Thankfully there was a lull in the snowfall and the roads were still clear enough for fast horseback travel, so a message was sent immediately to Duke Arec, apprising him of the situation. Arec's reply arrived after six days, and to Urss's relief he raised no objections. His sole interest was in securing the alliance, and the fact that his daughter's wedding would be a low-key and hasty affair didn't concern him. If Pola was disappointed, she would simply have to live with it.

The logistics of organising two major celebrations in such a short space of time were a nightmare to contemplate; but with the resources of Grand Mother Beck and her Sisters at his disposal, Father Urss believed they would cope. He explained the situation to the Imperator and Prince Kodor at a private meeting in the palace, adding his assurances that, with the God's blessing, all would go smoothly enough. Arctor nodded and sighed and said, yes, if that was what Duke Arec wanted, he would raise no objections. Let him be told what he must do and when, and he would play his expected part and be thankful when the whole thing was over. Kodor said nothing at all in his father's presence. He had not been asked for his reaction to the news, nor for his opinion of the hastily revised plans. But when Urss rose, bowed to the Imperator and made to withdraw, the prince asked if he, too, might be excused. Arctor acquiesced with a gesture and a vague, weary smile, and Kodor followed Urss out of the room. When the door had closed behind them, cutting them off from earshot of anyone, the prince said:

'Father Urss. A moment of your time, if you please.'

Urss paused. Though their encounters were always punctiliously polite, he and Kodor did not like each other. Their views often conflicted, and in Kodor's case the conflicts were openly expressed. Urss was not used to being argued with and took a dim view of anyone who tried. The Imperator did not try; he knew the proper way of things and had almost always been willing to defer to his advisors. Unfortunately, he had failed to instil the lesson into his younger son.

Urss made a slight, wary bow and said, 'Of course, Your Grace. How may I be of service?'

In the low light of the corridor Kodor's grey eyes looked like flint. 'Just one question, Father. Has my brother been told about this?'

Urss had not expected quite such a direct approach, but he didn't let his momentary discomfiture show. 'No, Your Grace, he has not,' he replied smoothly. 'Naturally, until the Imperator himself had been informed—'

'Of course. However, I wasn't referring to the new change of plan. I meant, has Prince Osiv been told that he is to marry?'

Father Urss's eyebrows lifted with an eloquence that was an answer in itself, and Kodor smiled coldly.

'I see. So amid all this hectic efficiency, no one has considered that it might be worth informing Osiv of the changes that are about to take place in his life.'

Urss sighed. 'Your Grace, I trust you'll forgive my bluntness, but to inform Prince Osiv of anything outside the scope of his own simple concerns is . . . well, to put it delicately, it is a little *challenging*. His affliction—'

He was interrupted. 'Father Urss, I'm probably more familiar with Osiv's affliction than anyone else at court, so I'm well aware of his limitations – and his capabilities. If matters are explained to him carefully and patiently, I'm quite sure that he'll be able to grasp the basics. At the very least, it seems only the merest courtesy to try.'

Urss was too skilled a politician to allow his irritation to show, and he made an acquiescent gesture. 'Naturally, Your Grace, if that's what you wish, it shall be done.'

Kodor nodded. 'Thank you. But I merely wanted an answer to my question; now that I have it, I'll tell Osiv myself.' He paused. 'And what of his bride, Father? I know nothing whatever about the chosen girl – what should I tell my brother about *her*?'

Urss's irritation evaporated as, belatedly, he saw the nature of the game. This concern for Prince Osiv was a charade to disguise Kodor's own curiosity. Pride prevented him from asking openly and directly about Nanta EsDorikye, but he wanted to know, so he was using Osiv as an excuse. The ploy appealed to what passed, in Urss, for a sense of humour, and his face relaxed into an expression that was almost benevolent.

'Naturally, Your Grace, I'll be pleased to tell you anything I can. Prince Osiv's bride is of the north-eastern house of the EsDorikye family. Her sire and grandsire—'

'Yes, yes; I don't doubt her pedigree's impeccable, but that won't interest Osiv,' Kodor said impatiently. 'What does she look like? What is her character?'

Urss suppressed a smile. 'She is twenty years old, slight and fair-haired. I think anyone would judge her comely. As to her character . . . well, she is pleasant-natured; modest and docile, and her Academy tutors speak well of her. I can't imagine that Prince Osiv will take exception to her.'

'I see. But will she take exception to him, I wonder?' Kodor's look had hardened, and Urss saw a new and shrewd glint in his eyes. There was something more to this, he thought suddenly; something beyond ordinary curiosity. He looked quickly for a way to probe further, but before he could hone his thoughts Kodor said:

'She hasn't been told, has she? She still believes that Osiv is . . . normal.'

Ah, Urss thought, *we begin to move towards the nub of it*. Aloud, he replied, 'That's so, Your Grace. Under the circumstances—'

'Quite. We agree on that, at least. So she has no reason to doubt that one day, in the fullness of time, she will be Imperatrix in her own right. Which we, and certain others in my father's court, know can never happen in any real sense.'

Father Urss's face was very still. For several seconds he was silent, then, quietly, he said:

'Yes, Prince Kodor.'

'What will become of her then?'

Urss saw the light. Kodor wasn't thinking of Osiv – he was considering the implications of his own future. On the brink of marriage to Duke Arec's daughter, Kodor was in an unusual, and from his viewpoint potentially disadvantageous, position. As a wife the Marchioness Pola might theoretically be her husband's inferior; in reality, though, she was anything but. One day, she would be the rightful ruler of Sekol. Whereas Kodor was set to inherit only the position and title of Regent of Vyskir.

Unless, of course, some misfortune should befall his brother.

Urss had taken stringent precautions to ensure that no one outside a small, trusted cabal suspected the existence of a second and deeper dimension to the bargain made with Duke Arec. If the Imperator were ever to find out the truth, Urss and his abetters would die for their pains; and until this moment Urss had assumed, for safety's sake if nothing else, that Kodor would share his father's attitude. Now, though, it occurred to him that Kodor might view things in a different light. The Prince was an intelligent and energetic young man, with a sound grasp of politics, and a talent – when he chose to use it – for diplomacy. Though he would fulfil the Regent's task well, he was very likely to find the role frustrating. A Regent was, to coin a phrase, neither fish nor fowl; he had the responsibilities of a ruler, but not the true power and certainly not the popular admiration or respect. It might well seem to Kodor that the reward for his personal sacrifice in marrying Pola of Sekol was not entirely adequate.

Urss's thoughts took form in a moment and were slotted away in his mind as quickly, and with an unchanged expression he answered Kodor's last question.

'I don't think we need anticipate any real difficulties, Your Grace. Prince Osiv – in the fullness of time, as you say – will be Imperator at least in name, and I don't think his bride is ambitious. Even if she were, she is a woman, and whatever her status in Sekol, women cannot rule in Vyskir. Whatever her disappointment, it will make no difference to her position.' He smiled. 'Or to yours.'

The last words were bland but deliberate, a morsel of bait to test the water and see if the fish showed any inclination to nibble. Urss was far too skilled and shrewd a negotiator in the maze of court politics to take risks, and at this stage he had no intention of offering any further hints. The next move, if any, was Kodor's to make.

Kodor, too, was shrewd enough not to react. Urss expected that and was content with it. The seed had been sown; for now, that was all he required. If nothing came of it, nothing would be lost. But if it *did* germinate and produce fruit, one major snag in solving the problem of Prince Osiv would be removed. For while Kodor's opposition to the long-term plan was a dangerous factor, Kodor's support would be a positive asset. In fact, Urss reflected, Kodor could be the *ultimate* asset, for his co-operation was a sure route to success.

Still smiling, he said, 'I hope I've been able to put your mind at rest, Your Grace. If you have any further questions that I can answer—'

For once Kodor's habit of interrupting him did not grate. 'No, Father, thank you. For now, you've told me all I need to know.' He nodded once, briskly; a sign that the conversation was over. 'I'll speak to Osiv. And I shall also say a prayer for Nanta EsDorikye. Good day to you.'

He walked away, leaving Urss wondering just what his last remark implied.

Prince Osiv's personal apartments were in a secluded part of the palace, well away from the hub of court activity. Entering this private area was a little like stepping out of the real world and into an extraordinary and slightly disturbing fantasy. Here were bright, patterned carpets, simplistically colourful pictures instead of fine art in oil or charcoal, jewelled mobiles turning and shimmering in every window embrasure. No gold-and-grey-liveried footmen; instead, aproned nursemaids bustled and skimmed on softly shod feet, their smiles as bland as their surroundings were gaudy. The sour note in the studied banality – and it was sour indeed – was the understated but unequivocal presence of two burly male servants, both without a tongue in his head, housed in cramped cells at a discreet but pragmatically convenient distance from the prince's bedroom. Just in case of need.

Kodor did not glance at the mutes' cells as he passed them, nor at any of the rustling women who moved like wraiths through

Osiv's microcosm of a world. The last corridor before the main apartments was deserted; relieved at the sudden lack of surveillance, and allowing himself to relax, he headed for his brother's rooms.

Then abruptly paused mid-stride, as something anomalous shifted at the far end of the passage.

Instinct made Kodor move back against the wall, setting one of the pictures askew, as the anomaly shifted again. For one moment his vision seemed to slip out of focus, so that he was seeing the thing not only with physical senses but also with another, subtler perception; and in that moment he almost – almost, but not quite – had its measure.

A face. Human yet not human; too delicate and knowing and primordial to be mistaken, by a wise mind, for anything mortal. Its bones were too thin, its skin too fluid, its hues too close to the edge of the visible spectrum for it to be real. Yet it existed. It looked at him. It smiled a smile that could have been interpreted as mocking or conspiratorial. Then the face and the small, wiry body beneath it twisted and inverted, and the apparition was gone. In the space where it had been, a glittering movement as of snowflakes falling against moonlight showed briefly before it, too, ceased to exist.

Kodor felt a cold flush of perspiration breaking out on his skull and down his spine, coalescing unpleasantly at a point on the small of his back. A frost sprite, one of the strange, elusive servants of the Lady, who according to catechism existed and moved in the mortal world at her bidding. Bearers of her word, harbingers of her will . . . Only those with a psychic sensitivity saw them. Kodor knew he had such sensitivity, but even so nearly a year had passed since he had seen such a manifestation; and the last occasion had been a far lesser thing, more like a waking dream than a genuine experience. But this was not imagination.

He had to force himself to walk on along the passage. He did not want to pass through the space where the sprite had materialised; in dreams he had done that, and by the time he realised the nature of his mistake the icy hands were reaching out for him and it was far, far too late to repent his foolishness.

But dreams were only dreams. This was reality.

Kodor made his legs move. As he neared the spot there was a palpable drop in the air temperature, and a moist, chill sensation prickled his skin where his clothing did not cover it. Another step and he trod precisely on the spot – his mind was of the turn to note such things very accurately – and he paused, waiting for the shift in his thoughts, the change of feeling and instinct that he knew would come. These beings never appeared to anyone without good reason; there would be a message in the form of a psychic mark on his emotions . . .

It did come, and it was anger. The Lady, *angry*? On a detached level Kodor was surprised and puzzled, but the surprise was quickly blotted out by the greater part of his consciousness, which absorbed the sensation and reacted accordingly. There was suddenly a hot, bitter taste in his mouth, and with it came a surge of a dark, primitive desire to lash out, hurt, *avenge*—

He caught his foot in a ruck in the carpet, and stumbled forward out of the sphere of influence. The fury vanished like a snuffed candle flame, and Kodor was left only with the memory of it, acrid, but without power.

Righting his balance, he looked back at the patch of carpet, then at the empty stillness where the sprite had materialised. *Anger*. It didn't make sense. Yes, he had been feeling a form of anger towards Father Urss; but that was a minor, contemptuous thing, born of mere dislike and hardly worthy of the term. The message the sprite delivered went far deeper. Something was in the wind; something that would touch him or one close to him. And this was an initial warning.

He walked on to his brother's suite of rooms. The outer door shone with care and polishing but bore no imperial crest or any other ornamentation to hint at its occupant's rank. Kodor knocked. One always did; it was the protocol. A little time passed, then the door was opened by a nurse.

'Good evening, Your Grace.' The woman curtseyed, and Kodor acknowledged the gesture with a nod.

'Good evening, Dorca. How is the Prince Imperial today?'

'His Highness is well as usual, sir.'

'Will he take amicably to a visitor?'

Dorca, who had been in imperial service since she was six years old and attendant to Prince Osiv from the day of his birth, smiled. 'Of course, Your Grace. He is always pleased to see *you*.'

The slight emphasis wasn't lost on Kodor. He returned Dorca's smile with just the faintest of edges, and allowed her to lead the way through several more rooms to the prince's personal chamber. This door had a brightly coloured mural painted on it, depicting a garden full of flowers. It was closed, and noises came from beyond; a banging and jingling that was almost, but not quite, rhythmic. Every few seconds the sounds would stop, then there would be a brief silence, as though someone was thinking hard, before the whole thing began again at a different tempo.

Knocking was not the protocol now. Dorca merely moved a simple but effective catch, and opened the door. The banging-jingling ceased instantly, and a voice said loudly:

'No! *Wrong!*'

There was a peculiar, hiccupping laugh, like water draining down a conduit, and in the room's lamplight a younger woman, hair dishevelled and a wide apron over her dress, straightened as the visitors entered. She was holding a tambourine; seeing Kodor, she bobbed to him, then hesitated, unsure of what was expected of her.

Kodor nodded as he had done to Dorca and said, 'You may go.'

The woman scurried out. Something clattered raucously, its source hidden by the bulk of the door, and the strange laugh was uttered again.

Kodor stepped into the room. He looked, smiled, and said: 'Hello, Osiv. What game would you like to play tonight?'

This, then, was the beginning of it. The quiet procession that made its way into the Sanctum chapel an hour after the Sunset Devotional had chimed comprised eight women, all dressed in blue to honour the Lady and all veiled. Grand Mother Beck led them, her hands clasped piously before her and her eyes under the layer of gauze taking in detail and missing nothing. Behind her, Nanta was flanked by the two women who would be her handmaidens at the marriage ceremony. She knew neither of them and had had no say in the choice; these were grace-and-favour appointments in which friendship had no place.

Nanta's mother followed, with Sister Marine at her side. The weather had taken a turn for the worse in the past three days and the EsDorikye party had only arrived in the Metropolis that morning after a slow and thoroughly unpleasant journey. Karetta EsDorikye looked, and was, tired; but her place tonight was at her daughter's side, and even if she could have excused herself – which was out of the question – she would not have been willing to do so. It was, she reflected, little enough, considering the fact that she and Nanta's father had been informed barely an hour ago that their place in tomorrow's proceedings was not to be quite what they had expected. They would of course attend the ceremony in the temple, and the celebrations and court banquet that followed. But despite the fact that they were the Bride's parents, they were to be relegated to the second stratum of guests who, however noble, were not exalted enough to be included in the imperial party. No explanation had been given, and though she dared not show it, Karetta was very put out.

Nor had she been permitted so much as a moment alone with

Nanta. She had asked, of course; any mother would *ask*. But her request had been firmly if politely refused.

She glanced sidelong at Sister Marine. Impossible to see her expression behind the veil, but Karetta had thought earlier that Marine looked ill at ease. Possibly it was no more than natural discomfiture at being thrown headlong into court life; Marine was a woman of Spartan tastes and attitudes and would not have found it easy to adapt. But Karetta was no fool. Something was awry; something that Marine knew about but she herself did not. She would give a very great deal to find out what it was.

She asked herself, not for the first time, what had prompted the Exalted Council to choose Nanta for this extraordinary honour, above all the other possible eligible young women in the Metropolis. The house of EsDorikye was an old and noble one, but not prominent; indeed, as far as court circles were concerned it was relatively obscure. Yet Nanta had taken the Council's eye. What especial quality had they seen in her? Karetta wondered. She had always been a strange girl; withdrawn and private and far from easy to understand. As a small child she had been prone to dreams and fancies that were quite beyond Karetta's comprehension. She had grown out of them, or appeared to, and for a while mother and daughter had been relatively close. But since Nanta entered the Academy they had had little contact, and now she was a virtual stranger. The thought that the dry, detached priests and officials of the court knew her own daughter better than she did discomforted Karetta. But perhaps it was only to be expected; perhaps, even, it was a kind of poetic justice. Because—

No. She thrust the unwonted thought down, aware of a momentary pang of something close to panic. She and her husband had kept that particular secret under lock and key for nearly twenty years; now, of all times, it would be unwise in the extreme to resurrect it. Nanta had been granted a great honour, and one which reflected on her family. They could only trust to the will of the God and the Lady, as they had done before, and give thanks for their good fortune.

They were all inside the chapel now, and the last two women in the group, Nanta's personal servants, closed the door. The chapel's quiet, slightly chilly atmosphere wrapped around them and the outside world became meaningless. Everything was white and blue and silver here: the tiled floor, the hangings and adornments, the marble carvings, the cushions set ready for worshippers to kneel and pray or sit and contemplate. There were no windows and only the one door. But light shone from the centre of the circular chamber, where the shrine itself rose in carved marble elegance from floor to ceiling. The shrine was simple; a statue of the Lady, twice human size, with face veiled to symbolise her mystery and hands outstretched in supplication to symbolise her role as intercessor between the God, her lord and consort, and his mortal subjects. There were vases and urns at her feet, and someone had managed, even at this time of year, to half-fill one with flowers. Mother Beck could not imagine who might have done such a thing, and suspected Nanta, with Marine's connivance. She herself could not remember when she had last set flowers in any shrine. But then Marine did not yet know what she knew. Marine might suspect; indeed, Beck was fairly certain that she did; but she did not yet *know* and, being Marine, would not under any circumstances ask of her own accord.

Which was, Beck thought, something that might need to be rectified in the very near future.

Beck returned her thoughts to the moment as she realised that the others in the party were waiting to take their cue from her. She moved to stand before the shrine, bowed her head and said with dignity:

'The tears of the Lady are the blessing of the snow.'

'*The tears of the Lady are the blessing of the snow.*' They repeated the words dutifully, Marine's voice rising a little more loudly than the rest. In turn, and beginning with Beck, each woman then stepped forward, lit a candle from the eternally burning devotional lamp set at the statue's feet, and placed the candles in the row of holders on the shrine floor. There were to be no group prayers; on occasions like these devotions were personal and silent, and with relief Beck stepped back from the shrine and moved to one of the high-backed chairs set by the wall. Sitting, she made a show of bending her head in private contemplation, while her ever-vigilant eyes kept watch.

As Beck withdrew, Nanta came forward and knelt down before the shrine. She was aware of Marine and her mother doing likewise, Karetta with a faint grimace as four days' jolting in a carriage took its toll of her muscles, but she did not look directly at them, only concentrated on the figure of the Lady before her.

So, then. Her final few hours before the die was cast for ever. Tonight she entered her vigil as Bride-Prospective; tomorrow she would go to the sacred altar and become Bride Imperial. And tomorrow night . . .

She knew in outline if not in detail what must take place tomorrow night. No one had instructed her as to the central duty of a newly married woman, but one of her new servants had a lively tongue and had taken little persuading to tell her mistress what she thought her mistress should know. It had small meaning to Nanta. She dreaded it, just a little, but she was not afraid. The servant had said it could be very pleasant, if the man was kind. Was Prince Osiv kind? A day from now, she would find out.

Bride Imperial. The prospect had become almost a commonplace, and it was hard to believe how little time had passed since she had been taken without explanation from the Academy and slotted into a completely new life. So much had happened, so many impressions, demands, obligations, that she had had no chance at all to stop, catch her breath and *think*. She was a cog in a wheel that turned faster and more urgently with every passing hour, and now the wheel had spun up to full speed and the journey was almost complete. A miracle that all was ready, but ready it was. The gown, the headdress, the shoes. The words she must say, the movements she must make. The public appearance. The banquet. What to eat and when, what to drink and when, whom to speak to and whom to acknowledge only with a nod or smile. Rank, precedence, propriety, etiquette. And titles. The Imperator would be 'Sire' or 'Majesty', now and always. Kodor, the younger prince, must be addressed after the ceremony as 'brother', while his bride-to-be (Nanta did not understand why that second wedding was to take place so hard on the heels of her own, and no one seemed able or willing to explain to her) was 'cousin' before her nuptials and 'sister' thereafter, when the title of 'cousin' would fall to her father, Duke Arec. So much to learn, so hard to remember each tiny but crucial detail. Marine had been a tower of strength in her austere way; indeed, without such austerity, like a rock in a stormy sea, Nanta believed that she would have been unable to bear the strain.

But for all her virtues, on a personal level Marine was not easily approachable. And Nanta desperately wanted someone to *talk* to.

She raised her head a little and looked surreptitiously at her mother, just visible beyond Marine's upright figure. She had barely had a chance to greet her parents, and then only with servants and a court official in attendance, before they were whisked away in opposite directions; they to be shown to their suite, she to undergo last-minute instruction from a High Father on the purpose of tonight's vigil. Nanta *knew* the purpose: to prepare her heart and soul for the solemnity of the marriage vows, and to pray earnestly to the Lady to make her worthy of her new role. Every bride and groom in every district of Vyskir held vigil on the night before their wedding, and she knew the form by heart. She *wanted* to pray. She wanted it so much that something inside her ached with the pain of it. But the comfort the Lady might bring her was not the same as her flesh-and-blood mother's comfort.

Besides, the Lady never answered her.

It seemed that Karetta intuitively sensed her daughter's turmoil, for she looked up at that moment and Nanta saw the gleam of her eyes behind the veil. Then, smoothly, Karetta rose to her feet. Skirting Marine, who appeared to be lost in her own prayers, she moved quietly towards Nanta—

'Ah, Karetta.' A shadow in the candlelight, and Beck was there, interposing her bulk like a cloud over the sun. She smiled a precise little smile that barely disturbed the jowls of her face. 'I may take the liberty, I trust, of addressing you by your God-name?'

Confounded, Karetta flinched slightly. 'Of course, Grand Mother.'

'Good; good. I see you have completed your devotions, and as Nanta and Sister Marine are still engrossed, this might be a timely moment for us to discuss a few last-minute matters.' She gestured towards the chair she had occupied. 'Shall we . . . ?'

Karetta was a strong-minded woman, but few people had the courage to defy Mother Beck. Nanta watched them walk away. She was saddened and disappointed, but the feelings were dulled, as if she was separated from them by a glass wall. The low murmur of Beck's voice reached her. Her mother's higher tone, replying. Then Beck's rich, throaty laugh, muted for propriety, that always sounded warm and kindly and in truth was anything but.

Marine sighed softly. It was only a reflex; the Sister was unaware of what had just taken place. Her eyes were closed, her mouth moved silently. Nanta felt a pricking in her own throat, the herald of tears, and fought the sensation back. No crying. She had nothing to cry about. She was tired, that was all.

She bowed her head, clasped her hands, and began to whisper, over and over again;

'*Lady, help me . . . Lady, help me . . . Lady, help me . . .*'

Beck, Marine and Karetta left the chapel an hour later. Beck saw no point whatever in staying; the formalities had been adhered to and there was no rule, written or unwritten, that obliged the entire party to undergo the vigil's full tedium and discomfort. The Bride would remain, and she had her hand-maidens and two attendants to supervise her. That was quite sufficient.

Marine and Karetta did want to stay, but Beck would have none of it. Marine had already earned a debit mark for her lack of vigilance that had almost allowed Karetta a private word with Nanta, and Beck wanted them both out of harm's way. So Marine obeyed a direct order, Karetta was easy to intimidate, and they left the chapel in Beck's wake like chicks following a daunting mother hen.

They progressed in silence up the spiral stairs to the Sanctum's main entrance hall. Under the glow of a huge chandelier that hung on chains from the vaulted ceiling, Beck stopped and turned to Karetta.

'Will you take some refreshment in my study, Karetta? I believe Exalted Father Urss will be there shortly, and I'm sure he is eager to meet you.'

Karetta returned her gaze uneasily for a moment before looking down at the floor. 'Thank you, Grand Mother, but if you will forgive me, I – I am rather tired. The journey was distressing, and tomorrow—'

'Is but a few hours away. Of course, my dear; I quite understand.' The mention of Father Urss had had precisely the effect Beck had intended. 'Your suite is in the palace's outer court, I believe? I don't suppose you know the way, so you shall have an escort.' She snapped her fingers and a blue-robed Low

Sister came hurrying towards them. 'Good night, my dear. My regards to your husband.'

Karetta was led away. As she disappeared, Marine said, 'Grand Mother, I—'

'Marine.' Beck cut across her, at the same time turning to give her a basilisk look. 'You were lax in the chapel. Did I not give you *explicit* instructions that Nanta and her mother are to have no private discussions?'

Marine flushed. 'You did, Grand Mother; but—'

'*But* is not a word I like to hear as an excuse, Marine,' Beck said relentlessly. 'Fortunately, I was able to intervene in time. And, I might add, able to invent enough trivial small-talk to divert the woman away from what might otherwise have become a trying situation.'

Marine looked penitent. 'I'm sorry, Grand Mother.'

'I'm glad to hear it. Now.' Dismissing the subject, Beck started to walk towards the main staircase. 'We all have a long day ahead of us tomorrow and an early night would be in order.' She looked back, saw that Marine was still standing uncertainly under the chandelier, and paused. 'Was there something else?'

Prudence urged Marine to say no, and forget the thoughts in her mind, but other words were on her tongue before she could stop herself.

'Grand Mother . . .' *You've gone too far now, Marine. Say it. You must.* 'Grand Mother, don't you think that Nanta should be prepared for what she will discover tomorrow?'

Beck stood very still. 'Prepared?' she repeated softly.

Marine twisted her hands together. She owed Nanta this, she told herself. Nanta, and her own conscience.

'Yes.' Her voice was small but, to her own surprise, firm. 'She has not seen Prince Osiv. She has no idea that he . . . is as he is. Yet tomorrow she must become his wife. It seems *wrong*.'

Very slowly Beck walked back towards her, and stopped when they were only a pace apart.

'And if the child did know the truth,' she said softly, 'what difference do you think it could possibly make?'

Marine was not prepared for that answer, and her face tightened. 'I – I didn't mean that it – that she—' she floundered.

'She would refuse him, is that what you're saying? Of course you didn't mean that; you know as well as I do that such a thing would not be permitted. So I ask again: what difference would it make?'

Marine knew her argument was lost, and the look in her eyes told Beck so. 'I only thought,' she said quietly, almost pleading, 'that to lessen the shock would be a kindness. As things are—'

'As things are, she has been thoroughly and intensively schooled to ensure that whatever shock she feels won't disrupt the smooth progress of the ceremony and all that follows,' Beck finished for her. 'She is a tractable and obedient child, Marine, which is the main reason why she was chosen. She will cope.'

'Yes, Grand Mother, I believe she will,' Marine said. 'But she is frightened.'

'Natural enough. All brides are nervous on their wedding eve.'

Marine shook her head. 'I don't mean nervous, Mother, I mean she is truly *frightened*. Tonight, in the chapel – did you not see how fervently she prayed to the Lady?'

'You've already told me she is devout.'

'Yes, yes she is; but . . . this is something more than devotion. I've observed her before. She prays with a kind of desperation, that runs far deeper than mere worship. I can't shake off the feeling . . .' Marine paused and looked at her superior, wondering whether what she was about to say would be derided as nonsense. To her surprise, Beck was staring at her very intently.

Beck said: 'Go on.'

Swim or drown, Marine thought. 'Very well, Grand Mother. I can't shake off the feeling that Nanta is beseeching the Lady to help her in some way. And that the Lady does not answer.'

Beck was silent for so long that Marine felt she had to fill the void, say something more.

'You see, Grand Mother, it occurred to me . . . If the Lady does not answer Nanta's prayers, there must surely be a *reason*. And if that reason should have some bearing on – on—'

The rest of the sentence failed her and she stared down at her own feet. Still Beck did not speak. The refectory hour had just ended and the entrance hall was becoming busy with a traffic of blue-robed women hastening to their next duties or, if no duties awaited, to the recreation rooms. Curious eyes looked at the still tableau of Beck and Marine, and though none of the women would dream of approaching them, Beck suddenly did not wish to be in the public eye.

'Come to my study,' she said abruptly. 'I have something to say to you.'

Neither said another word as they made their way along the blue-carpeted corridors to Beck's private room. A cold, leaden knot of disquiet was sitting in Marine's stomach, while Beck had made a blunt decision and wanted the necessities of it over and done with. Marine suspected enough to be told the rest. Her last, half-formed question had given her away, and whatever Father Urss thought, Beck believed she could be trusted. So, then: let Marine have the secret, and have joy of it. She would never divulge it to another living soul. She would never, ever dare.

Beck's chatelaine was in the study, tidying papers and making up the fire. Beck sent her away with a word so sharp that the woman flinched, and signed to Marine to sit down. Then she lowered herself heavily into the chair behind her desk, and folded her hands on the desk top.

'What I have to say can be kept brief, and I think we would both prefer it that way. "Nanta is beseeching the Lady to help her, and the Lady does not answer." Your own words, Marine. And you are perfectly correct.'

She could see the tension spreading from Marine's face through her shoulders and arms and into her entire body. The woman *radiated* it, like a flame emitting heat. As well she might. Unclasping her hands, Beck poured herself a glass of wine from a flagon on the desk. She fumbled a little, which angered her. Then she took a sip from the glass and her body and mind were under control again.

'You know your catechisms as well as any Sister and better than most,' she went on. 'They tell us that the Lady in her mercy answers the petitions of those who come to her in the proper way and at the proper times. And we know this to be true. We have seen incontrovertible proof of the Lady's answers on many occasions. She sends miracles. She sends her servants, the frost sprites, to appear to her petitioners and guide them. To a fortunate few, she even manifests personally, in visions and revelations.' She paused. 'You yourself came to the religious life as the result of such a vision; isn't that so?'

Marine shivered with a blend of awe and joy at the memory. 'She appeared to my mother and to me. She said—'

'She *said*,' Beck interrupted. 'That is the crux of it, Marine. Not *says*, but *said*. Tell me this. How long is it since you have had any experience – your own, or through others' reports – of a manifestation of the Lady?'

Oh, yes; oh, yes. Marine understood. Her pockmarked face lost what little colour it had and took on an unhealthy greyish tint. Her lips became bloodless, and her eyes – her eyes looked like the eyes of a betrayed child.

'I thought . . .' she began, in the tiniest of whispers.

'Don't think, Marine. Just listen. And be aware that you must *never*, on pain of your life, speak of this to anyone. Do I have your promise?'

'Y . . . yes . . .'

'Then hear me. Those of us in the highest religious office have struggled long and hard to ensure that not one rumour, not one *hint* of the truth should ever be suspected by the people of Vyskir. That struggle *must* be maintained at all costs, for the truth would threaten the very fabric of our society and stability.

'The truth is that, for twenty years past, the Lady has been silent. She answers no prayers. She sends no visions. The seasonal manifestations of her presence, such as the Corolla Lights in the northern sky, are no longer seen. Even the frost sprites, her servants, are absent; I know of no one who has seen such a being in all that time. The Lady is no longer with us, Marine. She has gone.'

Marine was shaking. Her mouth quivered, and it took all the will she could muster, finally, to speak.

'What have we done, Grand Mother? What have we done wrong, that she should turn her face from us?'

You poor simpleton, Beck thought. She shook her head, quite gently.

'No, Marine. We have done nothing wrong. We – those few among us who know of this – believe there is another reason.

'We believe that the Lady has ceased to exist.'

71

Chapter V

The gown was in place. Nanta stood before the wide, tall glass, staring at herself, but what she saw was not the reflection of anyone she knew. A stranger was looking back at her; a stranger who had taken her identity. The Nanta she had known all her life was gone for ever.

Perhaps, she thought, it was the drink they had given her that was having this effect. One of the servants had brought it just before the imperial dresser arrived to begin her work; a cup of red-brown liquid with a strong herbal taste, which the servant said would reverse the weariness brought on by lack of sleep. Nanta had not slept at all in the night. She had kept to her place on the floor of the Sanctum, kneeling while she could and then sitting when she became too numb to maintain that position, and had prayed until her mind lapsed into a dreamlike state in which reality lost its meaning. When Marine came for her an hour before dawn she had found her glassy-eyed and chilled through, and only a return to the warmth and bustle of the familiar apartments had brought her, eventually, out of the self-induced trance. Then came the drink and the dresser, and now – at least outwardly – Nanta was herself again.

But inwardly . . . She suppressed a shudder of revulsion as her thoughts focused on the travail of the past hours. First, there had been the ritual of being bathed, her hair washed and dried and tied into the tight complexity of braids and knots that must be endured if her headdress was to keep its proper place throughout the ceremony. Then she had been put into the shift. The shift was of silk, and had been worn by every Bride Imperial for centuries past. It was the colour of old bone, and time and the exigencies of rigorous preservation had given it a cold, slimy patina as repulsive as the feel of any ancient relic. Nanta's skin had crawled to its touch as the ghosts of fifty predecessors seemed to step silently into her body and take their places with a strange, dead anticipation. The shift clung greasily to her torso and thighs as the dresser next brought the bodice; encrusted with so many gems that it was as rigid as armour, and laced at her back and under her armpits and crutch until she was a stiff, tiny-waisted doll. After the bodice came the cage of the farthingale; spikes like lances radiating stiffly out from her hips to make her remote, inaccessible, a creature inhabiting an alien and rarefied world and untouchable by common hands. The skirt that overlaid it was timeworn cloth-of-silver, and smelled of sweet herbs and the charnel-house. Ropes of pearl and diamond and moonstone and zircon and sapphire were twined among its folds and clipped into place, and they and the jewelled hem clinked as frostily as sleigh bells if she dared to make the smallest move.

The sleeves were tied on to her arms. Vast, ballooning constructions of sapphire velvet and more cloth-of-silver, they flowed over her wrists like cataracts, hiding her silk-gloved hands and making her fingers all but useless. The dresser had clucked and fussed over the precise way in which they should trail, and only when she was satisfied was Nanta permitted, at last, to let her arms rest upon her farthingale and relieve their throbbing ache a little.

Another servant had brought the shoes. They had been fashioned to fit Nanta's feet with absolute precision, and the height of their blocks was also perfect, to ensure that the gown's hem would graze the floor, but no more and no less, as she walked. Not that she could walk in any recognised sense. As a child, she had once been taken to see a troupe of acrobats perform in the market square of her birth-town, and the antics of the stilt-man had made her laugh. She had no desire to laugh now. Oh, she had rehearsed this and rehearsed it until every movement was a catechism in her dreams. But this was not a rehearsal. This was *real*. She was no longer a woman, or a girl, or a person in her own right. She was the Bride. In two more hours she would go to the sacred altar, and she must not fail in any way.

In the mirror from which the stranger stared out at her, Nanta saw Marine. Marine had been peculiarly quiet all morning, and the few words she had spoken were brusque even by her standards. Nanta wondered what preoccupied her. She also wondered what would become of Marine when the solemnities were over; whether she would return to her own sanctum or stay on in the Metropolis, perhaps as Mother Beck's assistant or possibly even with a role in the imperial household. Nanta hoped, privately, that Marine would stay. She was kin; the only contact with her family that she could hope to have in the future. And against the odds, Nanta had begun to trust and – almost – like her. To lose her would be to lose a lifeline.

Marine was far too preoccupied to be aware of Nanta's thoughts. Outwardly, she was performing her duty with the precise and unshakeable efficiency for which Mother Beck had so shrewdly chosen her; inwardly, though, she felt as if a part of her, the only part that had any relevance, had turned to dust.

Last night's revelation had not, in truth, come as an earth-shaking shock, for, as Beck had suspected, the seeds of doubt and fear were already sown in Marine's heart. But to hear it stated so flatly and calmly, almost as though it were a common-place thing, had hit at the root of Marine's confidence in the world and all it contained. The Lady, consort of the God, mediator and mentor and the rock on which the foundation of Marine's entire life had been built. Gone. Departed. Ceasing to exist. *Dead*. It went against all reason; it was *impossible*. Yet

Beck and Father Urss and all the highest and wisest and most cognisant of the inner religious cabal believed it was so. Marine desperately did not want to share their belief, but the evidence was compelling.

She had cried for two hours. Not in Mother Beck's presence, for she knew what her senior's reaction to that would have been, but later, alone, at the nadir of the night. Then, when there were no more tears left, her own nature had come to her rescue and she had tried to think logically. *Could* a divinity die? No script or prayer or catechism suggested that it was possible; but catechisms were written by men, and even men like Father Urss were not omniscient. The lower beings of the God's realm were known to have a natural lifespan – but the Lady was immortal. Surely she was immortal?

Two more hours of desperate mental wrangling had brought neither relief nor solutions. *The Lady answers no prayers. She sends no visions. The Lady is no longer with us.* Beck's words were fixed in Marine's memory like an acid etching, and she couldn't deny them because she had experienced their validity for herself. *That* was the hardest part of it; to know on a deep, intuitive and irrefutable level that Beck was right. Even Nanta, in her small way, had contributed to the certainty. Nanta's fervent and frequent prayers, coupled with that air of bewilderment and an almost secretive refusal to share the joy that devotion should have brought her . . . there *was* no joy in Nanta's devotion, Marine realised now, because the tide of it flowed only one way.

Back in the night she had had to fight a seditious but powerful urge to return to the Sanctum chapel, rouse Nanta from her contemplation and tell her the truth. It was unthinkable, of course; even as the idea arose, years of conditioning had awoken and hauled hard on the reins, and now the thought was dead and buried as it must be. Beck knew her profession and she knew Marine, and the secret she had divulged was safe. It was a matter of necessity, prudence and security, and the penalty for treason did not need to be spelled out.

Besides, Marine could not have found the words to speak to Nanta. This morning she had watched her gradual change from a vital personality to a cipher, and each stage of the transformation widened the gulf between them. There was more to come, far more than Nanta knew, and any chance Marine might have had to defy Beck and follow her conscience was lost now. She had her duty to perform. All she could do was think of that and play the part assigned to her.

The dresser bustled into Marine's field of vision then, saying something that did not register.

'What?' Marine looked up, and the dresser recoiled slightly at her sharp tone.

'The *balance*, High Sister. Unless it is absolutely right, the headdress can't be guaranteed to stay in place throughout the ceremony.'

'Then make sure the balance *is* right.' Marine felt an irrational flare of anger and quashed an urge to push the woman away from her.

The dresser looked irritated. 'That is why I have just asked you to *help* me, High Sister! It needs two of us to put the frame in place, and then——'

The rest of her explanation was eclipsed, for at that moment the bells began.

Marine physically jumped and her teeth clamped together with shock at the sheer volume of the sudden clashing din. Orders had been given that the wedding peals should begin precisely at noon, and by a piece of extraordinary serendipity the ringers posted throughout the Metropolis had judged the moment to perfection. The temple, the Sanctum, the Academy, law houses, moot squares, watchtowers; almost every belfry in the entire city joined the first exultant onslaught in a tidal wave of noise that flooded into the room. A few seconds later the single gigantic bell of the imperial palace added its magisterial boom to the tumult, and Marine clapped her hands over her ears, feeling as if her bones were being shaken out of their places. The dresser agitatedly mouthed something, but the idea of listening or replying was ridiculous; all anyone could do was stand still and wait until the bombardment ended.

It went on for ten minutes, and the cessation was almost as well-timed as the start had been. Everything stopped on a crescendo that reverberated away in scrambling echoes punctuated by just a few lone, dissonant clangs – then there was extraordinary, unbelievable silence. Marine found herself gaping like a stranded fish; the servants were shaking their heads, still hearing the ringing in their ears, and Nanta stood rigid before the mirror, her eyes tightly shut and her hands clenched into fists.

The dresser broke the spell, as Marine could have predicted.

'Already past noon!' Her voice was piercing in the quiet. 'We are behind schedule, High Sister, and this will not do! Help me now, please – the headdress—'

The bells would ring again at the next hour, and again at the next, and the fourth time they rang they would not stop until the ceremony was over. Half the city's populace would be deaf by the end of this day, Marine thought.

And none of them would know what she knew.

She saw Nanta's face in the mirror. She had opened her eyes again and was staring at herself. Her face was utterly expressionless.

'High *Sister*—' the dresser began.

'Yes, yes; the headdress. I'm coming.' Marine broke her gaze from the mirror and walked briskly across the room.

The marriage ceremony of Osiv, Prince Imperial of Vyskir, and Nanta of the house of EsDorikye began with a jubilant fanfare that rang to the highest vaults of the Metropolis temple. The trumpets climbed to a dizzying top note, and as they held it, the massed voices of the Academy Choir joined them to create a vast, triumphant crescendo that drowned even the thunder of the bells in the great tower overhead.

The two sets of massive bronze doors on opposite sides of the altar opened at precisely the same moment, and everyone in the congregation craned for the first glimpse of the twin processions. First came the heralds; Osiv's in the grey and gold imperial livery, Nanta's in the blue and silver of the Lady. Then came the attendants, two men and two women who would stand beside the bridal pair and witness their marriage pledges. Osiv's attendants were Kodor and (another shrewd political move on Father Urss's part) Duke Arec of Sekol, both resplendent in bronze half-armour, crested coronets and gold-threaded cloaks that swept the floor behind them. As they appeared, the choir launched into the opening phrases of the Benediction Anthem – and, seated high on gold and silver thrones borne on the shoulders of six powerful, proud-faced men apiece, the nuptial pair emerged.

Marine, who sat with Grand Mother Beck in a cubicle to one side of the imperial box, felt dazed and vertiginous as she gazed through her veil at the scene unfolding below. It was a fantastical masque, and at its centre the prince and his bride were not mortal beings but dolls, automata, created by strange alchemy and given a semblance of life that did not quite convince. Osiv was a glittering, dazzling figure of gold, his headdress, in the shape of a rayed sun, surrounding him like a huge and grotesque exaggeration of the head it framed. His face was all but invisible, covered but for mouth and eyeslits by a golden mask without features, symbolising that he was chosen by and beloved of the God. He sat very still, not even turning to look about him, but despite his docility Marine saw that both Prince Kodor and Duke Arec were watching him as hawks might watch a sparrow.

And Nanta . . . Though Marine had helped with every detail of her preparation for this moment, she felt now, as Nanta had felt earlier in the day, that she was gazing at an absolute stranger. Smothered under the rigid planes of the gown, dwarfed by the towering headdress with its huge silver-filigree snowflake emblem and swaths of silver veiling, Nanta was being carried passively to her fate like a heifer to the autumn cull. As the two thrones reached the altar and began the slow, ponderous process of being turned and set side by side, Marine felt a terrible inward pang that for a moment she almost believed was a heart seizure. Beck, beside her, hissed sharply, 'Marine? Are you unwell?' and Marine shook her head wordlessly, making a negating gesture. This wasn't anything physical. It was simply the culmination of strain, shock and the misery that had been in her like a solid weight since last night. It would pass; and if it did not, then she would simply have to bear the burden.

With timing as perfect as Father Urss both expected and demanded, the thrones were set in their places as the last note of the Benediction Anthem shimmered away. The sound of the bells came back, muffled by the weight of stone between the temple amphitheatre and the dome but still painfully reverberating like a vast, throbbing pulse. The throne-bearers were moving backwards like an ebbing tide, Father Urss was taking his place at the altar. He raised his arms, and to the echo of a second fanfare, the rite began.

Nanta was frozen in a dream. She had rehearsed every moment of this until her performance was flawless, but now that the rehearsals had become reality, her conscious mind could no longer make any connection. She knew, on a subliminal level, that all was proceeding as it should. But it was if she observed it from a vast and impersonal distance, and with senses that barely functioned.

The veil obscured her view of the temple and made it impossible to gain any worthwhile impression of Prince Osiv. He was just an unmoving figure on his throne, and even his responses to Father Urss's promptings as the solemn declarations were made and the vows sworn were inaudible to her. She couldn't even see his face. Was he fair or dark? Handsome or ugly, or merely unremarkable? She thought that he was quite small; taller than herself but slight, though well-formed. Pleasant? Cruel? Lively? Dull? There was no way of knowing. Nanta stared at him through her veil as Father Urss led her through the words of her own pledges; then, too confused and numbed to stare any more, she looked without interest at Osiv's two attendants. The older man must be Duke Arec. The younger was Prince Kodor. Kodor was watching his brother very intently, and Nanta vaguely wondered why. Then she recalled that Kodor was himself to marry in a few days (two? Three? She couldn't remember). So perhaps he was observing, to learn. Perhaps that was it. It wasn't important.

She turned what little attention she could summon to Osiv again, and saw a faint sparkle of wetness on his jaw. It looked suspiciously like a tear and it surprised her, for if he was crying it must be because he was greatly moved by the occasion. A sensitive man, then. Was that good? She thought so.

Kodor, too, had seen the sparkle, and uttered a silent, fervent prayer to the God that no one else would notice it. It was usually a bad sign when Osiv started dribbling; more often than not it meant that he was building up to a tantrum. He had, in fact, done remarkably well so far, largely because Kodor had gone to great pains to convince him that today's events were a new game which they would all play together and he was certain to enjoy. Osiv accepted his brother's word more readily than anyone else's and had been content enough, with the help of his physician's drugs, throughout the preparations. He had not liked being strapped into his throne (a necessary precaution, or he would have lost interest in the proceedings and tried to wander off a long time ago), but by using the lure of the game again Kodor had managed to persuade him to submit. Now, though, he was bored, and threatening to become fretful. Kodor glanced covertly at the Bride, whose name he had forgotten again. Swathed as she was, and probably terrified half out of her wits into the bargain, there was little chance of her being alerted. The main body of the congregation was too far away for anyone to make out more than an overall picture, and the eyrie of the imperial box, where his father was sitting with those dignitaries who for reasons of protocol couldn't be placed anywhere else, was also distant enough to be safe. Nonetheless, the sooner the ceremony was over and Osiv could be pacified with some new distraction, the happier Kodor would feel.

Turning his head fractionally towards Father Urss, he was relieved when the priest caught his eye and gave the smallest of nods. Urss comprehended. He would bring the ceremony to a close as fast as was diplomatically possible – Osiv's replies to most of his prompts had been nonsensical anyway, so the appearance of the thing was all that mattered – and then there would only be the hurdle of the procession through the city to overcome. Osiv was likely to enjoy that, though he would see little enough through the coach's screened windows.

The Bride, though . . .

Well, Kodor thought, at least that part could be over and done with before they reached the palace. The girl would have time to get over the shock and compose herself again. She had done well so far; she was unlikely to cause trouble now, and the rewards of her new position would compensate for the failings. Kodor would do what he could in the short time he had before his own marriage, and if Nanta was then left to sink or swim, she was probably intelligent enough to swim.

He would meet his own bride soon. In a faintly indolent way, he was looking forward to that. Certainly he was curious to see if the reality of Marchioness Pola matched up to the legend. He didn't like Duke Arec, but then he had not expected to. Though an improvement on his ambassador, the man was still vulgar almost to the point of boorishness; he boasted about the value of his possessions as though that were some proof of nobility, and his daughter was blatantly included in the list. Still, he would be gone back to his own domain soon, and Vyskir would be secure. If it all came down to prices, Kodor reflected, he could have made a far worse bargain.

He realised how far his mind had wandered when the sudden resurgence of the choir made him visibly start. They were singing the Valediction – Urss must have cut the ceremony short by a good half-hour. Grudgingly acknowledging that the man had truly excelled himself this time, Kodor risked a quick, raking glance over the congregation. No one seemed to realise that anything was awry. Like him, they were probably just thankful that the tedious part was over and the secular celebration could begin.

Osiv said, loudly, something childish about his bladder, but his complaint was providentially eclipsed by a sudden crescendo from the choir. The attendants were flowing forward, preparing to lift the thrones and carry them down the long aisle to the temple's vast main entrance. Pulling his mind away from diversions, Kodor took his own place next to Arec as the cumbersome process of turning began again. The congregation was on its feet, a sea of faces in the flaring light, and the mingled sounds of the choir and the bells swelled like a tide. There had been no sign, no omen from the God or the Lady, Kodor reflected. Probably just as well; anything the God might have to impart about this particular pairing might be better left unrevealed.

Father Urss was leading the exodus from the altar; grunting and straining, the throne-bearers lifted their burdens and followed, and the attendants fell into step behind as the nuptial procession began its slow, solemn way down the aisle.

The coach had been prudently designed to travel on wheels or runners, depending on the weather. Winter had not yet advanced enough to make runners necessary, but two hours ago it had begun to snow again and now the white flakes were falling thickly. The eight caparisoned horses, four chestnut and four dapple-grey, stamped restlessly in the shafts, disliking the tickling wetness of the snowfall, but nothing touched Nanta and Osiv as, in a private courtyard, their headdresses were removed and they were helped out of their thrones and into the coach's plush seats.

The coach interior was gloomy and Nanta was still veiled, so even now she could see little of her husband. He *was* well-made, she could tell that much; sturdy but slim, with a fresh and youthful air about him. His face, though, was still hidden from her. On entering the coach he hadn't spoken to her, or indeed seemed the least interested in her; instead, he had turned his attention immediately to the window, rubbing away condensation with a gloved fist and peering out with the air of an eager puppy. Nanta watched his back uncertainly. Should she say something, try to breach the barrier? She had received no instruction about that, and was still debating with herself when, to her surprise, Prince Kodor climbed into the coach. He was holding something in his hand; he glanced at her, his features vague and his expression invisible thanks to the gloom and her veil, then took a seat opposite his brother. The door closed; the coach lurched on its springs and began to move.

Osiv turned round at last and Nanta saw his face for the first time. He was handsome – good bones, a wide, generous mouth, clear blue-grey eyes with a lot of humour in them – and she felt a tingle of relief mixed with sudden hope. But there was one anomaly. His skin was extraordinarily, almost bizarrely smooth. Like a small child's, without a single line of care or experience.

And then, like a child, Osiv thumped both clenched fists down on his own knees and declared in an extraordinary, high-pitched voice, 'Want some *cake*!'

Nanta started, then froze. Kodor was looking at her again;

after a moment he broke the contact and held out the thing he had been carrying.

'Here, brother. Sweetmeats.'

'*Cake!*' Osiv repeated mulishly. 'You promised!'

'I know, and as soon as we're back in the palace you shall have as much cake as you like. But you must be good until then. You remember that, don't you?'

Nanta stared in horror as the truth began to dawn. She couldn't move, couldn't outwardly react in any way; the noises of clattering hooves, clanging bells and, distant but growing closer, the cheering of the vast crowds lining the processional way through the Metropolis seemed to fill not only her head but her body and mind until she thought she would burst apart with the pressure.

Osiv snatched a sweetmeat and crammed it into his mouth. He chewed it, made a satisfied noise and demanded another. Kodor gave it to him, all the while watching Nanta clandestinely. Then, lowering his voice as far as was possible in the general background clamour, he said:

'They didn't tell you, did they?'

Nanta tried to reply, but all that came out was a feeble, throaty whimper. They were out of the courtyard, rocking and swaying towards the temple's outer precincts, and there was enough light now for her to see Kodor's young, slightly harsh features, and the strain in them.

'No,' he went on. 'I see they didn't . . . He's harmless. Very gentle, in fact, if you learn how to handle him. You can make him like you, if you're patient and kind.'

Still Nanta couldn't answer. Kodor spoke again.

'I can't see your face, sister, but it doesn't take genius to imagine your expression, and I've no doubt that you're grateful for a veil to hide it. I must ask one thing of you. Show nothing; above all, show nothing to my father, the Imperator. He's ailing, and it would not be good for his health to have any . . . distress attached to this occasion. What must be must be, and we all have our appointed roles to play. Play yours. Do I have your word on that?'

His words, and the fact that he had probably prepared and rehearsed them, passed Nanta without truly registering – but for one thing. He had called her 'sister'. Illogically, it made her feel that in this sudden and grotesquely unexpected twist of events, he was prepared to be her ally.

She was able, at last, to force a single coherent word out between her colourless lips. It was a surrender, an admission of total and hopeless defeat, but it was all she had.

She whispered, 'Yes . . .'

Chapter VI

They had married her to an idiot. A man with the mind of a five-year-old child, who would never grow up but would exist in his own infantile world, unfit to rule, unfit to have a wife, unfit for anything but to be protected and cared for to the end of his days. The knowledge pounded in Nanta's head like a litany, a cruel lyric accompanying the melodies of the orchestra players who filled the palace's vast ballroom with their music, entertaining the wedding guests. No matter if Osiv was kind. No matter if Osiv was handsome. He was an *idiot*.

The Imperator's immediate party were secluded in a smaller gallery above the ballroom, aloof from the livelier celebration beyond yet another filigree screen. The ordeal of being presented to Arctor on their return to the palace had been a small one; lifting back her veil as she had been told, Nanta had been confronted by a tired, slightly bemused man with kindly eyes, who spoke a few vague words of welcome to her before patting her hand and nodding his permission for her to move on. She had had no further contact with the Imperator, despite the fact that they now sat side by side on gilded chairs while the rest of the gathering moved around them like quiet satellites.

There were no more than twenty people here, few of whom Nanta recognised. Father Urss was in conversation with Duke Arec, while Prince Kodor seemed more interested in the selection of wines than in anything else. To Nanta's great surprise Sister Marine was present, in attendance on Mother Beck and looking extremely uncomfortable and out of her depth in formal court clothes. Nanta had tried desperately to catch her eye, but Marine seemed unwilling or afraid to respond, and Nanta dared not move from her place to speak to her, or to anyone else.

Prince Osiv was not in the gallery. The progress through the Metropolis had passed, for Nanta, in a daze of shock, as had the lengthy trial of the formal presentations at the palace. Nanta and Osiv, their headdresses restored, had been set like exhibits in the colossal grandeur of the entrance hall while a seemingly endless queue of nobles and dignitaries filed past at a discreet distance, each one bowing or curtseying and offering their felicitations. The distance, and Kodor's close attention, had avoided any trouble with Osiv, but the whole thing had taken upwards of two hours and by the time it was over Nanta was reeling with strain and exhaustion. A drink proffered by one of her attendants had restored her strength somewhat – the Lady alone knew what manner of drug was in it this time – but then, as the Imperator's party prepared to retire to this gallery, Osiv had started to cry.

The memory of those few minutes still made Nanta shiver. Torn between pity, embarrassment, anger and disgust, she had pretended to notice nothing as Kodor and several servants made valiant attempts to pacify Osiv, and then, when that failed, hustled him away through a side door. She had stood rigid in the terrible gown, looking and feeling like a waxwork and politely ignored by everyone, until Kodor returned to announce blandly that Prince Osiv was tired and would rest in his rooms rather than join the festivities. Nanta felt ashamed of her own relief.

But now Osiv was gone and the proceedings in the gallery were a little less fraught as a result. None of the guests in the ballroom, of course, had the least idea of what had transpired. Nanta had a black desire to tell them; run to the screen, throw it back and scream down to them all that their Prince Imperial, her husband, was a helpless and hopeless imbecile without chance of redemption, and that they might as well abandon their revelry now, for there was nothing, nothing, *nothing* in the world to celebrate. The desire swelled and ebbed: each time it swelled she forced it back; each time it ebbed she blinked away the tears that started under her veil, and gazed at the floor until her composure returned.

Though Nanta thought herself isolated in the stiff formality of the gallery, several people were in fact watching her closely. Grand Mother Beck's interest was no more than pragmatism laced with a little mild curiosity. Her task was to see that the Bride Imperial behaved as she should, and to dispatch Marine – who was here solely for that purpose – to deal with any unforeseen problems. Prince Kodor was also curious, but on a more personal level. He had gleaned some idea of the depth of Nanta's misery and was surprised, for it implied that there was a little more to this girl than cynicism and experience had led him to expect. Title and position seemed to mean nothing to her; she was genuinely frightened and disillusioned, and rather to his own surprise Kodor felt sympathy in his heart.

And Pola, Marchioness of Sekol and heir of Duke Arec, stood with her chaperone and watched both Nanta and Kodor. A tall, slightly mannish figure in her stiff Sekolian court dress, Pola had not yet been presented to her husband-to-be; protocol demanded that they would not exchange their first words until the great banquet began at midnight. But what she had seen thus far, she liked. Kodor was not handsome in any classical sense, but his face was well-modelled and his looks and colouring attracted her and made a good match with her own black hair and olive complexion. Pola was aware that she was not a beauty; but she was not ugly either, and she dared to think that when her veil was finally put aside and Kodor saw her face, he would be content with it.

She turned her attention again to the Bride Imperial, lost and lonely on her magnificent chair. Pola had learned about Prince Osiv's affliction when her own marriage contract was first being negotiated, but she gathered that Nanta EsDorikye had never been told, and had only discovered the truth once the marriage bond was sealed. Pola pitied her deeply. When she and Kodor were wed and Nanta was her new sister, it would be a kindness to try to make a friend of her.

Last of those watching the Bride Imperial was Father Urss. As far as anything ever truly pleased him, he was pleased with her conduct today. She had behaved impeccably, fully justifying Mother Beck's forecasts, and though she now knew the truth abut Prince Osiv she showed no outward sign of anything amiss. The first test had had a more than satisfactory result. The second – well, that was a matter for Osiv rather than for her, and Urss was confident of the outcome. Later tonight they would know, and if all went according to plan then the girl could gradually be prepared for the third and most delicate stage. The ultimate stage. Duke Arec had dropped another of his unsubtle hints soon after their arrival in the gallery, and though he disliked the man and despised his lack of finesse, Urss knew how vital it was not to try his patience more than necessary. The girl would be compliant, he was sure of that now. When the time came, she would put no obstacles in his path.

Or, if she did, she would soon learn the folly of it.

A voice at Nanta's elbow said, 'Your Highness. It is time to take your leave.'

Nanta was not accustomed to her new title, and for a moment did not realise that the words were being addressed to her. When she did realise, she turned and saw Grand Mother Beck at her side, with Marine hovering a few paces away.

'The banquet will begin in less than an hour, and it takes time to seat all the guests,' Beck continued in an undertone. 'The progress to the nuptial chamber will occupy several minutes, and—'

'*The nuptial chamber?*' The words were out before Nanta could stop them, in a sharp, hissing whisper that expressed a mixture of revulsion and disbelief. They could not think, surely they could not expect that she and Osiv would—

'Appearances must be maintained, Your Highness.' Beck's expression was impassive, but her eyes looked like steel. Unseen by anyone else she slipped a hand under the drape of Nanta's sleeve and took hold of her arm. In principle this was an unthinkable presumption now; in practice, Beck knew that Nanta had neither the courage nor the experience to object. She was right. Nanta allowed herself to be ushered from her chair and steered in a discreet semi-circle to approach the Imperator. Nanta curtseyed. Arctor nodded and smiled and made a limpid gesture that could have meant anything. By the door, Nanta saw now, her escort was gathering; men and women holding garlands of silk flowers and leaves. They would accompany her to the door of the nuptial chamber, they would festoon the garlands about her head and shoulders, and then she would go in to where the Bride Imperial's appointed handmaidens would be waiting to prepare her for her marriage night.

Nanta almost wanted to laugh. But she did not. Instead she went with Beck, who was taking care to make it look as if Nanta and not she were leading, and took her place. All the company bowed or curtseyed to her; even Kodor. One last image of the scene was imprinted on Nanta's mind as, below, the orchestra struck up another stately dance tune. Then she was moving like a sleepwalker (*no*, she told herself, *no, don't think of that* . . .) out of the gallery and away towards her new lodgings.

The apartments prepared for the Prince and Princess Imperial were in fact Osiv's own rooms, hastily but thoroughly redecorated to accommodate the new scheme of things. The crude, gaudy pictures had been taken down, and Osiv's toys now occupied only two rooms instead of being strewn liberally throughout the suite. Nanta had a bedroom, dressing room, bathing room and office of her own; the dressing room abutting Osiv's bedchamber and connected to it by a gilded door.

The women who waited for her were both elderly. One was hatchet-faced and intimidating, the other powerfully built, kinder looking but silent. They removed her headdress, setting it carefully aside, and untied her hair from its dragging knots so that it fell about her shoulders once more. Then began the long process of disassembling the gown and all its fitments. The relief when the blocked shoes were finally unlaced and she was permitted to kick them away was like a physical shock; Nanta gasped from sheer thankfulness, then, testing her own authority, timidly asked for a glass of wine. It was brought instantly and without demur or disapproval, and a shred of confidence began to return to her. Prince Kodor had said that Osiv was kind; and in everything but years he was a child. She surely had nothing to fear from him – indeed, he was probably asleep by now, and would remain so for the rest of the night. She could at least look forward to a few hours' rest, and tomorrow could be faced and coped with when it came.

The layers of her skirts were off now and the farthingale being lifted away. Only the bodice with its painful lacings remained, and under it the ancient slip. The thought of being rid of that foul thing was like a balm. Nanta wanted to scrub every inch of her skin to rid it of the half-rotted silk's taint. Doubtless she would not be permitted to bath tonight, but tomorrow . . .

Someone knocked on the outer door. The women looked up but neither seemed surprised; the hatchet-faced one picked up a blue velvet wrap and draped it around Nanta's shoulders, while her silent companion went to answer.

Prince Kodor was on the threshold. He gave the silent servant a meaningful look and she backed away, allowing him to walk unhindered into the room. Nanta opened her mouth to protest, but before she could speak Kodor addressed her other maid in a courteous but cold tone.

'I wish to speak to my sister alone. You may return in two minutes.'

Nanta said, 'No, wait—' but the women were already departing. The door closed gently but emphatically behind them, leaving her alone with Kodor.

Nanta's fear and confusion combined suddenly into outrage, and it overcame her awe. Hugging the wrap defensively around herself she faced him, her cheeks white but her eyes angry.

'Your Grace, I protest! To intrude on me here, without warning or – or invitation; it—'

' "Brother",' said Kodor. 'Not "Your Grace"; "brother". Remember?'

He had taken the ground from under her feet and she turned from him in frustration. 'Please,' she said after a few moments, 'go away, Prince Kodor.' A pause, then: 'I can't *cope* with anything more tonight!'

'I know you can't, sister, and it's the reason why I came.'

Struggling, Nanta tried to remind herself that in the coach Kodor had been kind to her after a fashion. It was only fair to give him the benefit of the doubt and accept that his intention, now, was similar. Her shoulders sagged and she said indistinctly, 'Forgive me. I'm . . . a little overwrought.'

'We all are, I believe. May I say what I came to say?'

'Please.' She made a helpless gesture.

'Thank you. It's simply this. I . . . sympathise with your situation, Nanta. As Osiv's blood brother and your marriage brother, I wish only to help you both. Please, remember that; and if you have need of a friend, think of me.'

There was silence for several seconds, then, slowly, Nanta turned to look at him again. 'That is all?'

'That is all.'

She swallowed. 'Then I – thank you, Your G . . . brother. I thank you for your kindness. And I'll remember what you've said.'

A discreet cough announced the return of the handmaids, but Kodor's business was finished. The pretext of his reassurance to Nanta had achieved the end he wanted; he had, finally, seen her face.

The impulse had come in the minutes before her departure from the gallery. Kodor didn't know why it had happened, or why it mattered so much to him. He did, however, know better than to try to quash it, for an all too familiar intuition told him that it was something far more, far deeper, than mere curiosity. There was a reason for this; it was a presage, a sign that he couldn't ignore. He *had* to know what Nanta looked like.

And the effect of the discovery was devastating.

His own face showed nothing of his feelings; Kodor was too well-schooled to make that mistake. As far as Nanta was concerned he had simply come to offer her brotherly support, and the only boundary he had overtly breached was that of etiquette. Nanta, though, did not know what was now seething in Kodor's mind. For she had never been a party to the dreams that had plagued him since childhood. She had never heard the voices that he heard in those dreams. And she had never seen her own face, framed in a scene of ice and darkness, looking at him and offering him the sole hope of salvation from his recurring nightmares.

Kodor said, 'Good night, my sister.'

Nanta lowered her head. She did not reply.

The women led her in to Osiv ten minutes later.

The Prince Imperial was not asleep. He was kneeling on the huge expanse of the nuptial bed, arms flapping at his sides as he bounced up and down on the thick goosedown mattress. Seeing Nanta he stopped, cocked his head sideways and gave her a look of candid and guileless curiosity. He seemed to recognise her. Then he smiled and said:

'I was flying.'

His smile was sweet, the smile of an infant who had never known anything but comfort and care. Nanta said, 'Yes . . .'

'Can you fly?' Osiv's arms started to flap again. 'Like this! Look!'

Nanta glanced at the women and said in a small, tight voice, 'Leave us.'

Again she was surprised when they obeyed her instantly. Osiv watched them go, then as the door closed behind them he put both thumbs in his mouth, stretched it and stuck out his tongue. 'Don't *like* them,' he declared.

In spite of everything, Nanta felt a tiny bubble of laughter trying to rise in her. Masking it with a discreet cough, she told him, 'Neither do I. One looks like a hatchet, and the other—'

'Hatchet! Hatchet-hatchet-hatchet!' Delighted with what was clearly a new word, Osiv tried to spring to his feet, got tangled in his cloth-of-gold nightshirt and collapsed on the bed in a kicking, laughing heap. The laughter ceased as suddenly as it had started, and, on all fours now, he pointed across the room.

'Look at my bricks!'

The cloisters of the Academy had given Nanta very little contact with and less experience of children, but at that moment she began to understand her husband. Kodor had said he was gentle, and Kodor was right. Humour him, play with him, indulge him, and he would be her devoted friend. These first moments alone with Osiv were lifting a little of the darkness and terror inside her. What *was* there to fear?

'They're . . . splendid bricks.' She took a hesitant step towards the bed. 'May I – could I—' Something caught in her throat; she cleared it. 'Would you like to play a game with them?'

Osiv's face lit like a sunrise. But before he could speak, with no announcement, not even a knock, the door to the outer offices opened and Father Urss walked in.

'Your Highness.' He looked directly, almost challengingly at

Nanta, and though he used her title there was no deference in his tone.

Osiv screwed his head round and stared at Urss with a look of open dislike. Straightening slowly, Nanta tried to summon the courage to react as a princess. 'Exalted Father . . .' Her voice was too high-pitched; she forced it to drop a few semitones. 'Would you please explain this . . .' She wanted to say 'intrusion', but Urss's impersonal eyes intimidated her and the sentence trailed off unfinished.

Then she saw that Urss was not alone. Grand Mother Beck stood behind him, and with her were three more priests; all High Fathers. Urss glanced over his shoulder, nodded, and Beck moved past him into the room.

'Make yourself ready, please, Your Highness,' she said briskly. 'This need not take long.'

Nanta stared at her. 'What do you mean? What need not take long?'

Beck didn't answer the question. 'Your robe, please,' she said.

'My robe—?'

'Yes. Please take it off and lie on the bed.'

The Fathers had converged on Osiv; there seemed to be some small altercation going on, and abruptly the bones of the truth dawned on Nanta. 'Grand Mother, you're not expecting to – that I – that Prince Osiv should—'

'Naturally, Your Highness, in the circumstances of his condition nothing is *expected* of Prince Osiv.' Beck's smile was icy. 'Nonetheless, we must leave no room for doubt.' She indicated the bed. 'If you please.'

Nanta was too astounded to resist as Beck took hold of her shoulders and started to pull away the blue velvet robe. Beneath it, the maids had put her into an elaborate cloth-of-silver nightgown that scratched and tickled her skin as she was steered towards the mattress. Then came a frightened wail from Osiv.

Nanta's head snapped round, but apart from one flailing leg her view of him was eclipsed by the priests' bulks. They were trying to pick him up between them; Osiv wailed again, then started to cry like a baby.

'Grand Mother, this is a travesty!' Nanta said desperately. 'He's a *child*!'

Beck was implacable. 'The formalities must be observed, Your Highness. Or if they cannot be observed, the fact that they cannot must be witnessed and made a matter of record. Come, now. If you co-operate, it will be over in a few minutes.'

She pushed Nanta respectfully but firmly on to the bed and made her lie back. The priests had control of Osiv now; ignoring his howls, they manhandled him across the floor, and as they approached, Beck leaned down, grasped the skirt of Nanta's nightgown and in a single, unceremonious movement pulled it up to her waist. Nanta shrieked a protest as her body was exposed to the priests' gazes; in shame and terror she tried to hunch into a tight, foetal position, but Beck had powerful arms and hands and a white-haired Father came to help her, grasping Nanta's ankles and forcing her back to her previous position. Father Urss looked on, but his eyes were focused on Nanta's face and his expression was glacially disinterested.

They all but threw Osiv on to the bed beside her, pulling his nightshirt over his head and leaving him naked. Nanta knew little enough of men, but even to her it was pathetically obvious that Osiv hadn't the least idea of what a bridegroom was expected to do. All he knew was that the Fathers were coercing him and hurting him, and he screamed his grievances with helpless desperation. Twice one of his thrashing hands caught Nanta across the face, the first time bruising her mouth, the second stinging her eyes; once, she herself tried to fight as he was doing, but Beck and the white-haired Father stopped the rebellion. At last her will went under and she could only submit, lying rigid and immobile in a waking nightmare as with relentless hands and harsh voices the Fathers tried to force Osiv to perform a duty that he could not even comprehend.

It was a grotesque and degrading farce that spared no humiliation and no trespass. But finally – though after far longer than Mother Beck's prophesied few minutes – it was over. The priests lifted Osiv away from the bed; Nanta felt Beck pulling her gown down to her ankles once more and she wanted to scream with hysterical laughter: *Yes, Mother, cover me, preserve my modesty; you've debased and abused me but the formalities must be observed . . .*

Father Urss said frigidly, 'Good night, Your Highness,' and in disbelief Nanta saw him make a bow to her. Her mouth worked but she didn't reply; didn't know any of the obscenities that were the only words she could have uttered to him at this moment. Osiv was in a corner, hugging himself and sobbing. He had lost control of his bladder during the ordeal; Nanta's thighs were wet with the result and there was a large dark patch on the magnificent bedcover, but Beck and the priests pretended not to notice. They were withdrawing, the Fathers making lower bows than Urss had done, Beck not bowing but pausing at the door to tell Nanta that if she should want anything during the night, the bell by the fireplace would summon her maids. Then the door closed.

Nanta didn't move for some time, but stared blindly at the opulent room. If she should want anything. *Want* anything. What could she possibly *want* from these cruel and brutal manipulators? What could they give her that would be of any value? Comfort? Understanding? A reverse of time, so that this travesty had never happened?

She laughed then, loudly and chokingly, and it broke the inertia that had held her. It also triggered another reaction, and with one violent movement she fled from the bed and ran through the connecting door, leaving it wide behind her. Her bathing room was an extension of the dressing room; by the time she reached it Nanta was retching uncontrollably, and with hands cupped to her mouth she doubled over the ornate basin, just visible in the dim, cold glow from the snow-filled sky.

She had eaten almost nothing all day and her stomach was empty of anything but bile. The retching seemed to go on and on, tearing at her muscles and burning her throat; but at last the spasms receded and, finally, stopped.

Nanta raised her head slowly, gasping, her skin and hair dank with sweat. The marble bath had a ewer of water set beside it. The water was cold and only filled the bath ankle-deep but she didn't care. She would have bathed in ice, flung herself into snowdrifts, plunged into the river with its currents and its creaking, frozen sheets, just to be *clean*.

She was crouched in the bath, hurling water over herself and shivering with far, far more than cold when the door was pushed open and Osiv came in.

He had managed to don his nightshirt again, though it was badly creased and put on back to front. He stood in the doorway, staring at Nanta with tears streaking his cheeks and a face so innocently and tragically bewildered that any hostility Nanta could have felt towards him instantly dissolved.

Osiv said: 'They hurt me . . .' Then his face crumpled and the tears started to stream once more.

Nanta got out of the bath and took him in her arms, rocking him gently from side to side until his tears began to subside. She was crying, too. Then she washed him, all the while talking soothing nonsense in a voice that only quavered and cracked a little, and took him back to the nuptial chamber, where she threw aside the soiled bedcover and tucked him beneath the blankets. Her cloth-of-silver nightgown she screwed into a ball and flung to the furthest corner of the room. Tomorrow she would order it burned, and if the servants refused to comply she would do the deed with her own hands.

Osiv grasped hold of her thumb as she settled him, and put it in his own mouth. She didn't protest, only waited until he was asleep before carefully pulling her hand free. Osiv sighed and mumbled, but did not wake.

Nanta put on her blue robe. The room felt hot; though there was no fire in the hearth the great underfloor furnaces that kept the palace's imperial suites free from winter cold had been stoked high, and the air was stale and oppressive. She wanted to walk out of this sumptuous prison, out into the night and away, walking, walking, until she *forgot*. She wanted to find someone who would – or could – *explain* this mockery to her. She wanted her mother. She wanted to take a knife and thrust it into Father Urss's heart.

She had moved to the empty fireplace and was sitting on a settle padded in gold velvet, though she had no memory of how she had got there. Candles burned brightly everywhere; they would probably last until morning. Nanta felt a twisting pang in the pit of her stomach, and the feeling rose, clutching at her, intensifying . . .

She lowered herself to the settle until she was lying full length, and her arms curled around her head, as though to shield her from the light.

Then quietly, exhaustedly, she cried herself to sleep.

Chapter VII

Grand Mother Beck summoned Marine to her office an hour before noon the next day.

Marine was not feeling well. The banquet had not ended until dawn, and it had been made quite clear to her that to leave before the finish was unthinkable. She had finally found her bed as daylight was breaking, but had spent four miserable, wakeful hours suffering severe indigestion. She disliked wine and was not accustomed to rich food, and the banquet's seventeen courses and as many toasts, none of which could possibly be avoided, had taken a heavy toll. Her stomach was leaden, her eyes ached and prickled, and she felt as if someone had attempted to tie a tourniquet around her skull. But she answered the summons, as she must. Her only consolation was that she had at last been able to change her intricate court dress for the simpler, comfortable gown of her calling.

Beck looked none the worse for the night's excesses, and greeted Marine briskly, waving her to sit down. She was signing letters; after a minute or so she looked up and regarded the younger woman with a penetrating gaze that made Marine wonder apprehensively if she had committed some infraction last night and was in disgrace. However, Beck's scrutiny had another purpose.

'Marine.' Beck put her pen aside. 'There has been a change of plan.'

'A change, Grand Mother?'

'Yes. My original intention, as you know, was that you should chaperone the new Princess Imperial until the time of her marriage, after which the duty would be taken on by more experienced palace servants. However, Father Urss and I now feel that it will be in the Princess's better interests if you stay on.'

This was so unexpected that Marine's expression gave her away before she could mask it. 'Oh . . .' she said in a small, dismayed voice.

Beck raised her eyebrows. 'I'm aware that the prospect doesn't please you, Marine. I know you prefer the cloistered quiet of a sanctum to the – animation, shall we say, of court life. But there are good reasons for this decision. And of course you have your own future to consider.' She smiled her familiar, hard little smile. 'I have a robust constitution, but I'm seventy now and I won't live for ever. I might even choose to retire before too long – and before I do, I want to make sure that I have a worthy successor as head of the religious women.'

Marine was stunned. She knew Beck's political skills, knew that she herself had no such abilities; yet Beck was giving out a clear hint that she was in line to take her place.

If she co-operated now. That, Marine thought, was the crux of it. Beck wanted something from her, and this was the bait. A promise of the ultimate advancement, the highest ambition that she could achieve.

At a price.

Flushing, and looking down at her own tightly clasped hands, Marine stammered, 'I – I truly don't know what to say, Grand Mother. The honour – to think that you might consider me suitable—'

'Don't pretend that flimflam with me, Marine,' Beck interrupted testily. 'You know perfectly well that I'm satisfied with your abilities; as well I should be, seeing that I trained you myself. You have your flaws, but that's largely a matter of experience and can be corrected. What matters above all is the fact that I can *rely* on you.'

Marine was silent. As Beck spoke of reliance her gaze had briefly slid away, as though she was uneasy or unsure of herself. The lapse lasted only a moment before her normal composure returned – but it told Marine more than any words. There *was* an ulterior motive behind this, and it had nothing to do with Nanta. Marine guessed that a new and possibly dangerous political game was in the wind, in which Beck was one of the principal players, and Beck needed an ally whose loyalty could not be bought or corrupted. Such people, Marine imagined, were few and far between in the intrigue-ridden circles of the court. So Beck had chosen her, not for her skills but for her integrity.

It was a compliment, but Marine felt uneasy. She disliked intrigue and politics and had no desire to be embroiled in either. All she truly wanted, as Beck knew, was to return to her sanctum and take up the reins of her familiar, peaceable routine again. But three factors stood against her. Firstly – and this in itself would have been enough – one simply did not refuse a proposal like this; not unless one wanted to find oneself suddenly and inexplicably transferred to some remote community in the bleakest mountain regions, to spend the rest of one's days teaching surly peasant children their letters. For all her austerity, Marine had no desire to follow *that* path. Secondly, there was Nanta to consider. For all the change in her station, blood was still blood, and Nanta needed friends now as never before. Marine liked to think that she was Nanta's friend, and that, even if this appointment was purely pragmatic, Nanta might well be glad of it. And the third reason . . .

The third reason was the hardest of all to face, but she forced herself to face it. How could she return to her community of women, and continue to lead and instruct and inspire them in the name of the Lady, if the Lady was no longer there? It would be a hollow farce, a mockery. An *obscenity*. She would be unable to maintain the lie, and it would break her.

Beck showed no sign of impatience as she waited for Marine to speak. She had an accurate idea of what was going through the other woman's mind, and knew it would not be long before Marine ran out of options and made the only viable choice. Her own short but significant conversation with Father Urss after the episode in the nuptial bedchamber last night had focused her mind on plans which would soon require positive action; and the sooner Marine was established in her new role, the better. Marine, of course, would not be told the truth. But her compliance – even if she were never to know precisely what it was she had complied with – would make Mother Beck's work a great deal simpler.

Marine's capitulation came a few minutes later. She was horribly aware of the length of her silence, and growing increasingly nervous as a result. Finally, she couldn't hold out any longer. With a tight, unhappy feeling that did nothing to help her queasy stomach, she said quietly:

'I accept, of course, Grand Mother. And I . . . thank you.'

I very much doubt that you do, Beck thought, but didn't voice it. Aloud, she said, 'Then the matter's settled. I'll have the necessary documents prepared for your assignment to the imperial household – and it will be as well, I think, to elevate you to the level of Mother, to give you sufficient authority.'

Marine blanched. 'If Exalted Father Urss thinks it fitting—'

'Oh, I'm sure he will.' Beck knew too many of Urss's political secrets to have any doubt on that score. 'So; that's all we need discuss for now, I believe.' She smiled. 'Congratulations, Marine. I'm sure you'll be a worthy addition to our numbers.'

'Th . . . thank you, Grand Mother . . .' Marine hesitated. 'What should I do now . . . ?'

'From the look of you, I'd suggest getting a few hours' sleep,' Beck told her. 'Your time is your own for the present; when you're needed I'll waste no time in telling you. Oh, and you can continue to use the suite you've been occupying until new quarters are arranged. That might take a day or two.' She reached for her pen, then, seeing that Marine was still hovering, added, 'Is there something else?'

'I only wondered, Grand Mother . . . if . . . that is . . . How is Nanta – I mean, the Princess Imperial – this morning?'

Beck looked faintly surprised. 'Still a virgin, but beyond that I really have no idea, Marine. She has been left in privacy, for which she is probably grateful.'

'Might I call on her?'

'Of course. That is, after all, what you're here for. Just don't forget to address her as Your Highness from now on, yes?'

'Yes, Grand Mother. Of course.' Marine backed towards the door. 'Thank you . . . Good day . . .'

'Yes, yes; good day, Marine.' Beck had already returned to her letters.

Marine felt exposed and insecure as she made her way through the corridors of the palace's imperial wing. She had been stopped three times by haughty and, in one case, downright rude servants demanding to know what business she thought she had in this most private of areas, and only by claiming her contingent new rank of Mother had she cowed them into letting her pass.

She wished she hadn't left it so long before making this visit. The day was all but over; meaning only to snatch a brief rest, she had slept through half the afternoon, and now all the nobles and dignitaries who had lain abed after the banquet were up and about again. For all that they took little notice of her, Marine found it hard not to scuttle away out of sight whenever one passed her by. It was a foolish instinct that she would have to learn to overcome, but the learning would take time.

Still, she managed to keep up an appearance of confidence as she approached the Prince and Princess Imperial's apartments.

The great ornate doors were daunting, but at least there were no guards; in fact there was no one in sight at all, which Marine found surprising.

She hesitated outside the doors, not sure of the proper form and trying to decide whether to knock or to wait until someone came along and could announce her. As she dithered, she had a sudden and distinct feeling that she was being watched. A chill sensation at the nape of her neck, a prickling . . .

Drawing a quick breath, Marine looked over her shoulder.

She didn't see it clearly; it was gone before her brain had time to register what her eyes were absorbing. But she knew instantly what it was.

A frost sprite. Phantom, mirage, call it what you would; but it was unmistakable. It had been many, many years since Marine had encountered one, and she felt a rush of heat and cold as the shock belatedly hit her. *The Lady's servants* . . . her mind said incredulously. *But how can this be possible?*

She was staring, mesmerised, at the space where the sprite had momentarily been when someone said:

'Pardon me, madam, but can I help you?'

Marine jumped visibly and turned to see a pleasant-faced elderly woman standing at her elbow. She realised that her hands were clutching and crumpling the skirt of her gown; hastily she forced them to relax and found her voice.

'Ah . . . yes, yes; I trust so. My name is Marine. I'm here to enquire after the Princess.'

The woman's face broke into an understanding smile. 'Of course, Mother; forgive me for not recognising you at once. I am Dorca, personal servant to Prince Osiv. Will you be so kind as to come with me?'

Wondering how the woman could possibly know about her advancement when she had only just learned of it herself, Marine allowed Dorca to open the doors and curtsey her through. Dorca followed her, closed the doors again firmly, and smiled.

'If you'll please to wait, Mother, I'll tell Her Highness that you're here.'

She went through to an inner chamber, leaving Marine to gain her first impression of Nanta's new quarters. This room was obviously intended as an outer office, the public face of the establishment. It was full of heavy, dark and, in Marine's opinion, extremely ugly furniture: cabinets laden with old and valuable porcelain, carved screens depicting historical events, shelves housing enough glowingly polished silver and bronze and pewter to buy half a city. The rugs and curtains, of which there were many, were patterned in the imperial gold and grey, which looked sombre in this oppressive setting. The curtains hung motionless, lifeless. The overall atmosphere, Marine decided, was very depressing.

There were sounds in the distance, but they were muffled by walls and the curtains and hard to interpret. Someone laughing; peculiar laughter, with a hiccup in it, then the murmur of women. Looking about her and trying to judge the direction of the noises, Marine noticed what looked like a velvet surcoat discarded on the floor, half hidden behind one of the formidable cabinets. Instinctively offended by untidiness, she moved to pick it up and was folding it neatly when the inner door opened again and Nanta appeared.

'Sister Marine . . .' Her voice was tight and stilted, then quickly she added, 'Your pardon – Dorca tells me you are Mother Marine now.'

Nanta looked more like a doll than ever, dressed as she was in a stiff brocade gown that covered her from throat to feet and with her hair all but hidden under a velvet gable hood. Her face was pallid, her eyes tired and her expression distracted and a little vague.

Remembering Mother Beck's admonitions, Marine dropped a deep curtsey, and Nanta's expression changed.

'Please don't do that!' Her cheeks flushed hectically.

'Everyone does. *Everyone*. It disconcerts me; I – can't get used to it.'

Marine was chagrined. 'I'm sorry, Your Highness.' She saw Nanta flinch at the use of the title; but what could she do? 'I didn't wish to upset you. I merely called to pay my respects.'

'Oh.' Nanta looked at the floor. 'I see. Yes. Thank you.' There was an awkward pause, then she glanced uncertainly at Dorca and seemed to have to pluck up courage to speak. 'Will you leave us, please?'

'Your Highness.' Dorca bobbed, made to go, then paused. 'It will be time for His Highness's meal in half an hour, madam.'

'Yes,' said Nanta defensively.

'Shall I send your dresser to you in a while, madam?'

'*Yes.*'

Dorca might have had a third comment to make, but something in Nanta's tone forestalled it. She bobbed again and hurried out, and with what seemed a great effort Nanta forced herself to relax a little.

'Come through to my own rooms,' she said. 'Please . . . they are more private.'

Few people were ever privileged to enter these personal chambers, and Marine felt uncomfortable as she followed Nanta through a second inner door and along a short hallway. The suite was all that might have been expected: lavishly opulent, luxuriously appointed – and unequivocally oppressive. The drawing room overlooked a small courtyard, a floor below, with a central ornamental pool. In summer, filled with flowers, it would doubtless be a pretty if artificial oasis. Now, layered in snow and bare of any greenery, it was merely bleak. And there were bars at the window.

Nanta saw Marine looking at the bars and said, 'It's because of Osiv. He doesn't understand the danger; he might try to climb . . .' Her voice tailed off as she belatedly realised that she might have revealed too much, and Marine looked away from her face.

'I know about Prince Osiv.'

'Oh.' Marine could feel Nanta's gaze on her like the touch of hot iron. 'Did you know before the wedding?'

Shame made Marine's cheeks prickle. 'Yes,' she admitted. 'But I was not permitted to tell you.' A hesitation, then: 'I'm sorry, Your Highness.'

'Don't.' Nanta said it quickly, sharply. Marine looked up, and for a moment their gazes locked. 'Don't call me Your Highness. *Please*. And don't feel sorry. What else could you have done? If you *had* been allowed to speak freely, I . . . think you would have told me the truth.'

'Yes,' said Marine very quietly. 'I would.'

'Then there's no cause for blame, is there?' Nanta walked slowly to the window and looked out. 'He's very sweet. Osiv, I mean. Like a child. He cries a lot, but I suppose that's only to be expected. I haven't had much experience of children, you see . . .'

Marine didn't speak. She could think of nothing to say.

'I think he has taken to me,' Nanta went on after a few seconds. 'When we had our noon meal, we invented a game; there was a mould of quails in aspic and we scooped out doors and windows in the aspic to make a palace, then Osiv decorated it with fruit comfits . . .' Her voice caught suddenly in an odd, half-choking sound. 'He likes me to play with his toys. He has a great many toys.'

Helplessly, Marine said, 'But you are not—'

She was interrupted. 'I am well looked after. The servants are very attentive and I have every comfort I could possibly need. What else is there to say?'

What, indeed? But Nanta's voice had a harsh edge to it; a tone Marine had never thought to hear from her. She had grown up overnight, and it had been a painful lesson.

Marine's silk skirt rustled as she smoothed it down and tried to compose herself. She had something else to say, but she was less sure, now, of how it would be received.

'I came, Your Hi—' She stopped, cleared her throat. 'As well as to ask after you, I came to bring you some news.'

Nanta turned her head. 'What news?'

'That I shan't be returning to my own sanctum. I am to stay on in the Metropolis.'

'Oh . . .' For a moment Nanta's rigorous self-control slipped a little, and something resembling hope showed in her face. Her tongue appeared, touching her lips uneasily. 'You're to teach at the Academy?'

'No. I'm to be at court, as Grand Mother Beck's subordinate. And, if you permit it, as your companion.'

Nanta sucked in a deep breath and shut her eyes. '*Oh, Lady,*' she whispered. '*You have answered my prayer. . .*'

The words went through Marine like a knife, and almost undid her resolve. She teetered on the brink of an overwhelming temptation to tell Nanta the dreadful secret that had festered in her since the wedding eve. She wanted to share the knowledge, unburden herself, *talk*. She wanted it so much that it was a physical pain.

The moment passed, as such moments had done before. Training and discipline could not be cast away, and the pain was replaced by another: the cold ache of failure and a sense of her own cowardice. Marine said nothing. She only bowed her head, hiding her expression, and waited while Nanta collected herself. She heard the girl walk towards her; the brocade dress made an abrasive sound on the carpet. Then, to her surprise and consternation, Nanta reached out and laid a small hand over hers. She was gloved – she must, of course, be gloved – but the artless gesture spoke volumes.

'I'm glad you're staying, Marine. I would like to think I have a friend here.'

'I hope I shall always be that. Though our relationship must of necessity be at a distance.'

'No,' Nanta said. 'It must not. I don't wish it to be. We're *cousins*, whatever the supposed difference in our stations. I wish to be able to call you Marine, not Mother. And to you I want to be Nanta, not Highness.'

Marine was shocked. 'That would not do! If Exalted Father Urss were to hear—'

'*Rot Father Urss!*' Nanta almost spat the malediction, startling Marine into backing off a pace. Nanta's face, she saw, was ugly with some unnameable emotion; then abruptly she put a hand up to her eyes and the savagery died down.

'Forgive me.' The tight self-control was back once more. 'A lapse . . . I meant only to say that Father Urss is not my keeper, and he doesn't need to be privy to *everything* I do.' The fury threatened momentarily to surge again; she quelled it. 'I *want* you to call me by my own name. It is still *my* name.' Her fingers, hovering over her eyebrows, clenched briefly, then her hand fell to her side and she worked her facial expression into something softer. 'Osiv calls me Nanti. He actually says "Nandi", but he tries. In the Academy, we were reprimanded for using the diminutive.'

'You are not in the Academy now,' Marine said gently.

'No. No, I'm not, am I? And Prince Kodor calls me "sister", while I call him "brother". Marine, do you think that my mother and father will have to call me "Your Highness" now?'

'I truly don't know,' said Marine.

'Oh. I very much want to see them. I asked, but I was told there might be some delay. I don't understand why.'

So there was another small detail that had been kept from her. Marine wondered how the palace servants could bear to live with their consciences; every move they made seemed based on dishonesty. Well, if others would not tell Nanta the truth, she must.

'I'm sorry, my dear,' she said. 'But your parents have left the Metropolis.'

Nanta's eyes widened. '*Left?*'

'Yes. Early this afternoon. I didn't know of it; I discovered the fact quite by chance, after they had gone.' *And too late to speak privately to Karetta. They took great care to ensure that.*

Nanta was stricken. 'But I have had no *time* with them! We hardly exchanged a word – and there's so much I want to tell my mother, so much I need to *talk* to her about!'

'Perhaps,' Marine suggested delicately, 'it's as well you did not. For their sakes.'

Nanta looked piercingly at her as she realised what her words implied. Her parents did not know about Osiv, and it was imperative that they should not find out, lest their tongues should prove unreliable. The inner court coterie could be trusted; Nanta, now, could be trusted; but the EsDorikyes were a wild card, unpredictable.

'The most important thing of all,' Marine continued, 'is that the people of Vyskir should not discover the truth about their Prince Imperial. If they did, it could threaten the stability of the kingdom.'

It was so obvious, yet Nanta had not once thought to look at it in that way. She was aghast at her own naïvety, and she felt an utter fool.

'I didn't consider . . .' she said indistinctly. 'It didn't even *occur* to me.' A frown creased her face. 'Osiv can't rule, can he? When the Imperator dies. It won't be possible.'

'No, it won't. Prince Kodor will become Regent in his place.' Marine paused. 'And you will be Imperatrix in name only.'

Nanta nodded. 'It's little but a name anyway, isn't it?' Then she gave a short, sharp laugh. 'I'm glad, Marine, do you know that? Glad that I won't have to face what it really means to be Imperatrix. It must be very, very frightening.'

111

Marine privately agreed but did not say so. Instead, she asked, 'Have you met Prince Kodor?'

'Yes. Twice, now.' Nanta had in fact half expected Kodor to visit the apartments again today, but he had not. 'I don't know if I like him, but he spoke kindly to me. And I think he is very fond of Osiv.'

Marine had heard as much. 'And the Marchioness Pola,' she said. 'Have you met her, too?'

'She was presented to me at the reception, but I didn't speak to her and her face was veiled,' Nanta replied. 'I believe I'm not to meet her properly until after her marriage. They tell me she's not the least like Duke Arec.'

That, Marine could well believe. Pola of Sekol had also been present at the banquet, which Nanta had not attended, and when she lifted her veil during her brief formal introduction to Prince Kodor, Marine had seen her face quite clearly. She wasn't the conventional beauty everyone had been led to expect, but she was a handsome young woman, with a fine if sallow complexion, a generous mouth and very expressive dark eyes. At a guess she was in her early twenties; of a similar age with her husband-to-be. For the rest of the night she had seemed tense, and every move or gesture she made was performed with rigidly schooled decorum. No; she was certainly not like her father. But beyond that certainty, she was as yet an enigma.

Thinking of enigmas, Marine abruptly recalled the frost sprite. It gave her a small shock to realise that she had put the incident out of her mind, and suddenly it seemed vitally important to tell Nanta about it. But the chance had passed, for even as she groped for a way to broach the subject, Dorca returned.

'Your Highness. Mother.' Dorca curtseyed to them both in turn; a deeper curtsey to Nanta. 'The dresser is waiting, Your Highness. It's nearly time for the Prince's meal.'

Nanta looked as if she would have liked to snap a vitriolic reply, but instead her lips only tightened a little and she said,

'Very well.' She looked at Marine, her eyes expressing all that she couldn't voice in front of the servant. 'Thank you for coming, Marine. And thank you for your news. I'm more glad than I can tell you.' She took Marine's hand again, scandalising Dorca, and to avoid trouble later, Marine curtseyed and bowed her head.

'Your Highness. I am at your disposal at any time.'

When Dorca had closed the door on her with a final disapproving look, Marine surveyed the passage in both directions. There was nothing untoward to be seen now. Could she have imagined that momentary glimpse of the sprite? She was overtired, probably overwrought; it was quite possible that there had been nothing there at all.

She started to walk back towards the public area of the palace and, wanting to distract herself from thoughts of the sprite, considered the changes in Nanta. There was a strange anomaly about the girl; the unworldly innocence was still there, but underlying it now was a new and almost harsh strength that Marine would have thought quite foreign to her nature. Anger, she could understand – but the old Nanta would have been too timid to show it in any way. This new girl – this new *woman* – was different. The mouse was showing signs of turning into something much fiercer. As Imperatrix, Marine thought, Nanta might well have surprised a great number of people who thought they had her measure. The results would have been interesting. As it was, though, she must be consigned to a lesser role, while another fulfilled her duty. It crossed her mind to wonder exactly what Nanta's role in the court *would* be in future.

It did not, however, occur to her to wonder about Prince Osiv's.

Chapter VIII

T he marriage of Prince Kodor and Pola of Sekol took place two days later. This second imperial wedding was in stark contrast to the first, for apart from the bells and the lengthy temple ceremony, the whole thing was a very low-key affair. There was no public procession, no formal presentation, and the banquet took place in a lesser chamber than the ballroom, where the relatively small number of guests would not be dwarfed by the vastness of their surroundings.

There had been one major alarm when it seemed that the Imperator might not survive to see his second son married. On the morning before the ceremony Arctor became ill – the result of a fish dish that hadn't been properly cooked – and though the sickness lasted only a few hours, it left him badly debilitated. Father Urss immediately ordered half the kitchen staff to be imprisoned pending enquiries, then decided that if the worst did happen he would have the Imperator's corpse carried to the temple tomorrow, and maintain the illusion of life until the nuptials were safely over. Fortunately, though, Arctor was much recovered by dawn, and the physician – no doubt with more than a thought for Urss's wrath – pronounced him strong enough to play his part.

The Prince Imperial did not attend the ceremony. But the Princess did. Nanta was seated beside Arctor in the screened box, with Duke Arec flanking her on the other side and a row of dignitaries whose faces and names she did not recognise behind

114

them. Arec occasionally made a jovial remark to her, but the Imperator spoke to no one; in fact through most of the ceremony he appeared to be asleep. The flesh of his face had become even more sunken since yesterday's illness, and his skin had a blue-grey tinge.

To satisfy either decorum or his own religious conscience, Father Urss made up for his haste in conducting the previous marriage ceremony by drawing this occasion out to the fullest possible length. How Pola withstood it Nanta could not imagine, for the Marchioness had no throne to support her but was obliged to stand throughout the entire proceeding. She wore a simpler reproduction of Nanta's blue and silver bridal gown, but her cloak and train were the crimson of the Sekolian ruling house. She looked stiff and uncomfortable, and Nanta noticed that she cast frequent glances at Kodor, who seemed either unaware of or indifferent to them.

So the bells resounded and the protracted solemnities went on, until at long last the closing anthem began and the newly married couple left the altar to the accompaniment of a magnificent chorale. The sound of the massed voices sent a pang through Nanta, reminding her of her own years in the choir and the pleasure and elation she had found in singing. Never again; not now. For a member of the imperial family to practise any arts, even in private, was unthinkable.

The combined volume of choir and bells stirred the Imperator out of his doze, and Nanta rose and stepped out of the way as attendants came to help him to his feet. This time, thankfully, they were to return to the palace by the private tunnel, following the bride and groom; then would come the repeating pattern of the reception and the escorting of the newly-wed pair to their chambers before she was finally allowed to take her leave and sleep.

As the party made their way at the Imperator's slow pace through the tunnel, the thought passed through Nanta's mind that Pola's wedding night would be very different from her own. She was right. But she did not guess at the whole truth, or anything resembling it.

Apart from the fact that the bridegroom was present this time, the second reception was a scaled-down duplicate of the first; though its stultified dullness was increased when, after proffering his blessing to the couple, the Imperator fell asleep once more. From then on voices were hushed and movements kept to a minimum to avoid disturbing him, and the hours passed with an awkward stoicism that the muffled, distant noise of the wider celebrations did little to relieve.

Kodor and his bride sat to right and left of the sleeping Arctor. They could not speak to each other for fear of waking him, and for the same reason no one else dared approach close enough to make conversation possible. Pola sat meticulously still, seeming hardly to breathe; under her veil her mood was impossible to read. Kodor, ignoring frequent censorious glances from Father Urss, twined his fingers in a game of his own devising and made little attempt not to look as bored as he felt. He did, however, take care not to show the other feeling that was slowly but surely growing in him as the time crawled on. A feeling of acute and gnawing resentment.

He knew that the resentment shouldn't have been directed at Pola, for none of this was her fault. If he wanted to blame someone he should blame Duke Arec, whose covert threats to Vyskir's security had brought this situation about. But Duke Arec was out of his reach, while Pola was not; and his increasing animosity demanded a target of some kind.

Kodor gave a sudden, sharp sigh, drawing an apprehensive look from Pola and a mumble from his father. After a moment Arctor's head drooped again, but Pola was still looking at Kodor, and he forced down the irrational anger that her attention roused in him. She was *not* to blame. She was not ugly, not unintelligent; her personality seemed pleasant enough. Three days ago he had

had no complaint at the prospect of marrying her. For a pragmatic alliance, he could have done a great deal worse.

But that was before his first meeting with Nanta EsDorikye.

Kodor's gaze shifted sideways to where Nanta sat; not by Arctor this time but alone on a chair placed especially for her a little way off. She was veiled, as convention dictated, but the veil was a light one and some detail of her face was visible. Kodor stared fixedly at her without realising it, until a discreet cough from a few paces away broke the trance. Father Urss was watching him, and so was Duke Arec. It was Urss who had coughed, and the message in his eyes was ferociously clear. For Kodor to show such blatant interest in a girl younger and lovelier than his own new wife was foolish – and, in the presence of his wife's father, potentially dangerous. Arec would not be slow to take insult, and Father Urss was issuing a timely warning.

Kodor heeded it, and for the rest of the evening took great care not to so much as glance at Nanta again. But neither Urss nor Arec nor anyone else could censor his thoughts. And his thoughts continued to dwell on her almost to the point of obsession.

He did not – *could* not – believe that her startling resemblance to the unknown girl who had haunted his dreams for so long was nothing more than coincidence. Dreams were sent by the God for a purpose, as Father Urss never tired of telling him – so what conclusion should he draw from this? What message was the God sending to him?

Last night during his pre-nuptial vigil Kodor had prayed for an answer, but no answer had come. No manifestations, no revelations, no sign that the God so much as heard his entreaties. Father Urss had presided over the vigil, and at the high point of his frustration Kodor had been sorely tempted to confide everything and ask the priest's advice. He had not, of course. One confessed to Urss; one did not confide in him; and Kodor's dislike of him made him the last man in the Metropolis to whom

117

he would ever reveal anything as personal as his dreams.

So he had emerged from the vigil with his dilemma unresolved, and had gone, as he must, to marry a woman in whom he had no interest. How could he even pretend interest in Pola, when his every thought, waking or sleeping, was fixed on Nanta? It wasn't that he was in love with the girl; he barely knew her. But he wanted to know her; *needed* to know everything about her, to unravel the mystery and find out how a vision from his past could have stepped so shockingly and unexpectedly into the reality of the present.

For the rest of the evening Kodor managed to avoid any more indiscretions, and sat counting the crawling minutes as he waited for the reception to end. It did end at last, and he steeled himself to put on a cheerful face as the escort formed up to usher him and his bride to bed. The Imperator was gently woken and stirred himself enough to mumble a blessing, then the small procession left the room in formal line. Arec caught Kodor's eye and winked at him; Kodor forced an answering smile, but his eyes were cold.

The walk to their suite of rooms was conducted in silence except for some giggling from the younger women of the escort. Pola moved with stiff dignity, ignoring the muffled sounds. Neither she nor Kodor looked at each other, and Kodor wondered fleetingly whether she knew what was expected of her and, if so, whether she was afraid. Then, finding himself indifferent to the answer, he shrugged the thought off.

At the door of the suite the silk garlands were draped over them, and within another minute the door closed between them and their attendants. Women flurried to whisk Pola away to prepare her, and Kodor resigned himself to the attentions of his own male servants. It was all so predictable. The cloth-of-gold nightshirt, the flagon of wine, which he was expected to share among the servants so that they could drink to his health and prosperity and to the getting of many children. Kodor's mood was darkening further with every moment, and by the time the men left him to make his way to the bedchamber he felt as if a thundercloud were hanging over him, building pressure and waiting only for the smallest excuse to discharge a colossal bolt of lightning.

The bedchamber was lit by fifty candles, and a fire roared in the grate. Pola was not yet ready, and Kodor sat down in a chair near the fire and opened the book he had brought with him from his dressing room. It was a treatise on political history; hardly riveting reading but better than staring at nothing while he waited. He was halfway through one of the dry essays when there were noises from the adjoining room, whispering voices and a burst of feminine laughter, quickly stifled. Then the connecting door opened, and Pola came in.

Kodor's first thought as he turned his head and regarded her was that she looked angular and mannish. It wasn't true; it was simply her height and the fact that her face was handsome rather than beautiful. But he was comparing her to Nanta, and the contrast was so acute that irrationally, unjustly, it offended him. The women had loosed Pola's hair, and the heavy, uncompromising blackness of it made him think of Nanta's corn-fairness. Pola's eyes, too, were very dark. Nanta's were blue-green; even in candlelight, which was the only light in which he had seen them, he had noted their colour. In blue and silver, Nanta was exquisite; Pola was not. The colours didn't suit her but only emphasised the sallowness of her skin.

She was gazing at him uncertainly, standing between the door and the bed like an animal at bay. Then she cast her gaze down and said in a low, diffident voice, 'Husband . . .'

Something inside Kodor squirmed. He shut the book with a snap and stood up, still looking at her. She knew what was expected of her; that much he had seen in her eyes before she broke the contact. And she expected the same of him. Why should she not? They had been tied in marriage for a purpose, and if the purpose was not fulfilled the whole point of the union would be negated. Pola knew her duty.

He didn't speak to her but wordlessly indicated the bed. Pola had been schooled well; she made no pretence of maidenly hesitation but slipped off her robe and slid between the silk sheets. He had a brief glimpse of her legs under the silver nightgown; they were long and well-shaped, and despite his hostility towards her he felt a stirring of physical interest. He was human, he was male; he had a healthy sexual appetite, as a number of highly discreet women inside and outside the court could have testified. If Pola's father now effectively possessed Vyskir, why should he not claim his own share of the bargain? It didn't mean anything, but it would have its compensations; and if he got her with child quickly, the political factions would be content.

With a suddenness that startled Pola, he pulled off his nightshirt. He hated the twice-damned thing anyway, always preferring to sleep naked. As his body was exposed, Pola shut her eyes and he saw her tense nervously. She was a virgin, of course; as Arec's sole heir she was a valuable property and would have been kept firmly under lock and key until now. Kodor had had two virgins in the past and had enjoyed the experience.

But then Nanta was a virgin, too . . .

Suddenly, and without any warning, the thundercloud in his mind spat its lightning in the form of sourceless, savage anger that homed in on the young woman lying before him. For one blinding moment Kodor hated Pola, and the feeling triggered a reflex that he made no attempt to quell. He wrenched the bedcover back, throwing it to the floor, and she gasped as her body took the crush of his entire weight. Kodor didn't kiss her or touch her breasts; he didn't even look at her face, but took the mass of her black hair in one hand while the other thrust between her thighs, probing, exploring, pushing her legs apart. She writhed under him, but in shock rather than passion; he felt resistance and liked it; his fingers explored more forcefully and she whimpered a protest.

'*No!*' Kodor hissed at her. He wouldn't let her fight him; he intended to take her, and if she proved unwilling he would be brutal. When he was finished she could think what she pleased of him, but she would have no cause to complain of neglect. That thought spurred him, and with a grunt he pulled her into a better position. She wasn't aroused – far from it – but he was, and it was enough now to overcome her body's opposition. He held her down, pinning her with an arm across her ribcage, and worked his hips against her groin, feeling through the coarse tickle of hair to prise at her.

It was simple enough to break his way in, though her dry tightness was uncomfortable and didn't improve much as he had her. He hurt her, he knew; she didn't cry out, but when he glanced at her face it was contorted and ugly with pain, and she was biting hard on her lower lip.

The whole thing lasted just a few minutes, and culminated in a release that relieved Kodor's body and repelled his mind. He withdrew from her and slid out of the bed, wanting to get away from her and pretend that she didn't exist. An embroidered silk robe lay over a chair back and he put it on, tying the sash tightly and welcoming the cold feel of the material on his hot skin. Then he walked to the fireplace and stared at the flames. No sound from behind him, but he knew she was watching; he could feel her gaze like a physical touch, and it made him tense and angrier than ever. At last, unable to stand it any longer, he swung round to face her.

Yes; she was watching him. She hadn't pulled up the bedcover but lay as he had left her, naked and limp and passive. In the candlelight her eyes were huge, smudged by shadow so that they looked like charcoal. Her face was a still, expressionless mask. And tears were streaming down her cheeks.

Guilt stung Kodor, clashing with the anger. He wanted to turn and walk out of the room, leave her to her misery and find a corner somewhere in the apartments where he could simply lie down and sleep and forget this whole wretched fiasco. The guilt stopped him, for he owed her something, some explanation, however paltry, for his attitude. This was *not* her fault. She was an innocent party, used as he had been used, and he was compounding the wrong already done to her. A spark of compassion awoke, and Kodor started to ask himself if he might not make some kind move towards her, say something, reassure, apologise, *explain*.

Then in a soft, unsteady voice thick with tears, Pola said:

'Why do you hate me?'

She couldn't have known the nature of her mistake, but the words she chose, and the fact that she had spoken before he could, smashed the pity that Kodor was trying to nurture in himself. Suddenly he resented and despised her again, and all the venom of the reaction was in his voice as he replied, 'I don't hate you. I'm indifferent to you.'

She flinched as though the words had been a physical blow. 'I'm your *wife* . . .'

'Not by my choice. Or, I imagine, by yours.' Even her voice affronted him; it was contralto, with a Sekolian accent, and he told himself that he had always disliked both. 'But we're encumbered with it now, and we've done our duty to our fathers and our countries. If I've got a child on you tonight, well and good. If not, then I'll take you again until a child does result, and once it does you'll have nothing else to fear from me.'

Pola sat up. 'I don't want to *fear* you, Kodor! Don't you understand? I hoped—'

He cut across her. 'I understand as much as I need or want to, thank you, and I'm too tired to engage in a debate about it. You'd better go to sleep.' He paused, looking at her. 'And put something on.'

122

It was intended as a small bridge across the gulf between them, a suggestion that she should keep herself warm, but Pola misinterpreted. Her face flushed scarlet with shame and anguish and she flung herself from the bed, snatching up her nightgown, wrenching it on, hurling the blue robe around herself. She faced him again, just once, her eyes flaming through the disordered curtain of her hair. Then with a trembling attempt at dignity she walked to the connecting door, opened it and disappeared into her dressing room.

Kodor stood staring at the door. No sounds came from the far side, and after a while he turned away and started to snuff out the candles. The bedchamber sank gradually into darkness, and when the last candle was out he felt his way to the bed and climbed in.

He lay for a long time staring into the dark, listening to the quiet. Pola did not return, and at last Kodor's eyes closed.

He hoped he would dream.

The vanishing bar of light under the door told Pola that Kodor had extinguished the candles, but still she waited for more than two hours before cautiously peering out from the dressing room. She prayed that Kodor was asleep; if he was not, and saw her, it would strip away the last shred of pride that she had left. He must not think that she had come back like a fawning dog, seeking his favour. It might be true, but he must not think it.

She had sharp ears, and heard the muffled, uneven rhythm of Kodor's breathing as she leaned cautiously into the room. One of her servants at home in Sekol had been plagued by nightmares and breathed like that in her sleep. So, Kodor was dreaming. She would have given a lot to know what he dreamed of.

Her eyes accustoming to the gloom, she moved silently across the carpet until she could just discern the outline of the bed and its occupant. Kodor had thrown off half the covers and was lying with one arm outflung across the mattress, and Pola curbed an instinctive urge to go to him and cover him so that he would not catch cold. Whatever happened, she would not let herself touch him without a clear invitation. Another rejection, another humiliation, would be more than she could bear. So instead she merely stood at the bed foot, staring at the husband who had claimed his rights in what amounted to careless and scornful rape, and whom she loved with a sick, helpless bewilderment.

Her body stung and ached from Kodor's assault, but the other ache, the ache in her mind and heart, went far deeper. All she wanted to ask, to know, to *demand*, was: *why?* She had done nothing to offend him. She was not hideous or deformed. She had been willing to become his in complicity and, she had secretly hoped, in pleasure, and though she had no experience of carnal love she had been eager to learn. But Kodor had given her no chance, and she didn't understand.

Unless the suspicion that had begun to gnaw at her during the past few hours was true.

She had seen Kodor watching Nanta at the reception, and the expression on his face had sown the first seeds. In love with his brother's wife. Was it possible? Likely? Certain? Pola didn't know, but the evidence, though not strong, was there, and it went a long way towards explaining his attitude now. This was, after all, a pragmatic marriage in which neither she nor Kodor had had any say, and if the God and the Lady had decreed that she should lose her heart to her husband, they did not necessarily also decree the reverse. It was cruel, but she had no right to expect anything better.

She became aware that she was crying again; hot, slow tears that trickled silently down her cheeks and which she knew would not be easy to stop. In truth she didn't want to stop them, for they relieved, just a little, the agonising ache in her mind. Let them come, she thought. Just as long as she made no sound that would wake Kodor and give her away.

She went to sit by the window, which overlooked a small,

sunken courtyard. Snow was still falling, drifting in fat flakes past the panes and settling in a dimly visible blanket on the ground below. Pola thought of the future, and her duty, which through all her life she had never failed to do. She would not fail now: she would maintain a pretence of contentment, say nothing of her sadness to anyone, and be to all intents and purposes the perfect wife and the perfect princess. Princess Pola. It sounded faintly ridiculous to her ears, whereas Princess Nanta did not. Pola did not hate easily – truthfully, she had never dared to hate anyone – but she felt the unfamiliar emotion growing in her now, for the woman who had stolen what should have been hers. It would be hard, so hard, ever to call her 'sister'.

Kodor had begun to mutter in his sleep, and she looked over her shoulder to the bed. He seemed to be twisting and turning, though in the dark it was difficult to be sure. A nightmare? If so, he deserved it – but then she crushed that thought and put it away as unworthy and unmeant. She started to rise, hesitant, wanting to go to him and offer him comfort but knowing she could not. Then, amid the mutterings, he called out one word. A name.

Her name.

Pola laid her head down on the window ledge and wept.

And she did not see the pale, shimmering and not quite human form that flitted across the snowbound courtyard, paused a moment to gaze up at her window, then was gone.

Chapter IX

The excitement and upheaval were over, the last of the visiting dignitaries gone, and though the Metropolis was still in a festive mood, life had largely returned to normal.

Both of the imperial brides had apparently settled into the regimen of the palace. Nanta had begun her routine official duties and spent many hours at the desk in her private office, quietly and obediently working her way through sheaves of documents that must be read and studied or signed on her husband's behalf. Quite why she should have so many of these obligations imposed on her she didn't know, and the reason for it was not explained to her. The vast majority of the documents seemed to concern trivial matters that could have been dealt with as easily and efficiently by some minor member of the Exalted Council, and she came to the conclusion that the sole purpose was to habituate her mind – or perhaps merely her reflexes – for a future in which, as Imperatrix, she must be occupied in some worthwhile way. It all seemed rather futile, considering Osiv's affliction; but appearances had to be maintained. The right things must be *seen* to be done, and Nanta hadn't the confidence to argue the pointlessness of it.

Pola, equally obedient, was learning the minutiae of her role as the future Princess Regent. This at least had some real value, for in years to come her husband would effectively govern Vyskir, and she would be expected – not least by her father, Duke Arec – to play an active part in his rule. So Pola studied history, politics, economics, statecraft, applying herself with a dour resolution that thoroughly satisfied her tutors.

The two women had very little contact with each other. They met when Arctor was well enough for the imperial family to be called together at the dinner table, but those occasions were rare, and when they did take place the atmosphere was too inhibiting for any real conversation. Nanta was disappointed. She had hoped to make a friend of Pola, but Pola simply either would not or could not unbend enough for even the first overtures. At the tedious dinners she was more stiffly formal than necessary, never looking Nanta in the face even when they sat opposite each other, and only speaking to ask for a condiment or refuse a second serving. In fact, Nanta reflected, she had more contact with Kodor than with his wife, for Kodor often came to visit Osiv and play with him for a while, and when he did he always invited Nanta to join them. Nanta was puzzled by Pola's remoteness. But in her innocence, it did not occur to her that she might be the reason for it.

Her own life was settling into a dull, predictable but not altogether unhappy routine. The early shock of discovering that Osiv was as he was had waned now, leaving her only with a residual sense of discomfort and, occasionally, confusion. If physical appearance were the only consideration, then a young man of Osiv's good looks and figure would have been a husband to delight in, and Nanta was aware that she could easily have fallen in love with him. But one could not love a child in that way: the possibility simply did not exist. *There* lay the confusion, the anomaly that she must live with and learn to accept. But the irony of it, which could easily have become an obscenity, was made more bearable by Osiv's sweet nature. He had decided now that he unequivocally liked her, and treated her as a cross between a mother and a playmate. Every morning he would wake her early by bouncing on her bed and throwing his arms around her neck for a hug, and at night he refused to go to sleep until she personally had told him a story. Nanta knew few stories and would quickly have run out of ideas, but Kodor had sent her a gold-bound and exquisitely illustrated book of legendary tales from his own collection, which would keep Osiv contented for a long time to come.

She had also seen less than she had hoped of Marine. Marine had caught a severe head cold a few days after Kodor's wedding, and she was so unused to being ill that it had taken her a long time to recover. When she did recover, she seemed to be constantly at the call of Mother Beck, and her visits to Nanta were infrequent and so brief that there was barely time to exchange news and pleasantries, let alone anything more. Nanta thought that Marine looked tired and preoccupied, and prayed every night for the Lady to grant her strength. She herself was in excellent health, and – to her surprise – there had been no more nightmares or, as far as she knew, sleepwalking episodes. For all its limitations, her new life was tolerable, and she was slowly coming to accept it.

Then, barely a month after the weddings, the Imperator took to his bed, and this time it was not a false alarm. The chief physician came personally to Urss's austere quarters as the sun was setting and told him quietly but unequivocally that, in his professional opinion, the reign of Arctor IX would come to an end before the night was out.

Urss sombrely thanked the physician and dismissed him, saying that before attending to the formalities he would spend a few minutes in private prayer for the Imperator's peaceful journey to the arms of the God. The man left, but instead of praying, Urss stood staring at a map on his wall, aware of a new feeling stirring in him. He would not have called it excitement; that would be unseemly in the extreme. Yet it had a strong element of eager anticipation, as he contemplated the final fulfilment of the scheme that he and his close confidants had planned and worked towards for a very long time. They had waited patiently for this moment. Now, at last, the reward was in sight.

He dropped his gaze from the map and turned his thoughts to more immediate matters. Protocol required that Osiv should be the first to be told of his father's impending death; a waste of time, of course, as the prince wasn't capable of understanding, but it was vital that the proper procedures should be seen to be observed. Next Kodor must be informed, and when the physician judged the end was an hour or less away the family would gather at the bedside to make their farewells and participate in the Rite of Passing. The Rite, too, would need to be arranged, and Urss pulled the bell-rope that would summon his secretary. The man, a stooped, short-sighted but reliably discreet Father, appeared seconds later, and Urss gave instructions for preparations to begin, nodding solemnly in response to the secretary's expression of sorrow at the news. Then, when the man had gone, he donned his chasuble and the gold-fringed sash reserved for the most solemn occasions, and made his way to the Prince Imperial's suite.

Nanta and Osiv were dining; though 'dining' was hardly the term for the blend of game and close supervision that Osiv's meals involved. The prince sat at a small table with a napkin tied firmly around his neck; he had eaten the dishes that he liked and Nanta was now trying to coax him into taking a few spoonfuls of those he did not like but which were necessary, according to the physician, for his good health. There were toys among the serving plates on the table and Nanta's own food was untouched and going cold. A flustered Dorca announced Father Urss, and Nanta rose quickly and defensively to her feet as, without waiting for an invitation, the priest came in.

'Exalted Father . . .' She had not come face to face with Urss since the ugly scene on her wedding night, and her face flushed hotly. Osiv used her distraction to remove a half-chewed piece of fish from his mouth, then gave Urss a suspicious glare and turned away.

'Your Highnesses.' Urss bowed punctiliously to the prince then made a lesser bow to Nanta, and as he looked directly at her she realised that this was something serious. 'I regret that I must be the bearer of sad news.'

Nanta's expression changed. 'The Imperator . . . ?'

'Yes, madam. I'm afraid that the end is very near.'

'Oh . . .' Her face became still, introverted; she knew that she should make some show of grief but, truthfully, what was there to show? She had met the Imperator on few occasions and exchanged only a formal sentence or two with him. She didn't *know* him, and on a personal level his imminent death meant nothing to her. At last, struggling for anything that would be better than silence, she managed, 'I am . . . greatly distressed to hear that, Exalted Father. Osiv – my – the Prince Imperial will also be . . .' Then it occurred to her that the loss of his father would probably mean little more to Osiv than it did to her, and the polite words stumbled to a halt.

Urss permitted himself a small, charitable smile. 'I quite understand, madam. Perhaps you would prefer me to try to explain to His Highness?'

'No.' She frowned. 'Thank you, but no. I will talk to him myself.' She glanced towards the table, where Osiv was now dropping pieces of diced vegetable into his cup of fruit juice. 'Though not immediately, perhaps.'

'Of course.' Urss watched Osiv's antics with a distaste that bordered on contempt. 'However, the Prince will be required to attend the Imperator before the end, so if I might suggest that the matter isn't delayed for too long . . . ?'

Nanta wondered if Urss had any concept whatever of kindness. To subject a child like Osiv to a deathbed vigil was unfeeling and unfair; it would do nothing to help either him or the Imperator. But she kept her thoughts to herself and only said, 'Very well. Has Prince Kodor been told yet?'

'My first duty is to the Prince Imperial, madam,' Urss

reminded her. 'When I have your permission to withdraw, I shall go to Prince Kodor and inform him.'

'My permission? Oh . . . oh, yes.' Nanta nodded, collecting herself. 'You have my permission, of course, Exalted Father. Please convey my sympathy to the – to my brother and sister. And when the time comes to – to attend—'

'I will send word at once, Your Highness.' Urss bowed again, took a precise pace backwards, then turned and swept from the room.

Nanta looked at Osiv. He had grown bored with his new game and was slouching in his seat, chin on chest and kicking his heels impatiently against the chair legs. She was just beginning to ask herself, helplessly, how she could possibly explain to him what was happening and what he would be expected to do, when Dorca returned. Her pleasant face was creased with anxiety and, approaching with nervous deference, she ventured:

'Is anything amiss, Your Highness?'

Nanta liked Dorca, but at this moment she did not want to talk to her. All the servants would hear the news soon enough; let her find out in her own good time. So she said, 'No, Dorca, nothing's amiss. I believe Prince Osiv has eaten his fill, and I am not hungry, so you may tell the footmen to clear the table.'

'Yes, madam.' Disappointed, Dorca returned to the door, then paused. 'Though if there *is* anything I may do—'

An edge crept into Nanta's voice. 'There is not. Just obey me, please.' Her tone softened. 'Thank you.'

Dorca paused another moment, then thought better of saying anything more and went out.

Kodor and Pola were also dining when Father Urss arrived; but the contrast with the scene in the Prince Imperial's rooms could hardly have been greater. This time, knowing Kodor's temper, Urss did wait to be announced, and he was shown in to find the prince and princess seated at opposite ends of an immaculate table, waited on in respectful silence and keeping silent themselves. At a gesture the footmen hurried out, and Urss made his bows. Pola raised her eyes to his face but only nodded acknowledgement; Kodor, however, half rose to his feet, as if he already knew what the priest had come to tell him.

When Urss gave the news, Kodor said, 'I see.' His jaw worked briefly and he swallowed. 'We can't pretend that it was unexpected, can we?'

'Sadly, no, Your Grace.'

'But perhaps a little sooner than anyone had thought. He seemed better these last few days. By morning, the physician says . . . ? Poor Father. Still, perhaps for him it will be a merciful release.' He glanced at his wife but she had cast her eyes down again.

'I pray so, sir,' said Urss urbanely. There was a pause. Then Kodor asked:

'Has my brother been told?'

'I spoke personally to the Princess Imperial, Your Grace. She wishes to explain to Prince Osiv herself . . . or at least . . .'

'Or at least try; yes, quite.' Another pause. 'How has my – our – sister taken the news?'

A change in his tone, a softening, alerted Urss, and his gaze slid sideways to Pola once more. Her mouth had tightened into a hard line, as though she was biting back some emotion that threatened to force its way out, and her dark eyes were suddenly bitter. But still she didn't speak, and after a few moments Urss looked away again. All was far from well between this couple, and he believed he knew the cause. It could, in potential, become a dangerous situation. It would need careful watching and, if it worsened, careful handling and – possibly – a slight adjustment to the long-term strategy.

Aloud, he said, 'Her Highness is saddened but quite calm, Your Grace.'

'Did she send any word, any message?'

This time Urss had no need to look at Pola, for her silent reaction soured the atmosphere as surely as if she had screamed it to the rafters. 'No,' he said, unmoved by the fact that he was lying. 'She did not.'

The prince was clearly disappointed, but shrugged it off with a skill that would have fooled any lesser man. 'Well,' he said, 'then we can only wait.'

'And pray.'

'Of course. Thank you, Father Urss. I assume I can leave it to you to make the necessary arrangements?'

'They are already in progress, sir.'

Yes, Kodor thought, *I'm sure they are*. 'Then I trust you'll send word to me as soon as my father is ready to receive his last visitors.'

Urss bowed again. 'Be assured of it, Your Grace.' Another bow to Pola, another dignified nod of her head, and Urss made his soft-footed way out.

Nothing broke the room's silence for some time when he had gone. Pola had set her knife down on her plate, at its usual precise angle, and Kodor stood staring at his own half-eaten meal. She knew that he had no intention of speaking unless she did – if then – but the tension in her was so great that she had, at last, to give way.

'I'm so sorry,' she said in a low voice.

She could feel Kodor's gaze boring into the top of her skull. 'Are you?' he replied. 'Why?'

'Because he is your father, and he was always kind to me.'

'You've met him barely five or six times.'

'I know; but he was kind.'

Kodor laughed cynically. 'Kinder than I am, is that what you're implying?'

Her head came up sharply. 'No! I meant—'

'Oh, don't trouble to explain! What does it matter? I don't

expect you to like me; you have no reason to, nor I to like you. Don't say any more. I don't want to talk.'

He sat down again, rang the bell to summon the footmen back, and told them to clear away the food. Pola sat still and mute. She would have liked another glass of wine but did not dare say so, for Kodor was clearly in a mood to vent his spite on her at the smallest excuse. In her present state of mind, that would have set the final seal on her misery.

The table was cleared and the servants departed. Minutes passed; then, forgetting or choosing to ignore his own earlier words, Kodor said, 'So, you'll be Princess Regent before long. Does that please you?'

Pola shook her head, not looking at him.

'Well, it'll please your father; we can be sure of that.' Cynicism laced his voice. 'I suppose we'd better do the thing properly and send word by a personal ambassador. Let's also hope that it isn't the only news we have to give him.'

Pola's cheeks flamed as, without knowing it, he put his finger painfully on the real cause of her unhappiness. Their first sexual encounter had not borne fruit; nine days ago her monthly flux had come as usual and she had confessed it to him. Kodor had not been pleased. Brusquely, he told her to inform him when she was, as he put it, 'clean' again, and last night he had taken her a second time. The act had been as cold and unceremonious as the first, and afterwards he had returned to his own bedchamber before she could even collect herself enough to sit upright. And the worst of it all, the terrible, tarnishing, degrading worst, was that Pola had *wanted* him. No matter how careless he was towards her, no matter how callously he used her, she had *wanted* him. And if the only way she could have him was by failing to conceive, then she would pray with all her heart for failure, and duty and dynasties and the expectations of Vyskir and Sekol could blow away on the north wind. That was the shame she could not face, and the thing that Kodor must never, ever know.

But now the old Imperator was dying and a new one would take his place. Osiv. They had kept her away from him – or him from her; the reasoning hardly mattered – and other than that he was a mental cripple, she knew nothing about him. Osiv the . . . Fourth? Fifth? She wasn't sure; she was still getting to grips with Vyskiri history. He would be the public figurehead, while Kodor ruled behind the scenes. As far as Pola knew, the title of Regent would not even be made official, so that the public pretence about Osiv could be maintained. But Kodor would rule. And part of her task was to satisfy her father's ambitions by becoming the mother of Kodor's successor and thus uniting her own and her husband's countries. It was planned, it was arranged, it was simple.

And she desperately, desperately did not want to conceive.

She stood up. 'I think I would like to go to my own rooms,' she said.

Kodor waved a hand, uninterested. 'As you please.'

'I would like to . . . prepare for the – the—' Oh, what did it *matter*? What did *anything* matter? The truth was that if she must endure Nanta's company at the Imperator's bedside, she needed time to compose herself, to make sure that her suppressed feelings would not suddenly and uncontrollably erupt.

Kodor was waiting for her to finish her sentence, with a faint air of one whose patience was being sorely tried. Pola looked at him, but any further words were dead in her throat. Turning away with a sharp movement, she went out.

Kodor rested his elbows on the table and put his head in his hands. A minute or so later, tears began to trickle between his fingers.

His Gracious Majesty Arctor IX, Imperator of Vyskir, died two hours before dawn, with his family at his bedside and the antiphonal voices of ten Brothers and Sisters from the higher echelons of the Imperial Choir resounding in his failing ears.

Just before he took his last conscious breath he focused his eyes on his elder son, who at that moment was sitting on the floor and plaiting the fringe of the richest rug into a ludicrous tangle. Perhaps sensing something of the look, Osiv glanced up with a quick, candid but vacant gaze, and smiled at him. Arctor returned the smile. Then one veined, unsteady hand groped to where he knew Kodor was sitting at his bedside.

'Take care of your brother.' They were the last words he spoke, and a minute later the physician nodded fractionally, his expression sombre.

Kodor rose, reached out to his father's face, and pressed his fingers lightly against the motionless eyelids. They closed; Kodor withdrew, then dropped to his knees beside the bed and pressed his brow to the coverlet, his lips moving in silent prayer.

Across his bent head, the gazes of Nanta and Pola met. Nanta tried to convey something: a fellow feeling, an openness, even an invitation. Pola's dark eyes reflected it back at her like a glass wall. Then she looked away.

An hour of ceremony followed the death as Father Urss conducted them solemnly through prayers, psalms and the laying-out of the corpse, all punctuated by antics from Osiv, who was bored now and demanding something or someone to entertain him. Nanta did her best to keep him in order, but when, finally, he threw a tantrum just as the assembled company were about to make their obeisances to him as the new Imperator, the proceedings ground to a halt. Father Urss pronounced the last valediction with irritable haste, and to everyone's relief the formalities were deemed over. Arctor's spirit had been sent on its way in unseemly chaos, but under the circumstances it was the best that could have been done.

Nanta saw Osiv put safely to bed, where with luck he would stay until well into the morning, then retreated to her private room. She was tired but knew she would not sleep. In a few hours she must go into the new ordeal of full mourning; before it began she greatly needed a respite, the chance, both literal and metaphorical, to breathe a little.

The apartments of the imperial family centred around one of the palace's tallest towers, a domed minaret that commanded a view across the Metropolis and the river to the south, and the distant mountains that divided Vyskir and Sekol to the north. Nanta had only climbed the tower once; her free time was too limited and the servants had also made it clear that such activities were looked on as unsuitable and undignified. Now though, she chose from her wardrobe a long wolf and ermine coat – one of several, and warm enough to keep the night cold at bay – and, after ensuring that Dorca was within call if Osiv should wake, took a lantern and slipped out of the apartment by a private way that avoided the main corridors.

As she began to climb the spiral staircase, Nanta felt tension ebbing and a sense of something like peace enveloping her. Solitude had become a rare treasure, and for the little of the night that was left, she intended to enjoy it to the full. The tower summit was a long way up and she had little chance for exercise these days, so by the time she reached the top her legs were aching and her heart labouring with the effort of the climb. But her first breath in the open winter night was better than any physician's nostrum. No matter that the air was bitterly cold; it tasted clean and fresh and *alive*, and she stood still on the circular parapet, eyes closed as she gratefully drank in the freshness before setting down her lantern and looking out at the huge vista spread before and below her.

The snow clouds had cleared briefly and the sky was starry, mirroring the soft twinkle of lights in the city that never completely slept. There was the Fathers' seminary, with many of its windows shining; there the Academy, darker but still showing a few lamps here and there. Further, in the lower city, a curving ribbon of small, bright eyes marked the great central thorough-fare, illuminated from dusk to dawn; and beyond that lay the dim, phosphorescent sheen of the river. A cargo boat was moving slowly against the current, arriving, probably, from some remote port in another part of the kingdom. At the docks men would be waiting to unload amid a bustle of noise and activity. But up here the activity was invisible, and the only sound was the soughing of the wind.

Nanta felt tension ebbing from her and a quiet calm moving in to take its place. Leaving her lantern behind, she walked slowly around the tower's perimeter until the aspect changed and the city gave way to empty night. By the starlight she could make out the snow-covered contours of the mountain foothills, like the humped backs of vast, somnolent beasts, and behind them the mountains proper were dim ghosts against the sky. The wind was blowing from the mountains tonight, stinging Nanta's cheeks with its frosty touch. She wondered how far it was to Sekol, and whether Pola was homesick and the sense of alienation she felt from her thus explained. She wondered how Pola would fare as Princess Regent. She wondered how they would all fare now that Arctor was gone. She wondered if she would ever grow accustomed to the title of Imperatrix . . .

She was lost in the reverie of inner questions that had no answer when Kodor found her. He had not come looking for her; it was simply that his own thoughts and impulses had followed a like pattern to hers. But his surprise on seeing her there, and alone, was almost as great as his pleasure.

She turned and looked at him in some consternation. Against the sky Kodor couldn't see her face, and he hesitated.

'Nanta . . . Forgive me; I didn't realise you were here.' Another pause. 'Do you wish me to go?'

Nanta shook her head. She wanted to be alone, but Kodor had as much right here as she. And his company was easy enough to share.

He came and stood beside her, though at a circumspect distance, and leaned on the parapet. Feeling that she should say something appropriate, Nanta ventured, 'This must be a very sad time for you.'

'Sad?' Kodor considered the word. 'I don't know. I truly don't. Father was old and tired, and I suspect he was glad to go.'

'May the God and the Lady give him peace.' Nanta bowed her head respectfully.

Kodor made no comment. Silence fell for a minute or so, then he asked, 'How is Osiv?'

'Sleeping.' Nanta's expression closed in a little. 'He doesn't understand. I tried to explain to him, after Father Urss brought the news, but I don't believe he even realises that the Imperator is . . . no longer here. And as to what that means for him – I don't know what anyone can do to help him.'

Kodor sighed. 'He'll be spared the funeral, at least. The people will be told that their new Imperator is too prostrated with grief to attend, and they'll love him all the more for that. The coronation is another matter; but that's probably the best part of a year away.'

'A year?' She looked at him quizzically, and he smiled a small, thin smile.

'It's the protocol, Nanta. Or are you too young to remember?'

'Your father's coronation was before I was born.'

'Ah. To tell the truth, I recall little of it myself; I was barely able to toddle at the time. But yes; it will be of that order. First comes three months of mourning, public and private; and after that our religious masters decree a decent interlude in which any form of rejoicing is looked on as bad form. Knowing Father Urss, I imagine he'll make the most of that. So there'll be time enough to prepare Osiv – and you – for what must be faced.' He paused. 'I don't envy your position, Nanta. I'm sorry for you. Your life will be harder still from now on.'

She didn't react to that, at least not outwardly, but only said with what sounded suspiciously like well-practised composure, 'The God and the Lady will give me strength.'

'Will they?' Kodor asked.

He hadn't meant to say it, but the words were out before he could stop them. Nanta's head came round so sharply that she looked for a moment like a hunting cat rather than the mouse to which some palace servants disparagingly compared her, and she stared at him. 'What do you mean?'

It was too late to back away or deny what he had said, and Kodor felt uncomfortable. 'Oh . . . it's my own tribulation; pay no heed to it.'

'No,' she said. 'Tell me.'

He sighed. 'It's simply that I sometimes wonder . . . if there is any point in turning to the God and the Lady at moments like these. Or at any other moments.'

She continued to look at him, and he saw that she was deeply shocked.

'You doubt the benevolence of the God and the Lady?' Her voice was small, frozen as the mountain ice-caps. 'How *can* you?'

He shrugged. 'Because I see no real reason to believe in it. Oh, I know all the stories; the prayers that are answered, the supposed miracles. But I see no worthwhile evidence of their compassion. So I find myself questioning whether they truly care for mortals at all. And at a time like this, the doubts become magnified.'

'At a time like this,' said Nanta quietly, 'you should be able to take strength and comfort from the God and the Lady. Not the opposite.'

'I know. And it may simply be the melancholy of the hour that causes it.'

'You're naturally grieving—'

'Yes, yes. *But not entirely for the reasons you think. As my wife is well aware.*'

'Prayer can *help* you, Kodor. I know it can.' Nanta hesitated. 'Unless you forbid it, I shall pray for you in the Lady's sanctum.

I shall ask her to intercede and to – to restore your faith.'

She hoped he had not noticed the slight snag in her voice, the momentary wavering as private memories of her own un-answered entreaties crept out from their crevices in her mind. Kodor had not noticed. He was watching her very intently, and all he said was:

'It is not in my power to forbid you anything, Nanta.'

Nanta saw only the outer and not the inner meaning of his words, but nonetheless her cheeks flushed. 'Please don't,' she said, then: 'I've never *wanted* to be Imperatrix . . .'

'Very few of us are able to have what we want. In the lower echelons it's called ill-fortune. In ours, it's called duty.'

Nanta didn't answer but turned away and looked northwards again, towards the mountains. There was a faint light on the horizon, Kodor saw; enough to halo her figure with a pale, cold nimbus. Dawn must be close, and he should . . .

The thought faded as he realised that he was not looking at the first signs of the dawn.

Nanta heard his sharp, quick intake of breath in the moment before she was brushed aside as he took her place at the parapet.

'Kodor?' Confusion and indignation warred. 'What is it; what's amiss?'

'That glow . . .' Kodor was staring fixedly at the horizon.

She frowned. 'It's only the dawn glimmer. The beginning of sunrise.'

'Since when has the sun risen in the *north*?'

Before Nanta could reply, or even consider what he had said, the entire northerly horizon flared into life. A ghostly wall of light, like a vast curtain in a celestial theatre, swept across the sky, and scarves of ethereal colour began to move in it, towering and swaying and merging in an unearthly dance.

'*The Corolla Lights!*' Kodor's face, faintly but eerily illumi-nated by the great phantasm, was a study in rapt and awestruck disbelief.

Nanta, too, could barely believe what she was witnessing. 'I've never seen them,' she breathed. 'Never . . .'

'No one has, for twenty years past! I was a little child when they last appeared. My mother took Osiv and me to her roof garden to watch them, and when they faded, Osiv cried because he could not command them to return . . .'

But Nanta was not listening. She had clasped her hands before her breast, and her head was bowed over her interlocked fingers as she whispered a fervent prayer of reverence and thanks. Kodor's ears heard the flow of her words: '*Sweet Lady . . . Your blessing . . . Healing . . . Our homage . . .*' but it meant no more to him than the murmur of snow falling. He was stunned, stupefied. Twenty years, and the Lights had returned – and on this night of all nights, as the old Imperator died and the new reign began.

Osiv must see them! The thought came to his rescue as fear threatened to take too strong a hold, and it allowed him to snap back into rationality. The Lights would vanish when the sun rose; Osiv must be woken quickly and shown the marvel. He would delight in it, and crow, and hold his arms out to its beauty, and—

His thread snapped as Nanta collapsed to the parapet floor.

'Nanta!' Shocked, Kodor could only stare at her for several bewildered seconds. She had made no sound, given no warning; she had simply dropped like a sack of grain, and now lay prone with one arm outflung almost to his feet. Swiftly he crouched beside her, raised her head – she was breathing but her eyes were closed and her mouth hung slackly open. A faint, or a fit – not stopping to wonder what might have caused it, Kodor gathered her up in his arms and started to carry her, awkwardly in the confined space, round the parapet to the door. At the top of the staircase he set her down again, and relief clutched at his stomach as she began to stir.

'Nanta!' He cupped her face between his hands, only just

refraining from shaking her. 'Nanta, what is it, what happened to you?'

'Nnh . . .' She struggled with her tongue, which didn't want to obey her. 'I . . . *fainted*.' She sounded bemused and almost indignant, though in a weak, childlike way. 'Ohh . . . so *tired* . . .'

Kodor wasted no energy, hers or his own, on further questions. She could stand, if only just, and he took his own lantern, leaving hers to burn itself out, and started carefully with her down the stairs. She leaned on him for support, but she was no heavy weight and his anxiety for her gave him reserves of energy. They reached the tower's foot, and as they emerged through a discreetly curtained door into the royal apartments, two women servants appeared.

And so did Pola.

'Kodor. I've been searching for you.' Pola's voice did not quaver, but everything she saw and surmised was written in letters of fire across her face. She drew herself up with wretched dignity, aware that the two women were keenly watching this encounter. 'The Corolla Lights have appeared. I thought you would want to—'

'I've seen them,' Kodor said curtly. He turned to the servants. 'The Imperatrix is unwell. She is under great strain, and tonight's events have exhausted her. Take her to her private rooms, and see to it that she is properly cared for.'

The women mumbled and curtseyed and shepherded Nanta away. She did not look back, but Kodor's gaze followed her until all three turned a corner and were lost from sight. Then, reluctantly, he looked around for his wife.

And heard only the quick beat of footsteps retreating into the distance.

Chapter X

By the time dawn broke and the Corolla Lights faded, the Metropolis was in a ferment.

Father Urss had only just fallen asleep when he was woken by his flustering secretary, who in turn had been roused from his bed by a gaggle of agitated Fathers and High Brothers. Climbing to the roof of the seminary, Urss watched the last minutes of the phenomenon in thoughtful silence, then returned to his quarters and began to dictate an amendment to the proclamation of Arctor's death, which was scheduled to be made an hour after the First Obligation chimes had rung. The gist of the amendment was that the return of the Lights was an unequivocal sign of the God and the Lady's blessing upon the new reign of Imperator Osiv IV. Twelve days of thanksgiving would therefore accompany the beginning of Arctor's official mourning period, and all citizens would be expected to devote a minimum of one hour each day to private prayers.

This last statement was superfluous, as the combination of awe, fear and bewilderment brought on by the Lights' appearance would be more than enough to cause a surge of mass piety. Urss, though, had more immediate and personal reason for concern, and the minutiae of the edict were of no interest to him. He authorised the document with a frown and a hasty signature, then returned to his bedchamber, giving a last, curt instruction to his secretary that he would see Grand Mother Beck in his office at the second hour before noon.

In truth, Urss was worried. For all his general cynicism, he didn't doubt for one moment that the Corolla Lights were a very significant omen. Tradition held them as a sign of the Lady's literal presence in the world – yet for some time past, Vyskir's high religiouses had believed that the Lady no longer existed. The Lights' reappearance after a twenty-year absence had thrown a proverbial cat among the pigeons of that belief, and the question that burned in Urss's mind and – as nearly as anything could – frightened him was: *why?* Had they been wrong in their assumption about the Lady? Or did the Lights have some other meaning; one they could not interpret? The timing, so close on the heels of Arctor's death, was ironic at the very least; and when Urss added certain other factors into the equation, the irony became downright unnerving.

However, it was not in Urss's nature to give way to irrational speculation, so he decided that the wisest course was to return to bed and try to sleep for a while, to allow logic to reassert itself in his mind. He did not sleep well. But when, in the morning, the proclamation was made and he was woken by the first sonorous sounds of Arctor's death-knell booming through the city, he showed no outward signs of disquiet as he prepared to receive Mother Beck.

When Beck arrived, Urss saw immediately that she too was worried. She lowered herself into a chair opposite his desk, and though her manner was composed enough, her eyes told him that she was as aware of the situation and its implications as he was. The cheerless and discouraging sound of the knell, tolled by the temple bells and the single great bell of the palace, was starting to grate on Urss's ears and nerves; doing his best to ignore it, he wasted no time but began:

'The Lights, Grand Mother. I presume you saw them?'

'No, Father, I did not,' Beck replied. 'My servants woke me, but at my time of life the climb to a suitable vantage point is not an option. However, I can reassure you that I know all I need to about the incident.' She paused. 'There is a great deal of turmoil in the city, I gather. Spontaneous displays of religious fervour are breaking out, and self-appointed soothsayers are already at work prophesying everything from glory to disaster.'

Urss grunted. 'Most of them are harmless fools, and those that aren't can be dealt with easily enough. I'm not interested in rabble-rousing nonsense, Beck. My concern goes far deeper – and I don't think I need to spell it out to you, do I?'

'No, Father,' said Beck. 'You do not.'

'Then I'll not waste my time or yours with speculation.' Urss wished he could rid himself of the sensation that an invisible presence was looking over his shoulder, and had to summon all his concentration to continue. 'We cannot allow the resurgence of the Lights to alter our resolve. In themselves, as an isolated incident, they mean nothing, and if the phenomenon is not repeated then popular excitement will soon tail off and the event can be consigned to history.'

'But if it *is* repeated . . . ?' Beck asked.

He frowned. 'As I said, in themselves the Lights mean nothing, whether they appear once or on fifty consecutive nights. We must therefore not be tempted to draw hypothetical conclusions from them, and until or unless the God should choose to grant us a clear revelation, we shall proceed as planned.'

Beck looked uncomfortable. 'Naturally, Father, I don't question your judgement. But . . .' She paused, and Urss prompted a little edgily, 'But what?'

'A minor matter, and probably it means nothing. But several of my Sisters have had strange experiences in the wake of the Lights' appearance. They say they were visited by frost sprites in the hour after dawn. And one even claims to have seen . . . the Lady herself.'

Urss stared at her. 'Under what circumstances?'

'A waking dream. The woman is one of my senior staff; highly reliable and not the sort to indulge in foolish imaginings.

146

I questioned her myself, and I have to say that what she told me was uncannily close to many documented accounts of a true vision.'

'And what did this "true vision" impart to her?' Urss was beginning to sound extremely testy by now.

Beck sighed. 'Nothing that could be interpreted as a message or command. But if it were to be—'

Urss interrupted her. '*If*, Grand Mother. *If*.' He folded his hands on the desk top, pressing the tips of his thumbs together. 'Answer me truthfully. Are you saying that you believe the Lady *did* appear to this woman, and that our own conclusions are wrong?'

'In truth, Father, I don't know,' Beck admitted. 'But I am uneasy.'

Abruptly Urss's black mood ebbed. Contrarily, and unexpectedly, her disquiet had brought an inverse reaction in him, driving away his doubts and replacing them with new confidence. It was only to be expected that a woman – even a woman like Beck – should be prey to irrational fears and illogical reasoning, and though he might disparage her weakness, he was generous enough to make allowance for it.

'Beck,' he said more cordially, 'I understand your anxiety, but it's obvious that this woman has *not* been granted a true vision. She and the other Sisters have simply been infected by the general hysteria surrounding the Lights' appearance, and I have no doubt that the effects will wear off in their own good time. If they don't, you must deal with the matter in your own way; or failing that, one of the High Fathers will speak directly to the Sisters and impose some penances that will bring them back down to earth.'

Beck visibly bristled. 'I'm quite sure that won't be necessary, Father Urss.'

'I'm gratified to hear it. Now, if your mind is set at rest, we'll return to the purpose of this meeting.' His own mind was clearer than it had been since early morning; he had no doubt now that his instinct was goading him in the right direction, and he continued with certainty in his voice.

'In one sense, Beck, this incident with your Sisters has highlighted the greater concerns about the Lights and their effect on popular thinking,' he said. 'As of this morning Vyskir has a new Imperator, and the fact that his accession was accompanied by such a strong religious omen will give him an especial status in the eyes and hearts of the public that we could well have done without.' He sat back in the chair, regarding his intertwined fingers. 'If last night's phenomenon is not repeated, that perception will wear off; our good citizens have a short attention span and soon tire of novelty. However, we can't afford to make any assumptions, and if the Lights *do* recur, and keep recurring, it will jeopardise our long-term strategy. To put it bluntly, Beck, we can't risk Osiv becoming a figure of adoration, or it will become too dangerous to remove him.'

Beck, too, had recovered her composure, and the old, cold steadiness was back in her eyes. 'Do I take it then, Father, that you intend to bring matters forward?' she asked.

'Yes. Or at least to plan for that contingency. We shall wait and observe for five more days. If during that time the Lights don't appear again, public interest will start to wane and we can keep to our original plan. But if they do, we must be ready to act. Flexibility and efficiency, Beck. They're both of the essence from now on.'

Beck nodded. 'What do you wish me to do?'

'Your most important task is to keep the new Imperatrix busy enough to ensure that she sees as little of her husband as possible.' Urss frowned with irritation. 'She seems to have taken a perverse liking to him and I'm told that they spend a lot of time in each other's company. That must stop. It's vital that she should guess nothing; however meek she may be, she can't be trusted – and besides, we must have unrestricted access to Osiv in case we need to move swiftly.'

Beck nodded a second time. 'Marine will be useful. As cousin to the Imperatrix, and something of a friend—'

'I'm not interested in the fine details,' Urss cut in impatiently. 'Just ensure, if you please, that the thing is done. And your second priority is to distract the new Princess Imperial.'

That did surprise Beck, and her face showed it. But then she began to see what lay behind the instruction, and her expression changed.

'Ah,' she said, more than a hint of interest in her tone. 'Then may I take it that Prince Kodor is not entirely . . . averse to the prospect of becoming Imperator in his own right?'

There was a long silence during which they held each other's gaze. Urss had not realised that Beck knew – or had guessed – so much of the truth, and he was more than a little chagrined. But then he reminded himself that he had chosen her as his co-conspirator for a very good reason. For her to have missed this or any other clue would have signified a failing both on her part and on his.

He relaxed a little, and even allowed his lips to smile. 'Ensure that Princess Pola is kept occupied, Beck, and I think you will have the answer to your own question before long.'

Beck returned the smile, satisfied. 'Thank you, Father. And I assure you of my absolute discretion where the Princess is concerned.'

'I supposed nothing less.' Urss rose to his feet. 'I have a great deal to do, and I don't doubt that you have, too. The God go with you. Good day to you, Grand Mother.'

Beck stood up and made a reverent bow. 'Good day to *you*, Father Urss.'

Nanta dreamed. She thought at first that her old nightmare had come back, for it began with the delusion that she was awake in her bedchamber and there was a funeral bier, coldly and eerily lit, in the middle of the floor. But the room was only a memory from her childhood, and she knew at once that the shrouded figure on the bier was not that of the Lady. Again Nanta felt the compulsion to lift the shrouds aside. For a moment she did not recognise the seamed face of the old man who lay there, and she spoke to him, asking him his name, though a deeper, rational part of her sleeping mind knew that he could not answer.

But he did answer. His dead eyes opened, looking at her kindly, and his dead lips parted in a vague smile. She knew him then: he was Arctor, Imperator; her husband's father. And he spoke to her; one word, an answer to her question.

'Osiv.'

'No,' said Nanta in her dream, and shook her head. Her hair stung and prickled her shoulders, and she realised that she must be naked. It didn't seem to matter. 'Osiv is asleep in his bed, with all his toys around him. You can't be Osiv.'

Behind her, a voice said, 'Nandi!'

She turned (very slowly; normal movement seemed to be impossible) and saw Osiv, in his cloth-of-gold nightshirt, standing in the open doorway. He grinned at her – then suddenly he was no longer Osiv but something else, something silvery and frosty and not quite human, that raised unnaturally long forefingers to its own face and pressed the tips against its eyes.

She woke then, suddenly. And found herself standing in front of a wall of her bedroom, with her nose a finger's breadth from the tapestry hanging.

The mental shock of realising what she had done was worse than the physical shock of waking. This was her first sleep-walking episode since she had been taken from the Academy, and she had begun to believe that she had finally put that terror behind her. Now, that hope lay shattered. It was beginning again. And there must, could only be a connection with the appearance of the Corolla Lights in the hour before the dawn.

A jumbled memory of the tower came crowding into her

mind and she realised that her last memory was of watching the Lights and offering a prayer of thanksgiving to the Lady. The rest was a blank; she didn't know what had happened, how she had returned to her rooms, who had or had not seen her. What hour was it now? What *day*? Candles blazed and the curtains were drawn; it might be noon or midnight or anything in between. She had no point of reference, and panic clawed like an inner animal, inducing a sharp, choking cry over which she had no control.

They must have been listening at the door for the first sound she made, for the cry was no sooner uttered than they came hurrying in; three physicians and two of her own women servants, chirping with anxiety and surrounding her like a suffocating blanket. In the confused jumble of the next few minutes Nanta discovered that it was past noon; the physicians then subjected her to a further hour's rigorous examination before pronouncing that she had taken no harm, and the women fussed and fawned and wrung their hands over her until Nanta could have screamed from their attentions. Amid the clamour she gathered that it was Kodor who had helped her down from the tower, but still she could remember nothing between the moment of her faint and the shock of waking.

Except for the dream.

She tried to recall it again as the physicians bowed their way out and the women began to dress her for what was left of the day. But the first clarity had been snatched away by the interruption and, now, would not return. Osiv and Arctor and a frost sprite . . . the images were tangling in her head and she couldn't make any sense of them; each time she tried they only became more confused.

Then one of the women called her 'Majesty'.

Nanta froze where she stood, half dressed and with her unbound hair falling over her shoulders. In a voice that she hardly recognised as her own she said, 'What?'

An awkward silence fell. Then Dorca, who had newly joined the others, said gently, 'Madam . . . do you not remember? The Imperator – the old Imperator – is dead . . .'

'Ah . . .' said Nanta. Of course. That was why she had climbed the tower. A final chance to be private, to be alone, before she was hurled into the turmoil of her new role. Nanta Imperatrix. She shivered despite the heat of the fire, which the servants had insisted on building up. Dorca saw, and she and the other women exchanged knowing glances before Dorca added, 'The vigil will have tired you, of course, madam; and I've no doubt that whatever the physicians say, you are suffering from the shock of your bereavement.'

Nanta's mouth pursed slightly. 'I expect I am,' she said. It was simpler to agree with Dorca than to try to explain that she had no feelings one way or the other, and suddenly she very much wanted to change the subject.

'How is Prince Osiv today?' Belatedly she remembered that she should now refer to Osiv as 'the Imperator', but Dorca did not draw attention to the lapse.

'A little fretful, madam. He had bad dreams and they have upset him.'

'Oh dear.' *So I wasn't the only one* . . . Another hesitation, then: 'I suppose his succession was proclaimed this morning?'

'It was, madam; after First Obligation.' Dorca smiled sympathetically. 'Though I don't think that was what caused the nightmares. He doesn't really understand what has happened.'

'No,' said Nanta, 'he doesn't, does he? He can't. No, thank you, Tariya,' as one of the women advanced on her with a comb. 'I don't want my hair arranged today. I will wear it loose, with no hood.'

'Oh, no, madam!' Dorca protested. 'Pardon me, but the imperial dresser is coming to discuss your morning gowns, and after that you're to receive condolences from the emissaries of the city Guilds and all the highest families. We must prepare you properly!'

Nanta sighed, giving way, and Tariya began to comb out her hair as Dorca chattered on.

'I know how tiring it must be for you, madam; but these are obligations that can't be put off. Mind you, I've turned away your other visitors, and given word that you shan't receive them today. I hope that was right?'

'Other visitors?' Nanta repeated. 'Who were they?'

'Well, Prince Kodor called just before noon, and earlier Mother Marine—'

'Marine came?' Nanta's voice was suddenly sharp. 'Why did you not tell me?'

Dorca looked surprised and a little offended. 'You were sleeping, madam! If I had known you wanted me to—'

'Yes.' Nanta could feel the tugging tightness of her hair being braided, and wished she could wrench her head out of Tariya's reach. 'Yes, I should have told you. I'm sorry, Dorca; you did the right thing, of course. Did Mother Marine leave any message?'

'Only that she might ask an audience when Your Majesty should see fit.' There was a faintly waspish edge to Dorca's tone now; privately, she thought that Mother Marine presumed too much for her station. But the Imperatrix seemed oblivious to Marine's faults, for she only nodded and said:

'Send word that I'll see her this evening, after Pr . . . the Imperator has his meal.'

'But madam, that is when the emissaries are coming. And before the Imperator's meal, you will be too busy with the dressmaker.'

A tight, hard knot of anger was welling up in Nanta. 'Then Mother Marine may join my husband and me at table,' she said.

That was unprecedented, and Dorca was shocked. 'But madam—' she began.

'Send word, Dorca. *Do* it!' Nanta breathed in harshly, struggling to control herself. 'Please.'

Dorca didn't press the argument. She drew herself up with stolid dignity, said, 'Yes, Your Majesty,' curtseyed, and went out.

Nanta allowed herself to breathe out again. Tariya was finishing her hair and setting the gable hood into place, but there was palpable tension in both the remaining servants now, and they maintained a careful silence. It occurred to Nanta that a change had taken place; small, but significant. As of this morning she was no longer merely a princess but the Imperatrix. In theory it should have little effect on her servants' deference; in practice, though, it had exposed the fact that as Princess she had not quite wielded the authority of her rank. Now, her rank had changed. Suddenly the women were *afraid* of her. Dorca had protested a command she disapproved of, but she had obeyed without the wrangling that would have ensued in the past. For the first time in her life, Nanta had genuine power.

Fascinated and unexpectedly heartened by the revelation, she stepped away from Tariya's ministrations, turned, and smiled at both the women.

'Thank you, ladies,' she said, with the gentle courtesy of true privilege. 'I will be alone now.'

No matter that her sleeve buttons were still unfastened, that the gable hood was askew and untidy wisps of her hair showed beneath the frame; the women made their obeisances and went without a murmur. When the door had closed behind them Nanta stood motionless for a few moments, savouring her new autonomy, which was like strong wine. She would not abuse it; she knew herself well enough to be certain of that. But in the coming times it would give her space to breathe when she sorely needed it. It would give her peace.

She sighed, flexed her arms and turned to look into one of the dressing room's many mirrors, meaning to adjust the lopsided hood. The glass showed her own figure and the reflections of the candles—

And something else.

Nanta froze, staring. Then, slowly, she pivoted around.

It was standing between her high-backed chair and the table where Tariya had spread her combs and brushes. No taller than Nanta's shoulder, it had a wiry, wispy frame, a slender neck supporting a head disproportionately large, and white-silver hair that seemed to be plaited into a myriad braids. It wore clothing, of a kind, but the garments were confused and insubstantial, like a motley of cobwebs draped haphazardly over torso and limbs, and the colours were pale and faded so that the overall impression was of a dull, frosty grey. Through the curves and angles of its body she could see, faintly, the outline of furniture and wall hangings.

It met her dumbfounded gaze with eyes the colour of ice, and it made a bow so strange and convoluted that a detached part of Nanta's floundering mind thought its trunk would snap in half. Then, in a thin, high voice, it said:

'Nanta Imperatrix!'

With a colossal struggle, Nanta found her voice. '*What are you?*'

It raised hands which had no thumbs but only four extraordinarily long, spatulate fingers, and made an incomprehensible gesture.

'No name. To serve. To serve Imperatrix.'

It wasn't a frost sprite, she told herself. At least . . . it had something of the sprites about it, but it was somehow *more* than they were. Or less? Her confusion was intensified by the fact that she felt no fear. Curiosity was her strongest reaction, and in the background of her mind, strangely, a stirring of affection. It was as if she knew this creature, had had many dealings with it and its kind. In her dreams? It was the only possibility; dreams which she had forgotten but which had lain

155

dormant in her mind, perhaps for years.

But if that was so, why had the being chosen to appear to her in her waking hours? And why *now*?

She thought then of the Corolla Lights. A harbinger of the Lady . . . Could this creature, like and yet unlike the frost sprites, be another? Nanta's breath caught in her throat and without knowing it she advanced a pace towards the apparition, reaching out her hands in entreaty.

'Did the Lady send you? *Did she?*'

It twisted its strange, lithe body again, almost like a fawning dog. 'Not send; not send. Come. Come to Nanta Imperatrix. Warn.'

Gooseflesh broke out on Nanta's skin. 'Warn?'

'Warn. Warn! Nanta warn, Imperatrix warn!' The being danced on noiseless feet, its arms describing flowing patterns in the air like a mime-show player. Then it stopped abruptly, raised its forefingers to its own face and pressed the tips against its eyes.

The gooseflesh on Nanta's body seemed to turn to a coating of solid ice. *Her dream – the frost sprite had made the self-same gesture—*

'Tell me!' She advanced on it again, frightened now and desperate. 'Why do you warn me? What is to *happen*?'

The creature put its head on one side and said: 'Osiv.'

'Osiv . . . ?'

'Osiv Prince Imperial. No harm. Osiv Imperator. Harm.'

A hammer had begun to beat against Nanta's ribs from the inside. 'What harm?' she demanded. 'What threat is there to Osiv?'

The being opened its mouth as if to reply – and stopped. It flicked a glance at the door, then abruptly sprang sideways, dancing towards the window.

'No!' Nanta called after it. 'No, wait, you must wait!'

It paid her no heed. It reached the window, sprang up on to

the sill, and melted through the patterned glass as if it had been water. Launching herself after it, Nanta's hands slammed against the panes and she found herself staring down at a bare, empty courtyard and a steady fall of snow.

Behind her the door opened and Dorca's voice said, 'If you please, Your Majesty, the imperial dresser is here.'

Nanta's breath was fogging the window and droplets of moisture condensed on her nose and forehead. *Control*, said her mind savagely. *Dorca mustn't know, she mustn't see . . .*

'Is anything amiss, madam?' Concern laced Dorca's voice, and Nanta turned round.

'No.' She paused. 'This room is too *hot*. I shall open the window.'

Dorca didn't reply with her usual litany about the bitter weather and her mistress's health and comfort, but only watched as Nanta flung the casement wide. Arctic air flowed in and Nanta breathed it gratefully for a few seconds before speaking again.

'The dresser is here, you say?'

'Yes, madam. And Prince Kodor has sent a message that—'

'Tell me later.' Kodor was the last person Nanta wished to see at this moment. Marine would come, though, and in the meantime Nanta had nothing do to but stand while the women fluttered and fussed and discussed and effectively ignored her. It would give her time to think.

'Send the dresser in, please, Dorca.' Her mouth smiled so pleasantly that Dorca did not notice the haunted look in her eyes. 'I'm ready for her now.'

Chapter XI

Marine arrived as Osiv was being coaxed to his dining chair. Dorca, with censure written all over her face, showed her in, accepted Nanta's dismissal with a sniff and retired to nurse her sense of outrage.

Marine had spent much of the day in the Sanctum chapel, prostrated in earnest prayer. She had seen the Corolla Lights; later she had heard the stories of the Sisters' visions and had even spoken with one or two of them; though not, to her deep regret, with the woman who had been granted a vision of the Lady. Now, she was confused and more than a little afraid. The Lights' reappearance went against everything that Mother Beck had told her; everything the high religiouses believed. What, then, was the truth? Marine had prayed fervently for enlightenment, but had received none. And if, as she feared, Nanta had summoned her here to ask for her spiritual guidance, she would have no answers to give her.

The fact that she was also in Osiv's immediate presence added to Marine's troubles. He was an idiot and he was the Imperator, and Marine had never in her life before had to contend with either. Not knowing how best to behave, she resorted to stiff and stuttering formality, uttering speeches rather than sentences and bowing her head every time Osiv looked at her. Osiv was hugely amused at first, but he soon lost interest, and as he turned to attacking his food Nanta was able to command Marine's attention for herself.

'Marine, I *must* talk to you. I need advice – I need it so sorely – and you're the only person I can turn to.' Seeing Marine's uneasy glance in Osiv's direction she added, 'Don't mind him. He won't understand; and even if he repeats a word or two of what he hears, it will be taken as nothing more than prattle.'

Osiv was methodically mixing three different fruit butters into a repellent-looking mélange on his plate; he looked up briefly at them both and smiled an angelic smile.

'Please, Marine,' Nanta said. 'I have little time; I have to see the Guilds delegates in less than an hour. And this *cannot* wait.'

She poured herself a glass of wine. Marine was surprised; to the best of her knowledge Nanta had rarely, if ever, tasted anything intoxicating before her marriage. Change wrought further change, it seemed.

Then Nanta's next words put all other thoughts out of her head.

'Today,' Nanta said, 'something appeared to me. It was like a frost sprite, but it was *more* than that. It appeared in my dressing room, and it told me that my husband is in danger.'

Stunned, Marine listened to the entire tale. Nanta did not mention her dream and the sleepwalking – that was part of the old secret, the one she would not reveal to anyone – but she told the rest with a frankness born of the desperate need to share her fear.

'I don't know what the danger could be or even if the creature lied to me,' she finished. 'But I *feel* that it told the truth. And I'm afraid, Marine. I'm horribly afraid.'

A sensation like being deep in an ice-cold lake was taking form in Marine's mind. Tautly, very quietly, she said: 'Frost sprites do not lie.'

'I know. But *was* it a frost sprite? Or was it –' Nanta spread her hands, trying and failing to express with a gesture what she could not express in words – 'something *else*?'

Marine had no answer to that question; her own experience was too limited.

'You see,' Nanta went on, her words coming headlong now, 'you see, I was at the top of the tower when the Corolla Lights appeared; I witnessed them, and I fainted, and when I was brought down I slept all the morning, and when I woke the last thing I remembered was praying to the Lady—'

'You prayed?' Marine said quickly.

'Yes. Oh, yes. I wanted to give thanks; I'd never seen the Lights before, you see, and I – I—'

Your faith was restored in that moment, Marine thought. *I know, child. I know.*

Aloud, she said, 'Have you been to your chapel?'

Nanta shook her head. 'I have so little *time*. Always there are people to see, papers to sign, things that must, must, *must* be done. And my ladies would want to come with me. I don't want that, I want to go alone; but what reason could I give for excluding them?'

'You are the Imperatrix,' Marine said gently. 'What reason do you need?'

Nanta recalled her brief and successful tussle with Dorca and Tariya earlier in the day, and uttered a peculiar, strained laugh that brought an answering crow from Osiv. 'You're right, of course,' she said. 'They *do* obey me now; they have no choice. So perhaps I am a coward. Perhaps I'm afraid to ask the Lady for enlightenment, in case . . . in case . . .'

'In case she does not answer?'

'Yes.' A hunted terror lurked now in Nanta's eyes. 'In case of that.'

Osiv said loudly: 'Cock-doodle-do! Doodle-doodle, doodle-do! Nandi, *you* sing it!' He looked piercingly at Marine. 'You sing, too! Doodle-do, doodle-do!' He giggled hiccuppingly, then his expression altered. 'You've got an ugly dress on.'

Marine blanched. 'Yes, Your Majesty . . .' she said helplessly. 'But it's—'

'*Ugly*. Take it off. Put something pretty on, like Nandi.'

'He seems to dislike religious garb,' Nanta told Marine in an undertone, forcing away the memory of why and how that had come about. 'I must distract him, or he'll become fretful and the noise will bring Dorca . . .'

Marine watched uncomfortably while for the next few minutes Nanta pacified Osiv with a simple guessing game that she allowed him to win. At last he returned to his meal, Marine and the ugly dress forgotten in the new pleasure of shovelling roasted goose into his mouth at a great rate.

Nanta sat back and sighed. 'You understand why it is so difficult for me to concentrate.'

'Yes,' said Marine. 'I understand.'

Someone, probably Dorca, was moving about in the next room with a lot of unnecessary banging and clattering; Nanta recognised the signal and knew that they would be interrupted again before long. 'Marine,' she said, 'I must ask something of you.'

'Madam, anything I can do—'

'Please, Marine, *please* call me by my name! I can't tell you how much it . . .' She collected herself. 'No; never mind; I realise it can't be easy . . . Marine, in your new position you have the freedom of the court, and you are far better placed than I am to move about without your every move being watched. I want you to look, and to listen, and to – to *feel* what might be in the wind.'

'Concerning . . .' For prudence's sake Marine didn't finish the sentence, but her gaze slid sideways, meaningfully, to Osiv.

'Yes,' said Nanta. 'Concerning that. Anything, any hint or clue, however small it may seem.'

Because the greatest rivers begin as a mere trickle, Marine thought. 'And tell you of it?' she prompted.

'And tell me of it. Me, and no one else. Will you do that?'

Marine had never before envisaged herself as a spy. But that, effectively, was what Nanta was asking her to become. Her ingrained sense of principle urged her to refuse – and that begged the question of whether she could achieve anything anyway – but as she looked at Nanta's troubled face she realised that she was her only resort. There simply was no one else Nanta could turn to. And the fact that she trusted Marine enough to ask this of her was a very significant factor.

She said, 'I will do whatever I can. Though it may be little enough—'

'It doesn't matter.' Just to know that she had an ally was enough for Nanta at this moment. She swallowed. 'I don't know where the threat, if there is one, might come from. But I don't want any harm to befall Osiv.' She looked at her husband, who had finished the goose and was now trying to use his blunt, round-ended knife to drink soup straight from the tureen. 'I don't want that.'

Marine didn't voice what was in her mind; that if any ill should come to Osiv, Nanta's own future would be far from secure. *Was* there a danger? It had an unpleasant logic; a convenient death had been mooted when Osiv was a child, as Grand Mother Beck had told her, and only the stubbornness of the old Imperatrix, his mother, had put paid to the idea. But she and Arctor were gone now. And Vyskir had a new alliance, through Osiv's younger brother, with a very ambitious country . . .

Marine was no fool, and in the crannies of her mind she had been aware of this possibility for a long time. But she had thrust it away and out of reach, not wanting to speculate, not wanting to know. Now, suddenly, Nanta had brought it into the open; and the sprite's warning added a powerful emphasis that couldn't be ignored.

She saw then that Osiv had grown tired of the soup and was watching her with renewed interest. Careful to avoid his gaze, she lowered her voice and said, 'I'll try my best for you.'

'That's all I ask. And anything you learn—'

'You'll hear of it immediately.' The handle of the inner door rattled. Dorca's hints were growing broader, and Marine rose to her feet. 'I must delay you no longer.'

Nanta nodded. 'Thank you, Marine. With all my heart.' She raised her voice. 'Dorca. You may come in now.'

Dorca appeared so promptly that it was obvious she had been hovering inches from the door. 'Madam, the Guild emissaries will—'

'Be arriving soon; yes, I'm aware of that. The Imperator has finished his meal, I think, so I shall prepare myself to meet them. Please show Mother Marine out.'

The outer door of the suite closed behind her, and Marine turned away along the plush-carpeted corridor.

At the first turn, she came face to face with Prince Kodor.

Kodor stopped. 'Mother.' He nodded graciously, but his grey eyes were suspicious.

'Your Grace . . .' Marine curtseyed, then remembered that Kodor's title, too, had changed. 'Forgive me – I mean, Your Highness.'

Kodor's mouth twitched in a thin smile. 'Either will do, thank you, Mother. Have you been to visit my sister?'

'Ah . . . yes, sir. The Imperatrix summoned me on a matter of . . . of . . .'

'Of a religious nature, I imagine. Quite.' He could see that Marine very much wanted to curtsey again and hurry on, but he continued to stand in her path. 'How is the Imperatrix today?'

A muscle worked in Marine's throat. 'She is . . . quite well, Your Highness.'

'And well in spirit?'

Marine was a little surprised by that question. 'Yes, sir. I would say so.'

'Good. Then you were not called to offer comfort, but for another reason?'

Marine cast her gaze down. 'That's so.'

For a few moments they were both silent, and Marine could

feel the tension between them like a palpable presence in the air. Then Kodor said:

'I imagine that my sister wished to talk of the Corolla Lights. To see them was a glorious and uplifting experience, was it not?'

Marine's head came up and she saw that he was smiling; a very genuine smile that suddenly, extraordinarily, lightened not only his face but his entire demeanour. He, too, had been deeply affected by the Lights, she realised, and she found herself responding spontaneously, catching his enthusiasm.

'Oh, yes, sir!' she said fervently. 'Indeed it was!'

It seemed that her answer was what Kodor wanted to hear, for his smile broadened a little and the last of the suspicion vanished from his eyes. He stepped aside, inclining his head again.

'Good day to you, Mother.'

'G . . . good day, Your Highness . . .'

Marine fled. For a few seconds Kodor stood watching her dwindling figure; then he walked away towards his own apartments.

Arctor's funeral rites began six days later, with the full pomp and solemnity expected for such a great occasion. With the new Imperator 'too grief-stricken' to attend, responsibility for public family mourning fell on Nanta and Kodor, and from the great procession through the Metropolis, accompanied by dismal horns and bells and wailing choirs, to the long, tedious hours in the throne room acknowledging condolences from a seemingly endless stream of dignitaries, they played their parts gallantly. By the time the rituals ended after two days and nights, Nanta was in a haze of exhaustion, surviving on little more than automated reflex and incapable of looking beyond the next hour.

She had seen little of Osiv and nothing of Marine. Kodor had made several attempts to talk to her as they carried out their duties; but always something intervened to stymie his attempts.

Nanta was thankful. She did not want to speak with Kodor, for in the wake of the frost sprite's warning she was beginning to fear him. Who, after all, had most to gain from harming Osiv? The answer was painfully obvious, and for all Kodor's apparent affection for his brother, Nanta had learned enough in recent days to be aware that outward appearances could rarely be trusted.

Then there was Pola. Pola did not attend every stage of the funeral observances, but when she was present Nanta felt haunted by her. Tall and sombrely silent in her earth-brown mourning clothes, her face completely obscured by the layers of heavy veil, she was like a spectre. No matter that Nanta herself must present a similar picture to any outsider; something in the nature of Pola's grim dignity made her as frightening to Nanta's tired and overstrung senses as Kodor was.

At last, though, the worst of it was over, and Nanta gave heartfelt thanks that all that lay ahead of her for the next few hours was a night's uninterrupted sleep. The imperial suite felt like a long-lost haven as dazedly she allowed Dorca and her maids to release her from the encumbrance of her clothes, then, too tired even to look in on Osiv (who had not the least notion of anything taking place outside his own small world), climbed with the last shards of her strength into bed. Dorca, after giving the strictest instructions that the Imperatrix was not to be disturbed until morning, retired to her room adjoining Osiv's, and all was at last silent.

Two hours after midnight, the Corolla Lights began their dance again.

Kodor was woken by his senior servant. He had ordered the man to rouse him instantly if this should happen, and despite the dragging weariness that blurred his eyes and made his body feel like lead, he pulled on the first clothes that came to hand and headed for the tower.

Passing the corridor that led to Osiv and Nanta's suite, he

paused. Temptation was tugging at him, urging him to wake Nanta and persuade her to come with him. Her women would be sleeping, and if the outer door was locked he knew how to deal with that. He wanted to share this wonder with her. He wanted to *be* with her.

But to wake her now would not be kind. More pragmatically, to be snatched out of sleep when sleep was so desperately needed would not endear him to her; and above all Kodor did not want to open any gulf between them. So, reluctantly, he abandoned the impulse. He would speak with her tomorrow. He *must* speak with her tomorrow. For now, though, let her rest.

He walked on to the tower door, opened it, made to light the lantern he carried . . . and stopped, listening, as his ears detected a sound somewhere above. There, again; faint, but recognisable. The sound of feet on stone. Someone else was climbing the tower steps . . .

An irrational hope that it might be Nanta sprang up in Kodor's mind and, forgetting the lantern, he started up the stairs in pursuit. The air in the tower felt unnaturally cold, but he did not make the significant connection until, rounding the fourth curve of the spiral, he saw his quarry ahead of him.

It *was* Nanta. Barefoot and dressed in nothing but a nightgown, she was steadily climbing the staircase towards the tower summit. A strange, pale aura shone around her; a glow strong enough to form dim shadows on the wall to either side. And hovering above her, like will-o'-the-wisps in the aura's light, were two frost sprites.

Kodor froze against the stonework, mouth open and eyes stark with shock. The sprites were either unaware of or uninterested in him; all their attention was focused upon Nanta as she moved on up the stairs. She was vanishing around the spiral's next curve now, the glow dimming as the wall's bulk obscured her figure. Hardly knowing what he was doing, Kodor followed. Instinct, awe and fear were screaming at him not to betray his presence, but no reasoning in the world could have stopped him from going after her; it was a compulsion, a *need*, something far beyond his own control.

Nanta came into view again. The sprites seemed to be drawing her upwards, as though guiding or guarding her, or both. Still they ignored Kodor, and he strove to see Nanta more clearly. Was she awake or asleep? Until and unless he could get closer it was impossible to tell; but the way she moved, languidly, almost gliding, suggested that she had no conscious knowledge of what she was doing.

They climbed on, the sprites leading and Kodor maintaining a cautious distance, while Nanta moved at her same steady pace between them. The door at the top of the tower stood open, as Kodor had left it after the previous incident; the sprites flitted through and Nanta walked under the lintel without hesitating. As he climbed the last few steps after her, Kodor could see the uncanny reflections of the Corolla Lights as they played across the sky and the city. Abruptly a new fear came; that Nanta would walk on to the edge, and the sprites would not stop her but would let her fall, unknowing, over the parapet wall and down, to be smashed on the stones of the inner courtyard far below. Alarm punched through him and he quickened his pace to catch up with her – but when he emerged on to the walkway, he realised that his terror was unfounded. Nanta had indeed continued walking; but the sprites were barring her way, their thin, unhuman fingers touching her and bringing her to a gentle halt. They took her hands, guiding them and moving them until they rested lightly on the parapet wall, then they drew back and Nanta stood still, gazing – or appearing to – out over the Metropolis to the northern horizon.

The mingled sounds of his own pulse and his own rapid breathing were harsh in Kodor's ears. He was hardly aware of the Corolla Lights' magnificent display; all he could take in was the small tableau of Nanta and her unearthly attendants.

Questions to which there was no sane answer were tumbling in his mind, and suddenly he was gripped by an overwhelming desire to make himself known to her, to be a *part* of this fantastic and mystical event.

He took a careful step forward, and the sprites saw him.

He felt their scrutiny like a corporeal touch, and the air around him, already bitterly cold, turned arctic. The sprites moved, positioning themselves between him and Nanta, and their strange eyes locked with his in a silent challenge.

Kodor retreated as memories of his old dreams came sharply back to him; dreams of danger and threat and a deadly intent. He half expected the sprites to attack him – but instead they stopped, and their manner became less hostile. They would bar his way to Nanta, but beyond that it seemed that they wished him no harm.

He drew a ragged breath and hissed, 'I must speak to her! I want—'

One of the sprites raised a hand, palm outward, to its own lips, and the other pointed a crooked finger at Kodor's face. The words broke off and Kodor found himself silenced as his will collapsed under their silent command. The first sprite shook its head, while the other closed its eyes with meaningful deliberation.

And Nanta, still gazing northwards, began to speak.

'Lady, hear my prayer.' Her voice wasn't like the voice Kodor knew; it had a strength and a timbre he had never heard before, and it carried as sharply as crystal in the freezing air. 'Sweet Lady, I beseech you to hear and to grant me true vision.' The pitch of her voice dropped and she bowed her head, raising her hands and clasping them before her face. 'Grant to me, Lady, knowledge of the peril that threatens Osiv, and let me be strong enough and wise enough to stand with him in the hour of his danger and to keep him from harm. I beg this boon with all my heart – please, please, hear me and help me.'

She bent forward, pressing her forehead against her hands, and though her lips still moved, her litany was silent now. Kodor stood paralysed. Though Nanta's desperate plea had been uttered in little more than a whisper, he had heard every word of it, and a sick sensation clawed at his stomach as he watched her. *The peril that threatens Osiv*. What did Nanta suspect, and where had her knowledge come from? His gaze flicked to the sprites, which now hovered to either side of her like faithful pets, and again he took an experimental step forward. The sprites paused, watching. Kodor took another step.

He didn't see them move but an instant later they were in front of him again, barring any further progress.

'No!' Kodor whispered harshly. 'I must speak with her. I'll do her no harm, but I must *know*!'

They raised their arms, crossing them before their faces and splaying their bizarre fingers, and shook their heads with a slow, explicit message.

'*Please!*' Kodor's own hands were clenched unconsciously and, impossibly in this cold, his body was sweating. 'Osiv is my brother – I *will* not harm Nanta!'

A pause, while the sprites appeared to consider this. They were intelligent, Kodor knew; though the nature and extent of their intelligence was uncertain. He waited, trying to contain his frustration but aware of the folly of making any wrong move at this moment. Then one of the sprites moved. It laid the palms of its hands together and, tilting its head, pressed its cheek against them in the unmistakable mime of someone sleeping. The second sprite touched its long fingers to its temples, and smiled.

Their meaning was clear. Kodor must go, and he must sleep, and if he obeyed that injunction a dream would be sent to him.

There was a tight sensation in Kodor's chest as he whispered, 'When? When will the dream be sent?'

The smile became a look of admonition, and the other sprite turned its head away. So, then: they would or could not say. But

169

the promise had been made, and as servants of the Lady the frost sprites always fulfilled their promises – and their threats.

Slowly, reluctantly, Kodor backed towards the tower door. The sprites made no move to hasten him on his way; they seemed to know that he had accepted their injunction and would obey it. From the doorway he looked past them one last time to Nanta, who still stood with bowed head, murmuring her prayer. She seemed lonely and insubstantial against the colossal backdrop of the Lights in their celestial glory, and a sharp pain snagged at Kodor's emotions. But there was nothing he could do; no approach he would be permitted to make.

He left the tower summit, and the sound of his footsteps diminished down the stairs. The sprites continued to watch until they knew that he had truly gone, then returned to their task and their purpose, of which they alone knew the true nature. They would wait, patient and vigilant, until Nanta's prayers were done. Then they would lead her, still sleeping, back down the long spiral, back along the empty corridors through which they had brought her, back to the safety and security of her protected rooms. All in secrecy, all unknown, and when she woke to another day she would remember nothing but a dream. For now, that was how it must be; for she had not yet found her true strength. But the sprites had learned patience. They had waited twenty years for this, and they would continue to wait. For a while yet.

Chapter XII

When, on the following afternoon, Father Urss received a message from Prince Kodor requesting his immediate presence, he was surprised and not a little curious.

Urss had summoned Mother Beck to his office that morning, and the discussion that took place had been brief and to the point. The second manifestation of the Corolla Lights had put the unwanted spoke in the wheel of their carefully laid plans, and Urss was resolved. Flexibility and efficiency, as he had said to Beck at their previous meeting, were now all-important, and the contingency he had outlined then must be put in train.

Apparently there had been some more disturbances among the Sisters. No visions of the Lady this time, which was one nuisance avoided, but further tales of frost sprites and other, less tangible manifestations. Beck had reacted quickly; calling all the women of the Sanctum together, she had delivered a homily on the physical and spiritual dangers of hysteria, adding a thinly veiled warning about the consequences of blasphemy.

Urss approved Beck's actions, said what he had to say and dismissed her, satisfied that she would do what was required. Now, though, came this summons from Kodor. Interesting, Urss thought. The obvious conclusion was that the prince wished to consult him about the significance of the Corolla Lights; but he believed he knew Kodor better than that. The Lights might have a bearing – but the motive behind the message would be something else entirely.

171

Accordingly, he presented himself at the Prince and Princess Imperial's suite, and was ushered into Kodor's private office. Kodor was not at his desk; instead he was standing by the fireplace, one arm resting on the carved mantel as he stared into the heart of a newly built-up fire.

Urss said, 'Your Highness . . .'

'Ah. Father Urss.' Kodor turned round, acknowledged Urss's bow with a nod. 'Sit down, please. You'll take some wine?'

Urss accepted deferentially, hiding his quickening interest. Considering their mutual dislike it was rare for Kodor to proffer this kind of hospitality; and besides, the prince had an excellent cellar. A servant was rung for and the order given – one of the finest old south-western vintages, Urss noted with satisfaction – and while they waited for the tray to be brought, he said urbanely:

'The Princess Imperial is well, I hope?'

'As well as usual.' There was no mistaking the caustic edge in the response.

Urss allowed a few seconds to elapse, then: 'She stood the strain of the funeral rites with great poise and dignity, if I may venture to observe.'

'She was trained to,' said Kodor. 'As were we all.'

Urss smiled a practised smile, aware that this might well be leading him in the direction of a clue. 'Nonetheless, for one unused to Vyskiri ways such things can't be easy. I gather that Sekolian custom is more . . . basic than our own.'

'If by that, Father, you mean it is crude and cursory, then you echo my own opinion,' Kodor told him. 'However, we must give credit where it's due, mustn't we; and as you say, my wife performed diligently. In that regard, at least.'

There was real acid in his voice now, and Urss understood. 'Ah,' he said, with a very precise degree of sympathy, 'then am I to understand that as yet there is no prospect of issue?'

Kodor scowled and hunched his shoulders. 'You have a remarkable talent for using twenty words where five would do for anyone else, Father Urss, but yes; you are to understand that. Pola is not with child.'

'A pity,' said Urss, baiting his trap. 'Duke Arec will be disappointed to hear of it.'

'He need hear nothing for the time being. My wife is too busy these days to write more than the occasional letter to him.'

'Ah, yes; of course. As Co-Regent, the demands on her time—'

Kodor interrupted, swinging round to face him full on. 'Yes, Father Urss, and that is what I wish to discuss with you.' He stalked across the room to his desk, and indicated the stacks of papers and ledgers that cluttered its surface. 'You see all this? Demands, as you observe, on my time and on my wife's. But I am still waiting word – *any* word – of the date set for the regency to be announced!'

It was exactly what Urss had hoped to hear, and he felt an inner glow of triumph. This was the turning point; the chance he had been waiting for, to judge the real truth about Kodor's loyalty – and his ambition.

Kodor was watching him, challenging him to give an answer that would amount to more than a platitude. Before Urss could speak, though, the servant returned with the wine. In a chill, stiff atmosphere they waited until two glasses were carefully poured, then as the man went soft-footedly out Kodor said, 'Well?'

'Your Highness.' Urss had not sat down as invited; now he held the glass and played his fingers gently over the delicate stem. 'I appreciate your concern—'

'You may put it a great deal more strongly than that, Father!'

'Indeed. I ask your pardon.' A slight, courteous bow. 'However, you above all others will appreciate that a matter like this must be handled with the greatest delicacy. To announce a regency, when the populace has no reason to suspect that the new Imperator cannot rule as normal, has considerable complications – and risks.'

Kodor was unmoved. 'You've known that from the start. I would have thought that you, of all people, would have found a way to resolve it by now.'

Urss coughed delicately. 'Yes, Your Highness. But one complication that we did *not* anticipate was the return of the Corolla Lights.'

'Ah,' said Kodor. 'That. I see.'

Urss was aware that he didn't need to go over the full reasoning, but he did so, largely to make quite sure that Kodor understood. The omen for Osiv's reign. The effect on Vyskiri citizens, who would naturally feel a greater respect and love for their new Imperator as a result of this apparent benediction from the God and the Lady . . . Kodor, he noted, listened very intently to the argument, and when it was finished, he nodded slowly and thoughtfully.

'You have a point, Father Urss, and I confess that I hadn't fully considered the implications. However.' He set his glass down and paced back to the fireplace. 'The nature and meaning of omens are not set in stone, are they?'

'No, sir, of course not.'

'They are open to interpretation.'

'Indeed.' Urss's pulse was quickening.

'Then it does not necessarily follow that this sign *is* a benediction. Am I correct?'

Urss paused just long enough to appear slightly reluctant. 'Yes, Your Highness. You are quite correct.'

Kodor didn't say anything more for a while. He was looking into the fire again, thinking, weighing. Urss sipped and appreciated his wine, patient as a hunter waiting for the quarry to gain confidence and show itself without fear. After two or perhaps three minutes his patience was rewarded.

'My brother,' Kodor said, 'is an infernal nuisance.'

The quarry was in the open. Urss gazed into his glass and replied judiciously, 'Indeed, Your Highness . . . ?'

' "Indeed, indeed" – it seems to be the favourite word of the diplomat! Yes, Urss, Osiv *is* a nuisance! It would have saved Vyskir a great deal of trouble if I had been born before he was.' Kodor paused. 'Or if he had not been born at all.'

Silence held for a few taut seconds. Then Urss said, 'When he was very young, Your Highness, it was recommended in some quarters that . . .' He hesitated, feigning reluctance to go any further, and Kodor looked at him keenly.

'You mean, the suggestion that an end should be made to his life? I know the details, so there's no need to be genteel about it. They say that Father might have been persuaded but Mother would not hear of it.'

Urss made a helpless gesture. 'The previous Imperatrix was very fond of him, Your Highness. One can understand her unwillingness; even in the greater interests of the kingdom.'

Kodor's eyes were like steel now. 'And do *you* believe it would have been in the greater interests of the kingdom, Father Urss?'

'With great reluctance, sir,' said Urss in a low voice, 'I do.'

Kodor turned away again and placed both fists on the mantel. His face was hidden but his voice was steady as he said:

'It is strange, is it not, that after years of disagreement, you and I have finally found a subject on which we are of the same mind.'

Urss touched his tongue to his lower lip. 'Your Highness . . . ?'

'Stop pretending. You know as well as I do that Osiv's reign is going to be fraught with difficulty. On the broadest level, and to be absolutely blunt about it, he is a threat to Vyskir's long-term future.'

Urss looked down again, in case Kodor was surreptitiously watching him. 'For the duration of his life, sir, I have to acknowledge that there's truth in what you say. But once the regency is properly and officially in place, the Imperator will be only a figurehead. You and the Princess Imperial will hold the real power—'

'And do all the real work, in Osiv's name.'

'Well, yes; that is true. But of course the new Imperator will have no issue.'

Kodor looked round sharply. 'You're sure of that?'

'Certain, Your Highness.' Urss smiled faintly. 'He will have no issue, so you are his legal heir, and in the fullness of time you will become Imperator in your own right. He is older than you, and—'

'By a mere few years. And his physical health is robust. He might live as long as I do. Or longer.'

'That is something no one can predict, of course,' said Urss. 'But even if he should – forgive me, sir, but even if he should outlive you, the eldest son of your own marriage will be Vyskir's next Imperator.'

There was another long silence then, while Kodor considered again. Eventually he walked away from the hearth, back to the desk, where he had left his untouched glass. Father Urss watched as he picked up the glass and drained half its contents in one swallow. Then he looked directly at the priest, a look of startling – and meaningful – candour.

'I don't think,' Kodor said, 'that Duke Arec of Sekol will wish to wait that long to secure his investment.'

The trap was sprung, and Kodor had given himself away. Urss felt a sense of achievement that was almost intoxicating; the vindication of the view he had long held about Prince Kodor's true nature. Kodor had a politician's instinct, and it had been honed over many years by a politician's education and training. Urss himself had seen to that; and at last the carefully tended tree of his labours was bearing fruit.

'On his deathbed,' he said, very quietly, 'the old Imperator, your father, charged you to take care of your brother.'

'Yes.' Kodor's expression did not change.

Urss cleared his throat with practised nicety. 'The last wish of a dying man is not one to be taken lightly, Prince Kodor.'

'I agree. However, such wishes can often be open to interpretation. You were witness to my father's final words – would you say that he clearly wanted me to act in Osiv's best interests – and Vyskir's?'

'Yes,' said Urss. 'Most certainly.'

'Then, as he is no longer here to guide me, I must come to my own conclusion as to what those best interests are.'

Kodor, Urss thought, was *indeed* a politician. He smiled slightly; 'I believe I understand, Your Highness.'

'I believe you do, Father.' Kodor did not match the smile. 'Osiv can have no life worth speaking of. He is not even a *person* as you and I understand the concept. But he could be a threat to the future security of our country.'

Urss nodded. He had just one more question to ask; one that would set the final seal on it.

'Prince Kodor,' he said, very quietly, 'do you love your brother?'

Kodor gazed steadily back at him. 'While my father lived, I did the duty he required of me. He wanted me to love Osiv as he did. But the term "love" is also open to wide interpretation. It is not easy – perhaps not even possible – to love a creature like my brother in the normal way. A more accurate term for it would be pity, as one might pity a crippled animal. And the best interests of a crippled animal are not necessarily served by prolonging its life.' A long pause. 'Does that answer your question, Exalted Father Urss?'

Urss returned the gaze with equal frankness. 'Yes, Your Imperial Highness. It does.'

'Then I think,' said Kodor, 'that we should both sit down. I believe we have a great deal to discuss.'

'So.' Kodor knelt on the thick carpet of Osiv's playroom, rearranging the scatter of bricks and little painted pewter soldiers into a new formation. 'It's to be poison, is it? No blood and little noise, and easy, if the right substance is chosen, to make it look like a natural death.'

Osiv didn't hear him; he was on the other side of the room, pulling books out of the shelves in a search for one whose pictures he liked the best. Even if he had heard, Kodor reflected, he would have made nothing of the comment. The idea of poison, or any other form of death, was utterly outside his sphere of thinking; he was too gentle and too innocent for his mind to have any room for such concepts.

Three more days, Kodor thought. It was little enough time to arrange everything he needed to arrange, but he believed he could do it. Would *have* to do it, anyway; any delay would be too risky and might arouse Urss's suspicion. Wonderful how necessity concentrated the mind; and very useful, too, for the framework of a plan was already taking shape. He needed help, but he was confident that the people he had in mind were trustworthy. Or if there was doubt, it wouldn't be too difficult to deal with that problem at a later stage.

He was becoming as ruthless as Urss, he thought, and smiled humourlessly to himself. That was the one thing the priest hadn't bargained for: the fact that when it came to strategy and cold-blooded calculation he had met his match. Probably Urss's arrogance wouldn't even allow him to consider the possibility, which from Kodor's standpoint was well and good.

Osiv had found the book he wanted and now returned, crawling on hands and knees because it was less bother than standing up only to sit down again within a few moments. He dropped the volume – painfully; it was heavy – on Kodor's foot and said, 'Want the bears one!'

'The bears one? Very well, then.' Indulgently Kodor opened the book and riffled through its pages until he found the tale of the long battle of wits between the hunter and the arctic bear. It was one of Osiv's favourites and Kodor must have read it to him a hundred times; the mystical significance of it was beyond

Osiv, of course, but at this moment it seemed a singularly appropriate choice.

Kodor spread the book on the floor, where Osiv could see the illustrations, and began to read aloud. He knew the text virtually by heart now, so as he read, his inner thoughts were able to keep track of the problem at hand. Though he was not a physician, he had learned enough about anatomy and chemistry to know the nature of the poison Urss intended to use. This particular substance killed fast and relatively painlessly, and left a spectacular signature in that it bloated and blackened the faces of its victims, making their features all but unrecognisable. By a useful coincidence, there was a disease that produced a very similar effect. It was thought that the disease had first been brought to Vyskir centuries ago, by a band of religious ascetics making pilgrimage to the Metropolis from some distant southern country. Dubbed the Pilgrims' Plague, it showed few if any symptoms until the final stage: a rapid and inevitably fatal seizure that killed the sufferer within minutes. It had been a feared scourge for two centuries; but stricter controls and quarantines imposed upon southerners attempting to visit the kingdom had finally taken effect, and for the past seventy years the scourge had been unheard-of except for an occasional and isolated case.

Recently, of course, the Metropolis had had an unusually high influx of visitors. With two imperial weddings and one funeral taking place within such a short time, it would not have been possible to apply stringent safeguards; the resources simply hadn't been available. One incubating case was all that was needed, and it could arise from anywhere. Disease was no respecter of rank, and no one need be blamed. Simply a terrible, unforeseeable tragedy. And the Imperator Osiv had been vulnerable; his health undermined by grief at his father's death. Impossible to have predicted that such a thing could happen. We must only give thanks to the God and the Lady that, though the

Imperatrix is not with child, the Imperator has a brother, who must now bear his heartbreak for the sake of duty, and take the throne in his predecessor's stead . . .

Kodor paused then in his reading as a foul, dark cloud of fury gathered in his mind. He stared at the book's gaudy illustration – the hunter with his bow and magic talisman, the giant bear rearing against a storm-racked sky – and resisted a huge impulse to rip the volume in two and throw the halves into the fire.

'Kodi! More!'

Osiv's protest at the sudden silence broke through the miasma, and Kodor looked up to see his brother pouting at him.

'More!' Osiv repeated with greater emphasis. '*Now!*'

'All right,' Kodor promised him. 'In a moment.' He needed that moment to regain his composure; the fuse inside him was still dangerously short. To distract them both he asked, 'Where's Nanti?'

'Nandi busy. They won't let her play; she said.'

So that part of it had already begun; keeping Nanta away from Osiv to ensure that she would suspect nothing. It was probably just as well. Kodor longed to be able to tell her the truth, but he dared not; as much for her sake as for his own. Father Urss believed that his plan could be accomplished without arousing Nanta's suspicion; he also believed that Nanta would be glad to be rid of her husband. It was vital that he did not find out how wrong he was, for one careless and probably unwitting hint during their discussion had warned Kodor of what would happen then. If Nanta guessed nothing, she could look forward to a secure if stultifying future as Imperatrix Dowager, kept in closeted luxury, treated with the respect and kindness that was her due, but otherwise forgotten. If, however, she *did* suspect the truth, the remedy would be quick and ruthless: she would follow Osiv to the grave. Far too dangerous, then, to confide in her, for if he did, one inadvertent word in the wrong quarter would sign her death warrant.

He forced himself back to the story book, and Osiv settled down as he continued to read aloud. Kodor only hoped that the frost sprites would not reveal the truth to Nanta. If he could warn them – but the chances of that were too remote to pin hope on. He had an intuitive feeling that the sprites would not communicate directly with him again. They had sent the promised dream last night, and its meaning had been unequivocal; but that was all they would do.

His mind conjured the image of Nanta as she had stood on the tower top, making her plea to the Lady, and he wondered if on waking she had had any conscious knowledge of what she had done. It seemed unlikely, and he could not ask her without giving his own involvement away. Last night, the dream sent by the sprites had been followed by another: the old nightmare again, in which he was beset by a terrible threat, and the face and voice that offered his only hope of salvation were Nanta's. It was, or so it seemed to him, another skein in a tapestry depicting a story that he could not begin to understand, and the thought brought a strange, chill feeling, part awe and part fear and part – perhaps the greatest part – helpless fascination. The dream, the frost sprites, the return of the Corolla Lights . . . somehow they were all tangled together in a web of mystery. Kodor ached to solve that mystery. It was a driving need, a fixation; the most important thing, or so he felt, that he could or would ever do. When these next few dangerous days were over—

'More, Kodi, more! Not stop, *no*!' The flat of Osiv's hand thumped hard and petulantly down on the open book, and it snapped Kodor back to the immediate moment. He blinked rapidly, clearing the disarray of his thoughts, and said, 'I'm sorry, brother. Here; look at this pretty picture for a moment or two, and then I shall continue.'

'*No!*' repeated Osiv mulishly. 'More, *now*!'

With an inward sigh Kodor resumed the story's slow progress. There was no point in attempting to distract Osiv from what he wanted; it would only lead to a tantrum. Besides, his hopes of seeing Nanta were so small that there was no point pursuing them. He didn't even know (briefly he glanced at the connecting door that led to the other parts of the imperial suite) if she was here. Dorca had been evasive, telling him only that her mistress had no time to receive visitors today and, no, with respect and regret she could not say when that situation would change. *Leave it*, Kodor told himself. *You have more immediate worries, and arrangements to make. Let well alone.*

'*Kodiii!*'

It was an angry wail, presaging trouble. Kodor forced his thoughts of Nanta away, and continued to read.

While Kodor entertained his brother, Nanta was in fact in the imperial family's private sanctum.

Since waking from what seemed to have been a restless and troubled night – though with no memory of anything more than vague dreams – she had been haunted by gnawing worry that was far worse than usual. She couldn't concentrate, she had snapped at her ladies at the least excuse, and finally she had pushed aside the documents set ready for her attention (for the past few days there had been so *many* of them) and told Dorca that she wished to pray and would brook no interruption for any reason whatever. Then she had sent a lesser servant hurrying with a message for Marine.

Marine arrived at the sanctum a short time later. This was their third meeting since Nanta had asked for her help, but so far Marine had discovered nothing that lent any weight to the frost sprite's warning. If there was danger, its source and its nature eluded her. Her only crumb of comfort was that Mother Beck had made fewer calls on her time during the past few days, allowing her to devote her energy to Nanta's wishes. But without results, energy was of little use. Marine felt she had let Nanta down.

They prayed together for a while, both struggling – though neither knew the other's predicament – to understand the unanswerable questions in their minds. Marine's confusion over the Corolla Lights' return was as great as ever; but, strangely, when she was in Nanta's company she found the confusion ebbing a little and a measure of her old faith returning. Perhaps it was the fervency of Nanta's religious devotion, or possibly it was simply the effect that this private and very peaceful sanctum had upon her spirit. Whatever the truth, Marine found comfort here, and but for Nanta's trouble she would have been content.

Nanta, though, was very far from content. Her fear for Osiv was growing by the day, and the fact that neither she nor Marine had been able to unearth any clues at all added fuel to the fire. The sprite had not appeared to her again (or so she believed), and her pleas for enlightenment still received no answer. Four days ago she had resolved to take steps of her own to watch over Osiv: spend time with him, be vigilant, protect him by the simple fact of being with him. But her duties had made it impossible. Since Arctor's death there had been a great increase in the official demands made on her, and very recently the workload had become heavier still. Always there were papers to be read, petitions to be answered, documents to sign; she barely had a moment to herself, and there was simply not enough time for her to spend more than a few minutes each day with Osiv. Even this interlude wouldn't have been possible if she had not insisted and given the servants no chance to argue.

She glanced sidelong at Marine, who appeared to be lost in her private contemplations. Another day of waiting and hoping, only for the hope to come to nothing again. It couldn't go on for ever. Something would break, sooner or later. Something would have to.

Which, perhaps, was what she feared most of all.

Chapter XIII

That night the Corolla Lights returned for the third time, and their appearance set the final seal on Father Urss's resolve.

Already, in the city, the omen was being interpreted as he had feared. The network of spies sent out by Urss and Beck to monitor public feeling reported that Osiv IV had become an object of huge attention, almost an icon, and the populace confidently believed that his reign would launch Vyskir into a new and wondrous phase of its history. It was time to prove the populace wrong.

Early the following evening a cryptic message was sent to the imperial physician from Urss's office in the seminary, and within an hour Urss had made the necessary arrangements. The physician had been party to the scheme from the start and believed that he had Urss's complete trust. He was, Urss reflected, a foolishly credulous man; in circumstances like these, trust – with one or two very particular exceptions – was not an option. But that matter could be dealt with later; at present he had a more important objective.

Everything was prepared now to the smallest detail; including the Imperatrix's guaranteed absence while the thing was done. Urss had decreed that a special ceremony was to be conducted in the temple, to give thanks for the Corolla Lights. The imperial family were to attend as a mark of the ceremony's importance, and for good measure Urss and Beck would also be present and on clear public show. Even Pola would be kept well away from the suite – Urss hardly imagined that she would shed a tear for Osiv, but it was just as well to take every precaution. So, all was ready; there was nothing more to do but wait.

Urss sent word to this effect to Kodor, and was surprised when Kodor responded by summoning him to his apartments. Curious, and just a little apprehensive, Urss answered the summons and was shown to an anteroom, where the prince was waiting for him.

'Thank you for your message, Father Urss,' Kodor said. His face gave nothing away, and Urss bowed.

'I hope the arrangements meet with your approval, Your Highness.'

'They do; but for one thing. The matter of who is to administer the concoction. I presume it will be the imperial physician?'

'Yes, sir. He'll go to the Imperator's rooms on a pretext, and then—'

'That, Father, is the problem. For one thing, I don't entirely trust the man – and for another, neither does Osiv.'

Urss pursed his lips. 'I understand your misgivings, sir; but I don't think there's any cause for concern. As you know, when this is over . . .' He let the sentence tail off, and Kodor, who had been taken into his confidence on that score, returned a hard smile.

'Yes, I *do* know what the physician's fate will be. But that's not the point I'm making. What if he should lose his nerve? He is, after all, going to assassinate the Imperator, and whatever he may think or say now, when it comes to actually committing the act he may see it in a very different light.'

Urss's eyes narrowed. 'You think that he might fail us?'

'I think it's a distinct possibility.'

Urss said: 'Ah . . .'

'And then we come to the second complication,' Kodor continued. 'As I said, Osiv does not trust the physician either; in fact he thoroughly loathes all his physicians, because he naturally

185

associates them with medicines and other unpleasantness. So when the man tries to give him a potion, he won't take it willingly. He'll have to be forced, and he's surprisingly strong. Too strong, I'd say, for the physician to cope with unaided. Add that to the first complication, and I think we might have a problem.'

Urss stroked his own chin, considering. He had not been aware of Osiv's aversion to physicians; used, himself, to being obeyed without question, it hadn't occurred to him that this difficulty might arise. Now he saw that Kodor had a point, and a potentially serious one.

Kodor said, 'There's only one way that I can see to get round the obstacle, Father Urss. Osiv must be given the potion by someone he trusts. And unless we take the risk of involving outsiders, that leaves us with only one choice.'

Urss looked at him. 'You . . . ?'

'Me.' Even in the soft candlelight Kodor's grey eyes looked as hard as stone. 'And I'm willing to do it.'

Urss left Kodor's suite ten minutes later. Kodor waited a further half-hour, then put on an old hide coat kept for purposes such as this and made his way, by a very convoluted route that few in the court were aware of, out of the palace and into the Metropolis. He had some final arrangements to make, and something to procure. When both were done, he would be ready.

'But I've spent so little time with him these past days!' Nanta protested wearily. 'I must see him, Dorca; I insist on it!'

'Your Majesty, there simply isn't the *time*,' Dorca told her again. 'The temple ceremony is to begin in an hour, and for the Imperatrix to be late is unthinkable!'

'Prince Kodor isn't even attending the ceremony,' Nanta said with an edge to her voice. 'Isn't that more unthinkable?'

'His Highness has a cold, I understand, and it's bad enough

for him to have taken to his bed. Otherwise—'

'Otherwise he would do his duty, as we all must; all right, I *know*.' She sighed heavily. 'Very well, I'll do what you all want of me. But I *will* see Osiv when the ceremony is over.'

'Of course you will, madam, and I'll make quite sure that nothing happens to prevent it.' Dorca bustled to where yet another new gown, still in the dreadful shades of mourning, hung ready to be laced on, and Nanta gave herself up to the inevitable. Four hours, the ceremony was to last. Four hours of sitting in the temple, closeted in the imperial box with only court dignitaries and her senior ladies-in-waiting for company. And Pola, who seemed incapable of even speaking to her. She would *welcome* Osiv's society when she returned; it would be a blessed relief.

'Tell him that we'll have our meal together tonight,' she said to Dorca. 'Tell him that I promise it.'

'I will, madam. Now, if by your leave we may just help you out of your day gown . . .'

When her dressers finally departed, satisfied that their mistress was ready, only five minutes remained before the escort was due to arrive for the royal progress to the temple. Dorca, who was also in the party, had gone to hastily put on her own veil, and suddenly something in Nanta rebelled. In a few quick strides she was at the door, and she hurried to Osiv's playroom, throwing back her veil as she went so that her appearance would not frighten him. She did not knock but went straight in.

And came face to face with Kodor.

'Sister . . .' Kodor's expression was one of startled chagrin. 'I thought you had left for the temple.'

'And I thought you were confined to your bed,' Nanta rejoined. 'It seems we were both misinformed.'

He shrugged, a helpless, almost boyish shrug that she thought was intended to be endearing. 'I confess; it was an excuse.

There's nothing wrong with me, except for a very powerful desire not to attend the ceremony.'

She smiled, though without humour. 'I wish I could be as defiant as you.'

'You're the Imperatrix; it makes defiance a great deal harder. I thought I would spend a little time with Osiv. I've brought a new toy for him; look.' He held out a small and brightly painted wooden wagon. 'It's for his fortress garrison; there are horses to go in the shafts, and twenty of his soldiers can fit inside.'

Nanta's annoyance faded. 'He'll be delighted.'

'I think so, too. I was going to give it to him, but he's asleep.'

'Is he?' That surprised her; at this time of day Osiv was usually at his most lively. 'Perhaps he didn't sleep properly last night.' She should have known if that was so, and should have done something about it . . . Nanta pushed the guilty frustration away and added, 'When he wakes, please tell him that I'll come to him as soon as I return from the temple.'

She thought Kodor hesitated a bare moment before replying, 'Yes. I will.'

A patter of footsteps heralded Dorca, agitated. 'Madam, the escort is— Oh!' She hastily curtseyed to Kodor. 'Your Highness; I had no idea – I thought—' But she was too flustered to know what she did think, and she turned to Nanta again. 'Your Majesty, we will be *late*!'

'Go, sister,' Kodor said, smiling at her. She had the strangest feeling that the smile didn't come as readily as usual. 'We'll meet again this evening.'

He bowed to her before she went out, and Nanta's last impression of him – a strong one – was of a look in his eyes that she could not interpret and which made her, without reason, uneasy. As Dorca flurried her like a mother hen towards the corridor and the waiting escort, she looked back. But Osiv's door had closed.

'Your *Majesty* . . .' Dorca pleaded desperately.

'Yes, Dorca, I am coming.' With one last, questioning look, Nanta went to do her duty.

Kodor leaned back against the door, shutting his eyes and allowing his pent breath to escape in a long hiss. He had not expected that, and should have been more careful to ensure that Nanta was gone before making his move. But time was against him; there was still so much to be done, and he himself would have to be back in the palace before the ceremony ended and the royal party returned. It would be a very, very close-run thing.

He walked back into Osiv's bedchamber. Osiv was, indeed, asleep; thanks to a quick-acting soporific that Kodor had brought back from his foray into the city. It would have been too dangerous to take the drug from the palace physicians' supplies; though the chance of discovery was slim, it couldn't be risked. The dose had been strong, and with luck Osiv would not wake until well into the night, by which time he would have reached his destination.

Bracing his muscles, Kodor lifted his brother from the bed and laid him gently on a chaise at the far side of the room. Then he went to the window, opened it and gave a soft, low whistle. Shadows moved among shadows in the gloomy courtyard below, and through a fine film of snow Kodor saw his two accomplices emerge from where they had been waiting. They looked up – the snowfall smudged the detail of their faces – and Kodor signalled over his shoulder. Gestures acknowledged that they understood, and he withdrew from the window and closed it again.

A few minutes later the two men arrived at the outer door. Kodor went to meet them, and stood back as they carried something long and bulky into the suite. Their burden was a rolled-up carpet; anyone seeing them would simply have assumed that Kodor had arranged for some new gift to be delivered for the Imperator. The men bowed but did not speak; could not speak, in fact, for these were the two mutes who, until

189

his marriage, had been a part of Osiv's entourage. After the wedding they had been given small pensions and dismissed, as their presence was considered unfitting and even distasteful once Nanta was installed in the apartments, but Kodor had known where to find them, and had known, too, their deep-rooted loyalty to their old master. Now they were to serve their master again, and in a more important capacity than they had ever done before.

Wedging the door so that it could not be opened from the outside, Kodor led the mutes through to the bedchamber, where they laid the carpet down and unrolled it.

A corpse slid out on to the floor. It was the body of a man, of similar age, height and build to Osiv, and with hair of the same colour. Its face, though, was unrecognisable, for it was twisted and horribly discoloured, the suppurating skin almost black, and so bloated that the eyes were invisible.

Though he had known what to expect and had steeled himself for it, a shudder of revulsion still knifed through Kodor, and after one look he turned away.

'You've done well,' he told the mutes. He didn't know, and didn't want to know, how or where they had found their victim; his only stipulation had been that they must choose someone who had no family or loved ones to grieve for him. There could be no room for guilt or remorse; Osiv's life was more important than that of any stranger.

The mutes nodded and bowed their thanks. They lifted the corpse on to the bed, and Kodor fetched one of Osiv's night-gowns. The man had been dead long enough for the rigor mortis stage to have passed (though not for decay to have begun) and dressing him was relatively easy. When it was done, they spread his limbs at sprawling angles to give the impression that he had suffered a violent fit, and completed the picture by rumpling the bedcovers. Squashing his fastidious instincts, Kodor took a detailed and critical look at their handiwork. He was satisfied:

no one could possibly tell that this was not Osiv. Father Urss would see nothing amiss, and the imperial physician's examination of the body would be a mere pretence. The deception was as foolproof as he could reasonably hope.

He nodded to the two men. 'That will do excellently. Now; help me with the Imperator.'

Osiv's next journey would be undignified, but at least it would be brief. The mutes laid him on the carpet, then carefully, reverently, rolled it up around him. In one of the palace's more remote courtyards a carriage was ready to transport them all out of the Metropolis, and once they were clear of the city Osiv would be transferred to a waiting dog-sleigh. Kodor would return to the city then, but Osiv would be taken on to the forest, to Kodor's own hunting lodge. The lodge had every comfort; and with the devoted mutes and two other servants to tend him, he would be safe and secure for as long as need be.

Dusk was gathering rapidly in the courtyard. The carriage was waiting, its driver – also trusted and well-paid into the bargain – muffled against the bitter cold. Inside the carriage were furs and rugs and hot stones, together with a basket of food and drink and another full of toys. Osiv was lifted in – then as Kodor made to climb after him, his eyes caught a flicker of movement at the courtyard's far side.

He saw it clearly in the instant before it dodged – or faded – out of sight. A frost sprite . . . Kodor's blood chilled and his hands were suddenly unsteady. Why had it been watching him? What did it *want*?

The other men had not noticed the creature, and Kodor suspected that it wouldn't show itself again. Nonetheless, when he was inside the carriage and seated beside the sleeping Osiv, he rubbed the fogged window to clear it and peered out, alert for any further telltale signs. There were none; if the sprite was still there it was taking care, now, to stay hidden.

The carriage springs sagged a little as the mutes got in and sat down. The door was closed and the coachman's face appeared briefly at the window. Kodor nodded. 'Move off when you're ready.'

'Your Highness.' More creaking and sagging as the man climbed up to the box, then slowly, quietly, hooves and wheels muffled by the snow, they were away.

The carriage drove soberly through the Metropolis, and the curtains stayed closed. People in the streets paid the vehicle little heed; it bore no crest and thus could not belong to anyone of particular importance, so there was no need to crane in the hope of glimpsing some eminent personage inside. They crossed the river (which was mostly frozen now, though the ice wasn't yet thick enough for the winter fairs and markets to begin) by one of the lesser bridges, then took the north-eastward road towards the forests. It was heavy going once they were clear of the city; the snow had thickened in the last few days and the ground was better suited to runners than to wheels. Kodor looked out at what little he could see of the passing landscape, and hoped they would be able to reach the rendezvous point.

Then, as he looked at the dark blurs of the roadside pines, he realised that something was following them.

It was no more than a shadow on the snow, cast by the carriage lamps, but from its shape Kodor knew instantly that it was no part of their entourage. This was something separate; fleet, running, keeping pace with them just behind the rear wheels. Whether it was animal or human or something else, he couldn't tell; sometimes it seemed to lope on four legs and sometimes on two, and it had an angularity that was disturbingly incongruous.

He pressed his face to the corner of the window, trying to see further back and closer in, to get at least a glimpse of the thing's substance. But the big, turning wheel blocked any view. There was just the unidentifiable shadow.

The mutes had noticed Kodor's sudden disquiet and were watching him anxiously. They hadn't the assurance to sign to him, but their gazes fixed on his face and their eyes were filled with questions. Kodor let the curtain drop and said tersely, 'What weapons do you carry?'

From beneath the seat the mutes produced shortbow, cross-bow, several knives of varying length, and a cudgel. Kodor nodded. 'Keep the shortbow and a knife to hand. We have company, and I don't know what it is.' It could be a wolf, he thought; though wolves travelled in packs, not singly. A rogue? Possibly. But then, what wolf was capable of running on its hind legs . . . ?

He looked out again. The shadow was still there, and for a moment he thought that a second one showed at the edge of the lamps' reach before merging back into the dark. Old tales of the forests' strange denizens came back to him; were-creatures, half-men, spirit-things that could change their shape and their nature . . . He tried to remind himself that most of the stories had been invented purely to frighten children into good behaviour, but that didn't change the fact that *something* was out there, following.

The mutes were alert now, one fingering the hilt of his sheathed knife, the other with the shortbow and several arrows laid across his knee. Kodor judged that they did not have much further to go. He did not think the mysterious followers would attack the carriage; if that was the game, they were likely to have made their move by now. But when they reached the rendezvous . . .

Osiv slept on, his mouth hanging open, drooling slightly. Without a word, Kodor reached forward and chose a knife from among the mutes' small arsenal. Then he settled back in his seat, and waited for the journey's end.

The carriage arrived at its destination half an hour later.

The driver shouted a command and the coach lurched and pitched as the horses began to slow down. They stopped with a final terrific jolt, and Kodor was on his feet ahead of the mutes, opening the door and jumping down into fine, smooth snow.

An acute, almost deathly quiet surrounded them. The horses were steaming, moist clouds rising into the cold air; here in the shelter of dense conifers the snowfall was reduced to a few patchy flakes and the ground covering did not even reach Kodor's ankles. The shadow was gone and there was no sign of any untoward movement among the trees; nonetheless Kodor made a complete circuit of the carriage before telling the mutes that they could bring Osiv out.

The sleigh waited in the lee of a massive pine whose branches spread overhead like a roof. Eight dogs were harnessed in the traces, their breath condensing from lolling tongues, their intelligent eyes glinting with a peculiar, nacreous reflection in the snowlight. The sleigh-driver, a squat man swathed in so many furs that he looked almost spherical, waddled forward to bow reverently to Kodor, then stood back as Osiv was carefully transferred from the carriage. Osiv stirred and mumbled, but the drug was still working and he did not wake. Kodor waited until his fur-wrapped form was safely stowed in the sleigh, then turned to stare back along the pale ribbon of the road.

And saw the two shapes that stood watching him from the cover of the trees.

They were grey shapes, intangible and ghostlike; and neither animal nor human but an uncanny meld of both. One had the ears of a wolf, and a bird's wings where its arms should have been; the other seemed part pig and part deer, but with a boy's face and an old man's eyes. They made no move either towards Kodor or away, but only gazed steadily at him, without hostility and without fear.

Then a third figure stepped out from the darkness between them, and Kodor recognised the frost sprite.

It was the same creature that had haunted the courtyard before their departure; he was as sure of that as he had ever been sure of anything. And it had been with Nanta on the tower, he knew that, too. Her guardian and her friend.

'Why have you followed us?' Kodor's voice carried like glass in the quiet. 'What do you want?'

No answer.

'My brother won't be harmed.' For reasons that he didn't understand, Kodor had to give that reassurance. But the sprite knew it already; it *must* know. Was this nothing more than curiosity on its part? Or did it have some obscure motive, some purpose of its own?

He flung a rapid glance over his shoulder, to where the mutes and the coach- and sleigh-drivers stood motionless behind him. The mute with the bow had nocked an arrow and held the weapon half raised; but he would not be so foolish as to shoot. To harm a frost sprite was impossible, and even to attempt it courted a lifetime's bad luck.

'Get into the sleigh,' Kodor ordered the mutes quietly. 'Look after the Imperator.'

He heard the shuffle and creak as they obeyed, and he looked at the frost sprite again. Now, for the first time, it did move; a slow nod of the head which seemed to signify approval.

'They'll take him to a safe place,' Kodor said aloud. 'They'll guard him. It's all I can do.'

The sprite nodded again, more emphatically this time. Then it raised its hands, pressed the tips of the spatulate fingers together, and made the slightest of bows. As it straightened, it smiled a small, cold smile; then the fingers touched its mouth, its eyes and its ears, as though to say: *nothing said, nothing seen, nothing heard*. It was a clear signal, the making of a pact of privacy between them. If Kodor kept his part of the bargain, the sprite and its strange companions would watch over Osiv in their own way.

He didn't see them go; they simply melted from sight like his own breath misting and vanishing. One of the sleigh dogs yipped uneasily and the rest started to whine until a snapped threat from the driver silenced them. The coachman was at the horses' heads; they too were suddenly restless and stamping, and a wave of sweating heat chased through Kodor's body as one kind of tension was replaced by another.

'Go,' he told the sleigh-driver. 'Quickly, before it grows late.' He forced something approximating a smile. 'And don't fear anything you might meet on the road.'

The squat man nodded understanding. He climbed aboard, then his whip cracked and the sleigh began to move. It turned a clumsy, wallowing circle as the dogs strained in their harnesses, then abruptly it was gathering speed, skimming away into the night with a hiss and a bow-wave of flying snow.

The carriage-driver needed no command from Kodor; he was already on his box and gathering up the reins. Kodor scrambled inside; even as he slammed the door the driver yelled at the horses. A minute later there were only two sets of wheel and runner tracks, and a patch of scuffed and footprinted snow, to show that anything had come to disturb the silence.

Chapter XIV

As the procession made its dignified way through the private tunnel between the temple and the palace, Nanta slipped a hand under her veil to rub at her eyes, which were prickling with the combined effects of tiredness and incense smoke. She longed to be free of the veil, the formal gown and the rest of the imperial entourage; all she wanted was to rest, with nothing and no one to make any demands on her attention.

The temple ceremony had been one of the most tedious she had ever attended, seeming to go on and on until she half believed that it would never end. Twice she had almost fallen asleep, and several of the ladies-in-waiting had certainly done so; one even snored until her shin was hastily kicked by Dorca. Only Pola had appeared to be unaffected, as far as anyone could tell. She had sat rigid as always, hands clasped tightly in her lap, not looking to right or left and never once speaking. Now she walked behind Nanta, still silent, her whole manner precluding any possibility of a friendly move. Nanta disliked being followed so closely; Pola felt like a second shadow and, irrationally, she couldn't shake off the feeling that there was some ill omen in her presence. She thought again of trying to crack the icy wall that existed between them – then, again, let the idea drop. She simply didn't have the energy.

Halfway through the tunnel, they heard running footsteps ahead. The men of the escort were instantly alert, hands moving quickly to the sheathed swords they carried – and abruptly Nanta felt an inward lurch of foreboding. She stopped walking, and the rest of the party halted too, Dorca and the other women gathering protectively around their mistress as the escort called out a challenge.

A voice shouted a reply, and brighter lights appeared ahead of them, swamping the dim glow of the wall lamps in their brackets. Then a group of people appeared, with Kodor at their head. Nanta had time to recognise the senior physician, one of his assistants, and three servants whose names she could not recall, before Kodor slid to a breathless stop.

'Find Exalted Father Urss, quickly!' He addressed the leader of the escort. 'Tell him to come to the Imperator's suite – *hurry*, man!'

The leader didn't argue but ran back towards the temple, and Kodor snapped to Dorca, 'The rest of you – go on to the suite. Don't ask questions; there's someone there who'll tell you what to do!'

Nanta's foreboding swelled into something far stronger and she stepped forward, throwing back her veil, pushing the milling women aside. 'Kodor, what's happened?'

He turned to her, his face pallid and strained. 'It's Osiv,' he said.

'What about him? *What?*'

He didn't answer the question, only approached and put an arm tightly about her shoulders. 'You'd better come,' he told her. 'Come with me; we'll go back together.'

Nanta had one glimpse of her bewildered ladies, with Pola standing immobile and isolated in their midst, before Kodor was hurrying her away along the passage. Behind them the paralysis of shock broke and the women started after them, twittering agitatedly, but Kodor didn't even glance back. On to the tunnel's end, through the door that connected with the palace, along carpeted passages, running now. Her own and Osiv's apartments – the doors were shut but there were people gathered outside, and a woman's voice was wailing and lamenting—

'*Kodor!*' Nanta dragged him to a halt, staring in horror at the scene. She had started to shake uncontrollably.

'All right.' His arm went round her again. 'All right; we'll go in, but I'm going to take you directly to your private rooms.'

'*Where's Osiv?*'

'In his bedchamber. But it's best if you don't go in there. Not now; not yet.'

He led her forward again, very slowly now. Nanta's feet dragged; she was reluctant to approach the rooms and the people, who were all gazing at her with shock and pity in their eyes. Then Dorca came running from behind; calling, 'Madam, oh, madam!' She tried to catch hold of Nanta's sleeve, and bemusedly Nanta saw that tears were streaming down her face. The physician was at Dorca's heels, his expression grave – and suddenly Nanta knew what he had already told her servant.

A strange, inexplicable calm washed over her and she stopped again. Voice perfectly level, she said, 'He's dead, isn't he?'

'Oh, *madam* . . .' Dorca covered her face with her hands. Nanta regarded her silently for a moment, then turned to Kodor.

'Was he murdered?' she said.

A stunned silence fell as those nearest heard her. Kodor's face turned white, and for a single instant Nanta saw horror in his eyes. The horror, she thought, of a man with a secret to conceal . . .

Then the incriminating clue was wiped from his expression as though it had never existed. He said softly, harshly, '*Murdered?* By the God, Nanta, of course not! Who in this world could wish to harm him? Get a grip on yourself!' He flicked a gaze over the company at large. 'The Imperatrix is greatly distressed. Leave us, all of you. Exalted Father Urss has been sent for, and he will take charge.'

The crowd parted like diverted water as between them Kodor and Dorca hurried Nanta through the doors and into the suite.

Her numb senses registered the familiar oppressive furniture, all so neat and well ordered; then they were entering the next room, and there were two more doors, one leading to her private apartments, the other to Osiv's.

The urge came so quickly and unexpectedly that she acted on it without pausing to consider. Throwing off Kodor's arm, evading Dorca, she ran to Osiv's door and through it. The playroom – but he wasn't here; Kodor had said he was in the bedchamber—

As she burst in, two servants and another physician started to their feet. Their faces registered alarm and they made as if to step between her and the bed; but their awe and Nanta's momentum cast any such thought aside. She reached the bedside unhindered, and stared down.

Osiv had been covered by a sheet. For an entangled moment reality collided with Nanta's memories of her old dream – the bier, the shrouded figure – but then the dream spun away. This was not a mere nightmare. She was fully awake, and this was *here* and *now*.

She reached out a gloved hand, and lifted the sheet back.

'Madam!' Dorca was there. Nanta had not heard her come in. Rank was forgotten and Dorca was trying to pull her away. Nanta stared, kept staring.

'Oh, madam . . .' Dorca's voice was breaking with grief and anguish. 'Come away, my lady, come away. You must. There's nothing in this world that you can do for him now.'

Nanta raised her head. Her eyes saw, though her mind did not register, the gilded, moulded ceiling, and the shadows cast by candlelight, and the reflection of the fire in the hearth . . .

Then, not knowing what she did, she opened her mouth and a shrill, ululating cry echoed ringingly through the imperial apartments, rising higher and clearer and more piercingly, until all who heard it felt it vibrate through their bones.

And from a sky still thick with falling snow came a fearful

and formidable answer as, impossibly, the sound of a gargantuan thunderclap bawled out over the Metropolis and rumbled away into the night.

The lights of the palace burned until morning. In the Exalted Council's main chamber Father Urss, Prince Kodor and all the senior councillors, physicians and high officers of the court were closeted behind doors guarded by grimly silent officers of the imperial household. At the temple, the highest Fathers and Mothers of the religious orders were kneeling in prayer before the image of the God, while devotional candles flickered in every cranny and the smoke of incense hung like fog in the air.

Beyond the city, far away to the north, the sky glared with the eerie luminescence of the Corolla Lights. They danced a ragged and unruly dance tonight, as if responding to some violence pent below the horizon, and in the wake of the isolated thunderclap they seemed to presage something very ominous.

In the imperial suite, Nanta lay pale and still in her bed. She had collapsed as the thunderclap roared above the city, and when she came round the senior physician had administered a strong sleeping draught before she was conscious enough to refuse it. Everyone agreed it was for the best. Sleep was a healer, of both the body and the mind; sleep would help the Imperatrix to recover from the shock of this tragedy and overcome her grief. And while she slept, they would not have to face the look in her eyes. So Dorca kept vigil with her, while on the other side of the bed Mother Marine knelt in silent and earnest prayer for the soul of the Imperator and the comfort of his widow.

Marine's arrival had been Grand Mother Beck's doing. No one had thought to wonder how Beck had heard of the calamity so quickly; there were too many other preoccupations for such a small anomaly to be noticed. Besides, Beck had sent such eloquent word of her personal sorrow that any possible suspicions didn't even arise. She had also sent Marine, 'to help in any way that she can'; and though Dorca did not especially like Marine, on this occasion she was glad of her company. The thunderclap had struck terror into Dorca; a deeply superstitious woman, she was unshakeably convinced that the God had sent it in direct response to Nanta's terrible cry. The presence of a high-ranking religious was, to her, like a safeguard against any further show of divine disapproval, and helped to ease her fear.

It did not occur to her that the thunderclap might have had another source entirely.

Marine was suppressing a fear of another kind; the twin burdens of guilt and horror. The frost sprites had forewarned Nanta that the Imperator was in danger, Nanta had confided in Marine and pleaded for her help – and Marine had failed her. She tried to tell herself that the failure had been inevitable; the Imperator had died of a sickness, not by an assassin's hand, and no one could possibly have predicted the occurrence, let alone prevented it. But the sense of her own inadequacy still clung to her like mire, and alongside her prayers for Osiv and Nanta she also included a plea for forgiveness.

Dorca, of course, knew nothing of this. And neither did she know, as she watched sadly over Nanta's still, quiet form in the great bed, that in her drug-induced sleep the Imperatrix dreamed. Nanta's consciousness was deeply buried, and dreams should have been impossible.

But she dreamed . . .

The clap of thunder was the first thing to come sliding out of her memory as the dream began. But now it was not thunder; instead it was a voice, booming down from the sky in a huge, distorted wave of sound, and the sound formed a word that vibrated into the marrow of her bones.

'*YOOOUUU.*' It was drawn out into a roaring tide of echoes, and Nanta fell to her knees in the city street, clamping both hands to her ears as tears of fright streamed down her cheeks.

'*YOOOUUU.*' There was a calm, appalling inevitability in the word; it was recognition and acknowledgement and accusation all three. Nanta struggled to cry back a denial, but she was dumb, and even if she could have uttered a sound it would have been deluged by the gargantuan voice from the sky.

In her mind she screamed: *Why are you angry with me? What have I done?* But the voice only boomed out its dreadful indictment once again. For twenty years it had been searching for her. Now, finally, it had found her, and it would not listen, it would not reason; for her, it had no mercy.

Now she was running, through unlit night streets where she was a stranger and no one came to help her; and something was pursuing her. She could not see or hear it but she knew it was there, far behind as yet but catching up. She couldn't outdistance it. It was tireless and she was not, and one day, however far in the future that day might lie, there would be no breath and no strength left, and she would stop, and it would move upon her and over her and then would come the eternal dark.

She cried for the snow, for she knew that the snow could save her. But though the city streets had changed to beaten tracks, and the buildings had turned into trees, the snow would not fall. Nanta tried to make it fall, calling it down with all the willpower she possessed. But it did not fall. The forest was laughing at her, mocking her terror and her grief (why did she grieve? She didn't know, she couldn't remember) as she ran like a hunted deer. Above her, flickering and leaping between the stark branches of the pines, the Corolla Lights danced their stately minuet. She thought she could hear them singing, sweet and clear and pure, and if she could only reach the place where they began, that far place behind the north wind, they, like the snow, would shield her from the thing of hate and vengeance that followed her through the night and would never, ever tire of the chase.

Onward and onward. Strange, small faces peeped out at her

from the green-black forest canopy, but she had no time and no breath for them and they darted away again. Once, she saw a sleigh, skimming fast in the air ahead of her. The dogs that drew it were grey and they yelped on a high, terrible note; the driver turned his head to look back at her and he was a tusked and bristling boar; and she knew that among his cargo was a dead man whose eyes could still see. She tried to race the sleigh, not knowing why she did it, but the driver laughed a grunting, snorting laugh, and the dogs yelped anew, and the whole vision curved upwards, upwards and away into the sky, leaving her far behind.

She found her voice then, and screamed to the frost sprites. They had come to her before; they had shown her, warned her, helped her – but on this dreadful journey there was no such help to be had. The sprites *wanted* to answer; she felt the pull of their presence and their urging. But they could not reach her. Nothing could reach her. There was only Nanta, and the thing of hate at her heels.

In the opulent bed in the palace the Imperatrix sighed, halting Marine's prayers and bringing Dorca to her feet. But the white face did not change, the eyes did not open, and after a few moments the watching women lapsed back to their patient vigil.

But in Nanta's dream, suddenly, there was snow.

She heard the singing of it first, like the pure voice of the Corolla Lights but smaller, closer and more intimate. Then the soft whiteness began to fall down through the trees. It covered the ground and the bending branches; it touched her cheeks and her eyes and her lips, so that she drank in its coldness as though it were sweet wine. She felt her strength returning as the snow cloaked her hair and arms, clothing her whole body, protecting her like a coat of ermine. The thing of hate was drawing closer, but she was no longer afraid. Her running steps slowed, slowed, stopped, and she turned to meet it as it flowed through the forest and bloated towards her, shapeless and nameless and yet cruelly familiar.

The vast voice boomed: '*YOOOUUU.*'

'I,' said Nanta. The forest answered her: *I, I, I.* And the thing of hate was still.

Ice cracked as Nanta raised her hands. Her pursuer could not harm her now; she had a strength that matched its own, and somewhere within her, locked away still but closer to consciousness than ever before, was the knowledge of how that strength could and should be used.

She said: 'Go. I am beyond your reach. Leave me. For I know what you are, and I pity you.'

It shrank from her; only a little but the shrinking was enough to tell her that she had won this battle, if not the war. Her head turned, to right, to left, and the frost sprites stood beside her, their gazes fast on her face.

'Go,' she said again, though more gently now. '*Go.*'

She felt it fade. Sadness tore at her as it went, but she put the emotion aside, and when it was truly gone she sank down in the snow. The sprites came to her, stroking her hair, touching her hands. Nanta smiled up at them.

Then the smile drained away.

'Who killed him?' she asked the sprites. 'Tell me. Who murdered Osiv?'

Darkness was closing in from the forest. The Corolla Lights were gone and would not return tonight, and a cloud-bank moved across the sky, blotting out the stars. The sprites gazed down at Nanta.

'Ask,' said one.

'Your brother,' said the other.

And in the bedchamber of the palace, Nanta opened her eyes.

For some time she did not move, only lay gazing up at the ceiling as the dream pieced itself together in her conscious mind. When the picture was complete, she shifted her gaze carefully first to one side and then to the other. On her left Dorca, nodding sleepily in a chair; on her right Marine, kneeling, head bowed and hands clasped. Nanta was glad to see Marine, glad that someone had sent for her. But there was one other person she wanted to see.

She spoke, startling Dorca out of her doze and bringing Marine's head up with a sharp movement.

'Where is Prince Kodor?'

There was a momentary pause, then Dorca scrambled to her feet and leaned motheringly over the bed.

'Oh, madam, you should still be sleeping! The physician said—'

'Where is Prince Kodor?' Nanta repeated.

Marine was staring at her in consternation, though she made no attempt to speak. Dorca's face creased and she replied, 'He is with the Exalted Council, madam. In the main chamber.'

Yes, Nanta thought. *He would be.* 'When the Council's business is finished, send word to Prince Kodor that I want him to come to me immediately,' she said.

She could feel the strain in the silence that followed. Marine's gaze had slid away and Dorca twisted her hands together nervously; she seemed to be struggling for a reply but was unable to find one.

'What is it?' Nanta asked sharply. 'Why don't you answer me, Dorca?'

'Madam, I . . . I can't send such a message.'

'Why not?'

'Because . . .' But Dorca started to flounder again, and it was Marine who finally spoke for her.

'He is no longer Prince Kodor. He is the Imperator now, and cannot be commanded.'

A frigid little knot seemed to form in the pit of Nanta's stomach, and she said softly: 'Oh . . .' She had known it, of course, but until this moment it had not really come home to her. Kodor was no longer a mere regent, ruling in his brother's name. The throne and the title were now his by right.

And in the wake of her dream, Nanta did not believe that he had gained that right by a stroke of chance.

She said: 'How *did* my husband die?'

Dorca sagged back on to her chair and began to weep softly, and Nanta noticed for the first time that her eyes looked sore and reddened, as though she had done little but cry for many hours. Which was probably true; for Dorca was one of the few in the palace household who had felt genuine affection for Osiv. She, if anyone, would tell the truth. But Dorca was too upset to answer the question with any coherence, and again Marine had to come to her rescue.

'The imperial physician believes that a disease was to blame,' she told Nanta quietly. 'The Pilgrims' Plague – it's very rare, but when it does strike, the effects are swift and devastating. I understand . . . I have been told . . . that it kills within a very few hours of the first symptoms' onset.'

'I saw his face,' said Nanta, triggering a choking moan from Dorca.

'Yes . . .' Marine replied pallidly. She had not seen Osiv's corpse – Father Urss had given orders that no one should come near once the physician began his examination – but she had heard the reports of those who had seen it, and though she was not squeamish the descriptions had turned her stomach.

Nanta said, almost detachedly: 'Is that what the disease does?'

Marine nodded. And Nanta saw then in her eyes what she had already detected in her voice: the fact that Marine harboured doubts of her own.

'I see,' she said. 'Yes. I see.' And wondered what Marine suspected that she either could or would not reveal. Had she learned, just too late, some vital piece of information that might have turned this bitter tide? Nanta ached to know, but could not ask until she had a chance to be alone with Marine.

'Dorca,' she said, 'will you fetch me some food?'

'Madam . . . ?' Dorca looked up, her face tear-streaked and her expression bemused. Probably she was shocked by the idea that her mistress could even think of eating, and taking pity on her Nanta made her expression soften into a smile.

'I need all the strength I can gather, Dorca,' she told the woman gently. 'I can't allow myself to become weak, can I?'

'No . . . no, madam, of course . . .' Dorca got to her feet. 'I'm sorry; I should have thought . . . I'll go myself – I'll fetch something to tempt your appetite . . . Oh, my poor little prince!'

She fled from the room, and Nanta and Marine heard her burst into a fresh flood of tears outside. They looked at each other, and Nanta said:

'So Kodor is Imperator now, and his wife is Imperatrix. What does that make me?'

'I believe your title will be Imperatrix Dowager,' Marine replied cautiously.

'Imperatrix Dowager.' Nanta nodded. There was a pause; then, in a perfectly ordinary voice, she added, 'Do you think that Kodor killed Osiv?'

Marine's grey eyes widened in shock, and Nanta realised that the idea, the possibility, had never once occurred to her. She was surprised, and a little disappointed. From a woman of Marine's intelligence and acumen she might have expected a greater degree of realism, or perhaps even cynicism; this reaction struck her as almost naïve. It did not occur to her that only a very few months ago she herself would have been as naïve and more.

She told Marine then about her dream. Marine listened with increasing dismay, and when Nanta finished she sucked in her breath with a soft sound.

'The omen is clear,' she said. 'But the thought that Prince Kodor – I mean, the Imperator –' momentarily she looked guilty at using the title – 'could countenance *murder* . . . He always seemed so fond of his brother.'

Nanta's eyes glinted. 'But less fond, perhaps, than he is of power.'

Marine didn't know Kodor well enough to form a judgement; all she had was the logic of her own small observations, which suggested that Kodor could not possibly be responsible for Osiv's death. Marine did not even truly believe that Osiv had been murdered. Yet the frost sprites' message to Nanta could hardly have been clearer. *Ask your brother*. Whom could they mean but Kodor?

Nanta spoke again, her voice suddenly low and urgent. 'Did you learn anything, Marine? Did you find out anything at all?'

Marine shook her head. 'I failed you,' she said unhappily. 'I thought I had done my best, but it wasn't enough. If only—'

'No.' Nanta interrupted her. 'You did all you could.' She looked around the room, frowning thoughtfully. 'Whatever lies behind this, it's hidden too well and too deeply for you or me to unearth it. But for the sprites I would have suspected nothing; so how can I blame you for any failure?'

'Perhaps,' Marine said, 'they will return . . .'

'Perhaps they will.' Then the fleeting thought went through Nanta's mind: *or if they do not, perhaps I shall make them*.

'Uhh . . .' A shiver assailed her, startling Marine.

'My dear, what's amiss?'

'Nothing.' The feeling, and the thought that had triggered it, were gone, leaving Nanta confused and unsettled. *Make* the sprites return to her? She could not do that. No one could; they were not subject to human will. And yet . . .

The train of thought was broken by the return of Dorca, carrying a tray laden with what she thought were dishes suitable for a newly bereaved widow. Delicate things, bland things; the kind of foods that the physicians had always said were good for Osiv but which Osiv himself had despised. Nanta did not want any of them; to appease Dorca, though, she made herself taste a morsel or two. There was no more talk for some time. Anything else Nanta and Marine might have wanted to say to each other could not be uttered in Dorca's presence, and Dorca now seemed so over-full with misery that she was unable to speak at all. From another part of the suite came unfamiliar sounds. Nanta surmised that the servants were laying Osiv's body out, making him fit – or as fit as was possible in the circumstances – to lie in state while Vyskir officially mourned him. The lying in state would occupy several days; she recalled that from Arctor's funeral. It seemed, now, an age since Arctor had died, though in reality it was a very short time indeed. Did she truly feel any more grief for Osiv than she had done for his father? Hard to say. She had been fond of Osiv, there was no doubting it, but the fondness had, of necessity, had its limitations. She pitied his fate and in a shallow sense would miss him. But there had been no scope for anything deeper. Maybe that explained the absence of any real feeling inside her, except only for a sense of guilt that she did not care more passionately.

But one flame was alight within her. She wanted to know, beyond any shadow of doubt, the truth about how Osiv had died. If her suspicions were right, she wanted to see the truth exposed and justice done. That was important to her. *Very* important. In fact, she knew with certainty that she would not have peace of mind until and unless it was achieved.

She set down her knife, pushed away the tray, then glanced at Marine. There was nothing more to be said, not yet.

'I've eaten my fill, Dorca,' she said calmly. 'You may take the tray away. And then both of you, please, leave me. I want to sleep.'

And perhaps, she added silently to herself, *I will dream another dream.*

Chapter XV

The days immediately following Osiv's demise were an exhausting and stressful time. To begin with there were now two Imperators to be mourned, which meant extra demands on the public face presented by the court and all concerned with it. Father Urss, efficient as always, orchestrated plans for national mourning on an unprecedented scale. Osiv's funeral would take place in fifteen days, and would be attended by rites and ceremonies the like of which had rarely been seen in Vyskir's history. In the meantime, behind the scenes and hidden from the public eye, the more practical formalities were quietly completed. Firstly, the imperial physician's diagnosis was confirmed and announced: the Imperator Osiv IV had fallen victim to the Pilgrims' Plague. The source of the infection was unknown, but stringent examination of all persons connected to the court had confirmed that it was an isolated case. There was no danger to any citizen of the Metropolis, and the populace were exhorted to give fervent thanks to the God that he had seen fit to spare the lives of all other members of the imperial family. Amidst this pious rhetoric, the accession to the throne of Kodor VI was duly and ceremonially declared, and on a morning bitter with frost, under a leaden sky threatening yet more snow, the new Imperator processed through the city streets to give thanks at the temple for his own deliverance.

Nanta played no part in these early rituals. It was accepted, even expected, that an imperial widow should go into seclusion during the first days following her bereavement. Messages arrived at the palace in their hundreds, and many of the wealthier citizens sent condolence gifts, all of which were solemnly accepted and placed on display in one of the palace annexes; but Nanta herself remained closeted in her apartments, away from the gaze of all but her personal servants.

Other demands, though, were made on her, and many of them were far from pleasant. After lying in state in the throne room for a day and a night, the corpse was returned to the imperial suite, where it and all its trappings were set up in the outer reception room. Nanta could not leave the apartments without passing through that room, and she quickly came to dread the sight and atmosphere of it. Brown carpets to deaden sound, brown draperies to block out what little daylight might otherwise have crept in, and a hundred brown candles burning night and day around the huge, ornate catafalque. The room was kept unheated to slow down the onset of decay, but even so a distinct and unpleasant smell was beginning to emanate from beneath the coffin's closed lid. Nanta had had no more portentous dreams, but she was beginning to suffer nightmares in which Osiv, wrapped in his shroud, came to her bedside and held out his arms to her, saying, 'Hug me, Nandi, hug me,' while the stink of putrefaction clogged in her nostrils and throat. Three times on the first night of these dreams she woke screaming, bringing Dorca and two other women running to comfort her, and by the third night she was too afraid to sleep at all, but sat by her window until dawn, staring down into the bleak little courtyard and trying to blank all thoughts from her mind. Dorca, greatly concerned, sent for the imperial physician, who prescribed a calming tincture. It tasted vile but it put a stop to the nightmares, and on the fourth night Nanta slept soundly and dreamlessly.

No word of any kind had come from Kodor. Rationally, Nanta knew she could expect none; with both his brother's death and his own new position to come to terms with, the demands on Kodor's time and energy were greater than on anyone else's. But the dream she had had on that fateful night was festering in her mind like an open sore. The thing of hate, pursuing her relentlessly through the city and the forest . . . What *was* it? In the nightmare she had known that it had been searching for her, waiting to find her, through the whole of her life. But what did that *mean*? What had happened, twenty years ago, that was returning to haunt her now? She prayed and prayed for a further revelation, but no answer came; and the frost sprites did not appear again, either in dreams or in her waking hours. She wanted to see Marine, to talk further about the suspicions that plagued her. But Marine could not come to her; Grand Mother Beck had placed her in temporary charge of the Sanctum, to oversee the Sisters' preparations for their part in the state funeral, and she had no time to spare for anything else. When the funeral was over, Nanta's servants assured her, things would be different. She would move out of this suite to a smaller apartment, kinder and cosier for her; her duties would be fewer and less onerous, and she could start to put the unhappy memories behind her. But until then, she must be patient. There was no other choice.

So Vyskir mourned, and the Metropolis made ready for its solemn farewell to Osiv. Since his death the Corolla Lights had not appeared again. Father Urss was surprised but not overly concerned; the Lights' absence could easily be explained to the populace as the God and the Lady's own grieving, and the fact that they were no longer dancing would help calm any residual unease in the city. For himself, Urss was more preoccupied with secular matters, including the forthcoming arrival – weather permitting – of Duke Arec and a large retinue. Word of the tragedy had been sent to Sekol by the fastest possible means, and this morning the courier had returned bearing an appropriate message of Arec's 'great sorrow', together with the news that the Duke would set out immediately for the Metropolis. There was a great deal of nonsense in the letter about Arec's desire to comfort his beloved daughter and son-in-law in their time of grief, but his real motive was obvious to Urss. Arec wanted to make quite sure that Pola's position – and the alliance – were thoroughly and properly assured. And he doubtless also had some 'advice' of his own to give to the new Imperator; advice that Kodor would do very well not to ignore.

On the fifth night of the new reign Urss was working alone in his study, drafting and approving documents for the next morning's meeting of the Exalted Council. The hour was late and his was the only light still burning in the seminary; nothing unusual, for he rarely took more than four hours' sleep and often went without rest altogether for two days or more. In Urss's opinion sleep was a waste of time that could be better employed in activity, and overcoming the need for it was merely a matter of discipline.

He had finally dismissed his yawning secretary an hour ago, and now, by the light of just two precisely placed candles, he worked tirelessly on. The pile of papers diminished steadily, until at last he signed his authorisation to the last of them, laid his pen down and sat back in his chair, looking with satisfaction at the result of his labours. For once, nothing else demanded his urgent attention; anything still outstanding could wait until tomorrow.

His normal custom when work was finished was to kneel down beside his desk and pray to the God before taking a few hours' rest. Regular prayer, of course, was a requirement of his calling and Urss observed it scrupulously, though more often than not his prayers were a token gesture. Tonight, though, he felt the need for a little more. He would, he decided, go to the Seminary chapel, where he could meditate uninterrupted for a while and refresh his spirit.

The chapel lay at the heart of the Seminary, below ground level. It was an imposing chamber, square where the Sanctum of the Lady was circular, and large enough to accommodate two hundred priests. At this hour it was deserted and, closing the door behind him, Urss moved soft-footedly to one of the benches reserved for the highest Fathers, and sat down to absorb the peaceful atmosphere before beginning his devotions. Candles burned softly in sconces around the walls, untouched by any draught. They cast peculiar shadows on the central statue of the God, and a more fanciful man than Urss might easily have imagined that the carved figure's blank face now sported features: piercing eyes, broad nose and relentless mouth. Urss, though, saw only the slight flaws in the stonework and the fact that there was a thin film of dust on the surrounding pedestal. He made a mental note to discipline the Little Brothers whose task it was to clean the chapel, then knelt down, hands clasped and elbows resting on the ledge before him. Wetting his lips, he started quietly to pray.

Proficiently, almost perfunctorily, he ran through a litany and a sanctification, then turned his mind to a more personal invocation. Then, in an obscure corner behind the statue, something moved.

Through half-closed eyes Urss glimpsed the movement, and the prayer stopped as his head came up sharply. Someone else in the chapel? It seemed unlikely. His gaze shifted carefully to either side of the statue – no untoward shadows, as of a lurking intruder. And the movement had ceased now. A trick of the light; it must have been. There was no one there.

A little annoyed at having allowed himself to be distracted, Urss bent his head over his hands again. But his concentration was gone; through the blur created by his latticed fingers it seemed that there was something wrong with the chapel's dimensions, and the anomaly disturbed him. At length he gave up the attempt to return to his devotions, and instead rose, stepped down from the bench and approached the statue on its plinth. He would light a votive candle, and use the flame as a focus for an exercise in self-control. That would deal with the problem.

He crouched down, a little stiffly, took up one of the unlit candles and touched it to the shrine lamp that burned ceaselessly at the statue's feet. Then, sitting back on his haunches, he focused his gaze and his mind on the small flame. It seemed to burn more brightly than was usual; and there was a crimson pinpoint at its heart, like a tiny, feral eye. Urss concentrated on the eye. He could feel his mind relaxing, the exertions of the day slipping away and settling to quietness, and he began to breathe with a controlled, regular rhythm. Better; the feeling of disquiet was receding and his equilibrium coming back. He would offer a prayer to the God, and then he would return to his quarters.

'Great lord, hear the words of your servant and envoy in this world of men.' His voice murmured through the chapel and the walls sent whispering echoes back. 'I pray for strength and guidance in this time of change, and ask your blessing upon our new Imperator as he begins—'

He stopped, as in his mind, silently, a voice said: '*Father Urss.*'

A shock like a knife-stab went through Urss. His gaze was still on the candle flame and suddenly he found that he could not tear it away. A force beyond his control was holding him motionless; he was unable to move, unable to speak . . .

'*Father Urss.*'

Sweat broke out on Urss's face and body; he could feel a rivulet of it trickling down his spine under his robe. He started to shake as, slowly, he realised what was happening to him. It had been many, many years since he had experienced this . . . but tonight, here in the chapel, it was happening once again.

The God was speaking to him.

'Lord . . .' Urss found his voice with a vast effort, though the word quavered. 'Lord . . . your servant hears you!'

'*Then listen, Father Urss. Listen, and take warning.*'

With an icy rush the paralysis that held Urss released its hold. His head jerked, the movement so violent that it almost threw him off balance, and he found his stare being pulled up, up, to the statue towering above him.

The statue had a face. Later Urss would be unable to recall even the smallest detail of it, but it was no trick of the candles. There were eyes, set in deep, dark hollows and burning into him like brands. There was a nose, high-bridged and arrogant, like the beak of a bird of prey. And there was a mouth, moving and curving in the slightest of smiles.

'I am pleased with all you have done,' the disembodied voice whispered. *'But you must have a care. Be wary of her, Father Urss. Be wary of the fair child. Your Imperator is young, and the young must be protected from their own rash follies. If such a folly threatens, I charge you to do what must be done. Do not displease me, Father Urss. Do not fail. Watch the fair child, and have a care.'*

As the last calm, indomitable sentence was uttered the voice began to fade, and the final words sank away into profound silence. Urss felt the power that had overtaken him sliding back, releasing him from its grip, but though his body was his own again he still stood motionless, gazing up at the statue, his face blank with shock and awe. The statue's face, too, was blank again, the shadow-features wiped away as though they had never manifested. But Urss knew what he had seen. He knew what he had heard. And he had no doubt whatever that he had experienced a true vision of the God.

Who had given him a timely warning.

Urss knelt, then dropped to the floor and prostrated himself before the carved figure. It was a mute thanksgiving for the God's approval of all that he had done – and a solemn acknowledgement and acceptance of the new task with which he had been charged. *Be wary of the fair child.* Urss understood; and the warning was a vindication of his own forebodings. Now though, he knew that he could freely act, if need be, to remove that danger. He had the highest sanction of all.

For some minutes longer he stayed prone and motionless, completing his silent prayer of gratitude. Then he raised himself, climbed with dignity to his feet, and moved with a measured tread towards the door of the chapel. He did not look back; there was no need. But he smiled to himself, a smile of certainty and contentment, as the door closed gently behind him.

Two days later, Nanta had an official duty to perform.

The summons came in the form of a folded parchment bearing the Imperator's seal, and was delivered by a sober-faced herald in full livery, who asked that he might wait for the Dowager's formal reply.

Nanta broke the seal and started to read the message. The first paragraph commanded her to attend the throne room that evening, where she would be required to pledge her allegiance to the new Imperator, Kodor VI, and his consort, the Imperatrix Pola. She had been expecting this; it was a necessary protocol, to put on record the fact that she relinquished any claim to power and acknowledged Kodor as her rightful liege, and once the pledge was made, Kodor would by right have the authority to decide and dictate her future. Effectively, she was throwing herself on his mercy.

It was simply an observance, and generations of imperial widows had done it before her. But as she continued to read, Nanta felt a cold premonition touch her. *Ask your brother*. The frost sprites' words; an unequivocal warning. What *did* Kodor mean to do with her now? She had no useful function; she was just a relict, and a reminder of things that Kodor, perhaps, would prefer to forget.

Then, as she reached the message's last paragraph, she saw that there was something more. When the ceremony in the throne room was over, the Imperatrix Dowager was invited to dine with her loving brother and sister in the small winter hall of the palace. The phrase 'loving brother and sister' and the use of the term 'invited' gave a kindlier impression, but Nanta knew that this, too, was a command she could not disobey.

Nanta went into her office, where she wrote a brief, stilted answer to the message. She had no seal of her own now, but signed the reply with a flourish and secured it with plain wax. Outside the herald was waiting, restless and in a hurry; she had seen him trying not to fidget. Nanta frowned at what she had written. She did not want a personal encounter with Kodor; she wasn't ready for it yet, not while there was still so much uncertainty in her mind. But a refusal was out of the question. She would simply have to make the best of it. And there was one consolation – by coming face to face with Kodor she would have the opportunity to watch and listen for any untoward hint, any small clue, that might betray his involvement in the death of Osiv. For Kodor *was* involved, she was sure of it. And no matter how long it might take, or what risks she might run by her investigations, Nanta was determined to find out the truth.

The strange, stiff masque of Nanta's formal pledge of allegiance took place as planned on the following evening. Everything was done according to custom: Kodor, looking sombre and a little uncomfortable on the colossal, gilded throne, sat unmoving as the veiled Nanta was led in by two high officers of the Imperial Household. Nanta then curtseyed to her knees and stayed down while the officers formally presented her to the Imperator and he, equally formally, made a stiff speech of welcome. Pola, also veiled, sat beside her husband on a lesser chair, while behind and to either side of them the entire Exalted Council, in strict order of rank, stood watching and bearing witness. Nanta saw Father Urss at the head of the assembly. His face wore a very thoughtful expression and he seemed to be watching her with an unusual degree of interest. But there was no time for her to wonder what might be in his mind; the officers were respectfully raising her to her feet again, and a cold fanfare rang from the gallery overhead, signalling the moment for her to approach the throne. Slowly forward, head bowed: six paces and stop. She had been carefully schooled this morning in the minutiae of the ceremony, and the words she must say came so easily that she was barely aware of them. Then down again, kneeling this time, to kiss the gloved hands that were extended to her; first Kodor's, his middle finger bearing the Imperator's ring of office, and then Pola's, which felt cold even through its velvet covering. The fanfare sounded again, and Nanta raised her head so that Kodor could reach forward and lift the veil back from her face. For one moment Nanta gazed into his eyes, and what she saw there startled her. There was sorrow in Kodor's look; sorrow and wistfulness and a strange, suppressed hint of eager hope. His eyes closed as he kissed her forehead, and he said, so softly that only she could hear, 'My dearest Nanta . . .'

Pola had also cast back her veil, and she too kissed Nanta's brow, though her smile was feigned and she did not speak. Again Nanta rose, and to the sound of a third fanfare she backed away six paces before making her final curtsey. Then the thin bark of the trumpets faded and died, and the ceremony was over.

Kodor rose and the entire company made obeisance to him, even the scribe who had been absorbed in noting the proceedings springing to his feet and bowing deeply. A nod, and the doors that led to the winter hall were opened. Kodor looked at Nanta where she waited, and he smiled.

'We shall dine now. Sister, will you take your brother's arm?'

What followed then was a small indiscretion, but it was noticed. By the correct protocol Kodor should have offered his right arm to his wife as he led her forward, signifying her precedence over Nanta. Instead, he gave her his left. Pola stiffened as sharply as if someone had slapped her face, and for a moment it seemed that she would spurn him and walk away.

But Pola was not the kind to make a public scene. Her face tightened into a look of dignified indifference, and as Kodor proffered his right arm to Nanta she looked straight ahead and smiled another synthetic smile. Nanta could only accept Kodor's arm and go with them both. But as they passed the senior councillors, she saw Father Urss again. He was watching her still. His face was as cold as a glacier . . . and in his eyes was a dark and dangerous glint.

Twelve people in total sat down to dine in the winter hall. Nanta was surprised; from the wording of her invitation she had assumed that this would be a private function for the imperial family, reminiscent, perhaps, of the meals they had all taken together when Arctor was alive. The fact that it was not was a relief in one sense, for those occasions had usually been struggled through in an awkward and stagnant atmosphere, with little conversation and many long silences. It also gave her more scope for observing Kodor without making her interest too obvious. She could, however, have wished for better table companions. Three were high-ranking officials of the Exalted Council; old men with prim faces and dry minds, who had nothing to say to her that was of any possible interest. Four were aristocrats of the court, two men and two women with exaggerated manners and glib tongues; invited, Nanta surmised, as a matter of grace and favour. The party was completed by Exalted Father Urss and Grand Mother Beck.

Kodor and Pola sat side by side at the head of the great polished table, with their guests in strict order of precedence down its length. Nanta was placed immediately to Kodor's left, and as she took her seat she was dismayed to find herself directly opposite Father Urss. Urss bowed to her before lowering himself on to his chair, but the bow was perfunctory and his eyes held more than a hint of disdain. Already, she thought, there was a subtle but distinct difference in his attitude towards her. While she was Imperatrix he had treated her with punctilious deference, but now that she was a mere dowager her status had been diminished. Though on the surface Urss would doubtless behave as respectfully as ever, there was a new authority in his manner, a tacit implication that the balance of power had shifted in his favour.

Matters progressed well enough, if dully, as the meal began. For all their pretensions the four courtiers had robust appetites, and Beck more than kept pace with them. Urss ate fastidiously, Pola barely touched her dish, and Kodor seemed to prefer the wine to the food. In fact he was drinking a great deal, and by the time the third course was served the effects had started to show. The look in his eyes became darker and more introspective with every glass he drained, and as conversation progressed along its bland, careful lines he made less and less effort to hide his boredom. When addressed by Urss or one of the nearer councillors his replies were terse, and on the few occasions when Pola spoke to him he did not answer her at all.

The one person he did wish to talk to was Nanta. Time and again he claimed her attention, and as the wine did its work the contrast between his interest in her and in the rest of the party became all too conspicuous. He smiled into her eyes, he told her stories and anecdotes; twice he even reached across the table to touch her hand. Nanta was acutely aware that both Pola and Father Urss were watching intently. Urss's eyes, when she ventured briefly to glance at him, were wrathful, while Pola only glared steadily and silently at her husband's display, her mouth narrowed to a thin, tight and painful line. Nanta was horribly embarrassed – and in her turn as angry as Urss and Pola. Kodor was manipulating her, using her as a pawn in some game of his own devising which seemed deliberately calculated to humiliate Pola. Nanta, too, felt humiliated. She tried to rebuff Kodor's attentions, withdrawing her hand from his reach and attempting to strike up a meaningless conversation with the councillor on her left. Kodor, though, would have none of it. He wanted to monopolise her and he would not brook rejection. Nanta desperately wished that she could get up and walk away from the table, leave the hall and let him find another target for his perverse amusement. But Kodor was the Imperator, and to snub him or give offence to him in any way was unthinkable; she had no choice but to stay and suffer this for as long as it pleased him to continue.

To her astonishment, it was Pola who eventually came to her rescue. One of the women courtiers had just asked Kodor a simpering and facile question, and for courtesy's sake he felt obliged to reply. Pola took her opportunity. She smiled at Nanta – outwardly it was quite convincing – and said in her clear contralto:

'Sister, I believe we owe you an apology.'

Kodor stopped in mid-sentence and looked at Pola in surprise. Father Urss was also alerted; he turned a surreptitious gaze on the Imperatrix, and Nanta saw his eyes light with a glint of sudden and considerable interest. She herself was nonplussed, and said, 'An apology . . . ?'

'Yes.' Pola smiled again. She seemed to find it easier this time, as though her confidence was growing. 'We have seen nothing at all of you since . . . well, since the tragedy, and now that we are all together we've talked only of trivial things. That must be hard for you. You have so much on your mind at present, not least the thought of what you might wish to do once the funeral and the mourning are over. I'm sure I speak for everyone here when I say that we want to help you in any way we can.'

There was a small silence. Kodor was openly staring at his wife now, and Father Urss regarded her with a look of frank admiration. Pola, it seemed, was more resourceful than appearances had led him to believe. By assuming the role – and Urss knew perfectly well that it *was* just a role – of the concerned and loving sister-in-law, she had neatly outmanoeuvred Kodor and

223

plucked control of the situation from his hands. Duke Arec's daughter indeed, Urss thought; but with an added subtlety that Arec couldn't have comprehended, let alone matched. Pola had learned a great deal since she came to Vyskir.

All eyes were on Nanta now, waiting for her to reply. Nanta knew as well as anyone that Pola's show was just that and nothing more, and she chose her words carefully.

'I'm very grateful to you, sister,' she said, 'Though truthfully I've not thought greatly about what I shall do.'

'Naturally,' said Pola, feigning sympathy. 'You must still be very distressed. I understand.'

Kodor opened his mouth as though to say something but changed his mind. Nanta fingered the stem of her wine glass and glanced at him before her gaze returned to Pola. 'It is, of course, for you and the Imperator to make the final decision,' she continued. 'I don't even know what the choices will be.'

'You've not been told?' Pola's surprise seemed genuine.

Nanta smiled thinly. 'No.'

Kodor did speak then, leaning back in his chair and giving Father Urss a look of undisguised and almost gleeful dislike. 'Someone has been remiss, it seems,' he said. 'Eh, Father?'

Urss was unmoved. 'The Council judged, sire, that the Dowager would need time to recover from her bereavement before we troubled her with such considerations.'

'Did it. Well, perhaps the Council was wrong. At very least it would have been a courtesy to approach my sister on the matter, rather than make judgements without reference to her.'

'I'm sure Father Urss acted only out of respect for Nanta's feelings, husband,' Pola said firmly. She smiled at him. 'As you or I would have done. Isn't that so, Father?'

Urss bowed his head. 'Of course, madam. But now that you have so generously raised the subject, then this might be an opportune moment to explain the possible options to Her Grace the Dowager, so that she may weigh them at her leisure.'

Pola had made an ally. She knew it, so did Kodor, and so did Nanta. For Father Urss it was an unexpected and very welcome development, but he had the skill and acumen to disguise his satisfaction as he made a second bow, to Kodor this time, and added, 'With Your Majesty's gracious permission, of course.'

It was obvious that Kodor did not want to give his permission; but he was cornered. With a careless shrug he said, 'If it pleases my wife to help –' the word had a sour sting – 'so be it.'

'Thank you, sire.' The councillors were attending closely now, and lower down the table Grand Mother Beck's chilly eyes had lit with new interest. Urss turned to Nanta.

'Madam, there are a number of choices open to you. As Imperatrix Dowager you will receive a stipend – a pension, as it were – to ensure that you may live comfortably for the natural span of your life. But as to *where* you will live—'

Kodor interrupted. 'Nanta will continue to live here in the palace. It is her home now.'

Urss inclined his head. 'As you say, sire, it is her home. However, the Exalted Council feels that—'

'I'm not interested in what the Exalted Council does or doesn't feel. *I* wish Nanta to remain here.'

Pola coughed delicately. 'We both wish it, of course, Kodor. But surely it's for Nanta to say what *she* wishes?'

Again she had outdone him, and before Kodor could find an answer Urss pounced on the opening she had provided. 'And I'm sure that Her Grace would like to know *all* the alternatives before she arrives at a decision,' he said, and turned with icy courtesy to Nanta. 'By your leave?'

Nanta's face had tensed. There was a feeling rising in her, forming out of nowhere and nothing, flaring into a peculiar, absolute certainty. But certainty of what? She did not know. She could not grasp it.

Urss was waiting for a reply. She nodded distractedly, hardly aware of what she was doing, and he bowed with unctuous gratitude. 'Thank you, Your Grace. So, then.' He leaned forward. 'To begin with, the prospect of your re-marrying is quite out of the question. The widow of the Imperator must be above all possible—'

The certainty in Nanta's mind suddenly and sharply focused and she said, 'I have no wish to re-marry. None whatever.'

Urss's look became pitying, and faintly patronising. 'In these early days of your grief it's natural that you should feel as you do. However, you are young, and we must take great care that—'

'No, Father Urss.' She cut across him again, startled to hear the hard edge in her own voice. 'I do not and will not wish it; not now, nor at any time in the future. Do I make myself clear?'

Urss was taken aback – and so was Nanta. She didn't understand why or how she could be so vehement; the words had simply come and she had uttered them without pausing to consider. *Not now, nor at any time in the future.* A certainty. An absolute. But *why* was she so sure?

And an inner voice whispered: *Because a part of you knows that it will never be possible.*

She gave a small gasp and put a hand to her temple as a wave of dizziness suddenly flowed through her. Kodor was instantly on his feet, moving to her side, reaching out; Urss stood up hastily, and Mother Beck and two of the servants also came hurrying. But the giddiness was passing, leaving only a faint, residual nausea, and Nanta waved all her would-be helpers back.

'No,' she said, 'no – leave me. It was a moment's light-headedness, nothing more.'

'Take some wine,' Kodor urged. 'Let me refill your glass—'

'No,' Nanta repeated more emphatically. '*Please.* Just let me sit quietly for a few moments.'

'Would you prefer to return to your suite?' Pola asked with apparent concern. 'I'm sure no one will take it amiss if you retire.' She glanced at Kodor. 'Certainly *I* shall not.'

He noted the faint emphasis and its meaning, and shot her a glare that Urss didn't fail to notice. 'Nanta shall do whatever she pleases,' Kodor retorted, and turned his attention to her again. 'Come, Nanta. Are you better now?'

Nanta opened her mouth to say that she was – and the words froze in her throat. Across the hall, standing between the table and the door, was a frost sprite.

'Nnh . . .' She half choked, pushing Kodor's ministering hand away, and her chair squealed over the marble floor as she scraped it back and scrambled chaotically to her feet. She stared at the sprite, mesmerised, and everyone turned anxiously to see what had hypnotised her.

Then turned back again, their faces blankly bewildered.

'Sister?' Pola said. 'Whatever's amiss?'

They couldn't see it, Nanta realised. To their eyes there was nothing there; nothing but the empty floor. Yet the sprite still stood, still gazed. It was *real*. She wasn't dreaming or hallucinating.

Then the creature raised one hand before its own face, palm outward, fingers splayed. It shook its head, a warning, a message that Nanta remembered from the fragments of an old dream. *Say nothing; tell no one*.

Nanta was shaking. She tried to stop the reaction, tightening her muscles, summoning her will. Through teeth clenched with effort she said:

'I . . . am . . . very tired.' Thank the Lady, the words were coming more easily now. 'If my . . . my brother and sister permit it, I think I would prefer to return to my . . .'

She did not finish. The rush of giddy darkness came so fast that there was no time to prepare for its onslaught. Nanta gasped on a sharp, indrawn note. Then her eyes rolled up in their sockets and she slumped forward, scattering her glass, knife and plate across the table, in a dead faint.

* * *

Grand Mother Beck sidled up to Urss as the sobered company watched two servants laying Nanta on a litter, ready to carry her out of the winter hall. The meal had been abandoned and the footmen were quietly and efficiently clearing the half-finished dishes. Kodor had ordered apple brandy to be brought, and Beck sipped from the glass she held in her hand before saying in an undertone:

'The Dowager seems a little prone to these fainting fits. I wonder what brought this one on?'

Urss did not reply immediately. He was pondering, and in particular he was keeping a close eye on Kodor, who, ignoring the guests, seemed bent on accompanying the servants to Nanta's apartments. Pola still stood by her place at the head of the table. She too was watching Kodor; not, now, with the mask of concern she had shown to Nanta, but with a bland and skilful detachment that efficiently hid any trace of her feelings. Urss noted her manner and added Kodor's present indiscretion to the mental list of others that he had already made tonight. The wine had had its part to play, certainly, but there was no doubting the fact that Kodor was taking less and less trouble to hide his infatuation with his sister-in-law. No one at the court was actually *talking* about it yet; but it would not be long before the whispers and rumours began.

'The Imperator,' he said to Beck, in tones as low as hers, 'is going to cause us a great deal of trouble, unless we do something, soon, to prevent it.'

Beck's shrewd eyes scanned his face. Several days ago Urss had summoned her to his office, and had told her of his experience in the Seminary chapel. She, like him, had no doubt that the 'fair child' referred to in the revelation was Nanta; and now she saw and understood what had been meant.

'An affair . . .' She mulled the thought over. 'Do you think it's possible, Father? Do you think the Imperator would really be so foolish?'

'People in the throes of a passionate fixation are invariably foolish,' Urss replied. 'The Imperator is also an obstinate and arrogant young man, and in my opinion his new powers are beginning to go to his head. Something must be done, Beck. And quickly.'

Beck nodded. 'Duke Arec will soon be arriving for the funeral. If he should see the way the wind blows—'

'Precisely. That must be prevented at all costs.' Urss glanced down at her. 'I presume the Imperatrix isn't yet with child?'

Beck shook her head. 'I understand from her senior lady-in-waiting that her menses began again this morning.'

'Mmm. That is not satisfactory. I'll have the imperial physician examine her, to see where the problem lies.'

'I suspect,' said Beck delicately, 'that it lies more in the Imperator's reluctance than in any failing on the Imperatrix's part.'

She saw that that hadn't occurred to Urss, and suppressed a cynical smile. For all his worldly knowledge and political skills, Urss was like a man in an ivory tower; too lofty to take the basic realities into account.

The litter was being borne out of the hall now, and Kodor was going with it. Pola made as if to start after them, then abruptly checked herself and returned to the table, where she sat down. Her face still gave nothing away.

Beck had another sip of brandy. 'Under ordinary circumstances, the Imperator could have had his dalliance and, provided it was discreet, no harm would be done. It's been common enough practice in the past. Unfortunately, though, we have Duke Arec and the alliance to consider.'

'You echo my own thoughts,' said Urss. The small hiatus as they watched the litter had given him time to collect his thoughts, and as the doors closed he added, 'Beck, I want you to ensure that the Dowager has as little contact with the Imperator as possible until the funeral takes place.'

'Of course, Father.' Beck bowed slightly.

'And I also wish to see you in more private circumstances. Come to my office tomorrow morning, after First Obligation. We will discuss the Dowager's options, I think, and decide which one she should take.'

Beck nodded. 'My own choice would be to put her into a sanctum,' she said. 'It's perfectly acceptable for a widow to enter religious life, and it will look well with the populace. They'll remember her with sympathy and affection, and she will be out of the Imperator's reach.'

'I'm inclined to the same view. However, there is one flaw. We must first persuade her to agree.'

Beck chewed her lower lip thoughtfully. 'I think she can be persuaded.'

'I'm not so sure. For all her meekness, there's a defiant streak in her; you may not have witnessed it, but I have.'

'Then she must be coerced,' said Beck firmly.

'Indeed. Or, failing that, more drastic measures will have to be taken.'

There was a brief silence. Then Beck probed cautiously: 'Drastic, Father . . . ? I believe I don't quite comprehend.'

Urss looked down at her. 'I believe, Beck, that you do. But this is not the time or the place for any further word on the subject. Allow me to refill your glass; I see that it's empty again. And then I suggest that we exchange our pleasantries with the Imperatrix, and put this little dilemma from our minds until tomorrow.'

Chapter XVI

Six days before the funeral, the imperial physician died, 'of natural causes', in his bed.

Father Urss received the news with a show of regret that convinced everyone but the very few, such as Grand Mother Beck, who knew the truth. It was a relief to be rid of the man, and a successor was appointed so smoothly and quickly that the transition was barely noticed.

The physician's removal did give rise to one small problem, but with Beck's help – and Marine as her unwitting agency – Urss believed he had solved it. After a great deal of deliberation he had reluctantly come to the conclusion that the 'drastic measures' he had spoken of to Beck were likely to be needed where Nanta was concerned. Despite their best efforts it had proved impossible to keep Nanta and Kodor apart; the lengthy rehearsals for the funeral ceremony demanded regular meetings between them, and it soon became obvious that Kodor had no intention of abandoning his overtures to his sister-in-law. To give her credit, Nanta did not respond as Kodor wanted; if anything she seemed as anxious as Urss to keep a distance between them. But with Duke Arec now ensconced in the palace the situation was looking highly dangerous. One way or another, Urss decided, the Dowager must be removed, and there were only two safe options. A sanctum – or death.

Urss had returned to the Seminary chapel on several occasions, praying for guidance and hoping that the God might see fit to grant him a second revelation. Nothing direct had happened, but he had begun to have strange dreams. Urss rarely remembered his dreams, and knew at once that this could only be the God's answer. But the message the dreams brought was enigmatic; strange words, stranger references and, underlying all, an atmosphere of simmering rage that brought Urss awake in a sweat as the dreams ended. Only one thread was clearly repeated time and time again. *Beware of the fair child. Take away the fair child.* And, in the most recent and most compelling dream of all: *Eliminate the fair child.*

Urss did not tell Beck about that dream. Beck argued strongly for the option of sending Nanta to a sanctum. She had no particular scruples about the other choice, but reasoned that three deaths in fewer months among the imperial family would give rise to unwanted talk and speculation. It was all well and good to proclaim that the Corolla Lights had presaged these great upheavals, she pointed out, but the Corolla Lights had not appeared since the night of Osiv's death, and it would be harder to use them as an excuse this time. Urss was forced to agree with her; or at least to allow her time to, as she put it, 'persuade the Dowager to see reason'. He granted her four days. But if by then Nanta had not complied with their wishes, the other remedy must be applied.

Beck began the process by enlisting Marine's help. In a friendly interview in her study she confided the problem of Kodor's interest in Nanta and the resultant threat to the Sekolian alliance. Marine's response was gratifying; as Beck had expected, she favoured the idea of a sanctum – doubtless she was delighted by the prospect of welcoming another lost soul into the fold, Beck thought cynically – and offered at once to do her utmost to gain Nanta's acquiescence. Certain that Marine could succeed if anyone could, Beck accepted her offer, and dismissed her.

Outside Beck's office, Marine closed her eyes momentarily and offered silent thanks to the Lady. She had not lied to Beck;

she *did* believe that a sanctum was the best place for Nanta. Or rather, the safest. That was the crux of it, and the thing that no power in the world could have coerced her to tell her senior. For Marine's own doubts had been growing over the past few days. There was nothing she could put her finger on; it was simply an instinct – but a peculiarly strong one – that Nanta's challenging question to her, on the morning after Osiv's death, had been valid. Frost sprites did not lie. And now there was the added ingredient of the Imperator's determined interest in Nanta, as Beck had just detailed. *Why* that? Beck had drawn the obvious conclusion, but Marine saw another possibility – that Kodor had an inkling of Nanta's own suspicions. If Osiv *had* been murdered, and Kodor *had* been involved in the deed, then Nanta's continuing presence in the court was a threat to him. To Marine, the motive behind Kodor's attentiveness to Nanta was all too obvious. He was looking for confirmation, one indiscreet word to tell him that she knew more than was good for her. And if he found what he sought, then Nanta's fate would be sealed.

Nanta *must* be persuaded to leave the Metropolis, Marine told herself desperately. She herself could go with her, perhaps even take her back to her own sanctum in the east, where she could be cared for and protected and kept far away from the court and its machinations. The alternative was unthinkable.

I have failed you before, Nanta, Marine thought. *But this time I will not. I will* not.

She turned and hurried away along the blue-carpeted corridor.

Marine's earnest campaign, however, was doomed to failure. Nanta was adamant: she would not consider the prospect of a sanctum, and nothing Marine or anyone else might say or do would ever persuade her. Her vehemence dismayed Marine; never before had she seen Nanta take such a stance, and it revealed an unimagined depth of strength and determination. But if it came to the worst, neither strength nor determination would be enough, and after two days of wrangling and pleading Marine realised that her only hope was to tell Nanta the whole truth. She had avoided that, half from fear and half from a desire to shield Nanta from the cruelty of it; but Nanta's obstinacy left her with no choice. She must be told that her life was at stake. That, Marine was certain, would make the difference.

She was wrong. As she haltingly revealed the full tale, Nanta listened with a strange, intent alertness, her head slightly tilted, her expression quizzical – and her eyes growing dark with anger. When Marine finished, there was silence for some moments. Then:

'Marine. Why did you not tell me this before?'

'How could I?' Marine said. 'The thought that the Imperator might wish you dead – or even that he could be responsible for your husband's death – how could I find the words?' She looked away, giving a small, self-deprecating laugh that held no humour whatever. 'I have always believed myself to be a strong, even a hard, woman. Now I am inclined to think that I'm merely a fool.'

'Not that, Marine.' Nanta was gazing thoughtfully at her; though her head was still averted Marine could feel the gaze, like something tangible. 'You, of all people, are not a fool. But perhaps I have been.'

'You?' Marine turned back to her. Nanta smiled.

'Yes. For not accepting what the frost sprites told me, immediately and without doubting. As you yourself have said more than once, they do not lie. I believe your suspicions, Marine; I think you're right. I am in danger.'

Relief swept through Marine. 'Then you'll leave the court?'

'No. I will not.'

The relief turned to cold crystal that seemed to freeze in Marine's stomach. 'But—' she began.

'I said, I will *not*. I'm grateful to you, Marine; more grateful than I can express.' Nanta paced slowly across the floor of her office. Her brocade skirt made a sound like frosted leaves, whispering and rustling, and for no rational reason it made Marine feel suddenly, deeply uneasy. Then Nanta stopped and turned to face her. She was not smiling now, but her eyes burned.

'I want him brought to justice,' she said.

Marine stared, appalled. Suddenly this was not the Nanta she had thought she knew; not a young girl, an innocent, but someone – some*thing* – else.

She whispered, 'To *justice*? But he is the Imperator!'

'I know. It makes no difference. If what we believe is true, and I think now we must both accept that it is, then I will not rest until that truth is revealed and he pays the penalty for what he has done.'

'Nanta,' Marine said desperately, 'You can't even think of it! It's *impossible*!'

'It isn't. It can be done. I will do it.' And in a dream there was a bier, and on the bier lay the Lady, and a voice was whispering: '*Vengeance*' . . . Marine knew nothing of that, nor ever would. But for four nights in succession now the dream had returned again, and Nanta had woken to find herself standing by Osiv's coffin. Now she knew why – and her resolve was set.

Marine tried. She argued, she beseeched, she even fell to her knees at one point and begged: but nothing made any difference. Nanta remained immovable, until finally, when Marine had exhausted every possible avenue, she reached out a hand, silencing the last frantic pleas.

'Don't be afraid, Marine. I'm not. The frost sprites gave me warning when I needed it before, and I know they'll do so again. They will protect me.' She smiled again, a smile that made Marine wonder if, at this moment, either of them was entirely sane. 'What more could I need?'

Marine dreaded Beck's summons for a report on her progress, but when it came after two days there was no credible excuse for ignoring it. She did her best to play down Nanta's refusal, and tried to at least hint that, with a little more time, the Dowager might be brought round; but she doubted that Beck would be fooled.

Beck listened without comment to what she had to say, and when it was done she nodded. Her expression was impossible to read; but then to Marine's surprise she said:

'So, you think that time is the key? Very well, Marine, I shall trust your judgement. Persevere for a while longer. After all, as Imperator Osiv's widow she can hardly bow out of public life before the funeral takes place, so we have a little more time yet.' She smiled comfortably. 'You've done very well. Continue the good work, my dear.'

Marine left, nonplussed but very relieved. And at her desk, Mother Beck wrote a note to Father Urss, asking that she might call on him as a matter of urgency.

Urss gave immediate permission, and within the hour Beck had her instructions. Again, Marine would be the conduit for what was to be done – but this time Marine would have no inkling whatever of the part she was destined to play. It was interesting, Beck reflected, that similar events so often happened in threes. There had of course already been three deaths; but Imperator Arctor had gone to his rest in the natural course of time, whereas Osiv and the physician had not. Poison in both cases; the first attributed to a virulent disease, the second, by a different concoction, to straightforward heart failure through overwork. Now, the third. This must be different again, to avoid any risk of questions. Not a sudden malady but a gradual decline, a sinking into weakness and frailty until the body could no longer support the spark of life; and thanks to her early training Beck knew exactly what to use. A certain herb, innocuous in occasional doses but not so when administered repeatedly over a period of time. One pinch each day, disguised in the Dowager's food, would see the process through to its eventual completion.

No pain, no side-effects; only the gentle slide towards death.

In a detached way Beck rather pitied the child. Under other circumstances she could have had great potential, and if she had not been so stubborn she might have been a decided asset to the Sisterhood in some symbolic role. A shame that that must now all be wasted, but there it was; there were more important considerations at stake than the survival of one young girl.

She returned to her office, and there chose a particular book from the shelves. She had not consulted this volume for a good while, as the traces of mildew on the cover showed, but now she took it to her favourite armchair by the fire and sat down to read. It did not take long to find and confirm what she wanted to know, and Beck put the book away again, satisfied. Then she rang for Sister Chaia.

'Ah, Chaia; come in, come in.' Beck beamed at her. 'I want you to run a little errand. Tell me; who is in charge of the Sanctum's infirmary at present?'

Chaia delved into her memory. 'That would be High Sister Ludia, Grand Mother. She qualified as an apothecary eleven years ago, and she—'

'Yes, yes; I'm sure she's very worthy in all respects,' Beck interrupted. 'Fetch her here, please, Chaia. Tell her that I have need of her services.'

When Kodor heard that the Dowager was unwell he went immediately to see her, only to be informed by a flustered Dorca that, if it pleased His Majesty, and with her most abject apologies, madam was sleeping now and the physician had advised in the *strongest* terms that rest was the surest and swiftest cure, and—

'It's all right, Dorca; I quite understand,' Kodor said, breaking gently into her anxious dissemblings. 'Just tell me; what's amiss with her? I trust it's not serious?'

Dorca's face relaxed into a look of profound relief. 'Oh, no, sire; not serious at all,' she assured him. 'Madam is simply fatigued, the physician says, in both mind and body. All the strain of these last days, and the grief, and all that she has been required to do—'

'Of course. Does she have all she needs?'

'Oh, yes, sire. Mother Marine attends constantly and does everything for her.'

'Does she, now?' Kodor's expression altered a little.

'Yes, sire.' Dorca noted the change, and made less effort to hide her pique. 'The Dowager seems to find Mother Marine's presence a great comfort.'

'Indeed. Well, when my sister wakes, kindly tell her that I came to enquire.' He made as if to go, then paused. 'Will she be fit enough to take her part in the funeral, do you think?'

Dorca's face clouded. 'Truly, Your Majesty, I have my doubts. It's only two days away now; and madam seems *so* frail. She says she will take part; but I fear for her strength in such an ordeal, I really do!'

'Then you must be listened to.' Kodor smiled at her. 'Don't worry, Dorca. I'll personally see that the Dowager is not obliged to do anything that might overtax her. If she misses the funeral, so be it. Her health is far more important.'

'But Father Urss will—'

'Father Urss,' Kodor reminded her gently, 'is not the Imperator.'

'No. No, Your Majesty, of course he is not! Thank you, sire – thank you, from my heart!'

Nanta was in fact awake when Dorca returned to the bed-chamber, and Marine was helping her to eat a bowl of soup. The new physician had ordered a special, invigorating diet for her, which Marine prepared in the palace kitchens, helped by a High Sister from the Sanctum who had been lent by Beck and was skilled in herbalism as well as cooking. Thus far the diet seemed to be doing little good, but the physician assured that time and patience would see a change in the right direction. Dorca and Marine watched with fond concern as Nanta struggled through most of the bowl's contents, then when she could take no more the tray was carried away and Dorca said firmly that she should sleep.

In the outer room, Dorca told Marine of Kodor's visit. Marine, too, was thankful to hear that Nanta would not be forced into attending the funeral; but her reasons went a little deeper than Dorca's. The funeral, like Arctor's, would involve a sequence of events and duties in which Nanta would be obliged to spend a great deal of time in the Imperator's company. Pola's presence notwithstanding, Kodor would have ample opportunity to probe, and in a distracted moment it would be all too easy for Nanta to make a mistake. In that sense this illness was an unexpected blessing, Marine thought. She hoped it would persist for just a few days more.

Nanta slept for much of the afternoon. When she woke, Marine was gone back to her duties; but Dorca told her that Kodor had called on her, and also gave her a box of sweets that had been delivered a short while later. With the sweets was a hand-written note, wishing Nanta a speedy recovery and signed by her 'loving brother and servant, Kodor'. Nanta consigned the note to the fire. But the sweets tempted her failing appetite and she shared some with Dorca before putting the box aside to be enjoyed tomorrow.

That evening, one of Nanta's ladies-in-waiting found her mistress doubled up in agony on the floor of her bathing room.

The lady-in-waiting's cries brought the other servants on duty running, and in the initial chaos while one woman went to rouse Dorca, another ran for Marine. Marine arrived in great haste to find both Dorca and the physician there before her, holding Nanta's head over a basin as she was violently sick again and again. The spasms seemed to be endless, but at long last they subsided and Nanta, barely conscious and moaning with shock and pain, was carried to her bed by Dorca and her ladies.

Marine grasped the physician's arm in a savage grip as they hurried after the women. 'What is it?' she demanded. 'What caused this?'

'I don't know, Mother.' The physician was younger than his predecessor, and earnestly dedicated; Marine saw from his face that he was as worried as she. 'Until I can examine Her Grace—'

'Then do so, and quickly!' Marine hovered like a bird of prey as the physician began to probe, checking Nanta's pulse, lifting her eyelids, pressing gently on her stomach. Nanta's moans had lapsed into the smaller sounds of laboured breathing; the physician finished what he was doing and reached for his scrip.

'What are you giving her?' Marine snapped.

He turned a surprised and compassionate gaze on her. 'A mild calmative, Mother, nothing more. It will lessen the pain she feels, and make her breathing easier.'

Marine subsided. In truth she didn't doubt either his competence or his intentions; but a sense of alarm was rampaging just below the surface of her mind, like a bird beating its wings in a cage. Something awry, something *wrong*. What was it? She didn't *know* . . .

At the physician's instruction Dorca was opening Nanta's mouth, and several drops from a phial were placed on her tongue. Within a few minutes the stertorous breaths grew quieter and less hectic, and Nanta's body began to relax. She was conscious, but her eyes were closed and her expression dull and weary.

The physician stepped back from the bed and looked from Marine to Dorca and back to Marine.

'I think,' he said, 'that it is still nothing more than sheer exhaustion. Her Grace has been under great strain, and her system is protesting against it. Has she been following the diet I prescribed?'

'Yes, sir,' said Dorca. 'Only she eats so *little* at the moment.'

'Well, you must try to persuade her to eat more. You have the list I made; keep strictly to it, and if need be give her the ingredients in liquid form. The soups, for example—'

'She had soup today,' Dorca told him. 'But she would not eat all of it, would she, Mother Marine?'

'No,' said Marine. She was looking around the room, her eyes alert, searching . . .

'And the Imperator himself sent her a box of sweets. She did take some of those.'

No one noticed Marine's sudden tension at that remark. The physician shook his head. 'It was most gracious of the Imperator, but unfortunately sweets will not help Her Grace's condition; her appetite is small and should be directed to more nutritious foods. Mother, if there is any of the soup left I suggest you see if you can coax her to take it. Then let her sleep the night through.' He gathered up his scrip. 'Send for me at once if there is any deterioration; otherwise I'll call again in the morning, after First Obligation.'

'Yes, sir.' Dorca glanced worriedly at Nanta. 'Poor madam . . .'

'Don't fear; she will soon be better.'

Marine escorted the physician to the door, and as she opened it for him she said, apparently casually:

'I wonder if the sweets might have upset the Dowager in some way.'

'It's quite possible,' the physician agreed. 'Rich confections and a delicate constitution are not a happy combination. Still, her body has rid itself of them, so I don't think we need anticipate any more trouble.' He made a small, courteous bow. 'Good night to you, Mother.'

'Good night.' Marine closed the door, stood staring at it for a few moments, then returned to the bedroom.

'Dorca.'

Dorca turned, surprised by Marine's sharp tone, and with an effort Marine modified it.

Louise Cooper

'Where are the sweets that the Imperator sent for Her Grace, please?'

'I put them on her dressing table, Mother. That box, there.'

Marine looked where she pointed. 'Ah, yes. The physician says that they're too rich for her and we should take them away. In fact, it's quite possible that they are what made her sick.'

'Oh!' Dorca was mortified. 'Of course! I should have *thought* of it; madam offered me several of them and they are so sumptuous – here, Mother, give them to me and I will put them somewhere out of Her Grace's sight!'

'It's all right,' said Marine. 'Stay here with Her Grace; I'll see to the sweets myself. And then I'll warm the rest of the soup on the fire. She shall have that. It will do her far more good.'

Bearing the box of sweets, she retreated to Nanta's dressing room. The fire needed making up; she saw to it, then placed the warming-trivet near the flames and set the soup pot to heat through.

So: sweets, was it? Sent in person by the Imperator, no doubt with avowals of his fondest affection and concern. What was *in* them? Marine took one out of the box, examined it carefully, then bit into it. It tasted of fruit and spice, highly honeyed and, to her taste, unpalatably sickly. But it was *only* sickliness. She could detect nothing dubious, nothing to suggest that the sweets were not as innocent as they appeared.

But then, Marine thought, if the sweets had been adulterated, would she know? She was not an apothecary; and besides, it was unlikely that all poisons had a detectable taste. The physician was the obvious man to ask, but that was out of the question.

However, there was High Sister Ludia . . .

Marine's interest quickened. Ludia was not only a herbalist but also a trained apothecary. And she was a quiet, self-contained woman, not the sort to indulge in speculation or gossip. Besides, Marine was her superior, and thus to be obeyed without question. Yes, Marine thought; she would ask Sister Ludia to make a more thorough examination of the sweets. A purpose would be easy enough to invent, and it need have nothing to do with either Nanta or the Imperator. In fact, Marine decided, she would seek out Ludia straight away.

A hiss from the pot on its trivet caught her attention then and she remembered the soup. It was beginning to simmer, and Marine drew the pot away from the heat. First things first; before going to Ludia she must see that Nanta had a little more nourishment and then was made comfortable for the night. Giving the soup a brisk stir, Marine poured a good helping into a bowl set ready. Dorca had left the tray; neatly Marine arranged spoon and napkin on it and placed the bowl in between. Then, balancing the tray in her hands, she rose to her feet and returned to the bedchamber.

Nanta was still awake, but drowsy, her eyes vague and her movements slow and not well co-ordinated. Marine sat down at her bedside and balanced the tray carefully on the covering.

'Here, my dear.' She smiled fondly at Nanta, dipping the spoon into the soup and holding it carefully out to her. 'Drink some more of this. It will do you good.'

High Sister Ludia had not expected her first visitor that evening, but the second was even more of a surprise. For Grand Mother Beck to call in person on a subordinate was highly unusual; her normal form was to summon others to her. But Beck, it appeared, was simply passing by on her way to the Sanctum chapel, and rather than trouble Mother Marine, who doubtless was very tired at present, thought to look in on Ludia and enquire after the Dowager's progress.

Beck expressed her sorrow at the news of the Dowager's relapse, then cast a detached eye over the work Ludia was doing and which she had interrupted.

'An experiment, High Sister?' she asked mildly.

'Oh – this, Grand Mother? Yes, of a kind. In fact it is for

Mother Marine.' Ludia indicated the box of sweets. 'She came to see me a little while ago and asked me to examine these for her.'

Beck picked up a sweet and examined it. 'Not Marine's taste at all, I would have thought.' She made to nibble the sweet, and Ludia said hurriedly:

'Grand Mother, I think it would be better not to eat them!'

'Oh?' Beck's hand paused halfway to her mouth. 'Why?'

'Well . . .' Marine had said that the examination was a private matter – but of course no Sisters or Mothers had secrets from Grand Mother Beck. Ludia smiled a little sheepishly. 'Mother Marine thinks they might have been adulterated. That is why she brought them to me; to find out what, if anything, is wrong with them.'

'Well, well.' Beck put the sweet back in the box. 'And what have you discovered?'

'Nothing as yet, Grand Mother. In truth I don't believe there is anything amiss. But Mother Marine was a little concerned.'

'I see. I wonder who gave them to her?' Beck chuckled, but her eyes were like flint. 'Someone, I imagine, who does not know her very well.'

'I had the impression that they were not given to her but to someone else,' said Ludia innocently. 'Though she didn't say who.'

'Or who the giver was?'

'No, Grand Mother.'

'Mmm. Well, if they're innocuous, as you surmise, I'm sure she will be very grateful to know it, High Sister. I will leave you to your analysis and bid you good night.'

'Thank you, Grand Mother. Good night.'

Beck had had no intention of wasting her time at the chapel; the excuse had merely been a ruse to allay Ludia's suspicions. She had come to gain information – and she went away with a good deal more than she had anticipated.

Sweets. It took little ingenuity to guess how such lavish confections had come into Marine's hands. A gift from the Imperator to his beloved sister; and tonight Nanta had been stricken with sickness. Beck knew perfectly well what the real cause of the sickness had been; and knew that the sweets were utterly harmless . . . but that was not the point. This development was a clear indication that Marine suspected something. So far, she was looking in completely the wrong place. But when that avenue proved fruitless, it could not be long before she began to look in the right one.

Beck pondered for a few moments, then made a decision. It was a breach of propriety to interrupt Father Urss without a prior appointment, but for once propriety could be damned. This was too urgent to wait for requests and replies. She needed to see him *now*.

With a swish of her skirt she set off at a rapid walk towards the Seminary.

While behind her, unnoticed, a patch of air shimmered and an ice-cold breath skimmed through the corridor. The frost sprite did not fully materialise. But, briefly, a pair of strange eyes watched Mother Beck's hurried departure, and the mind behind the eyes registered and considered what it had learned. Then the shimmer faded and was gone, and nothing more disturbed the stillness.

Chapter XVII

There was no reply to Beck's knocking at the outer door of Urss's quarters. In one sense Beck was relieved, for it must mean that Urss had dismissed his secretary for the night, which was all to the good. But if Urss himself was not there, finding him might be difficult.

She opened the door and went in.

The outer room was unoccupied and unlit. Beck looked around – and saw a thin bar of illumination under an inner door. His office . . . relief rising, she crossed the room and rapped sharply.

'Father Urss!'

No reply. Beck nibbled her lower lip, hesitated a bare moment, then opened the door.

Father Urss was there. He was on his knees by the imposing desk, his hands clasped and his head bent as though in prayer. At the sound of the door latch his head came up in quick surprise, and Beck started as she saw his eyes. They were utterly blank, as though they were seeing something far, far beyond his immediate surroundings. His features were twisted into a tight, almost grotesque rictus, like a madman's grin. And behind him stood a tall, wavering shadow that had no visible source.

Then in the space of a heartbeat the shadow vanished and the bizarre expression fell away. Urss's eyes snapped back into focus, and he scrambled angrily to his feet.

'Beck! What is the meaning of this intrusion?'

Beck held her ground, though she was still recovering from the shock of what she had seen. 'I must ask your pardon, Father,' she said hurriedly. 'But this could not wait. It concerns the Dowager – and Mother Marine.'

A second furious reprimand was bitten off as Urss took in what she was saying. He stared at her, an extraordinary stare that she couldn't interpret. Then he replied, quite matter-of-factly:

'Yes. I know.'

'You *know* . . . ?' Beck was so astonished that the words came out as a thin squeak.

Urss smiled with a cold joy that quite unnerved her.

'The God,' he said, 'has seen fit to speak to me again.'

It had happened without any warning. Urss had been at his desk as usual when suddenly the room darkened, as though a great shadow had been cast over it, and he felt a tingling sensation that seemed to start at the core of his body and flow outwards, until he was shivering uncontrollably.

Then, as it had done in the chapel, the great, silent voice spoke his name.

Urss did not reveal the exact words that the God had spoken to him as he knelt in awed reverence. But the message, and the warning, were explicit. Urss's scheme, for which he had already been granted the God's supreme sanction, was in jeopardy. Someone was meddling, and was in danger of uncovering more of the truth than the God wished them to do. That someone was a woman, a religious, close to the fair child – and her meddling must be put an end to. *She* must be put an end to. And as the God's faithful and devoted servant, Urss knew the consequences of failure.

Urss had been repeating a fervent thanksgiving and pledge of his obedience when Beck entered the room. The sense of the God's presence had vanished instantly, shocking him back to earth and momentarily unhinging him. Now, though, as he listened to what Beck in her turn had to say, equilibrium was restored in full and his mind worked efficiently and rapidly.

'The simplest answer,' Beck said, 'is to remove Marine from the palace – indeed, remove her altogether from the Metropolis. I can send her back to her old Sanctum in the east.'

Urss shook his head. 'It's not good enough, Beck. The God has made his wishes clear: Mother Marine is to be dealt with *irrevocably.*' His gaze slid towards the window, though in the darkness outside nothing was visible. 'Even at a distance she could still stir trouble, and we would have the disadvantage of not being able to keep her under surveillance.'

'But *four* sudden deaths, Father . . . there's danger in that, surely?'

'Not necessarily. The Dowager's decline will be slow, re-member; and in Mother Marine's case, we need not even resort to an apparent illness or disease.' He turned to look at Beck again, his eyes steady and rigorous. 'She could, as you suggest, be sent back to her Sanctum; or at least on a journey; a reason will be easy enough to find. And meet with an accident on the road. At this time of year, such a thing is perfectly feasible.'

Beck considered the idea. Though she was careful to hide her feelings from Urss, she was more than a little uncomfortable at the prospect of conniving in Marine's murder. Marine was her protégée; and despite her piety and the tiresomely upright attitude that she had never learned to modify, Beck was in a sense fond of her. And whereas Osiv, Nanta and the late physician were virtual strangers, Marine was not. As far as could be permitted in a subordinate, she was a friend.

But a friend who could, if left unchecked, be the death of her. And the God had given an unequivocal command . . .

She met Urss's eyes with a cold candour that matched his own.

'Very well, Father,' she said. 'What do you wish me to do?'

* * *

'No, Mother, I could find nothing at all.' In the Sanctum infirmary High Sister Ludia stifled a yawn and smiled apologetically at Marine as she handed her the box of sweets. 'As far as I can tell, they are quite harmless. Although, of course, my knowledge is far from perfect. Perhaps the imperial physician could—'

'No,' Marine interrupted. 'I don't want to trouble him with something so trivial. Your word is good enough, High Sister; it was merely a whim on my part, something strange that I thought I detected in the taste. Thank you for your efforts. You've worked long into the night, and I'm grateful.'

She was turning to go when Ludia spoke again. Grand Mother Beck's visit had aroused her curiosity and, seeing no harm in asking, she said, 'Were the sweets a gift to you, Mother? They are very fine.'

'No,' said Marine pithily. 'They were not a gift to me. I wish you a good night, High Sister Ludia.'

She shut the door behind her with a force that rattled the jars and bottles on Ludia's shelves. Ludia stared at the door for a moment or two, then shook her head and, thankfully, prepared to retire for what was left of the night.

Marine's annoyance turned on herself as she hurried back towards the palace and Nanta's apartments. There had been no need to be sharp with Ludia; her curiosity was understandable and the question she asked had been innocent enough. But Marine was on edge. She had been certain in her own mind that Ludia *would* find something awry with the sweets, and the fact that she had not had thrown Marine's deductions out of kilter. Still, Ludia herself had admitted that her knowledge was flawed. And Kodor, as Imperator, had recourse to far more skilled help if he chose to use it. So her theory still held. But where to go from here?

She yawned, as Ludia had done, and shook her head

vigorously to clear the weariness that was creeping over her. The hour must be very late; it had been well past midnight when she left for the Sanctum. Dorca and the other women would doubtless be sound asleep by now, and Marine longed for her own bed. She would just look in on Nanta and make sure that all was well, then she would try to have a few hours' uninterrupted rest.

She had instructed Dorca to leave the outer door of the suite unlocked for her return, and on arriving she slipped quietly in and padded towards Nanta's bedchamber, trying not to look at the catafalque with the glowing candles like sentinels around it. Through to the unlit office, and across the plush carpet to the bedroom door. Marine turned the handle with great care, anxious not to wake Nanta, and looked in.

Two candles burned on a bedside table. By their small light Marine saw the hummock of Nanta's sleeping shape in the bed.

And she also saw the dark, unrecognisable human figure that was bending over her.

The gasp of alarm was out before she could stop it. The intruder heard, straightened with a jerk – and Marine found herself staring into the face of Kodor.

'Mother . . .' In a single chaotic moment Marine registered the fact that Kodor was holding a pillow in his hands; then he flung it aside and strode towards her. Horrified and frightened she backed rapidly away, back into the office – a flame flared and Kodor followed her, carrying one of the candles. In her first shock Marine fully expected him to attack her; but he only set the candle down on a nearby shelf and said ominously:

'What are you doing prowling around at this hour, Mother Marine?'

'I – I—' Suddenly Marine's fear turned to anger, and for the first time she utterly forgot his rank. 'I might ask you the same question!' she hissed back.

'I came to see my sister. Not that that's *any* concern of yours!'

'I think – sire – that it is my concern,' Marine countered.

'Nan . . . the Dowager is in my care, and it is not only my duty but also my desire to protect her!'

Kodor's lip curled. 'Thus far, your "protection" seems to be doing her little good. She looks as pale as a frost sprite and as weak as a kitten. In short, good Mother, her health seems to be worse now than it was when you began your ministrations. And I for one would like to know why!'

Marine's lips turned white, and two spots of hectic colour came to her cheeks. The sheer *cunning* of it – she had come upon him at his mischief, caught him in the act, and he had the cold-blooded boldness to turn the accusation against *her*—

'I believe, Your Majesty,' she said savagely, 'that you are better placed to answer that question than I am!' And with a dramatic gesture she held out the box of sweets.

Kodor stared at the box. The gift he had sent – what in the God's name was it doing in Marine's possession? He didn't comprehend; didn't know what the woman was talking about, and abruptly the dark mood that had been bedevilling him since early evening, and which had driven him to come here in the first place, started to rise again.

He and Pola had dined with Duke Arec tonight, and the occasion had not been pleasant. Sandwiched between his wife and her father, Kodor had felt like prey caught between two hunters; on the one side Arec's blustering arrogance as he outlined what he now expected from the Vyskiri-Sekolian alliance, as though he and not Kodor were the Imperator; on the other side Pola, with her long face and longer silences, toying with her food and radiating discomfiture heavily laced with nervousness. Kodor had wondered if she had said anything in private to her father about their marriage, but decided it was highly unlikely. For one thing, he doubted if Pola would dare, and for another, if she had complained at his treatment, he would have known about it from Arec by now.

He had managed to get rid of his father-in-law at last, but

then had followed an argument with Pola, who for once was not prepared to meekly buckle down under Kodor's ill-humour. Kodor had drunk too much again and she told him so, and told him, too, that she was shamed and humiliated by his attitude towards her, and wished she had never married him, never seen him, never heard of Vyskir. A good deal more followed, much of it too garbled for Kodor to take in after the wine, but one clear drift was Pola's bitter hatred of Nanta. 'Send her away!' she had said. 'What use is she here? She's no happier than I am, and there's no useful role for her – unless you want her as your mistress, of course! Is that it, Kodor? Is that your plan; to keep your precious "sister" as a concubine, because your wife isn't good enough for you?'

Kodor had almost hit her then. Afterwards, when he had calmed down a little, he was glad he had restrained himself; but in the fury of the moment it had been a close-run thing. As it was, he only looked at her with withering contempt, said: 'Damn you!' and stalked out of the room, while she screamed a last, corrosive salvo at him: 'If you're so enamoured of her, why didn't you marry her instead of me? I wish you had! I wish you'd married Nanta, and I had married your poor, idiot brother! Then *I* would be the widow now, and I could be rid of Vyskir and everyone and everything to do with it!'

The slam of the door had been her only answer, and for some time Kodor had heard her crying as he prepared for bed. At last the muffled sounds stopped and he surmised that she had gone to her own private room. He poured another glass of wine, then, deciding that he didn't want it after all, threw the full glass out of the window and got into bed. But he had not slept. His head ached, and his mind ached. He couldn't even take any pleasure in inventing cruelties that he would have liked to inflict on Duke Arec. And the day after tomorrow, he must stand beside his unwanted wife and put on a proper show for the farce of Osiv's funeral.

Two hours had passed before Kodor acknowledged that he was not going to be able to sleep. Once he did acknowledge it, the thing that had been lurking at the back of his mind started to creep out from its hiding place and take hold. He wanted to see Nanta. He *needed* to see her. Not just for his own reasons – though they were strong enough – but to reassure himself that she was recovering, that everything that could be done for her was being done. To be *certain*.

The effects of the wine were wearing off, and Kodor's reasonable side protested that this was not the hour for visiting anyone and he was being both selfish and disingenuous. But another side, more cunning, argued that the timing was ideal. Indeed, if he wanted to see Nanta privately – which he did – and was not about to be put off again by Dorca or one of the other twittering women, this was the *only* hour to call.

So he had given way to the temptation, and now he was here in Nanta's suite, and this hard-faced religious, who called herself Nanta's friend and whom Kodor had never trusted from the beginning, had walked in on him and seemed to be accusing him point-blank of some wrongdoing . . .

The feelings and the fury combined together in a rush, and Kodor said with a ferocity that far outstripped Marine's:

'Woman, you forget yourself! *Whom do you think you are addressing?*'

Where the courage came from, Marine would never know. It was, by all rational standards, an insane thing to do, and if she had paused to consider it, her nerve would surely have collapsed completely. But she did not consider. Instead, she stood her ground, the box still thrust towards him, and said:

'I think, *sire*, that I am addressing the man who wants to murder my poor Nanta!'

For perhaps three seconds there was absolute silence, as Kodor's face froze into a look of shock that was almost comical.

He stared fixedly at Marine. Then softly, incredulously, he whispered:

'You are completely insane . . .'

'No,' Marine said resolutely. 'I am not.' She thought he was about to lunge at her and stepped rapidly out of reach, though Kodor had not moved. 'You see, I know where these confections came from. They were from you. She ate some of them. And tonight she was taken violently ill – as though with poisoning.'

'*Poisoning?*' Kodor was utterly thunderstruck, but Marine was too agitated to notice or, if she had, to realise what his reaction implied. She rushed on, headlong and defiantly: 'Yes, *poisoning*! And now, tonight, I return after only a short absence, and I find you in her bedchamber, about to suffocate her!'

Of course, Kodor thought, *the pillow*— 'Nanta had pushed one of her pillows off the bed in her sleep, and I was merely picking it up from the floor!' he shouted. 'God blind me, you madwoman, can you truly believe that I would do anything, *anything*, to harm her? *I love her!*'

His last furious sentence made Marine recoil as if someone had thrown cold water in her face. 'You—'

'I love her!' Kodor repeated, as vehemently but with considerably less volume. 'Damn you, Mother Marine, I've said the words aloud at long last, and it has to be *you* who bears witness to them!' He paced across the room like a caged bear, then spun on his heel and pointed a threatening finger at her face. 'And if you ever repeat them to any living soul, then I swear I'll tear out your tongue with my own hands!'

Marine believed him. And in a miasma of shock and confusion she believed, too, that his declaration was genuine. Kodor was not Nanta's enemy. He was, instead, the most devoted friend she had. Suddenly all the whispers that were circulating in the palace, whispers which Marine had staunchly tried to ignore as being slanderous and wicked, slotted into place. The attentions Kodor paid to Nanta. The fact that the Imperatrix Pola was not yet with child. The rumours of friction, even bitterness, between her and the Imperator. And something that was no longer mere rumour but certain knowledge: that Kodor did not love his wife.

No, Marine thought; Kodor did not love his wife. Instead, he loved Nanta. Loved her so much that he would do anything for her. Do anything to have her.

Including killing his own brother . . .

Suddenly the strength went out of Marine's legs. She didn't know how, but she found herself sitting on a chair, with the box of sweets at her feet and Kodor standing over her.

'Mother Marine,' Kodor said, in a more controlled but still dangerous voice, 'I will ask you one question, and I will have a frank answer. Why did you think that I – or someone – was trying to poison Nanta?'

Marine's mouth trembled. What could she say? What could she *tell* him? The picture she had been forming had been turned so suddenly and violently on its head that she was still floundering, unable to grasp at what could and what could not safely be revealed.

'I thought . . .' she stammered, '. . . I believed that . . .'

'You said she was taken ill,' Kodor prompted curtly. 'How? What happened?'

Haltingly Marine told him. 'And what did the imperial physician have to say about it?' Kodor demanded when she finished. 'Did he share your suspicions?'

'I didn't tell him of them, sire,' Marine admitted miserably. 'He said . . . he diagnosed exhaustion.'

'Exhaustion. Just that?'

'Yes . . .'

'And how is Nanta now?'

'Better, sire. The spasms passed, then she took a little food and was able to settle to sleep.'

Kodor had seen the new physician for himself, when Pola had insisted yesterday on calling him in over some trivial feminine

255

complaint, and thought him competent and intelligent. If he judged Nanta's sickness to be caused by exhaustion, in all likelihood he was right. Kodor sighed. How this rainstorm in a puddle had come about he could not imagine, and he wanted to berate Marine for thinking, for having the *impudence* to think, that he wished Nanta harm. But on the credit side the woman had proved her own loyalty, however misguidedly, and that counted for far more.

'Mother Marine,' he said, 'you have been extremely foolish, but under the circumstances I do not hold that against you. So we'll say no more of this.'

'Thank you, sire.' Marine's hands trembled in her lap and he could not see her face.

'Now that you realise your error,' Kodor continued, 'I trust you will continue to care for the Dowager as you have done until now – but this time without letting your imagination run away with you.' Odd, he thought as a private aside; Marine did not strike him as the kind of woman who *had* an imagination . . . Appearances could be very deceptive.

'Go to bed now,' he added, 'and sleep this nonsense off.' Bending, he picked up the box of sweets. 'And when the Dowager wakes, you may safely give these back to her.'

Marine looked uncomfortable. 'Sire . . . the physician *did* say that she needs more nutritious foods, to build up her strength . . .' she ventured.

'Oh, he did, did he? Well, I suppose we should bow to his superior wisdom. Give them to Dorca, then.' A faint, sly smile touched his mouth. 'Though I wouldn't mind wagering that she's already sampled one or two when no one else was looking.'

Marine started as she recalled something Dorca had said to her. *Madam offered me several of them and they are so sumptuous* . . . Dorca had eaten the sweets and suffered no ill-effects. *Oh, Marine*, she admonished herself, *you have been such a fool!*

But perhaps not entirely a fool. For tonight, she had come just a little closer to the *real* truth about Kodor...

She curtseyed deeply, a tacit apology as well as the proper obeisance, and Kodor bade her good night. As he made his way through the outer room, he noticed that someone had left a tray on a side table near the door. The tray was piled with used dishes: a plate, a bowl, two spoons, a cup, and a pot that, when he sniffed it, proved to contain soup. Annoyance flicked through Kodor's mind. Nanta's servants were becoming lax and lazy – to leave this here was disgraceful. There was a *coffin* in this room – did they want Nanta's food to be tainted by the growing smell of corruption? He thought of hammering on the door that led to the servants' quarters and dragging them out here in their nightclothes to put matters to rights; but the noise of his temper might wake Nanta. He would deal with it himself.

The thought of what anyone who saw him would think of their Imperator carrying a tray of crockery through the palace corridors made Kodor smile. But at this hour there was no one to see. The soup would not be fit for Nanta now, so he made a detour to the royal kennels, where he gave the pot's contents to a small hound, a favourite of his, which came wagging and snuffling to greet him. Leaving the dog lapping appreciatively, Kodor deposited the tray in a corridor leading to the kitchens, and returned to his own rooms. Pola, presumably, was asleep; no light showed under her door and no sound came from within the room. Not even bothering to take off his clothes, Kodor flung himself into his own bed, and closed his eyes.

One of the grooms found the dog at dawn, and reported immediately to the kennel-master.

'Dead?' the master repeated perplexedly.

'And colder than stone, sir. It must have breathed its last some while ago; and yet there's not a mark on it, so it can't be that it was savaged by any of the others.'

The master scratched his head. The dog had been quite a young animal, so the usual cause of a failing heart was unlikely. Still, if there was nothing to show, it must have been a natural death.

'There are traces of slavering, sir,' the groom said. 'But nothing else. No blood.'

'Ah, well. There's nothing we can do, so there's little point speculating. Probably the cold got it; it was bitter last night. You'd best burn the carcass, though, just in case of infection.' He sighed. 'It was one of the Imperator's favourites, too. He looks his dogs over, most mornings; when he comes today I'll tell him.'

'You don't want me to send word, sir?'

'No, no. It's not urgent, after all. Not really important at all.'

Chapter XVIII

Marine had had no more than three hours' sleep when she was woken by a vague and drowsy lady-in-waiting, who informed her huffily that there was someone to see her and they refused to be put off until a more civilised hour.

In the outer office Marine found Sister Chaia, Beck's messenger, waiting.

'I'm sorry for the disturbance, Mother Marine,' Chaia said, 'but Grand Mother wants to see you at once.'

Marine knew Beck's habits and was surprised and a little worried to receive such a summons at this time of day. She dressed hastily, and followed Chaia back to the Sanctum in the early daylight.

Beck was at her desk, and as the two women came in she looked up. 'Ah, Marine.' Her face was sombre. 'Sit down. I'm afraid I have some bad news.'

'Bad news, Grand Mother?' Marine blanched, wondering what it could be.

'Yes. I've just received a letter from the EsDorikye estate.'

Nanta's family . . . 'What has happened?' Marine asked anxiously.

Beck sighed. 'There's no point in trying to put it gently, I suppose; sadness is sadness however it's disguised. The Dowager's mother has died.'

'Karetta . . . ?' Marine was stunned. 'But – she was young – no more than fifty-five! And in the peak of health . . .'

259

'I know. It was very sudden; a storm of blood to the brain. I gather these things can strike at any age and can never be predicted . . . Her family are in great distress—'

'Of course!' *And poor Nanta*, Marine thought. *All she has had to suffer, and now this.*

'—and they naturally wish us to break the news to the Dowager. Or rather, they say, to the Imperatrix.'

'Oh,' said Marine uneasily. 'Then they don't yet know?'

'It would seem not. A letter was sent, of course, but there has been no reply to it, and I suspect that it had not reached them before this new tragedy happened.' Beck gave another, deeper sigh. 'One blow upon another . . . we must handle this with great delicacy, Marine; which is why I have sent for you.'

'You wish me to tell the Dowager?'

'No.' Beck steepled her fingers. 'I've already spoken to the imperial physician, and he feels that in the Dowager's present state of health it is advisable to keep the news from her for a while. The shock, he says, might cause a serious relapse.'

Marine nodded.

'However,' Beck continued, 'we must in all decency respond at once to the EsDorikyes. I want you to go to them, Marine.'

'To . . . travel to the estate?' Marine was appalled. 'But the roads at this time of year—'

'Are passable to a sleigh with a good dog team. You'll get there as quickly as any letter; and in circumstances like these a letter, anyway, is not enough. Someone must go in person, to explain the situation at the palace and to give them comfort. And you are family. You're the only possible choice.'

Marine shut her eyes briefly. Beck knew how much she hated travelling; the sickness, the fear of vast spaces – but she was right. Marine was family. It was her responsibility and her duty to go.

She opened her eyes again and said weakly, 'Yes, Grand

Mother, I understand and of course I shall obey.' A pause. 'When do you want me to leave?'

'A sleigh has already been ordered for one hour before noon. That should give you ample time to pack.' Beck smiled a mixture of sympathy and reassurance. 'You will have an armed escort, naturally; and the sleigh driver is one of the most skilled in the Metropolis. I'm sorry to have to burden you with this, Marine. But you see that it must be done.'

'Yes, Grand Mother.'

'Good; then all is arranged. Give my regards and condolences to the family when you arrive. And tell them that both Father Urss and I will say prayers commending Karetta's soul to the God's care. I'm sure that will be a comfort to them.'

Marine rose. Her legs felt weak. 'Yes, Grand Mother,' she said again.

'And remember, not a word or even a hint to the Dowager.'

Marine nodded. 'Of course, Grand Mother. I'll do exactly as you say.'

'That,' said Beck, 'is why I have such faith in you.'

At about the time that Marine, dazed and dejected, began her packing, the Imperator was in the palace's kennel courtyard, speaking with the kennel-master.

The dog's carcass had already been burned; but Kodor did not need to see it in order to work out how it had died. The empty bowl told its own story; the bowl into which he, in a misplaced act of indulgence, had poured the remains of Nanta's soup.

So Mother Marine was right. Poison. Not enough to kill a human being, at least not at once; but immediately lethal to a smaller metabolism such as a dog's. Kodor even believed he knew what had been used, and it fitted perfectly with Nanta's declining health over the past few days.

But *who*? That was the question he couldn't answer with certainty. Dorca in one of her chattering moments had told him that Marine personally supervised the preparation of all Nanta's meals; but if Marine was the culprit she would hardly draw anyone's attention to the suspicion that Nanta was being poisoned, as she had done last night. No; there was another agency behind this, and Marine was an unwitting pawn. And Kodor's mind kept ranging back to Father Urss . . .

The kennel-master was apologising wretchedly and profusely for the hound's death; abruptly Kodor cut off his flow of words with an impatient gesture and said, 'Enough! What's done is done, and I hold no one to blame. Go back to your duties – the matter is closed.'

Gratefully the man bowed his way out of the Imperator's presence, and for a minute or two Kodor stood alone in the courtyard, careless of the snow falling densely and heavily on him. Then he turned abruptly and strode towards the door that led back into the palace.

First, he would find Marine. From her he would glean what information he could; clues that she did not even realise were clues. His second move would depend on what she told him. Whether or not he would entrust her with what he knew was another matter; he had no doubt, now, that Marine and he were fighting the same battle, but he did not know her well enough to judge her reliability under pressure. For if Father Urss was behind this, it would take someone a good deal stronger than a mere religious Mother to stand against him.

Urss. Kodor repeated the priest's name to himself, silently and with increasing venom, as he walked. It was easy to see his motive; and he was, of course, already an experienced player in the game of political murder. Tomorrow's funeral bore witness to that; but this time Kodor could not hope to deceive Urss as he had done in Osiv's case, for a pretence that he had suddenly turned against Nanta simply wasn't credible. Another way must be found, then; possibly not using Urss himself but through one of his accomplices. Who were they this time? The old imperial physician was dead and the new one an unlikely candidate. Though Urss had never confirmed it, Kodor had deduced that Grand Mother Beck was a party to the plot against Osiv, so it followed logically that she was involved again now. Who else? He could think of no one in Nanta's personal entourage; they were either too vapid and thus unreliable, or, like Dorca, too fundamentally decent.

Duke Arec was here, of course. Arec was a distinct possibility; he must have known about the plan for Osiv, even if he had taken no part in it.

And then there was Pola . . .

Kodor stopped in mid-stride as the ugly speculation slid into place. Pola. She had more reason than anyone to want Nanta removed, for Nanta was the worm in her apple, the woman who – in her thinking – had stolen Kodor's affection and usurped what should have been her own place in his heart. The fact that Kodor had never loved Pola made no difference: Nanta was the focus, the rival, the dissonant note in Pola's personal symphony. If she died, Pola would shed no tears. Possibly, she was even foolish enough to believe that with Nanta out of the way, Kodor would at last turn in love to her.

Kodor looked down at his hands and saw that they were shaking. It was a reaction, nothing more; and when he exerted his will on it he was surprised by how swiftly it stopped. He did not want to believe that Pola was involved in this. His animosity towards her stemmed only from the fact that he had been forced into a marriage with her when his heart was committed else-where. In candid moments he admitted that that was not her fault, and he did not think that her nature ran to cold-blooded murder.

Unless, of course, she was a great deal more cunning than he had ever realised . . .

Well, he thought, time and some investigation would tell. First things first: find Marine, talk to her. Only then would he be in a position to decide how to progress.

He walked on towards the imperial suite.

'I'm so sorry, Your Majesty, but Mother Marine isn't here.' Dorca looked up at Kodor, and her expression became uneasy as she saw, or at least sensed, something of his mood. 'She's gone to the Sanctum, sire, to pack and then to pray for a while in the chapel before she departs.'

'Departs?' Kodor frowned. 'What do you mean?'

'For her family estate – oh, but of course, you'd not have heard, sire; Grand Mother Beck only received the letter a short time ago.' Dorca's face became tragic and tears welled in her eyes. 'Madam's mother has died.'

'The God blind me!' Kodor was shocked. 'Poor Nanta – I must see her; I must offer her comfort—'

He started to push past Dorca and into the suite, but she barred his path, flapping her hands in agitation.

'No, Your Majesty, please! She doesn't yet know – the physician says that the shock might harm her, and she isn't to be told until she is stronger!'

That made sense, and Kodor subsided. 'Nonetheless,' he said, 'I will see her.'

'She's sleeping, sire,' said Dorca nervously. She did not, dared not, tell him that Nanta had talked with Marine an hour ago, and afterwards had given her servants the strictest orders that the Imperator was not, under any circumstances, to be admitted to the suite. 'Perhaps when she wakes . . .' she dissembled desperately.

'Very well. Send word to me. Now: you say that Mother Marine is going to the family estate? Why?'

'I don't know, sire. She said she was required to go in person – I believe that the EsDorikyes don't yet know about – about the Imperator Osiv; the letter could not have reached them before this new misfortune happened. So Mother Marine is to tell them. Grand Mother Beck has made the arrangements, I believe, and Mother Marine will leave at noon.'

Grand Mother Beck . . . Oh, yes; the picture was becoming clearer now. *Was* Nanta's mother dead, or was this a lie, a ruse to remove Marine from the scene for a while?

Or even permanently . . . ?

His eyes focused on Dorca again and the look in them made her quail. 'Which chapel will Mother Marine go to?'

'The Sanctum chapel, I imagine, sire. She is of course free to use the imperial chapel at any time, but . . .'

The words tailed off, and Dorca blinked in confusion at Kodor's diminishing back view.

The Imperator's arrival in the Sanctum had much the same effect as a fox's arrival in a henhouse. The Sisters were thrown into a fluttering clamour of awe and terror, further confused by the fact that Kodor was also breaking the unwritten but long-established rule that men simply did not set foot in this house of women. Kodor ignored the commotion, the curtseying and scurrying and twittering and hiding. Catching the arm of a Low Sister who could not run away from him in time, he demanded directions to the chapel, listened to the stammering, tearful reply, and strode on as behind him the girl dropped to the floor in a dead faint. Through corridors, down a flight of stairs and into the building's foundations. Someone, of course, would go running to Mother Beck; probably had done so by now. If Beck believed them, she would investigate, so he must find Marine quickly, before her superior arrived on the scene. He had already made one detour, to check a certain fact, and that had delayed him. Time was of the essence now.

The chapel door was ahead of him, marked by the Lady's snowflake emblem. Kodor smacked it open and barged in.

There were some ten or a dozen Sisters at their devotions in the chapel. As one they looked up at the unprecedented crash of

265

the door, and their faces froze with wide eyes and open mouths as they saw him. Marine was kneeling by the statue of the Lady. She was as stunned as the rest, and started to scramble to her feet as Kodor advanced towards her.

Kodor raked the other women with a glare. 'Out,' he said. 'Every one of you.'

'Sire—' Marine began to protest.

'Be quiet, Mother.' He raised his voice. 'I said, go! *Now*!'

They fled like a flock of birds. As the last of them vanished Kodor said, 'Does that door have an inside lock?'

'Of course not! It's a *chapel* – it is open to all!' Marine's composure was in tatters, and deference had flown out of the door. 'Sire, this is an outrage! To intrude on the Sisters at prayer—'

'Stop being a fool, Marine!' Kodor interrupted. 'You know full well that I wouldn't have come here unless it was vitally urgent. What are you denying? What are you afraid of?'

'Nothing.' But Marine's eyes gave the lie to it. She backed away from him. 'I'm not afraid.'

'Oh, but you are! Why? After last night—' Then suddenly it dawned on him. The confrontation last night had put one set of suspicions to rest, but there was another, still seething in Marine's mind. Kodor could see the train of her thinking as clearly as if she had written it in letters of fire on the wall. He loved Nanta, Nanta was Osiv's wife, and Osiv had conveniently died. To Marine, the connection was obvious.

'By the God!' Kodor almost exploded with pent frustration and impatience. 'You think I murdered my brother, don't you?'

'I – I don't—' Then Marine covered her face with her hands. 'Oh, sweet Lady, how much more sorrow will there *be*?'

'A great deal more, unless you and I do something to prevent it!' Kodor shouted. 'Look at me, woman; don't stand there trembling like a sheep at the slaughterhouse!' With an effort he got his temper under control. 'Look at me, and *listen*.'

Tremulously Marine obeyed, and Kodor made a decision. It was a risk, but the risk must be taken.

'Mother Marine,' he said. 'There are three facts you should know. Fact one: the sweets I gave to Nanta were not poisoned. But the soup *you* gave to her was.'

'*What?*' Marine's face turned the colour of the marble statue.

'You had no knowledge of it; I'm aware of that. *Listen*. Fact two: there has been no letter from the EsDorikye estate. I've questioned the palace officers, and Beck lied to you; the roads are blocked and no message could possibly have got through. Nanta's mother is not dead.' He drew breath. 'And fact three: neither is Imperator Osiv.'

To his relief, Marine had the mental resources to take in the skeleton of the tale in a few crisp sentences – and to grasp immediately the significance of what she had been told. The pieces of the picture fitted together, now, like a hand in a tailored glove, and Marine's first thought – as Kodor had anticipated – was for Nanta.

'Sire, she is in far more imminent danger than I had ever dreamed!' she cried. 'I must go to her – I must do something! But what *can* I do?'

'There's only one solution,' Kodor told her. 'You must take Nanta away from the palace. Out of the Metropolis, to a safe hiding.'

'My own Sanctum –' she began eagerly.

'Too far; and it's also the first place that Urss will think of. No; you must take her to the hunting lodge where Osiv is living.' His mind skimmed rapidly over a plan. 'Beck has arranged for a sleigh to take you – in theory – to the EsDorikye estate. You'll use that; but with my driver, not Beck's. I'll give the order.'

'But will the order be obeyed, sire?' Marine asked worriedly. 'If Mother Beck or Father Urss hears of it . . .'

Then they would intimidate the servants and override the command, unless he was there in person to gainsay them. If he did that it would bring everything into the open, for there was no plausible excuse for such an action. That must not happen; not until Nanta was safe.

Frustration surged again, and Kodor paced tigerishly across the floor. 'We need help!' he said through clenched teeth. 'The frost sprites – the God knows I've tried to communicate with them so often since that encounter in the forest, but they won't answer me!'

Marine, who knew nothing of the encounter, looked at him with wide eyes. 'I've prayed to the Lady,' she said. 'But she—'

'Oh, *prayer*! What use is *prayer*? We need *power*!' Kodor wanted to strike out at something, anything; raising his voice he shouted to the chapel roof, 'Damn you, you capricious creatures, where *are* you when you're needed? *Where are you?*'

An ice-cold breath whispered through the chapel. From behind them, a thin, strange voice said:

'We know. We serve.'

They both spun round.

The frost sprite's eyes were the colour of ice, set in a grotesquely oversized skull which in turn was framed by a mass of silver braids. Its body – spare, wiry, a child's frame – was draped in what appeared to be frosted cobwebs, in which faint rainbows danced like moonlight reflecting in icicles. Through its translucent form the outlines of the chapel were dimly visible.

Marine uttered a shocked gasp and reflexively her hands clasped together. 'The tears of the Lady are the blessing of the snow!' she whispered.

The sprite inclined its head. 'True, Mother. True. The snow is blessing when the Lady weeps. We shall help. We shall not let her die.' It looked then at Kodor. 'She must only call, and we come.'

'Go to her!' Kodor urged. 'Go now – protect her!'

But the being raised both hands before its face in a gesture he remembered. 'She must call. You are her brother, but we are not of you. *She* calls, and we obey. We are of the Lady. That is how it must be.'

'Sire, they are waiting for Nanta to ask them,' Marine whispered breathlessly. 'It isn't caprice – they have no choice!'

Kodor's mouth tightened into a hard line. 'Then go to her, Marine. Tell her everything, tell her what to do! I will keep Urss and Beck busy; I'll summon them to the throne room and—'

He stopped as the frost sprite made a strange, shrill sound, like a warning whistle. There was a shudder of displaced air; in the space of a breath the being vanished—

And the chapel door opened.

'Your Majesty!' Grand Mother Beck made a sweeping curtsey to Kodor. 'When Sister Chaia told me you were in the Sanctum, I could hardly believe her – I beg your pardon that I was not here to welcome you, sire, and explain the circumstances; but I'm sure you will understand that the *protocol* . . .'

She let the sentence trail away unfinished, at the same time moving with dignity towards them. Kodor saw her eyes, saw what lurked there, and in a rapid aside he whispered to Marine, '*Follow where I lead. Say as little as possible.*'

'Grand Mother.' He walked forward to meet her, schooling his expression into one of sober concern. '*I* must ask *your* pardon for this intrusion; I realise it is quite unprecedented. But when I heard the unhappy news of Karetta EsDorikye, I . . . well, I confess I acted without thinking. Dorca tells me that my sister has not been told – a very wise decision, I agree – and so I came in search of Mother Marine, in the hope that she could tell me the full story.'

Beck smiled. 'I'm sorry that you've been put to so much trouble, Your Majesty. *I* would, of course, have been honoured to explain everything to you myself.'

'I'm sure you would, Grand Mother.' Kodor was not intimidated. 'But I also gather that Mother Marine is to leave for the

EsDorikye estate today, and I want her to take them a personal message from me.'

'Ah,' said Beck. She seemed somewhat mollified, though Kodor doubted that she entirely trusted his reply. 'I understand, Your Majesty. It is most gracious of you, and I'm sure the Dowager's family will be greatly touched by your kindness.' Her gaze slid to Marine's face, and Kodor saw her trying to interpret what she found there. 'Marine, my dear, if His Majesty will permit, I think it is time to gather your belongings and make ready. The sleigh is prepared, and will be in the palace's south courtyard in less than an hour.'

Marine swallowed. 'Thank you, Grand Mother.' She glanced nervously at Kodor. 'If that is all, sire . . .'

'Yes, Mother Marine, that is all. You'll not forget my message?'

'Oh no, Your Majesty.' Her eyes flicked a meaning in which hope and trust vied with desperation. 'I'll remember every word.'

'Good. I'm sure you'll wish to make your farewells to the Dowager, so Grand Mother Beck and I will excuse you now. I wish you a safe journey.'

Beck clearly did not like the idea of Marine returning to Nanta, but she could raise no objection in Kodor's presence. She led the way to the chapel door; outside, Marine curtseyed to Kodor and hurried away, and Beck, too, would have taken her leave; but Kodor stopped her.

'Grand Mother Beck.' He smiled. 'I want you to attend me in the lesser throne room in . . .' He calculated. 'Half an hour from now, if you please.'

Beck was taken aback. 'In the throne room, sire? Yes – yes, of course. May I – ah – ask what is required of me?'

'I'll inform you of that on your arrival.' She would run straight to Urss, he was certain of it; and the chances were that the summons he also intended to send to Urss would arrive while she was in his office. Kodor smiled inwardly. 'Thank you, Grand

Mother. And now if one of your women will show me the way out . . .'

'It's a disturbing development, I agree, Beck; but not necessarily cause for alarm.' Standing at his study window and gazing down at the courtyard outside, Father Urss had the air of a predator contemplating its next attack. 'The reason the Imperator gave for his visit might well be true. And even if he has an inkling of something in the wind, he can have no evidence that would link us with his suspicions.' He turned and regarded her sternly. 'Unless *someone* has been careless.'

Beck drew herself up. 'I assure you, Father, that *I* most certainly have not!'

'Then we have nothing to fear. Mother Marine will soon be leaving the Metropolis, and that will solve one potential problem. High Sister Ludia, in her innocence, continues to include your special ingredients in the Dowager's food. No, Beck; we're safe enough.'

'But what about the Imperator's summons?' Beck asked. 'The timing isn't a coincidence, I'm sure of it. What does he *want*?'

Urss frowned, recalling his own message from Kodor and the haste with which it had been delivered. Beck was right; there was *something* odd about the timing. But as to what it portended . . .

'We'll only find that out by attending on him as he commands,' he said, carefully keeping the doubt from his voice. 'Which of course we shall do. As soon as—'

The words broke off in a gasp, and he clutched reflexively at his temples.

'Father?' said Beck. 'Are you ill?'

'*Nnn—*' Urss was trying to say 'no', but he could not make his tongue obey him. He gasped again, shutting his eyes tightly, then to Beck's alarm he started to sway like a drunkard.

'*Father!*' She hurried forward – and a force like a physical

271

blow rebuffed her, sending her tottering backwards across the carpet. Urss's mouth stretched in a terrible rictus; a bubbling sound came from his throat—

And a voice that was not his, but which emanated from his mouth, boomed:

'*No!*'

'*Ahh!*' The power that held Urss jolted away from him, and he collapsed on to his chair. The daylight dimmed as though someone had snuffed out a giant candle, and the voice spoke again, not through Urss this time but in a huge, disembodied echo:

'*HE IS TOO CLOSE TO THE TRUTH. YOU ARE FAILING ME, URSS, AND I WILL TOLERATE NO FAILURE!*'

Beck fell to her knees with a cry of terror, and through a stunned haze saw Urss, his hands clasped and his mouth open, look upwards to the ceiling.

'Great lord, I am your faithful servant!' he pleaded. 'I will not fail! Only help me, tell me what I must do, and *I will not fail!*'

'*I WILL TOLERATE NO FAILURE!*' the voice repeated ominously. '*OBEY ME, URSS. OBEY ME. THE FAIR CHILD IS TO DIE, AND THERE MUST BE NO MORE DELAY. GO TO THE FAIR CHILD, URSS. GO TO HER AND TAKE HER LIFE, OR SUFFER THE FULL MAGNITUDE OF MY DISPLEASURE!*'

Urss's mouth worked spasmodically. 'But great lord, the Imperator commands—'

'*THE IMPERATOR IS ALSO MY SERVANT AND MUST BOW TO MY WILL. GO TO THE FAIR CHILD. DESTROY HER!*'

Beck had covered her face now and was cowering in mortal dread. The echoes of the God's command clashed and faded; she felt the sense of a colossal presence whirling through the room, whirling past her and away – and suddenly all was still.

Urss rose to his feet first, though his movements were slow

and uncoordinated. Every limb trembled, and his face had taken on a deathly cast. He didn't speak; instead he moved falteringly to where Beck knelt, and helped her to stand up. Eyes burning with fear, she looked at him, silently but fervently projecting the question she had no voice to ask. *Why* did the God want Nanta to die? There had been such hatred in that voice, such rage; as though Nanta had committed a crime beyond redemption and the God was claiming his vengeance. Yet Nanta was a mere child, an innocent. It made no *sense*. Unless –

Beck's mind spun back over the months, to the time when she had been instructed to seek out a bride for Prince Osiv. The unnameable instinct that had guided her to Nanta – was there a connection between that guidance and the God's wrath? Had Beck unknowingly tapped into a matter deeper, greater than she or anyone else could have thought possible at the time?

She continued to stare at Urss and finally found her voice, though it was so thin and quavering that it was barely recognisable.

'What are we to do . . . ?'

'We must obey . . .' Urss struggled to regain his wits. 'The God has spoken to us. We must *obey*!'

'Yes, Exalted Father . . .' Beck whispered. There was another silence. Beck wondered if she was going to be sick. Then with a vast effort Urss seemed to pull himself together. His back straightened, the trembling diminished, and his face set into a grim expression in which there could be no room for the smallest shard of doubt.

'Beck,' he said, 'go to the throne room. Attend on the Imperator. I will do what must be done.'

'Wh . . . what should I tell the Imperator, Father? If you are absent—'

'You will not know the reason for it. Why should you? Pretend ignorance, and distract him. I need *time*.' He started towards the door, still not quite steady but with strength and poise rapidly returning – and, buttressing it, an unnatural, hectic energy. '*Go*, Beck! Don't waste a moment!'

The door slammed shut behind him. For several seconds Beck stood paralysed, her brain still seething with shock. But through the shock came something else: an old skill, a long-ingrained training . . . the instinct, against any odds and in the face of any threat, to *survive*.

The paralysis snapped, and she swept from the room in Urss's wake.

Chapter XIX

'Come now; come. We must hurry! Come, Nanta, before Dorca returns!' Coaxing, cajoling, Marine shepherded Nanta towards the outer door of the suite. Nanta's feet dragged and her movements were clumsy; though she seemed to understand the need for urgency, her body was too weak to respond as it should. There must have been another dose of the poison in her breakfast this morning, and Marine cursed her own ignorance and stupidity. If she had *known*, if she had *thought* – but 'if' was of no value now; things were as they were and she must make the best of them.

She wondered how much of the truth Nanta had taken in; or even how much she herself had understood as yet. In reality it hardly mattered; even if Nanta did not comprehend, she was obeying Marine like a small, sleepy child. But if they were to meet with any trouble on the way to the courtyard—

Marine slammed her mental shutters on that thought and concentrated on the task in hand. As they passed the catafalque Nanta tried to hang back; turning and staring at it she said, 'Osiv . . . ?' and Marine saw tears spring to her eyes.

'No, my dear, no; I told you. Osiv is not dead. You shall see him soon.'

'Not dead . . .' Nanta repeated vaguely. Hurrying her forward again, Marine offered a silent plea to the Lady that something, somehow, could break through this miasma. If they needed the frost sprites' help, and Nanta did not have the wit to call on them, everything could be imperilled.

'Come, my dear, come!' So little *time*, she thought frantically. The cryptic message from Kodor had told her only that the sleigh was waiting and the driver would offer her a password to prove his identity; Kodor would by now be in the throne room, waiting for Mother Beck and Father Urss. Were Beck and Urss there yet? Would they *stay* there? If they suspected what was afoot, would Kodor be able to command them?

With the questions boiling in her mind, Marine steered Nanta, at last, out of the door and away along the corridor. They passed three servants, all of whom stood back and bowed to the Dowager; with a pallid nod of acknowledgement Marine hastened on. Down a flight of stairs; not the main way but a lesser route, more convoluted but safer. It was snowing more heavily outside, she had seen through a window. Almost a blizzard. Would that work for them or against them? *The tears of the Lady are the blessing of the snow* . . . Let it be a blessing; oh, let it, today, be a blessing!

Strengthening her grip on the faltering, failing Nanta, Marine ran onwards.

Kodor paced the chamber, his eyes never leaving the dumpy figure of Mother Beck, who stood resolutely where he had commanded her to stand, beside the throne. At last he stopped and pivoted to face her.

'Well, Grand Mother?' His voice was ferocious. 'How much longer do you think we are to wait, before Exalted Father Urss deigns to grace us with his presence?'

Beck's face was expressionless. 'I'm sure I don't know, sire. I was not even aware that Father Urss was to attend, so—'

'You are a liar,' said Kodor.

Beck was visibly shaken. 'Sire, I—' she started to protest.

'Save your breath. I no longer believe a word you say to me.' Which was why he had sent a steward to escort Urss to this

276

room. Only the man had not yet returned.

'You see, Grand Mother,' Kodor began to walk in a slow circle around her, 'I know about your involvement in the murder of my brother. And I believe you have been Father Urss's accomplice in a number of other deeds. The supposedly natural illness of the Dowager, for example. And the planned accident to Mother Marine.'

Ah; he had struck the target. Just a flicker of fear in Beck's eyes, but it was enough.

'Unfortunately for you both,' he continued, 'Nanta has friends and guardians whose scope ranges beyond human abilities. Thanks to them, I have—'

The door opened, and Kodor broke off. Looking up quickly, expecting to see Urss and his escort, he was both astonished and angered to find himself instead looking at Pola.

'Husband?' Pola hesitated, then came in. 'Oh – good morning, Grand Mother Beck.'

'Your Majesty . . .' Beck's curtsey was perfunctory and her voice shook slightly.

Kodor said ferociously: 'What do you want?'

Pola's expression hardened. 'It is not what *I* want, Kodor, but what I have come to tell *you*. You seem to have forgotten that we were due at a rehearsal for the funeral an hour ago. I have been waiting for you, but you apparently neglected to inform anyone of your change of plan.'

'If I did, that's my concern!' Kodor snapped. 'Leave me, wife. I'm busy.'

With a caustic look Pola turned to stalk out; then paused. 'Oh, and I encountered your steward outside. For what interest it may be to you, he asked me to inform you that he can't find Father Urss.'

'*What?*' She was leaving; he called, 'Pola, wait!'

Perhaps she perceived the genuine fear in his voice, for she stopped and looked back. 'What is it?'

'Urss can't be found?'

Her brow furrowed in puzzlement. 'That's what he said. Why, is—?'

Kodor didn't listen to the question. He swung round and in four strides had reached Beck and grabbed her by the shoulders.

'Where is he? Where is Urss? You evil harridan, *answer* me!'

'Kodor!' cried Pola, horrified. 'What do you think you're doing?'

He flung her a wild glance over his shoulder. 'I'm looking for answers, and I'll have them!'

'She is a *Mother*—'

'She is a murderer!' Kodor yelled. If Pola already knew, if she was a part of this, he didn't care – it no longer mattered, for the veils of secrecy were being stripped away now. He shook Beck as a terrier might shake a rat; Beck cried out in pain and protest, and Pola came running across the floor.

'Kodor, *stop*! Have you lost your mind?'

'No! But two people are going to lose their lives unless this crone tells me where Urss has gone!'

'Sire, I – don't – know anything – about—' Beck choked out.

'*Liar!* Give me the truth, or by the God I'll smash every bone you possess!'

'*Kodor!*' As Kodor's hands closed on Beck's throat Pola threw herself into the fray, flailing, lashing out, struggling to drive him off. The three of them swayed together, tangling; Beck slipped and fell to the floor, and at the same moment a wild swing from Pola's arm caught Kodor full in the face. He staggered back, his cheek and jaw stinging – and suddenly reason crashed blindingly in on him. This was what Urss wanted! To waste precious time on Beck; time Urss could use for his own machinations – he was playing into the priest's hands!

He took off, racing towards the door. Pola screamed, 'Kodor, where are you going? What's *happening*?'

'Ask *her*!' Skidding to a momentary halt, Kodor pointed at

Beck, who was still on the floor. 'Ask her how she and Urss plan to murder Nanta and Mother Marine! Ask her about the poisoned food! Ask her about Osiv! And tell her – and your vulgar, arrogant, swaggering father – that *Osiv is not dead!*'

He vanished, running, leaving her gaping at the empty doorway. Osiv, not dead? Pola didn't understand, couldn't believe – Kodor was insane; it was the only possible explanation—

An awful sound snatched her attention, and she whirled.

Beck had tried to get up. But as she did so, an excruciating pain swelled in her chest and exploded through her. She fell back, face reddening, eyes starting in their sockets, and an inchoate plea for help bubbled between her lips.

'Grand Mother!' Pola dropped to her knees, horrified. She knew the signs of a heart seizure – Beck was suffocating, unable to breathe, and she ripped at the old woman's constricting wimple, at the neck of the gown beneath, tearing off buttons, trying to give her air. Beck gargled horribly; her tongue was protruding and her face had turned purple now. Her eyes rolled upwards and her arms twitched helplessly; uttering a Sekolian oath that she had never dared use in the palace before, Pola sprang to her feet again, hitched her heavy skirt and sprinted for the door.

'Help!' Her voice rang powerfully down the corridor beyond, and in the distance feet pounded in response. 'Help me, *quickly!*'

Kodor had just turned at a fast run into the corridor that led to the imperial suite when the frost sprite materialised in his path.

Kodor slewed, cannoned against the wall and rebounded, gasping. The sprite hovered, its head shaking and its hands moving in wild, quick gestures, but it seemed unable to speak, as though some force outside its control were holding it back.

'What?' Kodor cried. 'What are you trying to tell me?'

The sprite made a thin, high, whistling sound, but no words came. Then, like a snowflake vaporising in fire, it vanished.

Alarm flowered in Kodor; he ran on, reached the door of the suite and hammered on it.

'Dorca! Dorca, open this door! Let me in!'

There was a flurry behind the door, a scrabbling, then the door opened a crack and Dorca peered out.

'Oh, Your Majesty!' Relief lit her face like a star. 'I thought—'

He neither knew nor cared what she thought, but shoved the door wide and strode in. 'Where's your mistress?'

'She's gone, sire!' Dorca wrung her hands. 'I only left her for a few minutes, and Mother Marine was here; I don't know what happened, sire, I truly don't! And then when Father Urss came—'

'Urss was here?'

'Yes, sire. He came asking for madam, and when I said—'

'You told him she was gone?' Dorca nodded. 'What then; what happened?'

'He – Father Urss – he seemed so *angry*, Your Majesty . . . He shouted at me, and then he stormed off, and I don't *understand*!'

'Wait, Dorca, wait.' Marine had got Nanta away; she must have done. Kodor prayed that they had reached the sleigh safely – the driver had his orders and would not fail.

'Listen to me,' he told the distraught Dorca. 'Nothing has happened to the Dowager; she is in no danger. She is with Mother Marine, and Marine is acting on my instructions. All right, now; calm down and just tell me, did Father Urss say anything more?'

A shake of the head. 'No, Your Majesty, not that I remember. But he was so *angry* . . .'

He would be, Kodor thought. 'Thank you, Dorca. Stay here in the suite and don't worry. You'll have news of your mistress soon.'

He didn't wait to see if she had taken in his reassurance but turned and started back the way he had come. He realised now what the frost sprite had been trying to tell him; that Nanta was already gone. But why had it not spoken? Something to do with Urss? Was the creature afraid of the priest?

The question couldn't be answered, and it was irrelevant now. There was a short cut to the courtyard, one that Marine probably did not know. If he could reach them before they left, he would ensure that they got out of the city unhindered.

And then he would deal with Urss . . .

The sleigh was waiting, its bulk only dimly visible through what was now a dense veil of fast-falling snow. The cold of the outside air was a shock that knocked the breath from Marine's lungs; Nanta burst out coughing and tried to pull away, back into the shelter of the palace, but Marine hauled her bodily forward. They stumbled through calf-deep whiteness; ahead of them a dog yipped, and then the sleigh-driver, a small, squat man, was ploughing to meet them, arms held out to help Marine with her burden.

'Who lives at the hunting lodge, Mother?' he asked her.

Marine had forgotten about the password, and quickly searched her memory. 'The arctic bear lives there,' she replied, trying to stop her teeth from chattering.

The man nodded. 'Prince Kodor's given me my orders, ma'am. Come you, now; there are furs in the sleigh and you'll soon be warm.'

He had said 'Prince Kodor', Marine realised. Not 'the Imperator' but 'Prince Kodor'. Then it was true. Osiv was alive . . .

She had no time to ask questions, though, for the driver was lifting Nanta into the sleigh. Eight dogs, and big ones. They would travel fast. Marine only prayed they would be fast enough to elude Father Urss.

Nanta was secure in the sleigh; Marine climbed in beside her, unaided, and started to arrange the piled furs around them both. The driver took his seat, picked up his long whip—

'*You, man! Stop!*'

The stentorian roar came from the doorway. Father Urss was there. Shrouded in the whirling snow, he looked like a figure from a nightmare, and Marine reached out, clutching at the driver's coat as she screamed to him, 'Go! Move, get away, *now*!'

The driver knew enough to obey without an instant's hesitation – but his reflexes were not fast enough. Urss raised his hand, pointed – and to Marine's incredulous horror, the driver lurched as if something had struck him a violent physical blow. With a yell he pitched sideways from his seat, landing in the snow and almost disappearing. As he struggled to right himself, Urss came striding towards them. Marine could see his face now, see the demented expression on it; clutching Nanta to her she screamed again and shrank away as he towered over them.

'Get out of the sleigh, Mother Marine.' Urss's voice was as mad as his demeanour. 'Obey me, woman. *Obey*.'

Something tugged at Marine's mind; a compulsion to do as he commanded. This was not Father Urss: something else, something unhumanly powerful, had taken him over and was working through him. Marine tried to fight the power, but it was too strong; it was pulling her, dragging her, tearing at her—

She began to rise to her feet . . .

'*No*.'

A small, pale hand darted from beneath the piled furs and clamped on Marine's arm. Marine's heart seemed to plunge and turn over under her ribs. And Nanta said again:

'*NO!*'

She had sat up in the sleigh and was staring at Urss. Her eyes were wide open, wide awake . . . and they were no longer their familiar blue-green but the hue of sapphires. There was a new light in them, stone-hard and invincible. And on Nanta's fragile face was an expression of consummate loathing and contempt.

'We do not obey *you*.' Her voice seemed to cut tangibly

through the snow that clogged the air. 'You are nothing. Step back, little man. Step out of our path.'

The moments that followed burned themselves on Marine's memory like an insane, frozen tableau. Herself, held rigid, half sitting and half standing; the sleigh-driver on hands and knees in the snow, his mouth open and gaping. And Nanta and Urss, their gazes locked; Urss's in outrage, Nanta's in hatred. Nanta's conscious mind was still swimming with the progressive effect of the poison; on the surface she knew only that here before her was the man, the monster, who had tied her in marriage to an idiot child, and then degraded her and that child, poor Osiv, for his own cold, political reasons. But beneath the surface was something else; something she did not understand and at this moment could not even acknowledge. A strength. A *power*; not her own, but drawn from a far, far place, behind the north wind . . .

She whispered: '*Come to me, my sprites. Come to me.*'

The air shuddered. Marine saw their shapes materialising, forming a circle around the sleigh. She shut her eyes, overwhelmed, feeling that her own sanity was about to crumble; in her mind she sent a frantic prayer to the Lady—

Nanta's head snapped round. She gave Marine one look, and glacial reason flooded into Marine's brain, eclipsing the terror and wiping it out.

'*Driver!*' She yelled at the full pitch of her lungs. '*Driver, go! Get us away, NOW!*'

There was a scrabbling and a flurrying, and the small man leaped for his seat. Marine heard the dogs give voice, saw Urss's eyes widen in fury, as if he had snapped out of a dream to find himself besieged. Belatedly he lunged at the sleigh—

'*GO!*' Marine shrieked.

The driver cracked his whip, powering the dogs into their traces, and with a tremendous lurch the sleigh began to move. Through a bow-wave of snow Marine had one last glimpse of

Urss's gaunt figure as he tried to catch on to the sleigh's high stern, but the dogs were swerving for the gate and Urss was flung aside, rolling over and left behind. The gate was rushing to meet them; they were gathering speed, the driver yodelling encouragement to his team as the whip sang a shrill counterpoint. In a barrelling, rocking, yelping storm of energy the sleigh hurtled out of the courtyard, out of the palace, and away towards the Metropolis and the lonely forest road beyond.

Kodor reached the courtyard just in time to witness the sleigh's headlong departure – and to see Urss, covered in snow, clambering to his feet. Urss in turn saw him, and they both stopped, standing rigid and motionless as they faced each other.

'Exalted Father Urss.' Years of loathing, and something newer and far more personal, suffused Kodor's voice. 'You will come with me, Father. You will come *now*.'

Urss did not move. His face and figure were a blur in the snowstorm, but Kodor sensed an aura about him, an emanation of something dark and bleak and dangerous. Something not quite human . . .

'Do as I command you, Father.' But suddenly Kodor was unsure of himself. This was not the Urss he knew. It was as if the man he addressed was merely a body, an empty shell usurped and inhabited by an alien intelligence.

Then Urss's lips moved, and a voice that was not his spoke hugely in Kodor's mind.

'*You cannot command your Father.*' The priest's tall figure began to stalk towards him. '*I will have my way, Kodor Imperator. I will have the fair child's life.*'

This was *not* Urss. The face was clear now, and it was deranged. Kodor did not even believe that the eyes in the narrow skull were seeing him. He took a pace back, felt his heel come up hard against the stone step behind him.

'*You will not oppose me. You will not thwart me. The son*

obeys the Father.' Urss was looming out of the snow, and Kodor felt a vast, paralysing coldness knifing into his bones. Then the priest raised his hands as though to proffer a benediction—

A small tornado of blind energy picked Kodor up and hurled him across the courtyard. He fell with bone-shaking force into the snow, and as the energy spun away and he dizzily raised his head, he had a last glimpse of Urss fleeing into the palace, his robe billowing like dark wings around him.

'*Urss!*' But it was useless; Urss – or the thing Urss had become – did not hear and would not have heeded. Kodor scrambled upright. The snow had softened his fall and his body would suffer no more than a few bruises from it. He started to run after the priest – then recoiled with a startled shout as the driving snow in his path suddenly whirled into a maelstrom and a figure formed from it.

'No, Kodor, no, Kodor, no!' The frost sprite had found its voice and it danced in the air before him, a fantastic, twisting gyration. 'The tears of the Lady – in the snow, Kodor, in the snow! Help your sister! Brother and sister! He will kill, he will destroy! Help her, Kodor, you must help her!'

The sprite's frantic plea went home like a knife-blade. For a bare second Kodor stared at it, and in that second the last of his giddiness cleared and a terrible insight sheared through his mind. Urss no longer counted. This was nothing to do with Urss; it was something far greater.

He turned and ran, pelting, forging through the blizzard, towards the kennels.

'I don't care what you must do!' Pola's voice rose, sharp with strain and with furious, commanding energy. 'Enlist every servant in the palace, everyone in the palace! Find the Imperator, and find Father Urss!'

The officers ran at her bidding, leaving the huddle of stewards, ladies-in-waiting and physicians who had grouped round Pola and Grand Mother Beck in the throne room. The imperial physician was still kneeling at Beck's side; as the door banged echoingly he looked up and met Pola's hunted stare.

'I'm sorry, Your Majesty. It is too late. There's nothing I can do to help her now.'

Beck's eyes were open and she seemed to be gazing thoughtfully at the high, moulded ceiling. But she saw nothing; nor ever would again.

Pola turned away, putting the back of one hand to her mouth, and sucked in a long breath. Beck, dead; and Kodor had killed her. He hadn't intended that – she told herself fiercely that he could *not* have intended it. But he had killed her. *Why?* What had he *wanted* from her? That parting shot – *Osiv is not dead.* And a plot, to murder Nanta and Mother Marine – she *did not understand!*

She breathed in again, and when she spoke her voice was flawlessly controlled.

'Have Mother Beck's body removed and laid out in the Sanctum chapel. Tell the Sisters she must have the ceremony due to her. I am going to my chambers. The moment Father Urss's whereabouts are discovered, send word. And ask . . .' She paused. She had been about to say, 'Ask my father to attend on me.' But she did not want Duke Arec. She was Imperatrix, and she did not *need* him.

'No matter,' she said, and walked, tall and stately and dignified, from the room.

'The tears of the Lady are the blessing of the snow . . . The tears of the Lady are – are the blessing of the snow – oh, Lady help us, Lady protect us, sweet Lady let us come safely through this day!'

Marine's prayers were a desperate litany, barely audible even to her own ears over the hiss and rumble of the sleigh's rushing. Her mind and body had fused into one single chord of terror; the old horror of travelling, their breakneck speed, and, most fearful of all, the thought of what might even now be pursuing them from the Metropolis and along this forest road.

Tree-trunks were flashing past so fast that she dared not look at them for fear of the vertigo that threatened every moment. Though there was daylight beyond the branches, the forest was gloomy as dusk. And the snow drove, drove, drove in her face, freezing her lips and nose and brows, turning the fringes of her hair to a hoary white.

But amid all her terror there was a tiny shred of comfort and courage; for the frost sprites still raced with them. She had glimpsed their forms flickering and flying beside the sleigh, sometimes merging with the blizzard but always there, never tiring. And beside her, under the protection of the furs, Nanta stared ahead, her face a mask of snow through which her eyes burned, and a strange, sweet smile on her lips. Though it made no sense, she too gave Marine courage. The sprites had come for her and they would protect her; while they were together Marine knew, against all reason, that there was nothing to dread.

The sleigh careered on, the dogs tiring but goaded relentlessly by their driver. Far behind them on the road, a sled drawn by three animals ran like the wind, its lone occupant yelling his team on, his grey eyes fixed on the runner-tracks he followed. And in Kodor's hurtling wake, distant as yet but slowly closing, came something else. He knew it was there, he felt it like a roaring vortex; a thing of hate and vengeance that would never, ever tire. If it overtook him before he reached his destination, Kodor knew that it could, if it chose, destroy him. If it did not overtake . . . He didn't know. But there would be *hope*.

Far from the forest, in the palace, the search continued for Father Urss.

Who was crouching on all fours, like a wild animal, in a forgotten room where the searchers would not think to look. The mortal man that Urss had been was swamped and crushed to

287

nothing by the power that channelled through him, but he smiled a smile of joy and fulfilment. For the God was speaking and the God was commanding. The God was reaching into the mortal world, pursuing the one, the *special* one, who had been hidden in this world so long ago and who had eluded all his searching until the night when the Corolla Lights returned to dance in the sky. The Lights had shown the way, betraying their source and bringing the prey into the open. Urss understood everything now — and he was the God's faithful servant. Through the medium of his body and mind, the God wielded power. And he would prevail.

Chapter XX

The hunting lodge stood in a clearing created for it, surrounded by a high, gated picket fence that protected it from the forest's predators. As the sleigh slithered to a juddering halt, the gate was pulled open and through the snow Marine saw the glint of bobbing lanterns.

The mutes recognised the driver at once, and they hurried forward, signalling a greeting, lowering their weapons and hastening to help the sleigh's passengers. Expecting to find Kodor, they stopped in consternation as they saw, instead, the white faces of two women gazing back at them. One half-raised his crossbow again; the other turned to the driver in angry alarm.

'It's all right!' the driver said hastily. 'Don't you know her? Don't you—'

He got no further, for suddenly Nanta stood up, casting off the furs. She stepped from the sleigh, ignoring the fact that the snow was almost up to her knees, and walked straight towards the gate.

'Nanta!' Marine called. 'Nanta, wait! We should—'

Nanta turned and looked at her. She smiled. And Marine fell utterly silent as she disappeared through the gateway.

The driver stared after her with a strange, almost reverent expression on his face. The mutes stared, too, but their awe was tempered with a sense of their own duty. The woman – whom they still had not recognised – was going into the lodge, and in the lodge was their Imperator, whom they were pledged to protect against any threat. And now the other woman was trying to follow, and she was a religious, and their Imperator did not like religiouses.

They stepped into Marine's path, and she found herself looking at the deadly bolt of a crossbow, aimed at her waist.

'No . . .' She shrank back, raising her hands in supplication. 'No, please – I mean no harm, I am a friend!' Did they understand? 'The Imperator sent us!' she added pleadingly.

The mutes shook their heads disbelievingly, but the sleigh-driver came to Marine's rescue.

'She means Prince Kodor,' he said. 'Maybe she doesn't know yet, see? And what she says is true.' He pointed through the gate. 'That's the Imperatrix.'

The mutes' eyes widened. They started to lower their weapons; then abruptly from inside the fence came a joyful shout.

'*Nandi!*'

Going in at the gate, with one mute as escort while the other helped the driver to unharness the weary dogs, Marine was in time to witness Nanta's reunion with Osiv. Osiv was dancing in the snow, jubilantly hurling handfuls of it into the air and then rushing every few moments to Nanta and hugging her. Nanta stood still. She was staring at Osiv, and on her face was a look stranger even than the cold, sapphire stare fixed on her face throughout the hectic journey. It was a look of wonder, of certainty, of understanding; and mingled among those emotions was an excitement that communicated itself across the distance to Marine and stopped her in her tracks.

Nanta said: 'He knows.'

'Knows . . . ?' Marine was at a loss.

'*Yes*!' Nanta's excitement was increasing; it was as if her body could barely contain what was surging in her mind. 'This is why I was drawn here, this is why we had to come! Osiv knows. He has seen it all, in his memories and in his child's dreams. The *truth*, Marine. The truth about me.' She flashed a wild, alien look towards the forest, back in the direction they had come. 'The truth about *us.*'

Marine tried to say something, but there were no words to say. This was beyond her, far outside the sphere of anything she had ever known or envisioned.

Nanta turned to her again, and she almost recoiled from the harsh light in her eyes. 'When I was born,' Nanta said, 'were you there?'

The question seemed random, crazed, but Marine tried to answer. 'No . . .'

'Who was?'

Random. Crazed. Why was she asking this? 'I – I don't know! Your mother, Karetta, of course; but—'

'Was she?' Nanta smiled. 'I wonder . . .' Abruptly she turned again and, still smiling, extended a hand towards Osiv. 'We must go in.'

'Yes, yes, go in!' Osiv agreed, shouting. 'All go in!'

Nanta touched his jaw with one hand. Immediately Osiv quietened, gazing back at her with a quizzical, fascinated expression. The snow was falling on Nanta and she had no furs to shield her but only her gown and cloak. She looked, Marine thought, like a sculpture made of ice.

'Little one,' she said fondly. And walked into the lodge, leaving them all silent behind her. Marine stood motionless, staring at the lodge but not seeing it. Nanta's words: *Was she*? How could Karetta *not* have been present at her birth? It was a mad riddle, an impossibility.

But deep down in a forgotten pocket of her memory, a thought was stirring. A rumour. A hint. *Something* . . . Karetta had failed to conceive for so long, and then suddenly, almost when hope was abandoned, Nanta had come. A letter from another cousin; Marine recalled it now, in essence if not in detail. Gossip, or a sly jest; the implication that Karetta and her husband had not created a child at all, but had adopted a foundling, an unwanted

291

waif without pedigree or provenance. Marine had dismissed it at the time: the cousin had not married well and was known to be jealous of Karetta. Now, though . . .

Now . . .

A faint, strangled sound, like a half-formed cry of pain or shock, escaped from Marine's throat, and with jerking steps she started to flounder towards the lodge in Nanta's wake.

When Kodor reached the lodge, he knew that the thing of hate was not far behind him. He could sense it as an ache in his bones, bitter and ugly and insane; it had not found him yet, for it seemed that the snow hampered it; but it was seeking him and before long it would find what it wanted.

He was out of the sled even as it skidded to a standstill, and by the time the mutes with their lantern appeared he was through the gate and plunging through the still-deepening snow towards the lodge door. The sleigh was in the compound – so they were here, they had reached safety – and his heart quickening, Kodor clapped the mutes on their shoulders in thankful appreciation and hurried inside.

The lodge had six rooms, and in the largest of them Marine sat before a blazing log fire. She still wore her blue robe, but the soaked veil and wimple had been taken away to dry. Without them she looked very different: younger, almost vulnerable. She rose quickly to her feet as she saw Kodor, and he said without any preamble: 'Where is Nanta?'

Marine's gaze slid uneasily to an inner door. 'She is with her – with the Imperator, sire – I mean, Your Highness.'

Kodor smiled thinly. 'Titles are becoming confusing, Marine. Shall we dispense with them?' He started towards the door but she said quickly, 'Sir, please – I think it would not be wise to disturb them! Nanta has – she is –' She faltered, shivering despite the room's heat, and Kodor demanded,

'She is what? *What*?'

'I . . . don't know; I can't explain, can't begin to tell you – Since we departed – no, no; I mean, since we *arrived*, something has—'

Unable to bear her floundering any longer, Kodor interrupted. 'Is Nanta ill?'

'No. No, not ill. Not at *all*. She – she called the frost sprites. In the courtyard, when Father Urss tried to—'

'I know what Urss did.' *And I know what Urss is, now.* 'They came to her?'

Marine nodded. 'They ran with us on the journey; but when we arrived, they vanished. Yet I think Nan . . . the—'

'Nanta.'

'Yes. Nanta. I think they are – might be – with her now.'

Nanta, Osiv and the frost sprites . . . It was beginning to make sense. Suddenly a shudder ran through Kodor; not something from within himself, but from outside. A power, an anger – it was trying to touch him, wanting to use him as its conduit. The thing of hate and vengeance was almost here . . .

'I have to see her.' He strode for the door. 'No, Marine –' as she moved to block his way – 'don't attempt to stop me! This is between Nanta and me – it's nothing to do with you, and I'm only sorry that your mere presence here means you have to be involved.' His hands came down on her upper arms, gripping. 'You can do one thing for us. Just one.'

Her pale face gazed up at him. 'What is it?'

'Pray to the Lady. Not to the God; to the *Lady*. Pray with all your strength.'

He left her gazing bewildered at his back as he opened the door and entered the room beyond.

The shutters were tightly closed and the room was dark but for two candles that burned in a sconce near the empty hearth. It should have been bitterly cold – but it was not. There was a strange warmth in the air, and a scent that was almost but not quite familiar; like a forgotten perfume from childhood memory.

Nanta was kneeling on the floor, near the candles. Osiv was curled beside her. His head was in her lap and she was stroking his hair; at first Kodor thought he was asleep, but then he saw the faint gleam of his eyes, alert, watching. Nanta raised her head, saw Kodor. She did not greet him or smile. She only said, 'Osiv. It's time to play the game again.'

'Yes,' said Osiv. 'Play the game. Nandi and me. And Kodi.' He blinked. 'Kodi play too?'

'Oh, yes. I think he must. I think we all must.'

Kodor said: 'You know, don't you? You know what's coming.' She nodded.

'It followed me.'

'It had to. *He* had to.'

Something welled up in Kodor and spilled over. 'Nanta, how could we have—'

'Hush.' Nanta raised a finger to her lips, silencing him. 'We can't be sure of anything, not yet. We just . . . *feel* it.'

Kodor swallowed. A sense of oppression was beginning to build up, not in the room but around it; as though something was slowly, inexorably wrapping itself around the lodge like a suffocating blanket.

'What of the others?' he said softly. 'Marine and the servants . . .'

'I don't think he will harm them; I'm not even sure that he can.' She looked away. 'It doesn't matter, Kodor. This is for *us* to face, not them. They must do their best, but we can't consider them.'

He was a little shocked by her sanguinity; but then, perhaps, it was only to be expected. Then at her feet Osiv stirred again. 'The game, Nandi,' he said, a little crossly. 'Play the game!'

'What is the game?' Kodor asked.

Now, Nanta did smile. 'Osiv has been playing with the frost sprites,' she said. 'Since he was brought here, they have come to him and they have been his friends and companions. They drew things from his mind, Kodor; things he has seen, in reality and dreams, for all of his life, but could never communicate to anyone else. Now, with the sprites' help, he can show *us* what he knows.' She looked fondly down at her husband. 'Osiv understands far more than we have ever realised; far more than we do. I think perhaps it's his innocence; he is more willing to believe what to us – as we were – would seem impossible.'

Suddenly, swiftly, she stood up, pushing Osiv gently away from her. 'When I first arrived here, Osiv and the frost sprites played their game, and I played it with them,' she said. 'Now, we must play it again; and you must see it, too.'

The oppression was growing. The thing was so close now . . . 'Nanta, is there time?' Kodor asked uneasily.

'Yes, there's time. There has to be.'

Moving to the middle of the room, she took hold of his hand. Her touch sent a tingle through his fingers that spread into his arm and seemed to diffuse throughout his body. From the floor Osiv watched them, eyes wide with eager anticipation; still keeping the link with Kodor, Nanta looked at him.

'Come, Osiv. Shall we begin?'

To Kodor's astonishment, Osiv rose to his knees and began to sing. It was more of a crooning, but his pitch was perfect and the melody had a gentle, repeating lilt.

'I didn't know he had such a voice . . .' Kodor whispered.

Nanta only smiled at him. Then she, too, joined in the singing, and words formed: a calling, a summoning.

'Come you! Come you! Come you!' It was a sweet chant, their voices blending perfectly. 'Come you!'

Kodor felt the presence of the frost sprites before he saw them. When they appeared, he knew at once that they were the same ones who had guided and guarded Nanta at the palace. Her friends. Her servants . . .

The sprites each took one of Osiv's hands and lifted him to his feet. Then one reached out to Kodor. He hesitated; the sprite smiled, encouraging him, and he felt the icy touch of its long fingers clasping his. Nanta took the hand of the other sprite and they formed a circle, facing inwards. The chant fell away, changing now to a gentle, wordless humming in which the sprites joined with tones like tiny, frosty bells.

Then, within the circle of their linked hands, a light that was not of the candles began to grow. Pale, all but colourless, it strengthened gradually, forming a tall oval like a soft, frosted mirror; and an image took form within it. A bier; and on the bier lay a figure wrapped in an ice-blue shroud. White hands showed above the shroud, clasped as though in prayer.

Nanta had fallen silent since the sprites began to sing with Osiv, but now she spoke. 'Since I was a child,' she said softly, 'I have seen this image in my dreams. It is the Lady. And she is dead.'

She heard Kodor's violent intake of breath, and she squeezed his fingers tightly in a silent warning.

'I did not understand its meaning,' she continued. 'But today, Osiv and the sprites have shown me. Look, Kodor. Look, and see.'

A second figure was appearing in the mirror of light. Huge, dark, it stooped over the bier, and Kodor felt an appalling shudder run through his marrow. *A thing of hate and vengeance* – he could sense it, a part of himself and yet not a part; for it was something far beyond humanity and he was only human.

Or –

The stooping figure raised its head and seemed to look straight at them. A wave of rage and madness erupted from it, sweeping through the room, and with a shock that almost unhinged his mind Kodor saw that it had no face.

'*Great lord*!' The words of worship came automatically and he would have knelt in awe, but Nanta's hand clenched over his, her nails driving painfully into his flesh.

'*No!*' she hissed. 'Do not make obeisance to him! He is not worthy of it – *he killed her!*'

Kodor's senses reeled and he wanted to protest: No, that can't be, he is the God, he is all-wise –

And he is a thing of hate and vengeance . . .

The mental jolt froze him, crippling his limbs. As though from a vast distance he heard Nanta repeat, 'He killed her,' and her voice was calm and sure.

'Look again, Kodor. See now. Back in time.'

The bier faded, changed, became a bed within a room. Kodor knew the room, remembered it from his childhood. The royal suite of the palace, where generations of his ancestors had fulfilled their destiny. He and Osiv had been conceived and born in that bed; his mother and father had died there. And now, beside the bed, he saw a woman praying.

The old Imperatrix, his mother . . . He heard her desperate words: '*Another son . . . oh, dear God, grant me another son*!'

The song changed. The lilt fell away and now it was a sad dirge, wistful and heartbreakingly melancholy. There was a darkness flowing over the bed, over his mother's desolate figure. *Hate and vengeance* . . . It was coming to her, moving on her; Kodor saw her face uplifted in wonder and awe, and he knew what the God would do, how the Imperatrix's prayer would be answered.

A second son, to rule Vyskir where the first could not. But this son would not be Arctor's.

This son was not truly human.

And in the room within the oval, a small child with vacant eyes sat watching as the tryst was made . . .

'Ah, no . . .' Kodor started to back away. 'No, please – it can't be true – it *can't*!'

Nanta said: 'It is true.' And a raging, corrosive power swept over the hunting lodge, shaking it from end to end as though a hurricane had sprung from behind the north wind.

'You are the God's own child,' Nanta said softly. 'And so am I. But we did not have the same mother.'

He stared at her, unable to comprehend. 'Your mother was . . .'

'Not Karetta.' She was smiling, and her eyes were the colour of sapphires, imbued with an inner light of their own. Then, abruptly, her expression changed. The oval of light dimmed and flickered, as though lightning were dancing deep within it, and Nanta stared into its heart as her eyes became dark and dire.

'He slew her,' she said. 'The God slew the Lady. She bore him a child, and he refused to believe that child was his own. He claimed she was unfaithful.' A harsh laugh that made Kodor start violently broke from her throat. '*She* was not untrue. *He* was the unfaithful one, for he had answered the prayers of Arctor's wife and got a son on her. And he was driven by his own guilt; driven to accuse his true Lady, to cover and justify his own wrongdoing. I think that perhaps he was already mad then.'

Kodor was shaking, and couldn't make it stop. 'You . . .' he whispered, almost choking on the word as his throat tightened and constricted, 'The child she bore him . . . you are that child . . .'

She turned and regarded him once more. Her eyes were kinder now. 'Yes. I am.'

'But . . . how can you *know* this? Not through Osiv . . .'

'No. Your story is locked in Osiv's mind; my story is in my own. My mother placed the knowledge there, to be awakened when the time was right. It was the sprites who showed me. They opened the doors into the past, for me and for Osiv, and they set us free.'

Kodor understood. He understood what had been hidden away in Osiv's damaged memory for so many years. He understood the dreams that had plagued him and plagued Nanta – and plagued his brother, too, though Osiv could never tell of them. Osiv knew, and had always known. And when Nanta came to wed him, he, like Kodor, had recognised what she was. But unlike Kodor, Osiv had accepted without question, for he knew no other way.

And now that the truth had awoken, so had something else. A power that was dark and vast and mad, raging, coming through the snow as the daylight declined . . .

His father . . .

'Nanta –' He was trying to warn her, trying to express the horror and the fear he felt. But Nanta shook her head.

'Don't be afraid,' she told him. 'He is not here yet. And there is more . . .'

She turned again to the oval of light. Another image was forming. Snow; a blizzard. A fine house, surrounded by trees and with lights burning in every window. A figure was gliding towards the house against the furious drive of the snow. It was cloaked and hooded, and it held something in its arms . . .

Osiv's humming changed then to a new song; a song with words.

'Hide and seek, hide and seek!' He had put his head on one side and was regarding Kodor. 'Hide and seek, hide and seek! Never find, never find! Hide the baby, take the baby, give her to another lady!' The frost sprites hummed a counterpoint. 'No one know, no one see, gone is she and mad is he!' Then suddenly Osiv's face twisted into a wild, crazed look. He jumped on the spot, his feet thumping on the floor, and in a changed voice he yelled: '*Die, die, die! Die, die, die!*—'

'Enough, little one!' Nanta's command cut through Osiv's furious shouting, and instantly the outburst ceased.

'The Lady feared for me,' Nanta said, 'so she carried me to the mortal world. She cloaked me in the flesh of humanity, and she gave me into the keeping of the family I have always called my own. A foundling. A boon. The answer to a prayer . . . The Lady hid her daughter from the God's twisted vengeance, and because he could not find my hiding place, he slew her.'

Osiv was watching Nanta with solemn sadness, appearing to understand every word. The image in the oval was fading, and the light was fading too, dwindling in size and brightness until just a tiny spark, like a firefly, remained. Then the spark flickered once and was gone.

The frost sprites made a sighing sound, and Osiv looked keenly at Kodor. 'See, Kodi? They showed me the game. They're my friends.' He paused. 'But Kodi's my friend, too.' A seraphic smile spread across his face. 'Kodi's my *brother*.'

For several seconds Kodor remained absolutely still. He thought: *that isn't so. We're not brothers, not truly – the same mother bore us, but she – she –* Then suddenly the thoughts all collapsed in on themselves and in a violent movement he broke the circle and was across the floor, reaching out, hugging Osiv to him.

'Osiv, Osiv –' He couldn't say more; the confusion was roiling and nothing made sense, nothing seemed *real –*

Outside, in the gathering dusk, something howled.

Osiv sprang away from Kodor, and the look on his face changed. His smooth brow creased into a frown; putting his thumb in his mouth he scurried to the far side of the room and crouched down behind a chair. There were sudden noises in the next room; movement, footsteps, an agitated voice . . .

'He is coming,' Nanta said quietly. 'He has found his way to me at last.'

Kodor's heart pounded under his ribs. 'But he must have known . . . in the palace . . .'

'Oh, yes. On the night that the Corolla Lights first appeared, he knew who I was. I couldn't keep it from him, you see; for the Lights belong to the Lady and only she can summon them.'

'*You* summoned them?'

She nodded. 'I didn't know it. But I think . . . I believe . . . It was the night that your father died. I had never witnessed death before, and I think that it awoke something in me. Though I had no conscious knowledge of it then, another, deeper part of me . . . remembered my mother. And that part *knew* what had become of her. And he – our father – sensed it.' She looked up at him. 'But even though he had found me, he could not touch me. Until I recognised and acknowledged who I really am, I was beyond his reach.'

'But now you have acknowledged it . . . ?'

'Then I must face him. And I think I will destroy him.'

Her hand was on the door latch before Kodor came to his senses. When reason did return, it was in a single, slamming blow that rocked him to the core.

'*Nanta!*' He lunged after her. 'Nanta, no, *stop!*'

The howling came again, vast and desolate, echoed by a cry of fear from the outer room. Nanta turned, shook her head gently, and Kodor was halted in mid-stride, locked like a statue. He heard Osiv's delighted giggle – then Nanta was gone, the paralysis vanished and he collided violently with the door as it shut in his face.

He was there. She felt his presence, and she saw him in the wind that bent the pines and soughed in their high branches. The snow did not hinder her as she walked smoothly to the hunting-lodge gate; from the kennels a dog whimpered uneasily. The gate swung silently open; stepping through, she turned her gaze to the forest road and saw what was flowing through the dusk, her dream become reality, towards her. *Shapeless and nameless and cruelly familiar*. . . She heard his voice, her father's voice, the one booming word, malevolent, accusing:

'*YOOOUUU.*'

She said: '*I*,' and the forest answered in a thousand echoes. The snow fell on her. Ice cracked as she raised her hands. And far overhead, like spectral flames rising from the heart of a vast fire, the Corolla Lights appeared and the stately dance began.

'I know what you have become,' said Nanta, 'and I pity you.'

301

The bloating darkness was spilling into the clearing, blotting out the trees. But it could not dim the Lights, and nor could it stop the snow from falling. The snow was her mother's legacy, her mother's power, and the God had no hold upon it.

And far away in a forgotten room of the palace, Father Urss cried out, a hideous, agonised cry . . .

'Come you,' said Nanta, as softly as the snow. 'Come you now. You have no choice, for I am stronger.'

He was insane, she knew; and that was why she pitied him. His power was gone, wasted in the desert of jealousy and rage and, for many years now, grief and regret at what he had done. And he was lonely. *So* lonely . . .

'My father.' Scarves of strange colours swayed now around Nanta, as though the Corolla Lights had bowed down to earth, to acknowledge and protect her. She saw the darkness shrink in on itself, saw it become something else, a figure, like a man but not a man; a black silhouette of bitter anger and shame. He stood before her – he had no face, but she knew his face, and the pity swelled again – and the great, melancholy voice whispered through the forest:

'*I . . . HAVE . . . A . . . SON . . .*'

'Yes.' Kodor was there, at the lodge gate; Nanta knew it. He was watching. Now, he believed.

'And you have a daughter.' She took a pace forward, felt Kodor move behind her and sent a command: *No! Stay back!* This was for her alone.

'All these years you have longed to destroy me,' she said. 'My existence reminded you of *her*, and it reminded you, like a constant goad and pain, of what you did to her. The evil injustice you did to her.' She paused, then continued more softly: 'Did you want to destroy your son, too? Did he also remind you of your wrongdoing? You sent him dreams of menace and peril and hatred. But the sprites protected him, as they protected me. They were my mother's friends and servants, and now they are mine. We are stronger, Father. We are stronger, now, than you!'

She stepped up to the darkness, her father, and she held out her hands. She would not destroy him. There was no need; it would not put right the old wrong, and the suffering he had brought upon himself was punishment enough. But she could not permit him to rule. Never again. His reign was ended, and a new one must begin.

The dark made one attempt to envelop her, but the light was too strong and the struggle was over before it began. He raised his dark hands, and Nanta raised her pale ones. Their palms touched, merged for just one moment . . .

And the God, old and deranged and helpless, knelt before his daughter and touched his brow to her fingers.

The scream of mortal agony pierced through the thick walls of the forgotten room and echoed the length of the empty corridor beyond. But the searchers did not hear and did not know, for Father Urss had hidden himself well. He was merely human, and no human vessel could withstand such shock and pain. Perhaps, one day, they would find what remained of him; or perhaps they would not. It did not matter. It was ended.

There could be nothing more.

Chapter XXI

From the door of the hunting lodge Kodor watched as the dogs were harnessed into their traces. The servants were moving quietly about him, preparing the last of the baggage for loading, but they took great care not to look at his face as they passed, for what showed there was too private to be intruded on.

Inside the lodge, Osiv was trying to inveigle Marine into a last game before their departure. Marine's voice as she answered him was still unsteady, but she was bearing up remarkably well. A strong woman, Kodor thought detachedly. And devout. She would get over this in time, and though it would change her, the change would be to the good.

As for himself . . . yes; he was changed, too. More changed than anyone beyond these few witnesses would ever know. He had come into his heritage, and it was not the heritage he had ever known or dreamed to know. But it was *his*. And one day, like Marine, he might learn to accept.

Tears started to his eyes and he wiped them impatiently away, before they could freeze on his eyelashes. He wanted Nanta; wanted her so much that it was a physical pain within him. But Nanta was gone, and would never return. He would see her again, after a fashion: for the snow would continue its yearly fall, and the Corolla Lights would continue their eternal dance. But *she* – her face, her voice, her sweetness – would not be here.

'I love you,' he had said to her. And: 'I know,' she had replied. 'But our roads go different ways. And you are my brother. My *half*-brother.' She had smiled then, and he would always remember that smile, as she corrected herself. 'And that other half of you is human. It cannot be, Kodor. It is not what I want; for I have another and greater destiny. And you have a wife.'

A wife. Pola Imperatrix. Kodor almost, but not quite, laughed as he thought of Duke Arec and how he would react to the news that Imperator Osiv IV was alive and well. Arec would not like it at all; but then Arec had known about the plot to murder Osiv, and – unless he wished that knowledge to become more common – he would do well to hold his tongue and his temper. Pola had not known. Pola, indeed, was perhaps the most innocent of them all, and he had been unjustly cruel to her. He had, perhaps, misjudged her. And she was his wife . . .

He looked through the open gate. The place where Nanta had stood, where he had had his last sight of her, was just an unremarkable patch of the clearing floor. But he would remember it. He would build a shrine here, for the sake of that remembrance.

'I will watch over you,' she had said. Her last words to him. 'I will watch over you, my brother.' And then she had gone, and the old, broken God had gone with her. Back to the place of their origins, behind the north wind. A place where he could not follow, because a part of him was human.

'Kodi, Kodi!' Osiv came bounding from the lodge and grabbed Kodor's arm in a ferociously excited grip. 'Going to have a sleigh-ride!'

Marine followed Osiv to the door. Her veil and wimple were in place once more, and her face was very pale; but she managed a weak smile as he looked at her.

'The Imperator is very eager, Your Highness,' she said.

Kodor returned her smile. 'Titles, Marine, titles. Remember what I said?' There would be changes in Vyskir; great changes. He had never thought of himself as a reformer, but perhaps the talent had lain dormant in him all along. Osiv would be happy;

he would see to that. And Pola was intelligent; in fact, she probably had a political prowess to match his own. With her help, he could rule wisely and well, and if she would forgive him – as he believed she would – they could learn to get along together kindly enough. It was not what he had wanted, what he had dreamed of. But perhaps he had had enough of dreams.

A call from across the compound: 'We're ready, sire!'

Sire. Your Majesty. Your Highness. Your Grace . . . Kodor laughed softly. Changes. *Many* changes.

And Nanta would watch over him. The Lady is dead; long live the Lady . . .

'Come, then, little brother!' He put an arm around Osiv's shoulders. 'Time for our sleigh-ride! And then home.'

Osiv scowled. 'No medicine!'

'No. No medicine.'

Osiv looked at Marine. 'You've got an ugly dress on,' he said, then: 'Where's Nandi?'

Something caught at Kodor's heart. He pushed it down.

'She is here, Osiv. In a way. She always will be.'

Osiv tilted his head quizzically. Then he smiled.

'*I* know,' he said.

They walked together to the waiting sleigh.

EPILOGUE: ONE YEAR ON

The prospect of yet another great public occasion wasn't what the Imperator would ideally have wanted. There had been so many such demands over the past year that he felt glutted and more than a little overladen with them. Funerals, weddings, inaugurations; and, most recent and spectacular of all, the coronation and all that it had entailed and implied.

This latest celebration, though, was a little different to the rest, for it reflected a private achievement – and, though the feeling had taken Kodor a little by surprise, a private joy. It wasn't just the fact that he and Pola had fulfilled what might be seen as one of their prime obligations. It was what that fulfilment *meant*, and what it implied for the future, that gave him the greatest satisfaction.

The news of the Imperatrix's pregnancy had been received with enormous delight by the peoples of Vyskir and Sekol alike. Duke Arec was ecstatic, and had written of his intention to return to the Metropolis again as soon as the spring began, to 'play his proper role' in the preparations for his first grandchild's arrival. Arec knew, now, that his role was not and never could be as influential as he had intended it to be. But the alternative, as Kodor had privately and delicately pointed out to him some time ago, was a good deal less desirable. A month before that private interview, a servant had by sheer chance come across the remains of a human body in a rarely opened room of the palace. The body was badly decayed, and the imperial physician, choking back nausea, had declared that if he did not know such things were impossible, he would have said it had exploded from within. Kodor had made no comment to that. From the skull, clothing and teeth the corpse was identifiable beyond reasonable doubt as that of Exalted Father Urss. That was all Kodor needed to know, and it gave him a useful lever in his dealings with Arec. Arec might have played no direct part in the plot against Osiv, but he had been well aware of it and had given it his blessing. It would be a great pity if his compliance should be made known to the peoples of their countries. It would not reflect well on him. Both the prime movers were now of a certainly dead, Kodor had said; and if they were to be left to shoulder the blame alone, a little less interference in the affairs of Vyskir was surely a small price to pay. Arec was shrewd enough to know when he was outmanoeuvred, and had given way with a grace that was both a surprise and a relief to his son-in-law. He was learning to live with his disappointment, and without his meddling, or the insidious, manipulating influence of Father Urss to hamper them, Kodor and Pola were finding life a great deal easier and more pleasant.

So many changes. The diehards and pessimists still shook their heads and muttered about the folly of it all, but their influence, too, was diminishing and before long they would be consigned to history along with the jetsam of so many other pointless encumbrances. Rules were made to be challenged and, if found wanting, broken; and many things that in Arctor's day had been deemed impossible or unthinkable had proved astonishingly simple to achieve.

It had been Pola's idea that the populace should be told the truth about Osiv's apparent return from the dead, and about his affliction. Perhaps, Kodor thought, she had more faith in human nature than he did – which, under the early circumstances of their marriage was hardly surprising – and her earnest argument had hinged on her belief that to lie was wrong and they should trust and respect their people enough to be honest with them. Kodor had gambled on her instinct, and the gamble had paid off. Far from reacting with anger, the people had responded with sympathy, both for Osiv's plight and for his brother's. A wrong had been done, but the perpetrators, Urss and Beck, had been punished (for everyone's sake the truth been had diverted down a small tributary in that regard) and all was well. Osiv had officially abdicated. Such a thing had never happened before, but the innovation was readily accepted and Osiv was a figure of great affection now. The people had adopted him in their hearts, almost as children might adopt a pet, and had even given him the new and affectionate nickname of 'Vyskir's Baby'.

Osiv himself had voyaged through the turmoil and upheaval of political change like a bird on a summer breeze. His time was divided between the palace and the hunting lodge, and in his limited way he had blossomed as never before. Recently he had developed a strong affection for Pola, and viewed her prospective child as a personal gift from her to him, a playmate to be nurtured and protected. Now and then, in the night, he cried for Nanta; but Dorca alone knew that secret and kept a still tongue.

And Kodor . . . He could not yet, truly, say that he was contented, but as time passed he was becoming reconciled to a life which, as he privately acknowledged, was kinder to him than he probably deserved. Pola's forgiveness of his cruelties had been instantaneous and unequivocal; anyone knowing the whole truth and looking at the matter detachedly would have called her a fool. But it wasn't Pola's way to bear grudges; she loved Kodor, and slowly, gently, patiently, she was teaching him to love her. Time was on her side; they were both young yet. And if there was still a rival for his affections, that rival was now so far removed from the everyday world as to present no possible threat.

If Pola wondered at the revelations about Nanta's and Kodor's true natures, and feared them, she had never shown the smallest outward sign of it. Kodor had told her everything, and she had accepted the truth with a calmness that astonished him. To her, Kodor's heritage was unimportant; he was her husband, and to all intents and purposes as human as she. That was what mattered, and it was all that mattered. Besides, she had added in her quiet, thoughtful way, with the God's power broken and his presence gone from the world, Kodor's human self was surely strengthened. Let the past be; set it to rest, and look towards the future.

It was wise advice and Kodor tried to take it. Pola knew he was trying, so when in his dreams he called Nanta's name, or spoke of strange and intimate secrets not meant for her own ears, she only stroked his brow and pushed away the pangs of hurt, knowing that they had no real power. Pola Imperatrix was a patient woman, and an optimist. She had already won the day; now it only needed time to soften the harsh edges and make them smooth.

And, strange though it seemed, in that ambition she believed she had the strongest ally of all . . .

She did not know, and did not feel the need to question, why it was that she liked to spend a little time each day in the Imperatrix's private chapel of the Lady. But something about the still, quiet chamber seemed to call to her; it was a place of rest, of peace, and within the embrace of its walls Pola found a tranquility that soothed her soul. At first she had preferred to go alone, but in the present stage of her pregnancy she was suffering fainting fits and needed someone to attend on her. So her companion in the chapel now was Mother Marine. Pola had grown fond of Marine; despite the differences in age and background they had more in common than either might have guessed. And Marine was a restful companion. There was no need to speak at all unless either had something in particular to say; they could simply sit together, absorbed in their prayers and meditations, both content in the knowledge that the Lady heard them.

One day, Pola hoped, Marine would feel able to talk of what she had witnessed in the forest on the night that had so changed all their lives. As yet, though, the wonder was still too close and the awe too great for any words to be possible. Observing the older woman, Pola believed that it would be a long time before she recovered fully from the shock . . . but Marine was strong, and her years of self-discipline were coming into their own. And she had her work. The legacy of Grand Mother Beck's political and religious cynicism was already cracking under Marine's influence, and soon it would crumble altogether, swept away by the fresh and genuine devoutness of her successor. Where the chapels of the God now stood empty and all but disused, those of the Lady flourished as never before. For the Lady – the *new* Lady – looked kindly on her human worshippers, and would not forget them. *Even I*, Pola thought, *who misjudged her and was cold and did not understand. Perhaps it's for Kodor's sake, but no matter. The Lady blesses me. The Lady blesses us all.*

So now, tonight, in the chapel with Marine silently praying at her side, Pola Imperatrix was content. In their suite in the palace Kodor was playing with Osiv and probably getting a little too drunk for his own good. But she understood why, and when it led to laughter instead of anger, as it always did these days, there was nothing to forgive. When he fell asleep she might climb to the top of the tower, if her sickness and dizziness did not return, and watch the nightly dance of the Corolla Lights. And tomorrow she and her husband were to drive in an open sleigh through the streets of the Metropolis to show themselves to the citizens and be cheered from one end of the city to the other.

Pola's prayers were done, and smiling faintly to herself she rose and moved quietly to the foot of the shrine. She had brought a small bunch of evergreen leaves – all that could be managed at this time of year, but it was a daily ritual with her now and she would not dream of neglecting it – and crouched down to set them in one of the vases at the statue's feet. When the leaves were arranged she looked up at the carved, serene figure of the Lady rising above her. That veiled face, symbolising mystery . . . Pola smiled again. She knew what lay behind the veil. And when she whispered, softly, 'Thank you,' she knew, too, that her words would be heard.

I will watch over you. Nanta's last words to Kodor, and a promise to them all. Pola straightened, smoothed the folds of her skirt and moved back to where Marine sat watching her. They exchanged a look, then Marine, too, stood, and silently they left the chapel together.

The door closed, causing the votive lights to flicker briefly before settling back to their customary stillness. Then a soft breath exhaled through the chamber, and it might have seemed to an observer that the statue was no longer quite a statue but something more. Life stirred in the white marble; shades of blue and gold glimmered faintly and briefly, and for a moment, just a moment, the sculpted figure appeared to be moving. Then the mirage faded and was gone, leaving only an echoing sense of peace that spread like a ripple in a pool, out of the chapel, to encompass the city and the world beyond.